KLAVERN

KLAVERN
A Sherry Russell Thriller

JAMES K. RONE

Arno Press, College Grove, TN 37046

ISBN: 0615661688
ISBN-13: 978-0615661681

For Susan, Margaret, and Bill.

It is not easy to describe a crisis so profound that it has caused the most powerful nation in the world to stagger in confusion and bewilderment. Today's problems are so acute because the tragic evasions and defaults of several centuries have accumulated to disaster proportions.

The constructive achievements of…1955 to 1965 deceived us. Everyone underestimated the…violence and rage Negroes were suppressing and the…bigotry the white majority was disguising.

—Martin Luther King Jr., *A Testament of Hope* (his final published statement)

PREFACE

The Ku Klux Klan is perhaps the world's oldest terrorist organization. Its history, which will not be greatly detailed here, can be readily divided into phases: The first consisting of its origins in Pulaski, Tennessee, in late 1865, its wildfire spread across the Reconstruction South, as a blunt instrument for controlling through fear, violence, and murder the region's recently freed slave population, and finally its end in 1872 brought about a Federal crackdown, and even disbandment by its own leadership, concerned over the carnage, and the Klansman's increasingly low reputation.

The second phase, opening with a cross-burning on Thanksgiving night, 1915, in full view of downtown Atlanta, was the heyday of the Klan. Under the banner of protecting "traditional" values (i.e., white, native-born, Anglo-Saxon Protestant ones), the reborn KKK flourished from coast to coast, amid what was seen as the moral decay of the 1920s. Its ranks swelled to five million, to include the author's great grandfather. It was a political force at the Democratic National Convention of 1924. Soon after, though, mainstream America fled the Klan in droves, repulsed by its corrupt leadership and inherently violent nature: exemplified by the conviction in a sensation trial of the Indiana Grand Dragon in the horrific 1925 death of girlfriend, Madge Oberholtzer.

The third great Klan uprising erupted with the 1954 Supreme

Court strike-down of public-school segregation. Blacks and Jews were targeted, increasingly with dynamite. A late-fifties lull was followed by the 1960s ushering in full bore the African-American civil rights movement, to which the Klan reacted viciously. It grew to 40,000-strong but never enjoyed mainstream social approval as it had in the 1920s, its methods and rhetoric abhorrent even to middle-class Southern whites otherwise opposed to progress on the civil rights front. Klan power was again waning by 1966, as its own brutality ironically fostered passage of pro-civil rights legislation. The FBI meanwhile, however reluctantly (J. Edgar Hoover was an out-and-out racist as dedicated to destroying Martin Luther King as he was Soviet spies) and unconstitutionally, fought and won a pitched battle, leading to convictions of high-profile Klansmen previously immune to prosecution. True to form, the Klan decayed as well from within, strangling on financial irregularities, and a mutual distrust that was, in fact, entirely warranted.

Late 1967 saw a final spurt of violence that ended with what journalist Don Whitehead, famous for his book *The FBI Story*, called the "last gasp of a mortally wounded monster"—a convulsive firefight, 30 June 1968, triggered when the FBI and Meridian, Mississippi police collaborated in a Bonnie-and-Clyde-style ambush. The Bonnie-and-Clyde imagery is apt, because riding with a Klan bomber, that midnight, on a quiet Meridian residential street, was in fact beautiful 26-year-old school teacher Kathryn Ainsworth, a committed Klanswoman. She died in a hail of gunfire. The bomber, though savagely wounded, survived a wild running shootout, unfolding on foot and by car, the Klansman at one point blasting a submachine gun at pursuing officers.

The bombings and burnings stopped. The Klan slithered back in its pit, only to crawl out again for a fourth and a fifth time: respectively, the David Duke era of the late 1970s, focusing on blue-collar labor anxiety, and the right-wing extremism of the eighties and nineties targeting the Federal government, involving Klansmen, neo-Nazis, skinheads, other hate groups, and encompassing the events of Ruby Ridge, Waco, perhaps Columbine, and certainly Oklahoma City.

***

Klavern is a fictionalization of events during the waning stages of the third Klan uprising, specifically the late-1967 "spurt." No actual persons or incidents are depicted, though my descriptions of Klan activities, members, and language are intended to form an accurate facsimile of reality based upon published sources. For example, a number of situations, characterizations, and some saltier dialogue were suggested by accounts given by the famous FBI undercover man Gary Thomas Rowe in his book *My Undercover Years with the Ku Klux Klan* (Bantam Books, 1976). My depiction of a Klan rally draws heavily from and acknowledges two sources: *Ku Klux Klan: the Invisible Empire* by David Lowe (W.W. Norton, 1967), which is basically a transcript of a 1965 *CBS Reports* broadcast, and journalist Patsy Sims' frightening depiction of a rally she attended in West Virginia in 1975, published in her book *The Klan* (Dorset Press, 1978). For details of a Klan bombing operation I credit the *LA Times'* Jack Nelson and his excellent *Terror in the Night: the Klan's Campaign Against the Jews* (Simon & Schuster, 1993). Technical details regarding electronic-surveillance gear used in 1967 are accurate based upon *The Electronic Invasion* by Robert M. Brown (John F. Rider, 1967).

Additional sources I acknowledge and commend to those interested are as follows:

- "Playboy Interview: Robert Shelton—a Candid Conversation with the Klan's Notorious Imperial Wizard." *Playboy*. August, 1965.

- *Inside Ku Klux Klan* by Paul J. Gillette and Eugene Tillinger. 1965.

- "Snooping Electronic: Invasion of Privacy." *Life*. May 20, 1966.

- "A Testament of Hope" by Dr. Martin Luther King Jr. *Playboy*. January, 1969.

- *Attack on Terror: The FBI Against the Ku Klux Klan in Mississippi* by Don Whitehead. 1970.

- *The Orangeburg Massacre* by Jack Nelson and Jack Bass, 1970.

- *Hooded Americanism: The History of the Ku Klux Klan*, 3rd ed. by David Chalmers. 1981.

- *Let the Trumpet Sound: a Life of Martin Luther King, Jr.* by Stephen B. Oates. 1982.
- *The Ku Klux Klan: an Encyclopedia* by Michael Newton and Judy Ann Newton. 1991.
- *Backfire: How the Ku Klux Klan Helped the Civil Rights Movement* by David Chalmers. 2003.
- *There's Something Happening Here: the New Left, the Klan, and FBI Counterintelligence* by David Cunningham. 2004.
- *The Informant: the FBI, the Ku Klux Klan, and the Murder of Viola Liuzzo* by Gary May, 2005.
- *At Canaan's Edge: America in the King Years, 1965–1968* by Taylor Branch. 2007.
- *Hellhound on His Trail: the Stalking of Martin Luther King Jr. and the International Hunt for His Assassin* by Hampton Sides. 2010.

Lastly, neither my use of vulgar racist slang, nor my portrayals of bigoted attitudes, nor the well-meant but insulting racial paternalism (or maternalism in this case) exhibited by my protagonist, reflect the personal habits or opinions of the author. If the reader feels I have written any African-American characters unflatteringly, even stereotypically, I apologize and accept responsibility. However my intent and belief is that all of this—language, attitudes, character details—reflect accurately upon the time and place in which the novel is set, on the basis of my cited research, and my own recollections growing up in a middle-class, politically aware, white Southern suburban family in 1967.

To the extent *Klavern* commits to the page "strong stuff" in our politically correct, racially sensitive times—times that are not alas, post racial, in spite of President Obama's historic ascent to the Oval Office—I would remind all that to rewrite (or fail to write) unpleasant, despicable history, risks repeating past evils and mistakes. *Klavern* has only one goal—to be a page-turning, entertaining thriller. If it additionally reminds (or teaches) even one reader of where we've been, how far we've come, how far we still have to go, then my work will have transcended its intent, and I would take pride in that.

KLAVERN

CHAPTER 1

I WAS THE ONLY WHITE THERE—a tiny Negro church like you read about being burned or bombed. It was a dusty Friday late in July of 1967, the "Summer of Love," if you were a tuning-in-turning-on-dropping-out hippie. To the rest of us its more apt label was the "Long Hot Summer."

As for me, Sherry Russell Nates, one-time Tennessee debutante: it was simply prologue to a frazzled autumn.

Frazzled and bloody.

The pastor was a heavy-built pious man, not particularly tall. He had a long horse face and a flat nose with long deep crevices from his nostrils to the corners of a frown as fixed as the Rock of Gibraltar. Limping behind the lectern he swung out the bad leg, sweating already against accumulating heat, a *thromp* as his shoe dropped. Knobby thick hands grasped the pulpit; he leaned out over the single pine casket.

Just the one, because the deceased's pregnant wife had been eulogized and buried a full day before—her family having spurned any joining of the services, bitterly blaming Montie Collins for the quadruple murder. The other dead Negroes, a man and a woman, were not from the same congregation, and were thus inconsequential to the joint-service controversy. However, besides simply blaming Montie Collins, the wife's family—reasonably, to my thinking—had feared the turmoil and perhaps further racial violence Montie Collins' funeral was liable to beget.

It had been said of me most of my adult life—not without cause—that I was a young lady looking for trouble. I'd occasionally managed to find it. But I'd not driven two hundred miles, clear down to Lavonia County, Alabama, looking for more. Nor, frankly, had I known Montie Collins from Adam's house cat.

I knew his sister.

She was my "help."

I'd arrived late, amid a lurching lusty rendition of "Amazing Grace." Despite propped-open front doors, and raised narrow windows along both sides, the one-room church was stagnant with a heat that opened up all your pores. With all the swaying and clapping and music, I thought, it'd be a bona fide miracle if we got through without at least one good heat stroke.

I'd never been to a colored funeral but I'd heard wild stories all my life. A few women, up front, wore white—the rest wore the same heat-absorbing black I did. Some stopped singing upon seeing me backlit in the doorway. Row by row, rippling forward, hateful stares faced round, and fell silent. The choir kept belting it out though.

I had figured to thread around the periphery and grab a nice out-of-the-way, end-of-pew seat. Then I realized the congregation was split:

There was the howling-lunging majority, but braced across the back and up both sides was a cadre of young men, older boys. Jaws set, facies grim. *Militant* came to mind. The pews didn't seem so full these gentlemen couldn't have found seats. And pardon my cynicism, I didn't think they were just being chivalrous. There seemed a symbolic purpose in setting themselves apart.

A protest?

Tis the season…

At any rate, they didn't appear disposed to let me comfortably slip to the fringes. So I raised my chin, and gulped some air, and set off pocketbook swinging gently down beside me, straight up the center aisle. Thankfully, along about a middle pew, a medium-sized woman of indeterminate age made room, and I sidled inward, mouthing a *thank you*. She wore a gaucho hat, fanning herself with a paddle. She smelled of talc. While settling, smoothing my skirt, I offered polite, grave nods to those around me, then fingered back a sheaf of peroxided hair. Folded hands in my lap.

The choir stopped.

The minister was preparing to preach, scanning us through pince-nez glasses.

Until his large watery eyes alighted squarely upon me.

I verged on fleeing, declaring stillborn my noble gesture of racial solidarity, when the man suddenly reared back and sang in a great booming voice: "What a Friend We Have in Jesus." Summoning the room back on its feet.

The choir joined in, bucking and weaving, and the building itself came alive.

All except the stoics:

Young, granite-hard, black-skinned.

They didn't move or sing or care whether Jesus was a friend or not.

At the closing of the hymn the pastor cracked open his Bible, removed his glasses.

"The voice of the Lord from John 14," he began. "Let not your heart be troubled. Ye believe in God, believe also in me. In my Father's house there are many mansions: if it were not so I would have told you. I go to prepare a place for you." He lowered the tattered Bible and, replacing his eyeglasses, limped beside the lectern. "I want to speak to you from the subject of serving God with a broken heart."

"Go ahead!"

"Preach!"

The ladies in white.

"Many have fallen to the oppressions of this world. Two of our family have joined them, and our hearts fill with grief."

"Yes!"

"Say that!"

"Yet Jesus tells us we must continue to serve him."

"No!" cracked a savage voice like a gunshot.

I craned over my shoulder.

The pastor ignored the dissenter. "Jesus is the way."

"Tell us!" I faced front again, exhaling.

"Jesus is the truth and the life. No man cometh unto the Father but by him."

"That's right!"

"We have been cheated. Given second-hand clothes, and books. Told to sit in the balcony at the picture show. Given inferior education, poor housing"—a glorified bedlam was swelling the congregation—"unemployment, inadequate health care; we have been mired in poverty. Each is part of a bitter oppression that is our heritage. We have been lied upon, beaten upon, lynched…"

He calmed, theatrically.

"But Jesus says we have a home."

"My brother works for the mortuary," the angry voice roared. "He seen Montie and Dorothy, both'em butchered like white man's livestock!"

I half came out of my seat. He was black-gloved, fist thrusting, seemingly at God, in some bizarre salute. The others followed, one fist each, high, some left, some right, some stern, others tentative, a sloppy display, but a display. They began to chant something. I wasn't a particularly church-going woman, but even I deemed this unconscionable sacrilege. The rumble grew louder.

Two words.

Repeated.

Which, I realized, I'd heard before…

"Black Power…

"Black Power…

"Black Power…"

Nashville, three months ago:

The Fisk Riot.

Stokely Carmichael had spoken at the Negro university, triggering an eruption. A student shot, ten cops, seven others injured, eighty arrests. The rioters had shouted: "Black power, black power, black power…"

"To hell," Carmichael had said, praising the rebellion, "with the laws of the United States."

Black-gloved fist still up, others still chanting, the man came up the aisle: "'Nough preachin' Rev! Jus' tell us whose skulls to

6

bash!" And a seething current washed around me, a current not wholeheartedly disagreeing with the protester.

It had been an unspeakable murder.

I was so angry at my own kind, at whoever had taken the law into their own hands, and lynched Montie Collins for the killing of a white man—and slaughtered, to boot, the innocent people with him. They had, I feared, hammered quite a few more nails into all our coffins. The pastor dripped with patience:

"Montie and Dorothy have gone home."

"Amen!"

"And when we close our eyes one final time, we will also wake up—"

"Lay down, Rev? No *damn* way!"

"Sit down boy! You in church!"

My legs uncrossed and re-crossed with swishings of nylon, my eyes darting, seeing fanning hymnals and bulletins. "Resist not evil," preached the pastor, "but whosoever smite thee—"

"All you men, come with me. No mo' talk! No mo' marchin'! 'Cept to that white town to burn it. Burn it down, baby!"

A solid-built bald man shot up. "Sit down son!"

"Let him talk." Another rose. "Ain't sayin' he's right, but this gotta be decided."

I'd never seen a funeral hijacked. My heart rapped, and I felt awful for Ruthie Mae. My friend, Montie's sister, sobbing inconsolably in the front pew. Then came a thunderous hammering.

Heel of the pastor's shoe beating on the lectern.

À la Khrushchev.

Sudden stunned silence. "I hear your rage. God hears it." He paced with the limp, wielding the shoe. "As I prepared for today, I had my doubts. Doubts are not evil. I prayed for guidance. 'Show me how to lead them,' I prayed," he cried the words into the rafters.

"A—men," screeked one of the sisters.

The choir hummed. Swayed.

"And God answered."

"Praise be."

"With a telephone call."

"Yes!"

"It was the Reverend King."

"Praise the Lord!"

"He apologized for not joining us in our time of grief. He is in Cleveland registering voters, and he's backbreakingly busy with all the rioting. Dr. King wanted me to assure you we are in his thoughts, and prayers. His heart weeps. I confessed, ashamedly, my own doubts." A galvanized silence gripped even the black-power gang. "He said, Negroes have awakened to their rights and dignity, to the unutterable wretchedness of their lives. He said, Montie Collins behaved irrationally, but no more than those who expect injustice to be eternally endured. He said, to do little to relieve the agony of the Negro is as inflammatory as inciting to violence."

Sobs roiled up. "Montie Collins killed a white man. Blood is on the hands of Negroes. But what of the blood on the hands of Montie and Dorothy's killers. On the hands of white society. On the hands of Congress in Washington, and of President Johnson."

He caught his breath.

Slathered sweat, face sopping. "In the face of these realities," he puffed, "Dr. King appeals to the Negro community to act responsibly."

One last stab from Black Glove, calling King: "Da Lawd." Going on to condemn the civil-rights leader as out of touch, behind the times. Nobody was listening, however. The man dropped his fist. Prowled angrily from the church with no one following. As the daughter of a liberal newspaper editor, however, I knew dangerously increasing numbers disparaged Dr. Martin Luther King exactly as that young man did, as a once-great leader past his prime. Attacked from all sides:

Young militants for adhering to nonviolence.

Everybody else for his opposition to Vietnam.

LBJ no longer welcomed him to the White House.

The Supreme Court had ordered him jailed.

The country was coming apart, splitting into armed camps. Never before in the history of the civil-rights movement—my father had recently editorialized—had whites and Negroes stood so insanely polarized.

The Pastor was going on:

"...Naturally, there is hunger to retaliate, but it escalates! Nonviolent resistance is the only way. Nonviolence paralyses, confuses power structures. Forces the oppressor to commit his brutality openly. Nonviolence is the answer to the crucial questions of our time. Our need to overcome oppression and violence. Without resorting to oppression and violence. If man—black and white—is to survive he must evolve for all conflict a method that rejects revenge, rejects aggression, rejects retaliation. The final word will be had by unarmed truth and unconditional love."

CHAPTER 2

THE SERVICE MOVED TO THE graveside, surrounded by piney woods, red-clay hills, and songbirds flitting hither and yon. A scalding sun beat down as I paid my respects from beyond the rusting fence, back in the saw palmetto and grasshoppers and wafting dust. The clothing next to my body clung with perspiration. I dabbed my lipstick with a corner of Kleenex. I wore plain black rayon. My gloves were black. My pillbox hat and veil were black. What a blonde fish out of water I was.

And that didn't really bother me, want to know the truth, nor did the fact that I knew not a soul, besides Ruthie Mae, in a hundred miles. See, I'd once been Nashville's only female private detective, only one with her own agency, anyway. Thus, being out of the house, amongst strangers, felt oddly calming.

Compared, that is, to my current role of homemaker.

The service ended and I set off across grass and thistle. A white sheriff's deputy, shotgun lazed back across one shoulder, walked a guard post, protecting us from Klan mischief. An Alabama highway patrolman with him wore an army-surplus steel-pot helmet. Another watched from the church portico, both state men also brandishing shotguns. A splintery pair of bullet holes marred the sign:

BARBEE CREEK PRIMITIVE BAPTIST CHURCH.

A quarter mile east along the same road stood blackened timbers, another church, burned by mistake last week by Klan arsonists.

"Miss Sherry… Miss Sherry…"

Ruthie Mae's gasping voice. I pivoted, a weed snagging my black stockings. And there came my once-per-week maid, Bible cradled as she trotted. Followed I was surprised to see by quite an entourage—including, hands pocketed, trailing the main group, the pastor himself.

Ruthie Mae had helped raise her brother. She handed off her Bible and hugged me. I was introduced to a selection of siblings and cousins. One sported full Army regalia with a tall stack of yellow stripes up each sleeve, military medals studding his chest. All gave me embarrassingly reverential treatment. "Sorry for your loss," was all I could manage to say, while the pastor waited off to the side. I excused myself and tramped over, offering my hand. "I'm Sherry Nates, Reverend."

"I know," he said frowningly. "Ruthie mentioned you might come." He gave my hand a squeeze. I lowered my head and shoulders, being the taller of us, and said: "I pray everyone will continue to listen, sir; I could not have agreed more—"

"It is for your own sake you pray."

Drawing up, I shifted the handles of my bag in the crook of my arm. My hazel gaze flickered off to the others through my veil. "For all our sakes," I said, back in the Pastor's face. "Black, and white."

"Come, come."

"I didn't drive all this way," I snapped, "to have my motives questioned, sir."

"I'm told when you were in school, you participated in a Negro sit-in."

"Yes sir. Nursing school. That would have been…1960."

"Hmmph…" He nodded, pulling his pockmarked jawline. "Seven years…"

Sun glinting off pince-nez glasses.

"What have you done lately for the cause of freedom?"

My brows stitched. Cars were starting up and sending up more drifting dust clouds. I replied: "I don't think my husband would approve. Don't get me wrong, he's no racist but he has definite ideas about proper behavior for a wife."

"We are all racists, Mrs. Nates."

"Excuse me?"

"Dr. King has said racism is as native to our soil as pine trees, sagebrush, and buffalo grass."

I made a grim little face.

"Still, one must love, honor, and obey one's husband, mustn't one?"

"The Negro's great stumbling block," he said, "is not the White Citizen's Counciler or the Ku Klux Klanner, but the white moderate who is more devoted to order than justice. What do you say to that, Mrs. Nates?"

"I say"—I sighed, glimpsing wispy cotton-candy white clouds against brilliant blue—"I need to be heading back if I'm going to get home in time for supper. But before I go, I have one question, Reverend. Did you really talk to Martin Luther King last night?"

His turn to draw up.

"Why…do you ask?"

I shrugged with shoulders and eyes. "Your secret is safe with me. But some of that oratory was straight out of King's Nobel Prize speech. And you obviously have a working knowledge of his other writings. The reason he's not here isn't voter registration up north, or riots. He's not here because it would be ruinous to his reputation—a little shaky right now anyway—to show direct support for the acknowledged murderer of a white man? What you say to that, Pastor?"

"I say…"

He might've been chewing ten-penny nails.

"Have a nice supper Mrs. Nates."

CHAPTER 3

FRED AND I ARGUED THAT night. It started because my drive from Lavonia County—sixty miles west of Birmingham—took till nearly six-thirty, and Fred's truck was already in the carport. He hadn't been too keen on me driving all that way anyway, for a colored funeral, smack at the core of the latest racial brouhaha. That was just the chivalrously protective Tennessee grizzly bear I'd married. My late arrival, though, added fuel to that fire, as did the time it took me to preheat the oven and bake us a couple of Swanson's beef pot pies, which failed to receive the warmest of greetings when I did get dinner on the table. Anyway that was how it started. But it worked its way around to something that had been a long time coming.

It was July 28, almost four weeks since our first wedding anniversary.

I'd asked Fred to give me one year before we talked about children. He'd done that. Fred always did as promised. He worshipped me. He was absolutely faithful to me. He made a good living and was generous with my "allowance." He was there when I needed him, within reason, to open a jar or bend steel in his teeth. Now I was being asked to uphold my end. "I never promised I'd want to have a baby after a year; I just promised we could talk about it."

"We're talking!"

"No. You're yelling at me." Supper was over. Fred was in his swivel rocker drinking a beer, sock feet on the ottoman. He was six-foot-two and 235 meaty pounds. He kept in shape hauling, stacking, and loading fifty-pound sacks two at a time at the mill-and-grain company he ran for his father. *The Man From UNCLE*, his favorite show, was ending. "I'm sorry," Fred said, glimpsing up. "I'm not yelling now. What's wrong Sherry? Married people have babies. My parents—and your mother by the way—are asking questions I dunno how to answer. They want grandchildren."

"*They* want? That's a reason to bring a child into this world?"

My arms were crossed; I was pacing the pile-carpet in stocking feet, still wearing my black funeral dress.

"*I* want a child. Two or three in fact."

"I know," I said. "Let's just talk about one for now. And I'm not sure I want *that*."

"Why?" he roared.

Then, "Why?" in a civil tone.

My nostrils pulled some air through and there was a wheeze, probably nobody else could hear, that had been there ever since Sal LaRocca broke my nose. Knotting my arms tighter I considered my answer carefully. "If we have a child, Fred," I said, "you are going to go off to work every day like now. And I'll be here with the baby."

"Of course. You're the mother."

"Yes, and I just want to make sure I'm ready, before I assume such a huge responsibility."

"That's awfully selfish, Sherry."

"It's worse than selfish if I have a child and don't give it the love and attention it deserves because there're other things I have to do with my life. I'm trying to be smart. Maybe in a few years."

"There are dangers if we wait."

"I know."

"How long? Till you're thirty? Over thirty?"

"Till I'm ready."

"See, selfish: Thinking of yourself. Not me. Not our parents."

I screamed at the ceiling. Clawed my fingers. "Quit bringing up our parents! Yes, I have to consider your feelings. As for *my* mother, I stopped living my life her way long, long ago. And your parents—they have your sister's kids. They're taken care of."

"My *sister's* kids! My point exactly. Nobody to carry on the Nates name. My father and I are very concerned about that."

"Don't lay that on me."

"It *is* on you."

"These are reasons to have a child?" I said as if through a strainer. "Do you know there are three billion people in this world, and there's a population explosion. They expect six billion by the year 2000."

"Now who's dreaming up bizarre excuses?"

"Do you *listen* to the news? Not sure, selfish or not"—my hazel eyes flashed—"whether I'd feel right about having a child in this day and age. Let's see, what did I hear today, in the car? Detroit is burning. Army paratroopers are there. Martin Luther King is blaming white people. Ahh…let's see…there's a war some place called Biafra. We just got over one in the Mid East. Not to mention record casualties in Vietnam—"

Fred's head began to swing dismissively

"Bombing close to China," I pressed, "LBJ's sending more troops, and the UN says we're on our way to World War Three."

"There've always been wars, Sherry, and people still have babies."

"And some get slaughtered."

"That won't happen."

"You don't know that; you don't know a Russian ICBM won't land in this den five minutes from now."

"You're talking crazy. What are you really afraid of?"

My shoulders sagged.

A crime show called *T.H.E. Cat* was starting; I was staring at the floor. My head shook exhaustedly. "I've told you." I swept over the room. "These four walls," I practically screamed.

"I give you everything!" He roared, thrashing up from his chair. "Still it's not enough!"

He was a hundred pounds heavier than I was. Hands balled into fists. My heart should've been up my throat. Except, I refused to be afraid of the man I was married to. "You do everything and more Fred," I pleaded. "Maybe just talk to me more, sometimes, but that's not it. You do enough. You're a good man. A good husband. I love you."

I took a step.

Caressed the rusty hair blanketing his forearms, then took the callused hands, the fists opened. "I might...want to do some things for myself is all." I got up into his eyes. Willed them to see the seriousness in mine. But he tore away. "Like what?!"

I jerked. Rubbed a spot above the bridge of my nose.

"Maybe a few more nursing shifts. Maybe a case. Occasionally."

"No. Nursing fine. But none of that private-eye lunacy."

My eyes drifted.

"Lunacy..." I started out of the room, unfastening the tiny hook and eye behind my neck and starting to unzip the back of my dress. "I'm going to bed." Not looking back. "Leave the TV on long as you like."

"Sherry..."

I didn't turn.

"Sherry, I could divorce you."

I halted.

Like an ice pick stabbed between two of my vertebra.

From the hallway I craned back.

"No," I answered. Slow, methodical. "I used to work a lot of divorce, remember. The grounds in Tennessee are, let's see..." I stared up. "Adultery, cruelty, desertion, non-support, alcoholism, felony, impotency, pregnancy at marriage, violence, and indignities."

Then I twisted harder, sterner.

"That what you want?"

"*No*, of course not. Just trying to make a point." Fred's turn to look hurt. He liked that I was smart. That I had some college and he didn't. But not if he felt I was using it against him.

"You made it," I said.

Now wasn't the time to announce I wanted to go on the pill.

Nor that I'd been scolded that day for not doing enough to prevent a race war.

CHAPTER 4

IT WAS A TUESDAY IN September, Ruthie Mae McNair on lunch break from her mopping, waxing, and scrubbing. I had made us ham sandwiches and we were talking across my enameled kitchen table, drinking Cokes out of six-ounce bottles in knit holders my mother had sewn out of socks. Our house was a two-bedroom brick ranch off Greenland Drive in Murfreesboro, a college town of 19,000, southeast of Nashville.

It was my husband's and mother's hometown. I'd been born in Nashville but moved to Murfreesboro with my mother when I was nine after my parents divorced. I'd done a year of teachers' college at MTSC, then transferred to Nashville for nursing school. I stayed, working to support myself, until Fred and I got married.

I was an RN, turned PI, turned homemaker.

Living the American dream and Betty Friedan's nightmare. I'd read *The Feminine Mystique* when it came out. Shortly thereafter, by coincidence, I went through some trouble and left full-time nursing. Went off to "find myself" as a detective. One tough, case, though, plummeted me back to earth, and I up and asked Fred to marry me, figuring he'd never get around to it.

Had I *found* myself…?

Ruthie Mae wore a flowered apron over a yellow house dress. She was taller and broader than me. I knew her to be forty-six. By her looks she could've been a dozen years either side of that, true to my mother's maxim, you could never tell with "them." She carried a dignity and strength I'd admired even before the tragedy with the brother. She had four children, ages sixteen to twenty-eight, and was raising her eldest's out-of-wedlock son. Born in New York, the boy visited his working mother there annually during the broiling Tennessee summers. "They ain't found the men yet," she told me thickly, "who killed Montie'n'Dorothy."

I stopped to listen.

"My sister says the FBI give up."

"I doubt that."

She'd finished her sandwich, dabbing maroon lipstick with a napkin. "They made a show of it. All that glorified manpower from Washington. Driving out of town, one after another, big black cars. Like a parade announcin' to the Klan they was goin' and they could take the town."

"You told me Lavonia County wasn't Klan Country."

"Everything's changed. All the riots, cities burning, has whites scared, and I cain't say I blame 'em. They thinkin' they'd better arm themselves against us. And, hard as it is t'say, Miss Sherry, we ain't no better. We got Negro leaders, like that Carmichael, the Black Panthers, prodding our youths to kill and burn. It would help, least down there, if whoever killed Montie and the others got some of the punishment they deserve. Now there ain't even hope for that."

I finished my Coke.

"Why?"

"With the FBI gone...? Why would they do that Miss Sherry? How could they?"

I shrugged. "Guess even the FBI gets spread thin. What about the local sheriff? State cops? They kept the peace during the funerals."

"Only 'cause nobody with a lick a sense wanted a bloodbath. Bad for white business."

"You could give them a *little* credit."

"It's hard." She was rotating her bottle. I got up and carried our plates to the sink. Over my shoulder as I rinsed I said: "So? What about the sheriff?"

"Name's Turbeville."

I glanced back.

"Bobby Ray Turbeville. They call him Sheriff Bobby."

"Un huh…"

"I dunno him; he didn't settle in Lavonia till after the war. 'Bout the time I married Nathan and moved up this way. Me and most of my brothers and sisters got out. Fled to New York or Detroit, or the Army, most anywheres to make a living, other'n that dirt poor ol' county."

"You still have some family there." Plates done, I turned, resting the heels of my hands on the counter edge behind me. "What do they say, about this Turbeville?"

The muddy whites of her eyes swiveled up.

"Say he might be Klan. Course nobody never knows that for sure."

"Why might he be Klan?"

"They say he ran for election on how many…how many *niggers* he'd killed, wearing a badge."

"Oh," I said.

Stiffening.

"I see."

She'd said *niggers* with a snarly tug out one side of her mouth.

The word was never used in my household, nor by my parents. The unpleasant sound of it seemed to lodge somewhere, as I served us coffee. Then I brought over—hesitating, the frivolity feeling suddenly inappropriate—a plate holding two small white-iced cakes, decorated with fall leaves, in orange and brown icing. I'd bought a half-dozen from Home Bakery on South Church and Fred and I had eaten two each for dessert last evening.

Ruthie Mae and her husband had a small farm this side of Manchester. Each weekday she took the bus to Murfreesboro, or Shelbyville, or the outskirts of Nashville, to clean white people's homes. At 8:55 every Tuesday I drove through town, passing the old brick Rutherford County Hospital, to the Trailways depot at Burton and Walnut and picked her up. By three-thirty I'd drop her in front of Penney's on Maple Street and she'd shop until time to catch the bus home.

Wasn't sure I needed a maid.

Fred liked the prestige, and my mother thought one

necessary for any former debutante/lady of the manor such as myself. The maid also had to be black, according to my mother, which gave me the willies about what century she thought we lived in. To assuage my liberal-white guilt I insisted upon paying Ruthie Mae a quarter more than her going rate of $2.00 per hour, for a typical $14 each Tuesday. I considered her a friend, someone to talk to. I wasn't overly simpatico with my neighbors who seemed to pop out babies with disturbing alacrity. "Mary," she was saying, biting off a corner of cake, "who helps Mrs. Spurlock down the street…"

I nodded. "Yes."

"She says Mrs. Spurlock says you used to be some kind of cop, Miss Sherry."

I gave a slight grin.

My head a small shake. "Not exactly."

"You wasn't a detective?"

"I was private."

I swallowed some coffee. Got out a cigarette.

"Ma'am?"

"A private detective."

"Like on TV?"

"Not exactly like TV, but that's the general idea. I snooped, got the goods on cheating husbands and boyfriends. Divorce work basically." I lit the cigarette. "Something I got good at when my fiancé—not Mr. Nates, before him—stepped out on me. Became a living after I lost my nursing job. Actually my license got suspended. That's another story."

I was about to tell it when: "Mary says you told Mrs. Spurlock you had other kinds of cases."

"Uh…criminal cases you mean?"

I shrugged self-effacingly. Blew gray smoke at the ceiling. "Very little," I finally said. "There was a blackmail thing." That *thing* involved Pauline Prescott, the reigning queen of country-western, and had to stay super confidential. "I found a missing person, who was just a runaway. Minor insurance-fraud thing. I only told Brenda any of that because she looked down her snooty nose at the divorce business I'd mostly done." I rolled my eyes. "All I was doing was leveling—"

"I wanna hire you, Miss Sherry."

"What?"

"To look into my brother's murder."

CHAPTER 5

N OT SO FAST..."

"I'll pay you," she said.

"That's not the issue. Whatever I am, I'm certainly not a homicide detective. I do know a guy, though, on the Nashville Murder Squad. Maybe he—"

"I want you."

Slowly I was shaking my head.

"We—my family and me—don't trust the FBI. Even if we did, they gone. They all white. They got other business, like you say. Plus Montie *did* kill that white man. Think they go' go to the mat for him? Half of 'em probably glad it turned out like it did." As she spoke, I found myself recalling my father's well-heeled-attorney friend telling me, when I was working the Music Row extortion matter, not to trust the FBI.

Ol' J. Edgar, he'd opined, would never take a stand against organized crime.

I rose, tapped my ashes in the sink.

Surely this was different?

I turned: "The Feds did convict three Klansmen in the Selma case."

"White woman got killed."

"They're going to trial again next month, I read, in those Philadelphia, Mississippi murders."

"One black," she said, "two whites."

22

"Colonel Penn," I said irritatedly.

Lemuel Penn: Reserve Army officer, shot and killed by night riders, driving home from Fort Benning, Georgia. *What?*—I snagged some hair falling across my cheek—*three, four years back?* I took a pull from my cigarette. Ruthie Mae drank coffee. No doubt there was truth in her cynicism.

She had pretty hair. I'd told her so. Straightened, shiny black, pageboy. My natural color was a "dirty" variety of blonde, though I'd lightened it to a more flaxen to please Fred. Also I'd grown it out. Now it swept gracefully down the sides of my face, a big bouncy flip at the bottom, nearly to my shoulders. "I don't trust whites, Miss Sherry. Just don't. I'm sorry."

"I'm white. White as white gets."

"I trust you. You're a friend. If you'll pardon me saying, ma'am."

I twisted, darted my cigarette in the sink, then went over and sat with her again. Grasped her hand on top of the table. My eyes smiled into hers.

"That preacher put you up to this?"

"No." She waggled her head, smirking. "I promise. And maybe there ain't a lot you can do. Just talk to the sheriff. Maybe them knowing an interested well-to-do white lady is around will…well, kick'em in their asses, pardon my language, Miss Sherry."

I groaned, let my neck go lax, and head drop back. My wallpaper had roosters. My curtains behind the kitchen sink were lime-green check with white ruffled tiebacks and valance. I hauled my head up straight: "Being an interested white lady got Viola Liuzzo shot dead."

Her buxom chest rose and fell.

"I know this ain't your problem—"

"Sure it is. My friends' problems are my problems."

She grinned.

"Let me think about it," I said.

CHAPTER 6

I DIDN'T NEED TO THINK about it.
I wanted to do it.
I'd decided to do it.
I hadn't decided how to break it to Fred.

We were getting along. I mean, no marriage is perfect, right? He'd dropped the baby issue, and I was diving into my happy-homemaker role. Whenever the subject of children did come up, though, however accidentally, the air between us ionized. He'd soon get serious again. Fred had every right to want children, and I felt awful and guilty and sick and all of that. I loved Fred. I loved being married. Sleeping with him. In many ways this was the happiest I'd ever been. Why couldn't it go on, the two of us? I wanted to be all he needed. Was I jealous? Of my own not-yet-even-conceived child? Was I that much of a bitch?

Anyway, going to Alabama, tinkering at the fringes of what the papers called the "Lavonia Massacre," would be a welcome distraction. Also irked me to no end, what that pastor said:

What had I done for freedom in seven years?

How dare he, and his we're-all-racists-under-the-skin baloney.

CHAPTER 7

THE FOLLOWING FRIDAY, SEPTEMBER 15, Ruthie Mae rode the bus to Shelbyville and I drove south out of Murfreesboro, gassed up the Impala, and picked her up, eight sharp, off the steps of the Bedford County courthouse. I'd fried Fred bacon and scrambled him eggs in the grease, and made toast and—kissing me, looking up from his coffee and paper—he'd told me to be extra careful. I'd said I loved him. Ruthie Mae and I snaked west from Shelbyville to Lewisburg, rolling pastures gleaming with dew, like sterling silver, a cool morning, but where we were going the day would be in the eighties. Twenty miles from Alabama we took the southbound ramp onto I-65.

Ten miles from Pulaski.

Pulaski, Tennessee:

Cradle and manger of the Ku Klux Klan.

I knew little of the Klan, no more than any respectable white southerner. I knew it was a hooded society of bigots. I knew of cross burnings and white capes and pointy hats. I knew it had sprouted like a tenacious species of weed throughout the old confederacy, in the ruin following the "late unpleasantness"—to guard, supposedly, the purity of white southern womanhood, under grave threat from all those lustful, freed slaves. My late grandfather had been a member briefly when my mother was a girl. No one much talked about that, her divorce from my father

25

being scandal enough.

The interstate was open to Birmingham, except around Decatur, where we got gas at an Esso. Decatur was a small industrial city on Wheeler Lake, a wide spot along the Tennessee River formed by a series of TVA dams. Hydroelectric power had spurred development in this region of Alabama, transforming an economy that had, a hundred years ago, totally depended on farming. Worse, a single crop. King Cotton. Yet already Ruthie Mae and I had seen textile mills, an aluminum plant, a tire factory. Diversity meant jobs. Jobs meant money in workers' pockets. And relatively stable race relations. My father had taught me the two necessary cofactors for bigotry:

Ignorance.

And poverty.

On the whole though, Alabama was a poor state—fourth poorest, after Mississippi, Arkansas, South Carolina. So as we sloped off the plateau into the true Deep South of Alabama, I knew to be watchful traveling with a black woman. I carried in my handbag my .38 Special Airweight revolver. Hammerless with a two-inch barrel, weighing about a pound. Perfect purse gun.

Fred didn't know.

Nor Ruthie Mae.

And, no, Fred was not happy about this second field trip to Alabama. Especially since I planned to ruffle feathers, giving it the dual distinction of being possibly dangerous, and definitely unladylike. How then had I managed that pleasant, borderline X-rated, kiss goodbye?

Way to a man's heart...

Wednesday night I'd made us cocktails, broiled us steaks, baked us potatoes, which I'd loaded with sour cream, Blue Bonnet, and bacon bits. Served us on the patio, scooped ice cream for dessert, and when we were done, I'd left the mess and tugged Fred into the bedroom, where he didn't mind me getting unladylike. And I was very unladylike. I wasn't on the pill yet, but I'd just had my period. The morning after, my head atop his mountainous shoulder, my body small and naked up against his, I told him I wanted to go to Lavonia with Ruthie Mae. Talk to a few people. For a friend. For the cause. A cause he wasn't all that keen on. For crissakes he'd voted for Goldwater!

When I was done, I added, I might feel different about a baby.

I didn't believe that, but I'd manipulated my father all my life.

Why spare my husband?

He'd even offered to close the feed store for the day and go along.

A lovely gesture I managed to convince him was unnecessary, plus bad for the family business. What I didn't dare explain was that there were men, I'd been around the block enough to know, who would happily chew the fat, about almost anything, with a 35-25-35 blonde with gams like Marilyn Monroe's, who would just as soon throw a punch at, or run scared from, a muscular giant like Fred.

And neither reaction would learn us squat about the Lavonia Massacre.

Ruthie Mae directed me along a jagged collection of rural routes in and amongst the wooded hills leading to Haleyville. A good two-lane wound south from there through Boston, Brilliant, and Winfield. Hardwoods gave way to pines, signs marking coal-mining and logging operations up red-clay roads twisting back into the timber. A fading-in-and-out Birmingham radio station played "Ode to Billie Joe," "Pleasant Valley Sunday," "Penny Lane." Our appointment with the sheriff was for one-thirty. I was looking at my watch; I was starved, and wanted to bone up at the local library before the meeting, gather the basic facts of the case.

Cases, actually:

The murders of Montie Collins, et al.

And the murder Collins supposedly committed.

It was already a quarter to twelve when we crossed into Lavonia County, through some pinewoods, past fields gone to seed, and chapels belonging to one fundamentalist denomination or another—or if not the actual church, then a sign indicating it down some dirt road. Approaching Lavonia proper there was an American Legion Post, a general aviation airport, a clean-cut-looking county hospital. The city-limits marker stated a population of 4,227, and seals proclaimed local chapters of the

Lions and Kiwanis Clubs.

No mention of the KKK.

A lumber mill, a big cemetery—the white cemetery, Ruthie Mae noted—white high school, white funeral home. Churches galore, most Baptist or Methodist, one Church of Christ, one Assembly of God. Yellow-red dust skipped across unpaved side streets and a red light swayed and bounced from a nexus of power lines at Columbus Street, which gave all the appearances of being the main drag. Hardware stores, Rexall, barber shop, beauty shop. At Columbus and First stood a dry goods store called Savitz's. If anything, Lavonia's downtown was proportionally busier than inner-city Nashville—from where much retail had fled to the suburbs. For Lavonia, you see, had no suburbs.

You were either in the city...or the third-world country that was the rural South of 1967.

We ate at the drifting-cigarette-smoke-filled Mayflower Café. Hiked onto two stools at the counter, careful to sweep our skirts under us. I ordered a burger and fries, telling the girl to hurry. Ruthie Mae had the catfish blue-plate special. I lit a cigarette, shook out the match and dropped it in a glass ashtray. The noon news on a GE radio by the register reported LBJ pushing for gun control, Arabs derailing an Israeli train, and Red China halting their shelling of India.

"By the way, Miss Sherry..."

I glimpsed over.

Ruthie Mae palmed me a folded twenty. "Never did say how much you charge."

"I'm not taking your money." I placed the bill on the Formica, and slid it back, then I rotated facing her, elbow on the counter, cigarette shoulder level, pad of my thumb on the filter tip. "I want to help, that's all."

"Ain't asking for charity, Miss Sherry. I'll pay, 'less my money ain't good enough."

"That's not it."

"What do you charge? My family will chip in if twenty for the day ain't 'nough."

My chest rose and fell.

She was offering to pay me, it occurred, almost half-again as much as the fourteen bucks I paid her for a day's work. Hard work, at that. No sense rubbing it in, telling her I'd earned sixty per day—on one case, seventy—as a detective in Nashville.

I took the twenty.

Wrote her a receipt.

We parked on the public square two blocks north. West side of the square stood the courthouse. The post office was to the north, the old brick Lavonia Memorial Library to the south. The librarian, spine like a question mark, got me all the newspapers published locally as well as in Birmingham and Tuscaloosa, starting with July 18, day after the initial killing, and continuing through July 29, a week following the discovery of the four murders blacks.

That netted me two issues of the weekly *Lavonia County Broadcaster*, and twelve days worth of the two Birmingham papers, and the *Tuscaloosa News*. I set aside the two local papers and the others from the eighteenth through the twenty-third, and skimmed the remainder. Those papers aside, I took out a pad and Bic pen and jotted notes as I read the others. I wished I'd learned shorthand sometime along the way, but I'd believed the adage that a woman who knew shorthand would be a secretary for life.

The first stories led the morning papers of Tuesday, July 18.

The Tuscaloosa headline was plain enough:

White Farmer Gunned Down by Negro

Smaller type below:

Victim Blasted Seven Times;
Killer a 'Beast' Says Sheriff

CHAPTER 8

APPROXIMATELY THREE O'CLOCK MONDAY AFTERNOON, July 17, Mr. Jesse B. "J.B." Roberts, 52, a Bankston man, was shot to death in his barn, victim of apparent robbery. His wife, Ginny Seeley Roberts, heard shots—eight of them—and entered, finding Montie Roosevelt Collins, 26—a Negro (as each article went out of its way to detail)—crouched over the body holding, literally, a smoking gun. That gun was Roberts' own Army-issue .45, kept in the barn's tack room. Collins fled. Lavonia County Sheriff Bobby Ray Turbeville found him at his home elsewhere on the Roberts' farm at approximately 3:40 P.M. Collins confessed to having struck and robbed Roberts, and handed over the stolen cash. Deputies found the murder weapon in a stack of firewood outside. Collins was arrested.

Heel of a hand against the heavy ornamental table edge, I creaked the wooden ladder-back, disturbing library silence. I blinked, and used a manicured pinkie nail on an itch, careful not to disrupt my eye makeup. Then I took the Kents out of my pocketbook and lit one. I smoked, contemplating the crown molding, troweled over with about eight coats of paint. The cigarette moved to and from my lips with easy swivels of my wrist. Filter tip staining ever more deeply pink.

I got up.

Paced.

Something was already bothering me.

Too early, though, to start mixing up facts with interpretations.

Just the facts, Sherry, for now—the Jack Webb approach. The facts were, I knew from Ruthie Mae, her brother had been a sharecropper. He'd grown corn on a section of the Roberts' over sixteen hundred acres. Collins went to Roberts that day to discuss buying that plot of land he'd been working. This purchase, according to the family, had been the anticipated outcome of a longstanding handshake agreement between the men. However, that day, Roberts refused to sell. They argued, Montie demanding restitution for the extra share of his harvest he'd been handing over to Roberts for years. Five percent Montie had understood would apply toward his future acquisition of the property. Roberts claimed the markets had been weak, the money had gone to offset cash loans, and housing and equipment expenses. Collins had shamefacedly— according to the family—told his pregnant wife, moments before the sheriff's arrival, that he'd flown into a rage, convinced he was being cheated, and clubbed Roberts with a horseshoe puller.

And that was that.

Except for pilfering cash out of the unconscious man's wallet. Cash he reasoned he was owed. At which point he beat a hasty retreat, not having ever seen, much less handled, a gun.

Nor had he seen the victim's wife.

Glimpsing a wall clock, I was still finishing my cigarette when I retook my seat. Plowed through the remaining newspapers. Collins had been arraigned. Wednesday, July 19. Pled not guilty to murder. Bail set. Separate items covered Ku Klux Klan Grand Imperial Wizard John Riley Hobbs arriving from Tuscaloosa, promising his people would be "observing" and "assisting" local authorities. My introduction to what I came to know as a Klan trait: They considered themselves semi-official arms of local law enforcement. One article quoted Hobbs, holding an impromptu rally on the courthouse steps, saying: "People think of nigras as human because they have hands and feet. But the Bible don't say nothing about them having souls."

Concluding:

"Only good nigra is a dead nigra."

That very night, Wednesday, night riders shotgunned the home of a black school-bus driver for Head Start. On Thursday the parsonage of a Negro Methodist church in Lavonia was torched. On Friday, more fires: a grocery owned by a white ex-Klansman who'd become an FBI informant, and a Negro Baptist church, site of a Head Start program.

That same Friday, NAACP Tuscaloosa chapter president George Wesley came to town—with one thousand dollars raised by black congregations all over Alabama. He also brought a bondsman willing to post Montie Collins' remaining bail. Collins' release was delayed, however. The bondsman, having done his part, departed. George Wesley returned to the jail at seven P.M., accompanied by Dorothy Collins and Esther Malcolm, a local black school teacher active with the NAACP.

The librarian, thick bifocals, doddered through straightening things.

Whispered, "Need anything more dear?" Glancing up, I gave my head a shake. "That dress is such a pretty blue." I thanked her and drawstringed my brows, paging to the finish line of this horror story. Some further delay...reasons vague... Not till 8:05, around sunset, when George Wesley and the women finally left with Montie Collins. Headed south out of town on Route 171 in Wesley's blue Ford Galaxy. Intended destination: Wesley's house outside Tuscaloosa.

Wesley's wife reported them missing about ten P.M. The disappearance solved the next afternoon when three boys playing in the woods with coonskin caps and toy flintlocks, drawn by a sour odor, and the drone of thick swarms of flies, made a grisly discovery.

Four Negroes—two men and two women, one late in pregnancy—bound to trees in a circle. Shot to death. The Ford, gutted by fire, half submerged in the swampland bordering the Sipsey River three miles north of the Tuscaloosa County line. The last item I had time to read, from the *Birmingham Post-Herald*, Sunday, July 23, stated Lavonia Sheriff Bobby Ray Turbeville was investigating.

Aided by FBI resident agents.

Which, I knew, had come to nothing.

Poor little boys, I sighed. Recalling when the Biloxi Police showed me Woody Stinson's corpse dragged out of the Back Bay.

Into *this* world...

My husband wanted us to bring a child?

CHAPTER 9

THE SHERIFF'S HEADQUARTERS WAS A two-story brick building diagonally across from the square, pie-wedged between the post office and courthouse. The square was a small grassy park upon which spired a memorial to the county's Confederate war dead. Four cast-iron cannons stood guard; it was a nice little marker. I felt my Southern heritage, a temblor of pride—though, considering why we were there, I was sure I could never adequately explain that to Ruthie Mae. Not prideful of the bigotry, certainly not the slavery, but the heroism.

Fighting and dying for a cause believed in.

For one's home.

A larger grimmer structure of similar age and Italian Renaissance styling, roof parapeted, eaves boxed, backed up to the sheriff's department—the county jail, I deduced from the barbwire and rust-flecked window bars. We went to the front entrance on Second Street, up two concrete steps, and entered a foyer narrow, deep, and gloomy. Off came my Foster Grants.

On the left a counter was manned by a barrel-chested deputy. On the right clopping down a wide staircase was a fluffy blonde cradling a ledger. She hauled the ledger and her jiggedy rump into an office beneath the stairs, the deputy leering. I waved my business card, and the big head unscrewed to the front:

"Afternoon..."

His eyebrows needed a trip to the barber all on their own.

He stepped up, grinning out one side of his mouth—a blonde in hand is, after all, worth two in the bush—"How can I hepya, young lady?" I said the sheriff was expecting us. Slapped my card onto the countertop. Slid it with a finger gloved in beige crocheted nylon. Prying it up, he donned some drugstore cheaters. A window air-conditioner flustered bulletin boards and baskets. A phone jangled somewhere and a typewriter was touch-typed by someone who knew how. The deputy carefully, as if the letters were Phoenician, read:

"Sherry Russell."

I was licensed in my maiden name.

"Private detective."

The shaggy brows jumped.

"Yew joshing ol' Dudley?"

"No sir. I'm from Nashville." I glanced back at Ruthie Mae, telling him my client and I had an appointment. He consulted a schedule like it was a geometry proof. I snapped my purse closed. Eventually he agreed gleefully we were in fact on the calendar. First door on the left, he directed. Candy and cigarette machines flanked the door, which had a scalloped glass pane, and slanted stick-on mailbox letters spelling SHERIFF. A secretary on the other side had hair that was dyed brutally red. Walleyed, she nevertheless announced us, and soon after heavy footsteps approached from behind a plain brown door, which was snatched open just shy of being torn from its hinges.

A great ox of a man emerged.

He had a broad face, large ears and blue eyes behind thick-rimmed glasses. He was bald up front, dark-haired and wavy from the sideburns back, with graying temples. Forty-something, taller than my Fred, which would make him six-three or better. Heavier too, perhaps 250. Perhaps more. He would have more fat than Fred but plenty of muscle all the same. His right jowl bulged as if he stashed spare golf balls there, but from the pouch stuffed down his right breast pocket I deduced it was Red Man, not Titleist, misshaping his face. He wore khaki, a polished law-officer's star, and a gun belt studded with ammo for the revolver he was packing. I got a whiff of sour sweat as he grabbed and shook my hand. Hard like a politician, which is what, I reminded myself, sheriffs were.

"Bobby Ray Turbeville," he practically shouted. "Yuke'n call me Bobby."

"Sherry Russell. We spoke on the phone."

He bowed gallantly.

Then, quarter-turning:

"Must be Mrs. McNair?"

"Née Collins."

I backed out of the way; he took her hand, cupping his other on top.

"You're...Charlie's sister, Charlie's and Abigail's."

"Yes suh."

"My condolences."

Aching sincere.

Or excellently practiced, for a man who'd supposedly run for office on how many Negroes he'd gunned down. The Voting Rights Act meant for the first time in many parts of the South politicians had to seriously court the black vote. Turbeville had a long hot corner office with shag carpet and the mounted head of a large antlered buck on the long inside wall. "You hunt, Sheriff?" I asked.

"Aw, I do. Most ever'body round here does, I reckon. But I didn' shoot that—one of my predecessors left it and nobody's ever took it down. Sorta like my dep'ty." He grinned. "Reckon it's one of Lavonia County's trappings of power." Three tall windows, floor to ceiling let a lot of sun stream through. Two were on the right, looking out onto the post office and square. The third backlit the sheriff's desk, and viewed the north exposure of the alabaster courthouse. A lawyer's bookcase and row of file cabinets flanked a credenza that covered the lower third of that window. The desk was inlaid hardwood, too small to be a national monument. He indicated for us to sit in round-backed armchairs facing the desk, then squeaked back in his own swivel chair, large hands over his stomach.

I crossed my legs, smoothed my skirt so my slip didn't show, and took out my license.

Turbeville reached for it.

"Issued by the District Attorney General of Metropolitan Davidson County."

He gave a ponderous couple of nods and returned it between

two fingers. "Duly impressed," he said. A foot-tall *Playboy* wall calendar caught my eye, rather the half-nude brunette did, heart-faced, pink-negligéed. I blinked, gave my head a little shake. "Your man at the desk, Sheriff, didn't seem to be expecting us."

"Saw no reason to a'vertise. We just getting things settled."

"You mean the FBI leaving?"

He gave a dull shrug.

"Partly."

"Eight weeks have passed with no arrests in a crime the press calls the Lavonia Massacre."

I got a coarse look, then he leaned down his side—

Out leaping a long brown snake of tobacco juice. My mouth spasmed at both corners. A liquidly metallic sound as the expulsion entered what I gathered to be the maw of a spittoon, down behind the desk.

Facing front again, he said:

"Pardon, you were saying?"

I took out a cigarette and lit it. Blew smoke at the ceiling, tiled with tarnished decorative tin. "My clients are the Collins family. They're concerned..." He pushed an ashtray to the front edge.

I tossed my burnt match in it.

"They're concerned about—frankly sir—that lack of arrests."

His Red Man got some strong chews. His head shoved back, his eyes roaming. Maybe the buck's head had the answer. The windows were raised. An oscillating fan rotated. Ruthie Mae wore navy pumps and white earrings with a brown dress. Mine was an aquamarine Mary Lewis shirtdress, six pair of tiny gray buttons trimming the front. My shoes were patent-vinyl slingbacks. I flickered an eye at the nude calendar girl. Hard not to. Turbeville finally planted a black boot against his desk edge. "I'm a law officer, Mrs. Russell, not a vigilante."

"Yes sir."

"Ain't sayin' we ain't got vigilantes." He shrugged. "But we cain't go round arresting citizens, accusing them of vigilante killings. Now can we? Not without *probable cause*"—he extended one thick finger, focusing on each of us, one at a time—"*grand-jury indictments*"—a second finger—"*warrants*"—a third. "I operate this department, ladies, according to the procedures of the criminal-justice system of the State of Alabama. Now, Mrs. Russell, do the wheels of justice turn any different up there'n big ol' Nashville?"

I tapped some ashes.

"Not as a rule. What can you tell me about the FBI's apparent abandonment of the case?"

He shrugged. "My case, Feds or no."

"A turf war?"

"Wonna call it that—I call it the Constitution of the United States of America—in which the Founding Fathers intended the powers of the central government to be limited. Well, the FBI don't seem to limit itself too darn much when it comes to bullying states below the Mason-Dixon."

I felt Ruthie Mae stiffen.

I glimpsed over.

Then back:

"I'm as southern a gal as you're likely to meet, Sheriff, but state's-rights, far as race relations, became water over the dam about a hundred years ago. Little place called Appomattox."

"Neither you, nor me, Mrs. Russell, has ever held a slave."

"Racial injustice didn't end with slavery."

"What's wrong with *separate but equal?*"

"What's wrong!" Ruthie Mae roared.

He deflected her way.

"I do mean equal, ma'am. I'll admit, we haven't always achieved that ideal."

"We could argue this all day," I sighed. "What can you tell me about the FBI?"

"Nothing." He tilted and adjusted his eyeglasses. "They don't consult me. Hell, I'm probably a suspect. Point is, they bullied their way in. That's their job, I s'pose. But mine's same whether they're here or they ain't. So, to me, they was just in the way."

"The FBI has more manpower, resources, and expertise than any law-enforcement agency in the State of Alabama, right?"

"Sure."

"I'd think you'd appreciate having that kind of assistance. You can't tell me a quadruple murder is commonplace for this office."

"No, but you're naïve. Any help from the Feds comes with a

great many strings attached."

"I don't understand."

He huffed. "Lemme put it this way, ladies: In these parts, many people say F-B-I stands for Fed'ral Bureau of Integration."

"Oh my Lord," muttered Ruthie Mae.

Turbeville looked. "That's not me talkin', Mrs. McNair. It's the majority of the white population I'm sworn to serve and protect—equally. But all that FBI manpower, resources and expertise you're so impressed by—we pay for all that, all us, with our tax dollars. But…uh, looking up from down here, to a lot of folks, it all goes to support the Negroes and Jews, never the whites."

Ruthie Mae stirred.

I'd told her to let me do the talking—perhaps that had been insensitive.

"I investigate," Turbeville went on, "all homicides in Lavonia County: white, black, Creek Indian. Except what falls under police chief Rayburn's jurisdiction, and I help there *if asked*. Who prosecutes? The county solicitor. What it boils down to, ladies, is we don't need no FBI to handle a homicide. One homicide. Or four. And if I do need help, I'm quite capable of askin'."

"Your opinion then," I said. "Why did the FBI leave in so obvious a fashion? Even if you've given up, or have some place more important to be, does it seem good policy to advertise that fact. Unless, it was a ploy…?"

A strenuous shrug.

"I—don't—know."

He spat again.

"Look, Mrs. Russell, you yanked my collar, yanked it good, for making no arrests. Fine. Not the first time I been criticized, and don' reckon it'll be the last. But your FBI didn't make no arrests neither. They solve the case, I'll give credit where credit's due. But they made a lotta noise, disrupted a lotta lives. Got me made me out like some bumpkin with a tin star on national TV. And in all that they didn't get the job done. So, good gol dang riddance, I say to the FBI."

Ruthie Mae exploded to her feet. "C'mon Miss Sherry!"

"Wait—"

"Tawkin' this peckerwood's like tawkin' to that ol'

Confederate monument out there."

And she walked slammingly out.

For a few heartbeats, I stared after her, debating whether to follow.

In the end I rotated back to Turbeville. "Sorry," I sighed.

"Me too. Not your fault or mine. Lot to be upset with us about. Us whites, I mean."

I nodded. "Montie Collins's family? Or Negroes as a race?"

"Both."

I nodded. Lit another cigarette in silence. Studied the sheriff as I licked the smoke. "Mighty diplomatic," I observed, "for a man who doesn't mind blustering he's bitter about tax money supporting Jews and Negroes."

"I calls'em as I sees'em. Only way, in my opinion, for a man to operate."

I nodded.

"You a Klansman?"

"What? No. I'm not."

He spat into the unseen spittoon, then rolled back:

"If I was, though, I wouldn' say."

"I'll keep that in mind."

He studied me through his eyeglasses. I kept smoking. Car noises rose and fell. All through it hummed his electric fan. He rearranged in his snapping, popping chair. Adjusted the glasses. "You didn't come all this way, did you ma'am, to jaw with no peckerwood 'Bama sheriff?"

"No, sir. I wanna look through your case file on the massacre."

His eyes beetled. "That all?"

"Look, Sheriff—"

"Bobby, please."

"No," I said, "I prefer to keep our dealings professional."

He shrugged. "'Kay."

"Sheriff, I have no wish to get in anybody's hair. I doubt I can add anything. I've told Mrs. McNair that. I do divorce work. Not multiple murders."

His round head tilted.

Listening. In truth I didn't think so little of myself, but if I didn't schmooze the coach, I wasn't going to get to bat. "If I could glance through the file," I continued, as if the prospect bored me, as if I'd rather get back to tatting doilies, "enough to assure the family everything possible is being done, and then I can collect my fee, and you'll never see me again."

I feel so guilty when I lie.

Rocking slowly, thumbs knocking, Turbeville brooded.

Then came an eruption of rowdy laughter. Bowing the walls, reverberating. He swiveled and bucked. Coming to rest, shoulders spastic: "Now I heard ever'thing." He exploded an open palm onto the desk. I jumped. He flung back, grasping the chair's arms. "Past few weeks"—barely able to speak over his giddiness—"I've talked to *Life* magazine, been up to my neck in TV reporters, all the networks, Charles Kuralt even. I've had white community leaders, Negro community leaders, preachers, Rabbis. Had the NAACP breathin' down my neck, the CDR, the SPLC. But this is positively—"

Gave the chair arm a mirthful slap!

"—the first time a sweet young thing has come along with her maid no less and asked to take over my case. This is goddamn priceless." Twisting ninety degrees, clapping palms to his sweat-riveted forehead. "I got for crissakes Scarlett O'Hara and Mammy in my office!"

"Sheriff…" I said levelly.

"Say no more."

Mock surrender.

"Wanna look at files. Look at files. What the hell? FBI's probably gonna arrest me tomorrow, anyway, as a mass murderer, right?"

CHAPTER 10

TURBEVILLE ESCORTED ME TO AND grabbed open the door, waiting for me to go through. There was a padlocked gun rack as I went out, four shotguns and a carbine hunting rifle with a scope. The redhead passed me a message. Ruthie Mae had gone to her sister's. I wasn't to worry if I needed to leave; she'd manage a ride home. She apologized.

I was glad.

The case file would reveal gruesome details, hidden from the public, about the violent death of a boy she'd practically raised. I was dreading them, and I was an experienced emergency nurse. I was glad, though, humbled she was trusting me enough to let me do the dirty work. Dirty work, after all, was my business.

What I was getting paid the twenty bucks for.

Turbeville and I would reconvene in two hours. Generous, I supposed, considering I was being granted unfettered access to official records. It was also about as long as I dared devote to this project that day, not wanting to test Fred's patience too much.

"One other thing, Sheriff."

I rotated, lightly grasping the knob of the door with the scalloped glass.

"Done told you, call me Bobby."

"Okay. Bobby. The Roberts killing…"

"Yeah?"

The broad head tipped back.

With a pouty mouth and one shoulder, I shrugged:

Asking to skim that file also.

Air blew in and out, Turbeville resting weight on his gun belt which creaked. "Pretty thin," he finally said. "The file, I mean. That case, remember, was open and shut."

"It surely was," I said.

"Montie Collins was J.B. Roberts' killer. Got him dead to rights, eyewitness. And Collins' death—however tragic, however regrettable—his death made the first case moot."

"Yes," I said.

"It surely did do that, didn't it?"

CHAPTER 11

I WAS LOANED USE OF a long yellow oak table in a second-floor conference room that in summer you could have cooked a casserole in. Since it was mid September, slow roasting a pot roast was all I might've managed. There were peeling gray-green walls, and a single window standing open, facing one of the barred windows of the old jail. The fluffy blonde brought through her first armload from a shabby back corridor. One more trip, she told me with a pale-eyed glower, resenting pack-horsing for another mere blonde. A ceiling fan stirred the mugginess; fluorescent tubes flickered a gray light, giving me a headache. Nailed up with carpet tacks was a road map of Alabama and a U.S. Geological Survey map of Lavonia County. I studied them, and drank from a Coke, and thought about Turbeville leaving me unsupervised with all these official records.

Relating to, no doubt, the two biggest crimes ever committed in his jurisdiction.

That seemed, to me, either sloppy...

Or foolishly trusting.

Four brown legal-size folders—thick and heavy, bound with strong rubber bands, identical case numbers scrawled in Magic Marker on each—comprised the documentation, to date, of the Lavonia Massacre investigation. The murders of Montie and

Dorothy Collins, George Wesley, and Esther Malcolm. Two folders were devoted to the expected ghastly collection of black-and-white photos.

Every conceivable angle.

Every victim.

Three different stages:

As they'd been found—bound to trees, slumped forward in death—then unclothed at the mortuary, before and after washing.

There were zoom-lens shots of every wound.

And there were a lot of those.

In fact, to my untrained, horrified eye, it appeared these people had been machine-gunned!

That hadn't been in the papers, nor been told to me by Ruthie Mae. Other glossies detailed the scene: half-submerged, gutted Ford, bloodstained ground, bullet-scarred trees, footprints, tire tracks, clothing, fired cartridge cases indicated with little placards. Folder #3 contained autopsy reports, crime-scene log, sketched diagrams, complete with exact distances, estimated bullet trajectories, positions of victims and key evidence. One sketch noted that a certain five-by-one-foot smattering of ejected .45-caliber shells—average ten feet out, ninety-degree angle to the line of fire—was consistent with a Thompson submachine gun.

Jesus!

The fourth file was chock-full of reports, reports, reports. Handwritten, typed, originals, carbons. Authored by deputies, the sheriff, FBI. There were witness statements, dozens of transcripts from interviews. None stamped boldly: CONFESSION or PRIME SUSPECT. I didn't have time to read any reasonable sampling. Instead I jotted a list of interview subjects, in case I ran across someone just back from Mars who wasn't included.

And suddenly, I thought—

Maybe, I'd found just such a person.

Next I went back to the photos, the autopsy reports. Bullet riddled. Insect covered. Wrists wrenched behind tree trunks, bound with coat hanger wire, or twine. Ordinary bailing twine. There'd been a fruitless effort to track the purchaser. Other details, purged from family newspapers, were retchingly clear. The truth of racial violence too much for the public to stomach, least at the breakfast table. Both men: savagely beaten before being shot. My cigarette coiled smoke from between my first two fingers, my thumb massaging my temple in hard little circles.

They'd also been castrated.

The women stripped to their underclothes.

I was drawn to Dorothy's gravid belly jutting between her maternity bra and panties, vividly white against her deep brown flesh. There were abdominal contusions of a characteristic shape, the autopsy having confirmed cause and effect.

Baseball bat.

Male fetus's skull fractured.

Neither woman had been sexually assaulted.

CHAPTER 12

TEN AFTER THREE.

Fifty minutes left.

I put aside the Lavonia Massacre files, drained my Coke and extinguished a cigarette, ashtray spilling over with identical lipstick-stained butts. I pressed the heels of my hands into my forehead, and bent over the back of my chair to ease a cord of pain. Then I scuffed back. Paced, kneading my lumbar muscles, my heels light and sharp. I fingered a collar, and some hair back from my face. Bending, I stared across the alley, into the barred window of the jail building. Curious, but I saw no face leering back. I went and stood over a fifth brown manila folder.

"Why you wanna look at that file Miss Sherry?"

Ruthie Mae, caustically.

"Because I need to," I'd told her, driving down.

Traffic filtered up through the window. The case file of the J.B. Roberts murder was positively anorectic. "Don't Miss Sherry," she'd pled. "I know Montie killed dat man, and I feel racked all over with guilt 'cause I helped raise him. And…cain't help thinking, did I do sumptin' wrong? Sumptin' made him bad." Nobody thought that, I'd told her. "We've accepted what he was," she pressed, "but even if he did reap what he'd sown, the others didn't deserve it. We hafta carry that guilt too."

"I know. If I didn't I wouldn't be going."

47

"Why look at that file? Why drag up the bad?"

"You asked me to help," I'd said from behind the wheel. "Unless you've changed your mind, you have to trust me."

"That's hard." The words as if knocked out of her by a blow.

"The trust part?" I'd asked.

Glancing over.

Spastic nod.

"I know," I said, eye on the road.

"But I can only do this my way."

There wasn't much in the file so I took notes on almost everything. Example: the desk man, Dudley, had logged the call from Mrs. Roberts, reporting her husband's shooting, as coming in at 3:10 P.M. I looked at that again when I got to Montie Collins' signed statement. He didn't own a watch, so his timeline was vague. He did, however, claim the clock in his kitchen had read not quite a quarter past three, "shortly" after he'd arrived home. He'd remembered because he was eager for his wife to get there, which she usually did by 3:20 or 3:30. Elsewhere was a highway-patrol estimate that the circuitous route Montie had traveled home—including a four-minute stop by a freight train—would have taken him approximately thirteen and a half minutes.

Something was off. Maybe not enough to matter.

But there was nothing in the file to suggest the discrepancy had ever been reconciled.

Nothing to suggest it was ever noticed.

Twenty to four, I was having a cigarette, counting cartridge cases on a sketch of the crime scene. The sketch included a stick figure of the murdered man sprawled in the breezeway of the horse barn, off which faced rows of stalls. He lay outside the open door of a tack room. The sketch included blood stains snaking—

Heavy boots tromped along the corridor outside.

I looked up upon the blurry image of a big man in khaki filling the door's opaque window.

It was not, however, the sheriff throwing open my door.

Barging through, interrupting me, with all the decorum of a Tibetan yak. Barking: "Who the hell are you?"

I scraped my chair around.

"I'm from the Emily Post Institute. We're considering adding that to our list of acceptable greetings, when the new edition of the *Blue Book of Social Usage* comes out."

"Hunh?" he practically shouted.

Front teeth stuck out.

A younger smaller edition of the sheriff: thirty-five-ish, six feet, around 225. Same uniform, same bullet-studded belt, six-gun, black boots. Still on his head, in the presence of a lady, probably meaning the Emily Post reference was lost on him, he wore a very-sweat-stained white Stetson, with rolled-up side brims. He removed a pair of gold-framed sunglasses to lick me over with wide-set steel-blue eyes. He made a show of carefully folding the glasses, hooking them outside a shirt pocket. Then shut the rickety green door.

Locked it.

Swaggered up. He had a small grinning mouth; he half sat on the edge of the table. One boot on the floor, he swung the other. "Who are you, and wha's the meaning of all this?"

Twining arms, I introduced myself.

"As for *all this*, it's between me and the sheriff. Ask him, and please excuse me. I have limited time."

"Yappy little thing ain'tcha?" He brought a card from under the flap of a pocket. My card, the one I'd given ol' Dudley. Had to be. Chewing a wooden match, the lawman held it by the four-corners like a photo. Studied me, then it, as if comparing us. "Sherry Russell...*this* Sherry Russell?"

"Obviously."

"Private eye?"

"Yes."

He glanced around, then lowered the inbred pig-mouthed face and hovered close. "Why don't you jus' go'wn right now," he said. "I'll give your regrets to the sheriff. He'll understand."

My heart skipped.

"Git out. Go." His head tossed at the door.

I sat, gnawing my lower lip.

Pulled it loose.

"I'm not a dog," I said. "I am, however, a guest of the sheriff...Deputy, is it?"

"*Chief* Deputy."

He shoved his chest out.

Small pig mouth, still grinning. "Chief Deputy Cecil Loftin."

Half of me thought the prudent act would be to leave. I was alone, the door locked. Not in a way I couldn't unlock it from the inside, mind you, but in a way no one could get in from the outside if I were, say, screaming for my life. Certainly Chief Deputy Loftin would be easily capable of preventing me from reaching said door for any purposes of escape, if he wished. Chief Deputy Loftin could do anything he wanted to me, if I failed to get my gun out of my purse, before he drew his. The point being, Chief Deputy Loftin held…*most* of the cards.

But I didn't think he'd play them.

I decided to play tenacious.

After a few seconds he re-pocketed my card and spat away the splintered matchstick, then paced. He got out a pack of Marlboros, split it open, and shook one loose. "If you're the chief," I asked, "how many Indians are there?"

He turned, cigarette plugged in next to the grin.

"Sassy," he said. "Yappy and sassy."

"My husband's nickname for me—how'd you guess?"

He seemed amused by that, and answered my question:

"Full time, jus' me and Bobby Ray. Four part-timers though, and Dudley. All he does is run the desk." Loftin mined his shirt for a fresh wooden match. He fired it with his thumbnail and lit up, spewing smoke. The match extinguished with a shake, placed on the ledge. I tracked him, rotating. My elbow down the back of my chair. One thigh atop the other, my nylon-clad knee snagging leering attention. My left thumb absently twisting my diamond wedding set.

I imagined a call.

To Loftin, on patrol: There's this Nashville PI snooping into things. Loftin grilling the caller, hightailing it back. Call from who? Dudley on his shortwave. The sheriff. Why not the redhead, or the blonde? Did it matter? No proof it meant anything to the caller, beyond interesting office gossip. Loftin's reaction, though, was intriguing. He wanted rid of me and he thought barking some orders would do it.

Most people instinctively obey uniformed officers. He didn't know I wasn't most people. I might've done the same in his place. Which was what? Lawman with something to hide? I got my smoldering cigarette, tapped the ashes, and took a pull. Or just a little man with a big gut and bigger gun and a lust for throwing his weight around. His Marlboro sagged between two fingers, the other hand wedged down a hip pocket, sole of one boot against the peeling wall.

"Who was that Negress?"

"Mean, the lady I came with? My client."

Back of his eyes, something shifted. "You'd *work* for one a them?" he said with disgust of the sort saved for graphic discussions of sexual perversity. "You, a seeming decent white lady."

"I work for whoever needs me, and pays my fee."

I shrugged. "Besides, sometimes she works for me."

He cursed me with a strange word.

Out of his small mouth, through clenched teeth.

"Mongrelization."

He slung down his cigarette.

Ground it under. He unlocked and opened the door. Then paused, glowering back.

"Well, say one thing…"

He sighed.

"What's that?"

"Nigger lovers these days come in lot prettier packages."

CHAPTER 13

CECIL O. LOFTIN WAS THERE, at four o'clock, when I met back with Sheriff Turbeville in the long office. I knew the chief deputy's middle initial from paging through many signed reports. I shut the door behind me, and crossed the shag on my slingbacks, Turbeville rising. Past the gun rack and below the stag's head I glimpsed some photos and plaques and certificates clustered on the wall. One photo in a dime-store gold frame was of a young Turbeville, in combat gear, posed in front of a snowbound battle tank.

World War II?

Korea?

Loftin stood on the sheriff's right-hand side, stubby fingers laced across his chest, elbow atop a file cabinet. The dark glasses and white Stetson were in place. He blocked my view, at least, of the calendar girl who couldn't quite keep both her boobs inside her nightgown at the same time. Turbeville waited till I had sat, then reclined, hefting his left boot atop his right thigh, showing about an inch of hairy calf where his pant leg rose above the lip of the boot. He pulled the Red Man from his shirt and refreshed the bulge in his cheek, then explained Loftin had brought him some legitimate concerns.

"About…?"

"Outside mixers."

"Me?"

Loftin heaved straight and lumbered up beside and behind his chief, fatty pinkish arms crossed. Like a Mameluke. Glaring down along his pig snout, with that pig-mouth snarl. "You are a long way from home, ain'tcha?"

"On behalf of an old Lavonia County family."

"You say."

How could I argue with such nimble logic?

"Me and Deputy Loftin," the sheriff said, swatting dust off his boot shank, "was just talkin'bout how you could've sought out the Collinses. Exploited their time of grief to give you a foot in the door."

I nodded.

Unclasped my purse and took out my old pack of Kents. Gouged the last one out. I struck a match to it, then leaned back gravely with my knees crossed. Blew smoke through puckered pink lips. I'd bought a fresh pack for four dimes out of the lobby machine. I shrugged with my brows and cigarette. "Why would I ambulance-chase all this way? No offense, gentlemen, but if I want to see the countryside, there're prettier places a few miles from my house than anything Alabama's shown me."

"Might be wantin' to rile people," Loftin accused.

I snapped a look up.

"Incite'em to riot."

"Incite *who* to riot?"

"The Negroes."

I blew smoke.

Laughed out the window. "So I'm the next H. Rap Brown? Look, I'm obviously not black. And I've shown you my ID. I am no Yankee. Do I sound like a Yankee?"

"Nashville ain't exactly the Deep South," Loftin said, "now is it?"

"We…consider ourselves a progressive New South city." I was sounding brilliant, borrowing from my father's editorializing. "We've had problems. Violence, a bombing or two. If that pales compared to a Little Rock, or Birmingham, I'm proud of that. Look gentlemen"—I shook my head, snagged back some hair—"I'm not here to re-fight the Civil War. I'm helping a friend. You're worried I'll inflame your situation? I saw one burned church my first trip, and read in the papers today about two other church fires here in town, and a grocery store."

"We got a lid on things," declared Turbeville.

Framed in the tall window back of him, though I couldn't see all the way up, was the flagpole atop the courthouse cupola. Presumably the U.S. flag billowed there, state flag below it, but what I could see flapping and snapping gently was a third flag:

The stars-and-bars battle flag.

"Mean you have a lid on the blacks," I said, "while the Klan runs roughshod."

"Klan!"

Turbeville yanked the ankle of his black boot up his thigh, jerking an *Is-she-crazy?* look at Loftin, before blowing up at me: "Ain't no Klan in my county, not to speak of. Who said there was Klan? Tell me?" He pointed warningly. "That's second time today you brung them up. First time you accused *me* a bein' a goddamn Kluxer!"

"You said if you were you wouldn't tell."

"Well I ain't."

"John Riley Hobbs. Grand Imperial Wizard. Stood on those courthouse steps"—I pointed accusingly past the sheriff out his window—"and practically called for Negroes to be murdered. Two days later Montie Collins and three others left your jail— yours!—and were never seen alive again."

"Aww, Hobbs just come to make speeches, grab some headlines, sign up an ol' redneck or two. This ain't a Klan county, Mrs. Russell." Angrily Turbeville leaned and spat. I heard the ringing of it inside the spittoon. He rocked back. Glancing up: "That right C.O.?"

"It is, Bobby Ray."

"My deputy grew up in these parts. Knows this county like his backyard. Been a dep'ty ever since he come back from Korea. Served two elected sheriffs before me. Right, C.O.?"

"Yes, Bobby Ray."

"Now me! I was born'n'raised over by the Coosa River, Chilton County side. Halfway twixt Birmingham and Montgomery. Now that, Mrs. Russell, is Klan country. So between the two of us, Mr. Loftin and me know what we talkin'bout. We may be country bumpkins but we know 'bout the Klan."

"If not the Klan, then who would be burning churches and businesses, shotgunning homes?"

"Citizens!" Loftin flashed clamped teeth. "Frightened white citizens."

"If I go to the FBI in Birmingham, will they agree?"

"Or maybe Negroes and commies," Loftin laughed, "like that Martin Luther Coon, tryin' to make us look bad." Turbeville tossed his deputy a *shut-your-mouth* look, then sighed, adjusted his glasses, and offered: "Them Hoover Boys got Klan on the brain. You seem skeptical of us. Fine. Maybe that's a good thing to be. Just don't believe ever'thing the FBI's got to say neither."

I paused.

"Sounds like good advice. Look, Sheriff, you and Mr. Loftin should be pleased to learn I have no intention of asking a lot of bull-in-a-china-shop questions about the Lavonia Massacre. You've covered the bases, you and the Feds."

"I think we have."

"Take a wild stroke of luck, for me to contribute anything."

He neither agreed nor disagreed, just looked at me through thick-rimmed eyeglasses.

"I do intend, however…"

"Yeah?"

"To talk to J.B. Roberts' widow."

CHAPTER 14

I WILL NOT HAVE YOU bothering this county's leadin' citizen. You got no official standing here, Mrs. Russell. I have been very accommodating. But—"

"She's your eyewitness."

"I'm warning you."

I swallowed. Studied the smoldering tip of my cigarette. Stubbed it out. "Very well. One question though, Sheriff." My eyes flickered his way. "Was the Roberts crime scene searched thoroughly for evidence?"

"Of course."

"By who?"

"Me, C.O., part-timer named Free, but he mostly just stayed with the widow."

"No assistance from, say, the state?"

"No."

"You an experienced homicide investigator?"

"Yes," Turbeville gruffed.

He pointed vaguely to the cluster of nailed-up framed photos, and so forth. "Git down that certificate." I pushed up from my chair, following his gesture. "That one. Git that one down and read it."

I held a small black wooden picture frame that might cost a dollar. Under its thin glass was sandwiched an official document with Sheriff Turbeville's name typed into a blank space. It said:

CERTIFICATE OF COMPLETION
ADVANCED POLICE TRAINING
FBI NATIONAL ACADEMY

I raked my hair back.

"No offense, Sheriff."

He took the frame and laid it aside. "And if we was gonna get sloppy it wouldna been that day. This is a county of small farms, Mrs. Russell."

"Yes sir." I smoothed my skirt behind me, sat quietly.

"Whites and Negroes alike, scratch out a living raising chickens, pigs, few cows, grow a little corn and cotton and hay."

I nodded, took out my fresh pack of Kents, breaking open the cellophane.

"The J.B. Roberts' farm, on the other hand, covers close to seventeen hundred acres. He owned a fertilizer company, and the building-and-loan. He was the most important, richest man in these parts. We wasn't sleeping on the job that day, I promise."

Nodding, I threaded some hair behind my ear, then tapped and drew a cigarette from the pack. "In that case," I said, starting to light it, "maybe you can tell me…"

"What?"

"Why only seven empty shells?"

"*That's* bothering you?"

"Mrs. Roberts' statement said she heard eight shots. She was pretty definite. Plus the autopsy showed seven entry wounds, then there was the miss, that ricocheted, embedding in the wall." I shrugged. "Where'd the eighth shell go?"

He added his shrug. "We looked. Tack room. Stalls. Crevices between the breezeway floor and the wooden walls. Between wall planks. Pried some planks off to get a look behind. The dry lot outside. We checked the horses' hooves. Brung in a metal detector. Nothin'. We recovered seven forty-five-auto cartridge cases. Period."

"How do you account for that?"

"Maybe only seven rounds was fired."

"The pistol was emptied."

He nodded. "*Some* only load forty-fives with seven rounds—one chambered, six in the clip. Saves wear and tear on the spring in the clip."

"Seven entry wounds plus the ricochet. Seven plus one makes eight."

"Maybe the doc got it wrong. He's eighty-three years old. Miscounted, or got lazy, knowing what Mrs. Roberts said. Maybe he didn't want to make her out a liar, being the grand ol' southern gentleman he is. Maybe the ricochet passed through the body, then exited. Not all the bullets was recovered intact. Few shattered on impact with bone."

"No blood, tissue, fabric traces on the bullet dug out the wall?"

"None noted. Wudn't sent to the state lab though."

"Why?"

"No need. We got our killer. Visible traces coulda been knocked off in flight, the impact with the concrete, track through the wood."

"Could've? That pass muster with your advanced FBI training?"

He shrugged.

Elaborately. "Could more've been done? If I had a big city police department, a big budget, sure. I do my best with what I have and allocate my assets the best way I know. This is a poor county. Am I perfect? No. Was that investigation textbook? No. But there was no reason to spend time and money on trace analysis, or digging out and counting every fragment, or withholding the body from the grieving family. We had our man. Montie Collins confessed for crissakes."

"Not to the shooting," I said.

"To arguing with, striking, and robbing the victim seconds—*seconds*—before he was found dead."

"But not to shooting him."

Loftin unfolded. "Smart boy that one. He knew we had him. Eyewitness put him at the scene. Prints on the shoe-puller Roberts was struck with. On the man's empty wallet. The man's cash in his pockets when we arrested him."

"But," Turbeville chimed in, "if he confessed to the shooting, he'd win a trip to the electric chair for certain. I think he thought if he confessed to lesser offenses we'd be more likely to buy his denial of the capital crime. Of course, our penitentiaries are jammed with folks claiming they didn' do it."

"Back to that missing shell," I said. "You say it wasn't there…" I exhaled smoke. "But what if it was, and somebody took it?"

"Who?"

I shrugged. "Not an impossibility."

"Who's gonna take one cartridge case. You take one, you take'em all."

"By accident?"

"Sure, maybe a turkey buzzard flew in, carried off a shiny trinket. Maybe."

"No evidence," I asked, "of anybody else there?"

"No. Absolutely."

"Just the victim and Montie Collins."

"Yes."

"You looked?"

"Yes. Positively and absolutely."

CHAPTER 15

RUTHIE MAE WAS WAITING OUTSIDE. We talked while I was fastening faux-pearl buttons at the wrists of my gloves, and narrowing my eyes, spotting a pale green pickup two blocks up, past the post office and jail. Still distracted up the street, I asked what she knew about Deputy Cecil O. Loftin.

"Big po'-white-trash family," she said, "all up in the woods and hills round here, while I was growing up, but I dunno him."

"He didn't try to cover his bigotry." I turned to her, and began to dig for my Foster Grants. "Course, the sheriff wasn't much more subtle, was he?"

"You know poor white trash, Miss Sherry. Don'matter how lowdown, no 'count they be, if they hate all colored people, they automatically better, in their own heads, than a whole nother race."

I clipped my pocketbook shut.

Put on my sunglasses. The pickup hadn't moved. "Why, Miss Sherry? You so in'erested in that Roberts killing? I didn't ask you down here to look into the murder of no white man. Plenty people care about dat."

"Ironically," I said, "I'm not sure that's true."

"Well, I don't care…"

She hissed low. No bones suddenly about her being taller and heavier than me. "I don't care," she enunciated, and I thought what my mother would've. That if even the "good ones" were this angry, what must the country be sinking too. I paced, pivoted, tapping the toe of my slingback. Then I looked her in the eye. Threaded my handbag to the crook of my elbow. "You have to trust me; if you don't want me involved, say so—otherwise hear me out."

She gave a nod.

"I pieced through those files. Looked at the photos. Read the reports. You chose not to. I understand. But that means you have to believe me when I say everything humanly possible seems to have been done to find the killers. Either by these yokels, or the FBI. And the FBI surely hasn't shared everything they have with the sheriff. If those files are any kind of snow job, I can't see it, not based on a fast couple hours work anyway."

"Thank you, Miss Sherry."

"I'm not finished."

"Yes, ma'am."

"Nobody's talking. The police have asked a lot of questions, but they're getting no answers. Either nobody knows who the killers are—they're total outsiders—or the ones who do know are keeping very quiet."

"Because they scared?"

I shrugged.

"Of the Klan," she said.

"Sure," I said. "But I think it's only partly fear."

"Huh?"

"And partly a shield."

I paced more, sidewalk gritty under my shoes. The glare of the low sun kept me from seeing, even when I tipped up my glasses, if anyone was inside that green pickup. I rotated back.

Told Ruthie Mae cold and hard:

"I think the population here, the white population, silently supports the killers. Not that most would or could ever do anything so horrible. Not that most would wish a black man dead, even most of the ones who are, in some measure, bigoted themselves. But they understand the motivation. And, even if it's subconscious, they feel, on some level, justice was done."

"Because Montie killed that white man. Miss Sherry…"

Exasperated, reproachful.

"That sheriff told you right one thing. This is a nice county. It's poor, seedy maybe, but it ain't a Klan county. They around. They everywhere. But in the shadows, out in the hollows." Her face grimaced to make me understand. "Most folks hereabout get along fine. White and black."

"Until something rips off the scab," I said. "The death of a man like J. B. Roberts triggers a lot of anger. Some racial, some natural human anger. At the waste, the economic impact. Wealthy powerful man. Business owner. Provided jobs. Loaned money. His death means a lot in a small flat-busted-broke county like this. I can't break through all that," I said. "The cops couldn't and I—"

I got interrupted.

Chief Deputy Cecil Loftin, badge and gun jouncing.

Rounding the brick corner of the building. Small mouth and metallic eyes grinning down as he doffed the cattleman's hat, puffing. "Glad I caught up with you ladies." He eyed Ruthie Mae, crushing his hat from the sides. "Must be the sister. Poor Mr. Collins' sister. My condolences, yes ma'am."

Ruthie Mae managed to be civil.

He looked at me.

"Still wanna talk to the Roberts widow?"

"With or without your boss's permission."

"Her preacher might hepya," he said through gritted teeth. "Don't tell Bobby Ray, though, he'd skin me live."

CHAPTER 16

I FOLLOWED LOFTIN'S DIRECTIONS FROM the square, the green pickup tailing me, well back and slow. After a curl around City Cemetery we came to a stop sign at Tenth Street, the northern edge of Lavonia proper, where Loftin said to turn west. Past an auto body shop we came to where there were thick stands of tall pines on both sides and I slowed, watching the road behind me—long, straight, and level at that stretch—in the mirror. Waiting to catch the green pickup in profile, coming through the intersection.

Ruthie Mae was asking what I was doing.

I didn't want to worry her.

There it was, wide and slow, pulling out.

GMC half-ton fender-side, 1960 model, give or take. I knew because Fred had sold one a lot like it to an employee before we got married. Ruthie Mae insisted: "What in God's green earth is wrong?" I just gave her a smile as I picked up speed, facing front, and said I'd thought I'd seen something. I didn't say we were being followed as my eyes flicked back and forth to the mirror, my mouth twisting. She didn't register anything as odd, which was natural because it wasn't easy to spot a tail you're not looking for. I'd bird-dogged many a lothario all over Nashville, and don't claim to be that good, but none of my subjects, to my knowledge, had ever made me.

On our left was a fortress wall of brick and wrought iron. It bordered and protected, Ruthie Mae explained, the town's affluent white enclave. Resident's had even hired an armed security patrol since the trouble began. I nosed up to a stop sign, Columbus Street crossing Tenth obliquely. The lowering sun a shimmering silver-white crest over the woodlands ahead. The GMC was almost literally squirming behind me, not to get too close.

A hard left would end us up downtown and led also to Columbus, Mississippi, 41 miles west, according to the signs and arrows. I wheeled the other way and came immediately to a fork. The left fork was the continuation of Tenth which dead-ended, Ruthie Mae recalled, out in the country a mile or so. In the crook of the fork, in a thicket of pines, stood the Free Will Assembly Baptist Church.

The fork to the right of the church was a state highway to Crossville, 11 miles, and Vernon, 19 miles. I restrained my wanderlust: Fred, cooling his heels at home, was going to skin me alive as it was.

I parked in a pine-needle-and-sand lot behind the church, which had a square-cornered bell tower on the left, viewed from the front, and a small wing built off to the right of what would be the main chapel.

The pickup took the Crossville fork.

Accelerated flatulently away. I climbed from the Impala, the engine sound fading.

I'd been wrong about it…

Or it'd found out what it wanted…

Ruthie Mae chose to stay in the car—not happy with this detour, since it meant I couldn't take time for us to have supper with her family, and since the only point of it was to learn more about J.B. Roberts' killing, which she couldn't care less about.

I hiked in my heels to the front of the side-projecting wing. Clapped onto a tiny portico, a chapel window alongside.

I knocked, and was greeted, expected apparently, pipe in his white teeth, by the Reverend Horace Cothran.

CHAPTER 17

EFFUSIVELY THE SOUTHERN GENTLEMAN, COTHRAN had a voice like Foghorn Leghorn, and looked like the doofus senator in *The Manchurian Candidate*. Hard-looking, late-fifties, medium build, sporting a gray cardigan, and an actual string necktie. I'd lived in the South all my life and never seen one. I sniffed, everything smelling of cheap tobacco as I was ushered into the small office of a man devoted to work, and the Word. Bookmarked Bibles, notes, articles piled up. One too-small square window looking out. Knotty-pine paneling. No family photos. A double-barrel shotgun stood in one corner. A simple oak-wood cross nailed up on one wall, haphazardly framed copies of the Lord's Prayer, the Ten Commandments, and the Bill of Rights on another. A typewriter had papers rolled onto the platen sandwiched with carbons. He squeaky-wheeled the stand out of our way, commenting that he'd been "toiling over" his sermon for Sunday when "The C.O." phoned.

"The C.O.?"

"Deputy Loftin. We call him that."

He grinned. "Short for, Cecil Orval. He hates that middle name."

"You're friends then?"

He puffed the pipe, creaking down in his desk chair, Zippo lighter tipped over the bowl. "Acquaintances, I'd say"—sucking through the pipe stem—"I growed up"—sucking—"with his daddy and uncles." He spoke too loud like people did after a lifetime around heavy machinery. I could easily imagine him scaring the wickedness out of a congregation, spewing fire and brimstone. A black coat with tails hung by wire hanger off a coat rack. Quite a colorful character, this Pastor Cothran, down to the Confederate-flag vest on the same rack.

"Wear that preaching?" I asked.

Indicating the vest.

"Not reg'lar services," he said, "but revival meetin's, that kinna thing." He apologized for not having offered me coffee or tea, starting to rise. I thanked him, no, my time was limited. He flashed rows of teeth so straight and gleaming they had to be dentures. "The C.O. said you was a detective, Mrs. Russell." Settling back. "He failed, inexcusably, to add that God hath rendered you, no doubt, the loveliest of all detectives."

Wow!

He can flirt too.

Cothran was missing the fourth and fifth digits of his right hand and curiosity got the better of me. "You didn't, I don't imagine, lose those fingers battling sin and iniquity?"

"No," he huffed.

"The war?"

"Nor that." The dentures clacked onto the pipe stem. "I was a steel-mill worker in Bessemer for thirty years. Bar of pig iron dropped on my hand. Crushed them fingers. Took my pension and retired. That was nine years ago. I'd already been ordained."

"You attended seminary as a steelworker?"

"Never 'tended no seminaries, just got my credentials."

I nodded. "Why here?"

"Born here. Near here, anyways, plum out in the country. But farming weren't for me. Soon as I was eighteen I hitchhiked to find steady work. Railroad first, then I heard my true callin'."

"God?" I said.

"Blast furnaces. Ironic, ain't it? Closest thing to the fires of Hell on the earth."

I nodded, grazing some hair back. "Ironic. Mrs. J. B. Roberts is a member here?"

My skepticism was heavy.

"Ginny'n'me go way back."

"How's that?"

"My father sharecropped on ol' man Seeley's spread. Her father. So I knew her as a little girl, before I took off to find my fortune." He grinned; smoke puttered out around the pipe stem.

"This, Seeley spread: Same farm Mrs. Roberts has now?"

"Yes."

"Where her husband was murdered?"

"The same."

"*Her* family's property—not his?"

"Correct."

The typewriter table happened to be positioned in a way that I could read—upside-down—from where I sat, a few lines he'd typed, then rolled out. Wasn't sure I was reading it correctly so I got a cigarette from my pocketbook and asked Cothran for a light. Standing I met his reach halfway, got my light, then paced. Smoking demurely, eyes traveling to that typed page.

Yep—I'd read it right:

SERMON--SUNDAY SEPT. 17, 1967
Sex Perverts, Beatniks, Pinkos, & Communists

CHAPTER 18

M Y MOTHER WAS A MEMBER of the Churches of Christ. Prior to marrying Fred, when I'd attended services, that was where I had gone. Fred's family was Methodist and I went with him now, if I went. Suffice it to say, the Sunday sermons at the Free Will Assembly Baptist Church of Lavonia were more...shall we say, topical...than my church-going experiences.

Sex Perverts, Beatniks, Pinkos, & Communists!

Tape reels stood on a shelf in boxes crisscrossed with rubber bands. Labeled *Christian Identity by Dr. Wesley Swift*. Rotating, I let my eyes pick over Cothran's desktop. He seemed in no hurry to have me leave, or get to the point. He seemed to enjoy observing me, puffing on his pipe. I'd been wrong earlier. Hidden behind a large Bible *was* one personal photograph. Inside a tarnished frame, the snapshot was old, 1930s perhaps, of a young woman or teen, wearing short shorts and some kind of sailor top. Sitting before a low wall, cradling a house cat. "You're obviously busy..."

"You know what they say about idle hands." Several issues of some magazine, cheaply produced out of newsprint, were strewn over the desk. Articles underlined, jottings in margins. The publication had the size, shape, and consistency, essentially, of a comic book. "I'll get to the point," I said, weight on one hip, pulling off my cigarette. "I'd like to talk to Ginny Roberts.

About her husband's murder. Might you ask her for me? Perhaps this Sunday, if she comes to church."

"I can ask."

"Thank you." I had a business card ready. "I've jotted my home number and area code on the back. I'd appreciate her phoning to arrange something. Naturally, she can reverse the charges. Or perhaps you could call for her, if that wouldn't be imposing. If my husband answers, tell him who you are and ask for me. I'm happy to meet her at her house, or anywhere, anytime."

He was studying my card as if it read provocatively. His hair was dyed black, the eyebrows too, and he looked up from under them. "You're married?"

"Yes." I plucked a glove off.

Waggled my diamond. "That so hard to believe?"

"Does your husband approve?"

"Of?"

"This."

Indicating the card.

"He knows I'm here. Approve...mmmight be a strong word for what he thinks about it."

"What of Ephesians?"

Blandly I said: "I'm no chapter-and-verse girl."

"For the husband is the head of the wife, even as Christ is head of the church"—there was a stern furrowing of brow, and bend of his head—"therefore as the church is subject unto Christ—so let wives be to their own husbands in everything."

"Women's lib," I countered, "wasn't practical in Biblical times."

"Much in today's society is ungodly—don't you agree?"

For instance:

Sex perverts, beatniks, pinkos, and communists.

Bet now he'd add *feminists*.

"I'm not getting suckered into arguing with a man of the cloth. You guys have all the answers."

He grinned. "Mrs. Russell—"

"Will you ask Ginny Roberts?"

I had my glove back on, purse at my side, and a good grip on the doorknob.

"I will."

"Thank you." I advanced suddenly, a nagging in my chest. I stubbed out my cigarette. Then picked up, shaking away scattered ashes, an issue of the periodical that seemed to be right up there with the Bible as source material for Cothran's sermonizing.

I read the cover...

Cothran watching...

The Flaming Cross.

CHAPTER 19

A 1958 PLYMOUTH FURY, BUCKSKIN *beige with gold trim, idled alongside Route 18, opposite the Free Will Assembly Baptist Church. Between the men inside were two pistols, two sawed-off shotguns, an ax handle, a GI garrison belt with bolts and nuts screwed into it, and two chains twelve to sixteen inches in length.*

Behind the wheel:

Lee David Autrey, 34, divorced father of two, sometime used-car salesman, ambulance driver, and bartender.

Full-time hell-raiser.

Beside him was James Henry Sims Jr., 42, father of five, machinist and navy combat veteran. In back were Hubert Townsend, 38, a married childless garage operator and gun collector, and Jerry Lackey, 25, a service-station attendant.

"Devil with the blue dress, blue dress, blue dress..."

Mitch Ryder rang in Autrey's head. "Devil with the blue dress on..."

She came out the Preacher's office. Hair bouncy, carrying a handbag, down steps, rounding the building. It was Lackey, who was an imbecile, and had never ridden with them, who wolf-whistled loud enough for Blondie Blue Dress to snap her head their way. Hank Sims wasn't amused. "Stow that shit!" Autrey grinned back. "She ain't much, Baby Bro', not stacked up to that pair a unholstered thirty-eights I had me last night."

"Let's do this," Sims graveled.

And the Canadian Club was passed forward again. Autrey guzzling a large swig before punching the TorqueFlite transmission, and stamping the accelerator.

CHAPTER 20

ENGINE SCREAMING, SMOKE PEELING OFF whitewalls, the Fury spewed dirt and gravel, like a Navy Phantom cutting in afterburners. Weaving, fishtailing—it braked finally to a skidding stop, boxing my car in. I'd chosen to ignore the lewd whistle as just one of those things women put up with in this world, having already let my paranoia run amok over the GMC.

Batting a thousand Sherry!

My fear was they'd grab Ruthie Mae, climbing out of our car, frightened, and I raced forward, up to my wrist, in my purse, clasping the checkered walnut of my revolver.

Four men bailed from the big finned Plymouth, choking dust scudding over the car, from back to front. I couldn't abandon Ruthie Mae to run for help from Cothran, who in any case, I was far from certain hadn't helped set us up. The foursome fanned my direction. The one most threatening, most aggressively charging, looked to be in his late thirties, maybe forty. He was fat, mean-faced, and bald—like an enraged hippopotamus—an engine-grime-stained finger stabbing at Ruthie Mae across the Impala's roof: "Git back in that car, nigger, and you won't be laid a hand on."

I rooted myself, facing their advance, a brush of wind billowing my skirt against my legs. My bag was across my stomach, and remarkably they didn't seem wary of my hand being inside it, like they might be of a man keeping, say, a hand in a pocket. I told Ruthie Mae to do as they said.

"Miss Sherry…"

"I'll be okay."

The phalanx spread into a half circle.

Two of them—Hippo being one—rattled and twirled lengths of chain at me. Another had a tool handle of some type, and the fourth smacked his open palm with a canvas strap, folded double, studded with nuts and bolts. The man with the strap was the Plymouth's driver. He was the biggest of them at six feet, over two hundred. He had wavy reddish hair, a ruddy complexion, and rimless dark glasses. His shirt, spread at the neck, was lime-and-blue-paisley. He reeked of Aqua Velva or Hai Karate or the like, and carried himself in a manner suggesting he was fully prepared, as a public service, to scoop up in midair, like Superman, any and all women brought to swooning by his mere presence.

And, yes, he might've been Adonis-like, but for that nose: tip absurdly pointed, bridge collapsed. Called a saddle deformity, the result of a broken nose, inflicted in say a barroom brawl, receiving inadequate treatment.

I tried not to give ground.

One of Sherry's rules:

A woman playing a man's game shall play it like a man.

Right up until she turns the tables, and plays it like a woman.

Lady-Killer was on my far right. On my left, the chain men, sporting sweat- and oil-stained blue work shirts. The elder, Hippo, had dark stubble, and a big stomach trying to fall through his shirt. A strip of curling-up masking tape covered that embroidered name they always had. The younger then came up ridiculously close to me.

"Bro', git back here." Instead, grinning imbecilically, he came around and whapped me on the buttocks with a several inches of strong chain. "Ouch!" I skittered back, stinging.

He lunged to try it again.

I snatched for the chain.

"Goddamnit, Bro', stop that!"

Lady-Killer.

"C'mon, Lee—"

74

Hippo suddenly balled the smaller man's shirt in his fists. Shoved him bangingly against the side of the Impala.

"Oughta kill you!"

Pointing.

"*No names!*"

I registered, at a distance, a large engine turning over.

Reinforcements?

My chest fluttered at the prospect of that, my shoulders jerking. The one wielding the ax handle was oldest. Tall and rangy, but not as tall as Lady-killer, whose name was apparently Lee. Ax Handle wore a gray windbreaker, had a squarish, creased face with a large nose and small cruel mouth. "Go home, young lady," he instructed.

The tool handle loose-held down his right leg. "Quit takin' up for that nigra murderer."

I swallowed.

"Yes, sir," I managed.

Heart thumping.

"Technically, though," I said, "Montie Collins—"

That motor in the distance suddenly throttled, tortured with gas. If I'd even wanted to keep talking I'd have had to yell. All of us though, I and the four Klansmen—my assumption being they were Klan—spun toward Tenth Street.

The GMC!

CHAPTER 21

IT HAD CUT THROUGH SOMEHOW from the other fork. Almost literally jumped a drainage ditch bordering the churchyard and slammed down on its springs, the driver a certified lunatic. Gunning it, bearing down on, narrowly missing the driver's-side fin of the Fury, he fishtailed, plowing trenches, lurching to a creaky stop. I heard the handbrake ratchet and honestly, to that point, had not the slightest earthly idea what was happening.

"My God!" I burst in shock and surprise.

My hands clawed at my face.

Fred.

My Fred!

My *husband* Fred!

He exploded down out of the cab, boots hitting like some Green Beret out of the sky. He gripped over his head, rotoring it like something medieval, a large blackish-brown wrench.

He attacked Ax Handle.

I danced clear.

The Klansman—his name I later learned was Sims—swung the ax handle like Lou Gehrig at bat. Fred caught it in his hand then knocked the breath out of Sims butting the wrench in his gut. He fell retching. Speechless and shell-shocked, I shrank against the rear of the church. Fred pulled the ax handle from his fallen opponent's grasp and faced the chain men. Hippo lashed trying to split Fred's skull. Fred lunged back and blocked the strike, the chain winding tightly onto the ax handle. Fred chopped the wrench into the meat between the Klansman's shoulder and thick neck.

Grisly crunch of collar bone.

I grimaced, reminded of gladiators in *Spartacus* or something. Hippo slumped and staggered, clutching his shoulder in pain. With a yank of the ax handle Fred tore the chain from the Klansman's grasp, then cast both entangled weapons well out of the fray—a heavy thud as they hit, peeling back pine straw. The younger grease monkey ran hell for leather into the woods. Hippo cursed after him, arm dangling. He hooked a savage, drunken right at Fred's neck. It didn't connect well. Fred backed off, swung a looping haymaker beside the man's eye. Spun him into the fender of the Plymouth. Fred hit him again, throwing him against the open passenger door, slamming it shut, and laid him out cold between the cars.

Biting down I was on the verge of breaking my teeth. Sick and guilty over this bloodthirsty circus, over being its unwitting catalyst.

"Fred!"

Lady-Killer, aka Lee, had worked in behind him. Neither of us had seen it. Fred pivoted at my voice, Paul Bunyan beard and all. I snapped my arm, pointing, and he met Lee's attack. Red hair, saddle nose, paisley shirt. Oddly giddy to have Fred all to himself.

Canvas strap doubled up, he was ready to flog it.

At my husband!

I could see what I was calling a "strap" was a heavy military equipment belt, nuts and bolts added, of course, for the infliction of grievous harm. I yelled that to Fred, digging in my purse. Put a stop to this, I decided, but I didn't get my gun out before the big men clashed like Titans. By which point, I feared any interference might distract Fred at some fateful, even fatal, instant.

Fred took the blow from the belt outside his arm, shredding his shirtsleeve as if he were mauled by a lion. I could tell it'd hurt him. Lee was the only one of the Klansmen approaching Fred's physical match. Fred absorbed the blow, unleashing a powerful right hook, lot of weight behind it, staggering the Klansman. He came back with a right at Fred's head, a left jab to his ribs. The headshot Fred ducked. The body blow thudded home. With a jerk like I'd been hit myself, I watched Fred rock back, stagger. Fling sweat. He tossed aside the wrench, spattering dirt.

Was he crazy?!

But Lee followed suit.

I was amazed.

Threw the belt away, grinning hugely.

Some bare-knuckles honor thing. Bent low Fred charged and showered fists against Lee's body from inside the man's reach. Left, right, left, right. Working a heavy bag. All Lee could give back were weak poundings at Fred's back and flanks. Layers of muscle, heavy bone, and fat, shielding Fred like the armor on a Patton tank. Fred stayed in close, both men exhausting, grunting like battling wildebeests. Fred bobbed back like Muhammad Ali. Darted in. Lunged. Snapped the Klansman's head back. A right, left. Fred stepped out, shaking his right hand. Both fighters slick with sweat, slinging it with shakes of head, swings of fist. Lee's face bled, smeared brightly red. He kicked Fred in the groin; it half missed. Fred caught him with a right to the side of the mouth. Lee spit out a tooth. I grimaced, horrified.

Fred tackled him.

They rolled.

Ax Handle was on hands and knees.

Going for the wrench!

I darted for it in my aquamarine dress and heels, snatched it back.

Shook it threateningly at the man, who cranked a pale, sweat-beaded, gasping-for-wind face up at me. A distant siren. I threw the wrench away then skirted the wrestling men, side-skipping, to snag up the heavy military belt with my manicure, and heaved it with my own grunt and strain out of anybody's reach.

"Bro', hey, Bro'!"

Hippo.

I spun, same instant Ruthie Mae cried: "Miss Sherry!" The stubble-faced man was on his feet, half-closed right eye, yanking two sawed-offs out the Plymouth's backseat. Bellowing for Ax Handle who was struggling up, holding his stomach in.

"Hereya go, Bro', time to clean up this goddamn mess."

My .38 was out.

"Don't take a step!"

Elsa, the African lioness.

"Goddamnit," the fat man muttered.

"Guns back," I said. "Slowly. Shut the door. Lock it." I jerked my head. "Get over here with your friend."

He grumbled the Lord's name in vain yet again, and with us being behind a church and all. Obedience to southern womanhood not as high, I gathered, on the Klan virtues list as guarding our purity was. Fred and Lee were back trading blows, on their feet, moving in a slow circle. Much of the paisley shirt shredded, one sleeve gone entirely, Lee's chest drenched in blood. Fred was no pretty sight either. Oddly, for a man who seemed to be losing, Lee was taunting Fred. Relishing the brutal process, and I wasn't sure Fred was much different. Both crazy like feuding roughneck little boys at recess.

"Fred," I scolded. "Stop it."

If he'd any inkling that, while he played on, his frilly wife was holding two Ku Kluxers at gunpoint, there was no showing it. A white unmarked Chrysler Newport, flashing red light on the dash swung in. I shoved my gun away, yelling, "Fred it's the cops!" Maneuvering, braking to a rocking halt, Deputy Cecil O. Loftin was at the wheel.

Who'd called?

Cothran?

I slogged over to the GMC, which I now recognized to be, in fact, Fred's old truck. He'd borrowed it back, obviously, knowing I'd spot any of our vehicles tailing me. I reached in, killed the ignition, half nauseous from the exhaust. The motor tumbled to a halt, and I sighed, looking over. Loftin snugging on his cowboy hat, hiked his gun belt, like John Wayne swaggering up beside the continuing fisticuff. He surveyed it with small pink hands on his hips, glowered over under a big tree, at Hippo and Ax Handle, licking their wounds.

"Clear out boys," Loftin boomed.

Pushing a thumb in Lee's direction. "Drag this idiot with you."

"Right, C.O.," Sims raggedly sighed.

The two moved stiffly.

"Bro' let's roll, buddy, c'mon." But Lee paid no more attention than Fred had to me. Like a boxing match stalemated many rounds ago, the crowd clearing the arena, and nobody told the fighters. Moving with all the grace of a Rock 'Em Sock 'Em Robots set. I told Loftin about the sawed-off shotguns in the car. "That right," he said, then to the Klansmen. "For hunting, no doubt."

"Absolutely C.O.," confirmed Hippo. Loftin shook his big flabby head like he couldn't imagine such stupidity. Then dropped his hands from his belt and slogged straight into the waning vortex of pugilism.

Shoved the combatants apart: "Break it up!"

I tugged Fred, grasping his left biceps. "Fred," I said gently, "Fred, Fred." His arm was bigger than a five-pound pork roast. Too big for both my hands to encircle. He was slippery, gritty with dirt; there was an awful amount of blood. How much his? How much the other man's? Loftin was blasting the Klansmen as knuckleheads, sending them packing. Fred broke out of my grasp as if from a child's.

"Officer!"

"Deputy," Loftin corrected, facing Fred.

"I don't give a damn if you're Wyatt Earp, fella." Barely winded. "I want them arrested."

"Fred," I urged, "calm down."

"They assaulted my wife."

Loftin squinted, a side-leaning metallic-blue look.

"Mrs. Russell here...*is your wife?*"

"Russell?" Fred fumed over his shoulder.

I sighed. My head lowered, cowed, though my eyes were up and angry. "Yes, Deputy, this is my husband."

Loftin chewed some gum hard. Small mouth open, showing teeth.

"What he said right, Mrs. Russell?"

"She's Mrs. Fred Nates!"

"*Fred...*" I scolded. I could've killed him.

"Look, Mr. Russell—"

"Nates! Fred Nates."

"Fred, please," I said.

"Mr. Nates, then." Loftin's tone one of utter reason, diplomacy, even a buddy-buddy hand on Fred's big shoulder. "Whatever happened here, looks to me like you and them had ample time to…ah…settle things. I propose we call it even."

"They *mo*lested my wife."

"Oh God…"

I tossed my head skyward and staggered, as Loftin advanced, raking me with an official once-over for evidence of molestation. He adjusted his hat. "That what happened ma'am?"

I looked warily. Shamefully. At Fred.

"Not exactly," I said. "There was a misunderstanding—"

"Hold on." And Loftin went off and huddled with the Klansmen. I didn't look at or try to speak to Fred. I was watching Loftin, trying, not successfully, to lip-read. He came back. "Look. Their story is Mr. Nates here attacked them without provocation—"

"I was defending my wife. Her honor."

"That's your side—"

"That's the truth."

"Fred…" I groaned.

Loftin's hands raised. "Thing is, if they get charged, we hafta charge you too. Let a judge sort the whole rigamarole out. Now, you listen here boy, our solicitor is jus' liable to count that wrench you used, if it comes to that, as a deadly weapon—"

"They had chains," Fred argued, "and ax handles."

"And," I added, "those sawed-offs."

"Stay outta this!" Fred snapped horribly.

I blinked.

Stunned.

"You say, and maybe you say right, boy. What I'm sayin' is you could be hip deep in felony charges, 'less we think this thing out right. And I don't wanna see that."

"Neither do we, Deputy."

"I'll handle this Sherry!"

"Your decision entirely, Mr. Nates, but we don't get this settled, right here, there's a real good chance you'll spend the night in jail. And with the weekend comin' up, no tellin' how long after that."

Fred paused.

JAMES K. RONE

Considering the angles.

Like a carpentry problem.

Pulled air through exhausted lungs. Gave his beard a downward pull. Wiped blood from his lip with the back of a hand. Then he twisted down at me. He was prideful, but not unwise. But he had to be sure I was okay with him backing down, which of course I was. "You're all right?" he asked.

"Yes," I said.

That settled, the Fury was loaded with its walking wounded, and growled back towards town. Loftin tramped back, saying: "One other thing, ma'am, Mrs. Russell or Nates or whatever..."

"Yes," I said.

"Considerin' what just happened, I think it best you stay outta Lavonia County. Don't you?" Then to Ruthie Mae, her arms crossed, backside against the Impala: "You too, for a little while anyway, Mrs. McNair."

She looked away.

He came back down into my face.

Small pig grin chewing gum on one side. "Last thing we need," he whispered, "is another nigger killin'." Then up at Fred. "You'll see to that won't you Mr. Nates? These ladies stay home where they belong. You obviously care 'bout your wife." He guffawed, and chewed. "Wives like her need a lotta tendin' after, don't they? They surely do, and need to be kept on a real short leash. Ain't I right, big fella?"

CHAPTER 22

FRED AND I STOOD ALONE once Loftin had driven off. Clever, I sighed, looking, Fred borrowing back his own old pickup to follow me. Ruthie Mae paced near the Impala, careful not to crowd us, or appear to eavesdrop—wise with more years of marital ups and downs than I had under my belt. I blotted my brow with the back of a wrist, then raked back a curtain of blonde, which started over my right eye and swept over the left half of my face.

"You okay?" I asked, Fred looking at me with confused disappointment. I took his hands in mine. Palpating the bones for fractures. He was rancid with body odor. The knuckles reddened and bloody would soon swell, but nothing was broken. I looked up, swallowing, without expression. His lower lip was puffed, swelling around the left eye. Reaching up I thumbed the rim of the orbital bones. There'd be contusions, largely concealed by his woolly beard. I stood on tip-toes, ordered him to bend so I could check his ear canals for bleeding. I wanted to test his vision and ocular movements. He stopped me.

"I'm fine," he said.

I paused.

Nodded.

"Good. Fine."

"Sherry..."

My hands tossed.

I swiveled, set off for my car.

"See you at home. Expect me late. If you follow I won't come home at all."

"Sherry! Let's talk."

I spun.

Tremoring finger.

Hot in the face.

"No talk, Fred. We talk now I will say something I will regret."

Back down through town, little daylight remaining, we idled for a Southern Railway freight. City Hall on one side, Lavonia Gas Board on the other. We humped over the tracks and entered the Negro section, then a left on Third Street took us quickly out of town. A bridge crossed the Sipsey River, down the east side of which we zigzagged. The actual river lay well back through impenetrable forest. Occasional swampy fringes amoeba'ed close to the highway. Bald cypresses with Spanish moss, root systems kneeing up out of black water teeming, no doubt, with deadly moccasins, bloodthirsty mosquitoes. It was along in here, on the opposite bank, that Ruthie Mae's brother and sister-in-law and two other Negroes had been found slaughtered. She had me turn off at New Chapel Road. More zigzagging and finally a narrow dirt lane back into some trees, and we steered at last up onto Ruthie Mae's sister's house.

We had eight for supper at Abigail's—a home impoverished by any standards I'd ever known, including my days as a struggling single gal blackballed out of nursing. Still, the gaunt, corrugated-tin-roof structure was comfortable, meticulously kept, well appointed. Worthy of any woman's respect. I accepted their supper invitation with the proviso that Ruthie Mae and I had to be going no later than seven.

They wanted to show me their appreciation for all I was doing for Montie. I swallowed some very-cold, very-sweet lemonade.

Unsure I was doing anything for Montie.

Abigail's husband, Henry, arrived behind us. He spent the week away, employed by a limestone quarry outside Birmingham. The couple had three polite children and there was a cousin eating, too, who was a tenant farmer nearby. Henry worked with him on his weekends home from the quarry. Jesus, I murmured, sipping from my glass. Wondering if I or anyone like me had the foggiest idea what honest-to-God hard work was. While waiting dinner the cousins perched on either side of me, explaining how they were business partners. They leased the land, and purchased or rented their own seed, fertilizer, and equipment. I commented my husband ran a feed mill, just to be contributing. My head swiveled, giving each man equal time. They educated me how tenant farming differed from sharecropping, in which the farmer depended more upon the landlord for his supplies and equipment. Montie's arrangement with Mr. Roberts had been the latter. His ambitious plan, however, to buy his own acreage, would have thrust Montie way ahead of the pack. "Dang fool shoulda kept that hot head under control," Henry whispered. "Abby don't wanna hear nuthin'bout that, but that boy had it all, or much as any us ever go' get. And threw it away. Got poor Dorothy, and Miss Malcolm kilt right along with his dumb self."

"*You* blame Montie?"

I looked from Henry, to the cousin, then Henry again.

"It's awl well and good, Mrs. Nates——"

"Sherry, please, Henry."

He nodded nervously.

"Go on," I said.

"All well and good, Miss Sherry, for Martin Luther King to have a dream. For a boy like Montie to listen and get one too. The good Lawd knows I got dreams. But we gotsta live in the real world too."

I muttered:

"Yeah we do."

My brain derailed onto Fred. As brains are apt to do when one is married, in love. Either or both. *We gotsta live in the real world.* Philosophy from the pit of a rock quarry. In my case the real world was a schizoid one in which women could be simultaneously despised and revered, and almost never simply *be.*

I blinked tears, feeling an abrupt need to be away from men.

I rattled my ice.

Excused myself.

In the kitchen I placed the glass in the sink, composed, then offered to help. I was turned down by Abigail and Ruthie Mae in a race to see who could do it faster. "Much too nice a dress to risk getting grease spattered," Abigail added from the stove, her ebullient voice elevated over the popping from her large cast-iron skillet. "What kind of material is that?" Her cooking filled the house with a heavenly fatty smell.

"Ah...Dacron I believe, a little cotton."

"New isn't it?" Ruthie Mae said.

"Got it, Castner-Knott, this past spring." For sixteen dollars, but I didn't mention that. The sisters began discussing sewing a knockoff copy of my very sweated-in fashion statement. I rinsed my hands, and was handed a towel. The children were doing homework around the table. I read over the older girl's shoulder. Algebra. She twisted up and around and smiled. I smiled back. Then I turned and asked my hostess, unthinkingly, if I might use their bathroom. That triggered the fourteen-year-old being ordered to abandon her homework and take me into the dusk-lit backyard, where stood an excellently constructed—clean as they came, no doubt—tiny narrow building large enough for one adult. Inside was a toilet seat built over a hole in the ground. A different hole, I might've crawled my embarrassed self into, elbows on my knees, clamping my temples, as I used the facility. The running water inside, I learned, was pumped from a cistern under the back porch, which in turn was filled by rainwater off the roof.

Jesus...

We ate "jiffy" steak: cubed beef from Jitney Jungle floured and fried crisp with onions, in bacon grease, served with white rice and gravy from the pan drippings, black-eyed peas with snaps, and skillet cornbread. Digging in, probably violating a few Emily Post rules, I made conversation about Charlie Collins, the Army sergeant at the funeral. He'd spent a year in Vietnam, and had orders for another tour, shipping out after Christmas.

"Sorry," I said.

Ruthie Mae and Abigail, I learned from Henry, had another brother—half brother—who played defense for the Chicago Bears. "Really," I said, and told him I knew a guy in Biloxi who'd played for Chicago in the thirties. Along about then I noticed

Abigail's plate had no meat on it.

Never had.

The men had double helpings. I had one whole sizeable piece. The younger children shared a serving and the fourteen-year-old shared with her aunt.

Abigail had given me hers.

My jaw hung there and I doubt I would've been able to speak, even if I'd had something to say. Sourly, then, I just resumed eating, figuring it would be hurtful, and impolite to make an issue at this point. But I didn't enjoy it nearly as much as before.

We gotsta live in the real world...

Gingerbread was passed around but I dabbed my lipstick, saying we'd better go. Henry questioned my plan to start driving to the next state after sunset. Dangerous, I was warned, for two women alone. I pointed out that as a nurse I'd routinely worked nights at rural hospitals. They offered to put us up, or pay to get me a decent room. I explained I couldn't, or rather didn't want to be away from Fred all night, and Ruthie Mae cinched it when she said she had a housekeeping job laid on for Saturday. We'd already phoned her husband, told him not to bother meeting us in Shelbyville. I'd drive her home. The family gave us Cokes, hugs and handshakes. We were off.

I pulled into my carport in Murfreesboro shortly before eleven P.M.

CHAPTER 23

FRED WAS UP WATCHING JOHNNY Carson. Neither of us having uttered a word, I clattered my keys onto the coffee table, and stood, arms crossed, taking in a little of the show. Ironically, a tall-dark-handsome actor named Mike Connors was chatting it up with Johnny and Ed. I recognized him from an old show *Tightrope* my father had liked. He was promoting his new series premiering that weekend, some private-eye show on CBS. I looked at Fred, filled my chest angrily. It was the sort of show he'd relish. "You get something to eat?"

"Yep."

"Want some ice for your hand?"

"It's fine."

I nodded and paced.

"Know why I was upset," I said, "in the churchyard?"

He didn't take his eyes off the TV. "Guess you didn't want me brawling with your pals."

"Jesus Christ, Fred. They weren't pals."

He glared up. "Didn't seem too int'rested in being rescued, my dear."

I dropped my arms. "So, I get two choices when comes to men I'm not married to? They're either *friends*. Or I need to be *rescued?*" I shrugged elaborately. "C'mon!"

"I do not like my wife dealing with strange men. It's

dangerous. It don't look right."

"Do *not*, Fred, lecture me about propriety."

"Somebody needs to."

"You may not like me going off, meeting with folks, snooping in their business—we need to talk about that—but it's work. Whatever it is, it's work. I'm a detective. It's nothing sorted or salacious."

"That depends—on your definition."

I saw red.

Felt a little knife stab between my ribs.

"I'm going to pretend I didn't hear that."

"Pretend all you want."

"Fred," I moaned.

"I saw that jerk wallop you on the backside!"

"He gave me...like a *spank*. It happens to women. All women. You learn to put up with it."

His sock-clad foot shoved the ottoman.

It flipped feet up, center of the room, and I retreated as he towered. "I don't put up with it when it comes to my wife, goddamnit!"

"Fred!" My hands were up, clawed. It helped nothing I'd been awake eighteen hours, exhausted from driving. Fred too. "I appreciate," I began, caught my breath, "that you want to protect me. That you love and care for me. I love you for that. But—"

"But nothing."

I almost wept.

"You talk to strangers at the feed store. Do business with strangers. Some of them *women*. Do I get upset? I, as a nurse"— all five fingers of one hand pursed together jamming my sternum—"you've said you don't mind me working as a nurse. As a nurse I interact with all kinds of men. Some bad or worse than those polecats. And a heckuva lot more intimately—they might even be naked."

"That's different."

"Why?"

"You're a nurse."

"I'm a detective, too."

"No..."

"No what? I'm not a detective. Not really because I'm a girl. Fred, I have a license. I earned a living at it—a good one—before we got married."

His breathing heavy, he was straining.

How best to say what he was thinking?

"Lemme guess," I fumed. "Being a nurse is okay because it's—*right?*—proper work for a woman."

"Yes!"

A tectonic swell of relief.

Finally, thank the Lord, I was making sense.

"And being a detective is not."

"No."

I pivoted, paced between couch and coffee table. A hand cradled my right hip, the other massaged my temples, through to my brain. "Like the song says, Fred…" I turned. "The times, they are a changin'."

"Not that much, not in my house."

"My house, too."

I padded in front of the rolltop Fred used for bills and bookkeeping. He paced too. We circled, coming face to face. A neighbor's dog barked. My hands were clawing the hair on the sides of my head. I saw the resolve in Fred's blue eyes. It wormed a shiver through me. He then smiled.

Huffed gruffly. And placed callused gentle hands against the broadcloth of my dress, at the shoulders, gliding them to my elbows, caressingly down till he had my hands in his. So romantic, for him, he might've been going to repeat our wedding vows or something.

The fight was over as far as he was concerned.

Conceited bastard!

I backed up, pulling free. I sidled around him and stalked towards the kitchen then swirled back. He faced around, a harsh "What?" My eyes squeezed shut. I shook my head and smeared tears blurring my vision. "You still don't understand, do you? What you did today."

"Sherry, obviously you and I see things different. I see things like a man. And those scum today saw them the same. You may honestly believe the world has changed, that there was nothing unseemly about you going around talking to total strangers in a strange town. But they didn't respect you. They were toying with you, and *thinking* worse. Trust me. And if I, your husband, allowed them to continue, I wouldn't be deserving of any better in their eyes. And, say what you will, I will not be shamed. Not if there's a breath in my body to stop it."

I nodded, exhaling.

Eyes tumbling off Fred.

"You've made it clear," I said, picking my look eventually up off the floor, "what you think of me. Okay. You're not the first. I expected better, of course, from my husband."

"Sherry..."

"No. I listened." My head shook involuntarily. "I hear what you're saying. Maybe I even understand it, a little. You're telling me what I did to you. Okay. But you are going to listen to what I have to say. What you did to me."

His Adam's apple jumped.

"Okay."

Sonny and Cher were on TV singing "And the Beat Goes On."

Her in black.

Him in vertical blue and red stripes.

"First. That man. Lee. You beat to a bloody damn pulp."

"He held his own."

"He ordered the one who slapped me with the chain to leave me alone. And the one you slugged in the stomach with a wrench—he was talking to me, just talking. They were giving me a warning, Fred. Like little boys, on a playground, telling a little girl to stay out of their sandbox."

"Fine. Good." He lumbered around shrugging. "So I helped. I showed 'em they couldn't scare you off. They know you're not to be messed with. Ain't that a good thing?"

"No! They weren't going to hurt me. But no telling what they'll do next time. Not because of anything I did, you see. What you did. You talk about respect. This male machismo nonsense. Well you've guaranteed me more trouble with them. Because honor will demand it."

"Only if—"

"Lemme finish. Not only that but he, the man you attacked, was just *starting* to talk. Talk, Fred. That's what I wanted. To talk to people who might know something. That's what detectives do. Granted, he was trying to chase me off. But if I'd played him right I might've learned something. Or established some rapport, upon which I could wheedle something out of him, or one of the others, later. Now all I've got on my hands are enemies."

"*Rapport,*" he said savagely. "*Played him...*"

"Business rapport, Fred. Politics. Dale Carnegie 101. Winning friends and influencing people. You do it in your business. I do it in mine."

"That. Is. Not. Acceptable."

"You are so hardheaded! You don't get it."

"Get what?"

"I spent my entire day driving down, talking to the sheriff, then to this strange Baptist preacher. Not to mention hours researching official files the sheriff allowed me access to—me, Fred!—and newspaper accounts at the library. And finally. Four scumbags burble up out of the seedy underbelly of that county. People who *might* actually know what happened, or know other people who would know. That's what I needed, Fred, in order to get anywhere. And you ruined it. You made my job ten times harder. It's no different than if you went out to the farm and spent all day building a shed or something and I showed up and flattened it to the ground with a tractor."

My teeth gritted.

Lips curled.

"That's what you did to me Fred. Showed me complete, utter, total disrespect. No trust. You destroyed my entire day's work. Thank you very goddamn much."

CHAPTER 24

DOES IT MATTER?"

My face ticced, and I glared up at my husband, a lip quivering.

"Does it matter," I parroted, a sudden weakness in my gut.

Surely it was impossible he'd said *that*?

But he repeated it.

Utterly reasonable. Unemotional.

"How can you ask that?" My voice constricted.

"I just— I mean I'm sorry if you think I insulted you or something. I love you. I'm just saying it doesn't really matter if I messed things up if you're not going back. That's all I meant."

"Who says I'm not going back?"

"You did. You said those guys meant trouble, you had enemies. You can't go back."

"If you had something important to do you wouldn't let them keep you away, would you?"

"That's totally different."

Again my jaw fell slack.

I rattled my head.

"You don't get it. You don't get it."

"Get what?"

"We're not communicating, Fred."

I needed some distance. I stalked through the kitchen, a fast clip that jarred my high heels down through the linoleum. I crossed onto the carpet of the dining room, on through to the living room, and stopped. Fred followed, floors creaking, and I kept my back to him, knotting my arms, a crush of emotional pressure to start crying. I managed to contain it. But for a single spurt of tears, heavy and salty.

"What do you want?" Desperation booming out of him. He honest to God had no clue.

"I want you to let me do a job, not interfere." I was talking to my left shoulder. "Don't follow me. Don't try to hold an umbrella over me so I don't get wet. That's all. It's simple."

"You're not going back."

I rotated.

Set my mouth.

Cocked my ear.

"What?"

"You're not going back. It's too dangerous. Maybe that's my fault. You're right. I'm sorry. But as it is, you're not going back."

"Like hell."

"Anyway, that deputy—"

"He has no constitutional authority to banish me. Besides, unless I'm very wrong—"

"It's dangerous."

"I can take care of myself."

"How, Sherry, forgodsakes?"

"A gun, Fred. A gun in my purse."

He hadn't even seen me draw at the church, which likely had saved his bacon, by the way, from those other Klansman.

Klansmen with shotguns!

"I can shoot. You know that."

"At targets, Sherry. Can you shoot a man trying to kill, or...or...gosh darn it I'll say it. Rape you? Can you shoot a man trying to kill or beat or rape you?"

"Can you? Shoot a man?"

"I dunno. Never had to find out. But I assume, life-or-death, wouldn't be that different from hunting."

In my experience, actually, it was quite different from hunting, and I came within a hair's breath of telling Fred. He had no idea how strong I was. How strong women could be when they had to be, which was more often than most men realized.

"I'm going. Alone. Without you or Ruthie Mae. I'll stay in a motel; I'll use my savings to pay for it. Too far to drive back and forth."

"No. I'm sorry."

"I'm not asking your permission, I'm your wife."

"Yes," he said.

"Not your slave. Not a child."

"What are you after?"

"A sense of purpose, identity."

"What is it I'm not giving you?"

"It's nothing with you. I'm trying to grow, or at least not regress."

"Turn yourself into a man?"

"*No*," I said.

"What then?"

"Human." My balled fists shook. "I'm trying to stay a human being."

"Jiminy Christmas! Make some sense, woman."

And Fred stormed from the room rattling walls all over the house.

That Sunday while Fred was on his father's farm splitting firewood I got a call from Pastor Cothran in Lavonia. Ginny Roberts would see me two o'clock Monday afternoon. I told him I would be there, and went to pack a suitcase.

CHAPTER 25

ONDAY I DREW $200 CASH from my personal passbook account, tucked half of it in my wallet and fifty in the zip pocket of my handbag. The remaining fifty I folded and unscrewed the mirror inside the lid of my train case, and replaced it with the bills sandwiched behind. Then I drove to Alabama. I'd told Fred Sunday evening—following a Chef Boyardee out-of-the-box spaghetti dinner, doctored up with ground beef, Worcestershire sauce, Italian seasoning, and bell-pepper flakes—that I was going, and wasn't sure for how long. I apologized for the suddenness. Suggested some easy things he could fix to eat, or there was always the Acme Restaurant, or half-dozen others downtown. The laundry was caught up and ironed, and I promised to be back before he ran out of anything. If need be I could cajole Ruthie Mae into coming to his rescue, considering why I was going.

"No."

My eyelids sank closed, and I placed my Pabst on a coaster. I took my cigarette from the ashtray, drew a puff. Watched my hand tremble, smoke corkscrew. "I *am* going Fred. I told you two nights ago I wasn't asking permission. Only way to stop me," I said, "is by physically restraining me, or taking my car keys. Either, of course, would not be compatible with us remaining husband and wife. I won't be parented in my own home."

He rose from the table—I looked up—and he went in and watched the rest of Ed Sullivan in polar silence.

All of *Bonanza* the same way.

I had made a reservation, using a dog-eared winter-spring directory we had stuffed in a drawer, and checked into a Holiday Inn outside Jasper, midway between Lavonia and Birmingham. A/C year round, a phone, bath, TV in every room: what more could a girl want for eight bucks a night? I unpacked then put a collect call through to the feed mill and told Fred my room and phone numbers. He jotted these down like he would a grain order. "Fred—" I began but he hung up.

I'd hurt him. We were even. Friday night he'd practically called me a whore.

CHAPTER 26

I CONSULTED MY OFFICIAL ALABAMA Highway Map with George Wallace's picture all over it, filled up my gas hound, and drove southwest on Route 69 for ten miles, then forked onto Route 18. After hanging up on Fred's dial tone I'd had just enough time for a sandwich in the coffee shop, before setting off for my rendezvous with Jesse Roberts' widow. The road saw-toothed alongside railroad tracks. Craggy hills broke up through the timberlands like icebergs. There were twists and dips and clay side roads up into the trees. Signs marked logging camps, coal mines. Where I crossed into Lavonia County the road looped and climbed, straining even the Impala's V-8. The railroad tracks veered sharply away. There was a crest and a drop and a slow curvy descent. There came a river and then a four-way stop with no traffic. Across the intersection a highway sign read:

←TUSCALOOSA 35
NATURAL BRIDGE 35→
↑LAVONIA 17

I went straight and followed a fence for nine-tenths of a mile—per Horace Cothran's instructions—past a chained agricultural gate, until a mailbox came up on the left, the name ROBERTS on it. Signal clicking, windshield filthy, I wheeled up a straight rutted road, straddling a grassy center hump. Cotton as far as the eye could see on my left. On my right, a smaller field of white puffs, and where that ended, began a lush green lawn shaded by old oaks. The house on the lawn had been magnificently visible as far back as the highway.

The Seeley-Roberts House.

As it was known to local historical-society types.

Typical Queen Anne, yellow siding, brown and white trim. Palladian window, lots of spindlework, wrap-around porch. A once-ornate knee-high brick wall, weathered, worn, and crumbly, ringed the lawn. Trailing reddish dust I steered between squat brick pillars, a gravel driveway leading to a padlocked wooden shed or garage, set back from the house. I nosed up behind a blue Ford wagon, which was, in turn, parked behind a spanking new black Buick.

I shouldered my pocketbook.

It was hot and dry and rurally silent, broken only by the tinkling of my engine. Shading my eyes, I watched a hawk soaring and circling. Farther along the rutted, humped road I'd come down stood a large red barn with an overhung tin roof. Nary a soul to be seen, I turned and negotiated the loose footing of the driveway and crossed a strip of lawn, grass swishing against my shoes, to five brick steps.

I mounted the porch.

The yellow siding needed paint, on close inspection.

Peeling and wrinkling, age-spotted. Like an old lady's skin.

For my audience with the Grand Duchess of Lavonia County I'd worn a brown-and-white-check jacket-and-skirt set with a sleeveless back-zip blouse of white crepe. The jacket had two little pocket flaps, and a small gold chain linking two gold buttons across the front. My pumps were bone leather, open at the back, a tan strap over the instep. Two-and-a-quarter-inch heels tapped terra-cotta tile, changing to wood plank around the front of the porch. Soft spots and warped boards. More peeling and chipping. Despite this low-level state of disrepair, the porch had been broom swept spic and span.

I pressed the doorbell, wearing capeskin gloves.

It gave an old-fashioned continuous ring, for as long as I held it. Beveled glass in the heavy old door showed vaguely human movement. There came a crack of stuck wood, a shriek of protesting hardware. "Mrs. Roberts...?" I asked the face, pleasant but not overly pretty, looking out the screen. Small jade eyes. Features heavy and florid. Freckled by decades of sun. Eyebrows thick. "I'm Sherry Russell...

"Pastor Cothran spoke to you about me..."

After a beat, as if only then recalling our appointment, she unlatched and swung open the screen, with a now eager, heavy drawled "C'mon in" managing to shoehorn two syllables into the word *in*. "I'm Ginny Roberts. C'm in, c'm in."

Once inside, I waited while she refastened the hook-and-eye, then pushed the big door further on its hinges and dragged a brass umbrella stand to play doorstop.

"Might as well let some of this good fresh air in," she said, a little manically.

Good dragged out.

Goo-wood.

I paced. Large entry hall with a grand staircase darkened by time. It took a ninety-degree left two-thirds up. Reds, blues, and yellows sparkling down from a high stain-glass window. At my feet lay a large opening, covered by heavy iron grating. Below would be, I imagined, an oil-burning furnace. There were signs here too of compulsive housekeeping. No dust on the banister, no motes along the baseboards. The diagonal flooring planks had been recently waxed. Yet beneath the wax the hardwood was scratched and worn, through a once glossy varnish.

"So Miss Russell..."

The lady of the manor had finished fussing with the door.

"Mrs.," I said. Tugged off my gloves, raised my ring.

My nails a pale metallic pink.

I regretted, instantly, having emphasized my marital status, considering hers.

"*Mrs.* Russell. You wish to talk about J.B.'s death, I'm told."

"If you don't mind."

"If I minded I wouldn't have told Horace—that is, Reverend Cothran—to have you come."

She grinned shallowly.

Wearing very bright red lipstick.

***

Ginny Seeley Roberts looked the same age or little younger than my mother. Her dark hair I now saw to be flecked with gray, basket-weaved in back. I wasn't sure what I'd expected—most women didn't wear mourning clothes much past the funeral these days. But she wore a taupe brown pleated dress with a white linen portrait collar and a bow up front. The bow and belt were the same brown as the dress, which was a size too small for her bordering-on-plump figure. She wore a butterfly pin, and an enameled bangle bracelet.

"Shall we go into the parlor," she asked in an accent so stereotypical even I—a four-star southern belle—found it brain grating. The parlor was a tall room off the foyer on the right. Ginny walked me through a wide opening that could be shut off by a pair of sliding pocket doors. A second set of these doors, carved elaborately, sealed an identical opening across the entry hall.

"Lovely old home," I said.

Will you walk into my parlor?

Said the spider to the fly. I was struck motionless by a huge oil portrait, in a massive gilded frame, depicting a stern bearded gentlemen, against stormy blues and grays. He could've, for all I knew, been Rutherford B. Hayes. "My great grandfather," Ginny offered, heavy with reverence. "He built this house to replace the one burned by carpetbaggers after the war. He was a brevet major general under Hood, in the Army of Tennessee."

I wondered where the silver was that had to be buried to keep it out of the Yankee's grubby mitts.

Ginny had many photos, mostly framed in sterling silver. I studied them as I orbited the room packed with antiques. I came to a picture of a younger Mrs. Roberts—heavyish even then— and a tall man with plush light hair and a pleasant weathered face. By comparison, I thought Ginny's expression—sour?

"You and your husband?" I picked it up, twisting.

"Yes, our fifth anniversary. That would have been 1948." I nodded. Replaced the frame, and continued my tour. "Your children?" I said at a shrine-like cluster of photos of a boy and girl at various ages. She joined me, grinning delightedly, back of a wrist propped on her hip. "That's Dennis and Sandra," she said. "He's twenty-four now and going to medical college in

Birmingham."

"Must be very proud."

"Yes."

"And Sandra?" I asked, looking at a graduation portrait.

Ginny's smile bled right off her face.

She paced away.

"She's a hippy."

"Oh."

"In San Francisco."

"I see."

My father loved "Frisco," as he called it, having spent time there in the Navy. These days, however, it had become a rather strange place: Haight-Ashbury, Leary, be-ins, LSD, free love. "I didn't put her...her latest picture on display," Ginny Roberts said. "The one she sent us from there. Never did show it to her father either."

"Why not?"

She glared around, a kind of horror.

"Why? I thought this was about J.B."

"It is," I said. "Just trying to piece together an understanding of what was happening in Mr. Roberts' life—and yours—around the time of his murder."

She again faced away.

Nodded shakily.

"I'll show it to you, if you really want to look. I can't speak about it."

I waited.

If I hadn't wanted to, I sure did now.

Eventually she walked robotically to a window seat. Bending she lifted the lid. Came out with a glossy black-and-white snapshot. She shut the window seat with a soft bang and carried the photo to me, continuing past, no meeting of our eyes, stopping halfway across the Persian rug, staring at nothing. I looked at the photo.

Swallowed.

Two young women.

Friends, grinning at the camera, each with an arm draped huggingly over the other's shoulders, like war buddies on Guadalcanal. The photo was shot in full sunlight. They were barefoot on a sidewalk, a crowded urban parking lot in the background. One had short hair and wore a long peasant skirt. The other looked enough like the girl in the cap-and-gown for me to ID her as Sandra Roberts. Her hair, dark like her mother's, hung in two long ropey braids. A bandana was rolled tight and wrapped across her forehead, knotted in back to form a headband. She wore a pair of denim hot pants made by cutting off some old blue jeans about a half a scintilla below the crotch.

Neither woman wore a bra.

Nor for that matter—

Any sort of top.

Which left two sets of perky cone-shaped breasts complete with four plump nipples popping straight out of the picture. "I couldn't get her," Ginny said over a shoulder, "to come back for her father's funeral. Stoned out of her skull when I talked to her. She said 'good riddance' to him. If she even comprehended."

"I'm sorry."

I left the photo on an inlaid mahogany table. "Sandra sent copies to all her friends." She pivoted. "The whole county knows; how could she?"

"Sandra didn't get along with her father?"

"Hardly."

"May I ask why?"

"No."

I took a seat, with permission, on a Regency fainting couch upholstered in woven yellow silk. My hostess asked if I'd like a drink, offering me choices. Tea would be fine, I told her. While she was gone I opened my purse and pulled out my spiral pad and Bic and wrote on a blank page:

Sandra hated her father.

Twice underlined it. Then waggled the pen. This family had not come out of *Ozzie and Harriett.* I shrugged. Whose had? Rutherford B. Hayes was giving me the judgmental hairy eyeball.

Ginny Roberts returned, entering from an adjoining room, which in her absence I'd determined to be the formal dining room. There was a huge antique table, darkened and dulled by age. A china hutch loaded with elegant dishware. A sideboard. Both similar to the table in style and finish. There was a white-marble mantle and amongst the bric-a-brac, a tiny old photo in a little tarnished frame. It caught my eye because I'd already seen a larger print of the same photograph.

Teenager, short shorts, sailor-suit top, cat.

Ginny Roberts as a girl, I now realized.

The low wall behind her was the crumbling brick wall out front.

The Reverend Horace Cothran had this image framed and displayed on his desk—only personal photo of any kind he did have on display.

CHAPTER 27

MY TEA, PUCKERINGLY SWEET, CAME with a sprig of mint, in a highball with a yellow-and-brown bird on it. I placed the sweating glass, on a coaster, on a marble-topped Louis XIV table with cabriole legs. Mrs. Roberts disappeared again and returned with a sterling-silver tray holding cookies, petit fours, and Ritz crackers topped with lunch meat and Kraft cheese. Onto a napkin, I transferred a polite selection. "Tell me about *that* day, Mrs. Roberts," we began after she had settled, legs crossed, in a wingback. "If you don't—"

"Ginny. Call me Ginny."

"Ginny." I smiled. "Tell me about the day Mr. Roberts died." She sighed.

"You've read the police reports, talked to Bobby Ray?"

"Yes, ma'am. And you should know I arranged to come here over his objections. He didn't want you bothered."

"That's sweet of him."

"I felt it was important. You are, after all, the only living witness."

"Well..." Thoughtful. Quiet. "Not as if you can get Montie off, is it?"

"No, ma'am, I can't."

"Guess there's no harm."

I gave a one-shouldered shrug. "That's my thinking."

Taking some tea, I washed down a ladylike nibble of cake,

105

then smoothed my skirt and waited with my pad and pen poised. Contemplating, again, Turbeville not wanting me to talk to Ginny. Then Loftin (Turbeville's majordomo) sending me to Cothran, who in turn sent me to Ginny, and who had a sexy picture of a teenaged Ginny on his desk.

I thought about all of that.

But had not the foggiest notion what it meant.

"Maybe start by telling me why," I prompted, "you went to the barn that afternoon?"

"I drove out to return the checkbook to J.B."

"The checkbook?"

"He— I had just been to the Piggly-Wiggly. I'd borrowed it from him at lunch."

I nodded. Made a note. "You *drove* out. This is not the big red barn next door?"

"No, heavens, the horse barn." She sipped some tea. "J.B. trained and bred American Saddle Horses and Tennessee Walkers out there. They were his passion."

I nodded. "Where is this from here?"

"Out to the highway, make a right, next gate on the right." I'd seen it. "Go through and follow the road about three-quarters of a mile."

"So you drove out. Where were you when you heard the shots? Still in your car?"

"Ah...no, I was out of the car."

"Inside the barn?"

"Walking toward it."

"You were outside, when the shots were fired inside—you could not see in?"

"Not then, from that angle."

"Eight shots were fired," I said, "in rapid succession."

"Yeees...So?"

"What did you do?"

"Why, I went inside. Saw J.B. lyin' dead there...bloody...in the breezeway with Montie Collins knelt over him with the gun, pilfering through J.B.'s wallet. Stealing from it."

"Holding the gun *and* pilfering through the wallet?"

"Well...I mean...I guess he put the gun down to go through the wallet. Then grabbed it back up when I walked in."

"*Is* that what happened?"

"I just said so."

"All right. Did Collins say anything?"

"No."

"Did *you?*"

"No."

"You saw Montie Collins. In fact, you told the Sheriff, it *was* him. Identified him by name. That's how they made the arrest so quickly."

Her jade eyes fell. "Y-yes."

I chewed some cookie. "You knew Collins by sight. And by name."

"Yes."

"Because he was a sharecropper doing business with your husband?"

"Well, yes. But I knew him. I'd known him his whole life. He and Dennis, my son, played together. I helped him with his reading actually, later with algebra. I encouraged him to stay in school, for as long as he did. It was tenth grade, I think, when he finally dropped out to farm full time."

"Your family and Mr. Collins, then, were pretty close knit."

"Allowing for the differences. Us being white, him colored. My boy Dennis was, let's see, two or three years younger, but Montie was always around. Visitin' or doing odd jobs. His mother used to help my mother out."

"Meaning housekeeping?"

She nodded. "Me too, once I married J.B. And his father sharecropped for my father. Same plot, in fact, Montie was working."

"Was he a violent man?"

"*J.B.?*"

"Ah, no. Montie Collins."

"No. I always found him to have a gentle soul. Determined to make something of that land. Don't think he ever got into brawls, or thieving, like some."

"Like some colored boys, you mean?"

She gave a self-conscious nod. "So…" I swallowed a sweet drink of tea, melting ice tinkling. "Montie Collins shooting your husband, so brutally—eight times—must've been a shock. I mean, beyond the shock of your husband being dead, if that's possible."

"I know what you mean. Yes," she said mechanically, "yes it was."

I squinted: "Why do you think he did it? Peaceful man. Hardworking. Why kill off his livelihood? With a wife, a baby on the way."

"As I understand it, there had been a disagreement."

"Specifically: over Collins purchasing that acreage he worked, and you say his father before him. His claim being that he and your husband had a handshake agreement, that your husband cheated him. That he, Montie, had been accepting for years a lower share of the income from crop sales, in lieu of making a down payment on the property."

"J.B. handled business."

"Like the checkbook."

"Huh?"

"You'd just mentioned having to get the checkbook from your husband—for groceries—then having to return it."

"J.B. handled the finances. He had the head for it."

Yet you tutored—

I pondered with a curled brow.

—a young man in algebra.

"Did an agreement exist? Or did Collins lie?"

"My father respected Montie's father very much. He called him—and you're going to read this all wrong—but he called him a *good nigger.*"

I nodded.

"My father was not a bigot, Mrs. Russell. That was how everybody talked. But he respected John Collins. For his work ethic, his common sense, honesty, strong religious faith."

I sat listening. I had a feeling one of Montie's father's more stellar qualities was his deference to white society. His sense of "place."

"We were always good to them. Food for the poor, candy for the children, literacy programs, good wages for the pickers. Nobody ever had to go to the back door of this house. And I've always run my household the same way my folks did. With respect for all. Regardless."

Then she snatched a breath.

Small green eyes everywhere but on me.

"Hell of a way," I said, "for Montie Collins to repay you."

She drew up.

"I *didn't* say that."

"No." I smirked. "You didn't. What about Mr. Roberts? Was he as...racially magnanimous?"

"In his fashion. Like most people."

"Like most white southerners?"

"Yes. He didn't give them much thought one way or the other."

"Was he a bigot?"

"No..."

A *no* that was mewly and qualified.

"Did he hate Negroes?"

"Heavens no."

"Nor did he love them."

"No—*do you*?"

My brows lifted, eyelids closed. Then with my head cocking funny I rearranged on the silk upholstery. Exhaling. Let's say, there weren't that many white people I loved. In fact, in the four years since I'd been jolted out of my nice-Nancy-nurse psychedelia, I'd seen and experienced enough—bolstered by the daily bad karma read by Huntley and Brinkley—to work up an equal-opportunity scorn for most of humanity.

"Was J.B. Roberts in the Ku Klux Klan?"

"My gosh no. He despised them."

She was shaking her head like trying to toss off her curls, or get a buzzing bee out of her ear. "This isn't a Klan stronghold. Even my father cursed them. And he was a member when I was little."

"Really?"

"I remember the robes. But he quit in disgust, 'bout 1925, I guess."

I nodded. Made a note. "You never finished telling me about the agreement. In fact, you started telling me about your father and Montie's father."

She was looking at her hands, fortifying with oxygen. I wasn't sure what I was after. "My father and John Collins jawed about

John taking over that land for years. Nothing ever happened. I dunno why. Those days, all I was concerned with was frilly dresses and snaring a husband."

I nodded.

A long-playing record in another room.

Dizzy Gillespie.

"When Old Man Collins died, Montie took over. That's why he dropped out of school. None of his brothers wanted any part of this county or that farm, but he did and you gotta admire that. They went on to bigger things. Army. Football. Montie stayed here." She paused, blinking, something might've glistened. "My father…"

She cleared her throat.

Drained her tea glass.

"Want some more?"

I shook my head.

"My father didn't respect Montie. Young people in general he held in contempt. Montie wanted to buy that section from day-one—but my father said Montie had to prove himself. That he was dang lucky he let him keep working the property, period. 'Stead of handing it over to another tenant, who might be more productive. Then my father died, no more'n six months after Mr. Collins, and my mother maybe six months after that."

"Hard year," I said.

"Yes. J.B. and I inherited everything."

I felt my brain jerk.

"Mean…*you* inherited everything."

"No, actually."

She applied a false-looking smile. "Both my parents' wills—and, yes, I am an only child—stated I was to inherit everything, but if I were married, the property should legally fall under my husband's name. So, in fact, I did misspeak when I said *J.B. and I.* I meant just J.B. That's the way my father wanted it. He was not a bigot, Mrs. Russell, but he *was* a misogynist."

CHAPTER 28

OH, THERE WAS SOME WORDING," Ginny went on, "protecting me if the marriage were on shaky ground. In the event of a quickie divorce, the property would revert to me. That was not really to protect me, but to keep the land from being stolen by some gold digger. My parents were convinced they were the southern Rockefellers and that swarms of shady, greedy characters were going to lit upon me to get the fortune after they were gone." Her eyes animatedly rolled. "So anyway, legally, it fell to J.B. to deal with Montie's wish to buy his parcel."

"Did they have a deal?" I said.

"I thought they did. I was aware of J.B. keeping an account, in crops, of what was to be a down payment."

"Did you object?"

"To Montie buying a piece of our land?"

"To having a black man for a neighbor."

"I have lots of black neighbors. This county is fifty-percent black. No, I wanted Montie to have the land his father worked, soaked his sweat into all those years. Montie too. It would be like having family there. My children don't care about the farm."

"So what happened?"

"Like I said, J.B. didn't talk much, but he did mention once Montie was talking more and more about inking a deal. With the baby coming."

"What did Mr. Roberts think?"

"If he objected, he didn't *at the time* indicate it."

"At the time?"

"Well…"

I leaned in.

"Something changed." She shook her head, distractedly, uncertain. "I heard through the grapevine, at the beauty parlor, that Dorothy Collins, who was a very good seamstress, rest her soul. That she was upset because she thought we were holding out on them. Dragging our feet about selling."

"You ask Mr. Roberts?"

"He said we might not be able to sell to them. That he was still thinking."

"What had changed?"

She shrugged. "I pressed. A little. Much as I dared. He said some people didn't think it was a good idea."

"Idea?"

"For us to sell."

"To a colored man?"

"That was my impression."

"Who were these people?"

She jerked a shoulder.

"The Klan?" I pressed.

"I *don't* know."

"See anybody visiting?"

"No."

"Did you ask?"

"I could tell J.B. didn't want to talk."

"Later, then? Did you ask if he'd made his mind up? Or do more to find out who opposed the sale?"

"No."

"With due respect, why not? The land was *your* family's. You had known Collins, or his father before him, all your life. You knew your father's wishes with respect to the elder Collins. One might think you would have championed Montie's cause."

"Because—"

Spurting to her feet.

"Because I had bigger fish to fry with J.B. than Montie Collins!" She stormed before the mantle. Clamping her temples, cradling the other hand back on her hip.

The jazz had finished.

Another record dropped in place.

Ironically, Sammy Davis, Jr.

His "Body and Soul" could give one goose bumps. "I'm sorry," Ginny wailed. She was crying. I waited. Looking down at my hands, fingers laced, twisting in my checkered lap. Bigger fish to fry…. "Excuse me," she burst, rushing for the back of the house. When she returned, I hadn't moved. Her nose and eyes were red, but she was composed. "Sorry."

"Don't suppose," I ventured, "you wish to elaborate on what you meant by *bigger fish*?"

"No." She moved, pleated skirt swaying, to the serving tray, selected the last lunchmeat-and-cheese Ritz.

She took a nibble.

"Very well," I said, re-crossing my legs, tugging my skirt hem. "When did you became aware of Mr. Roberts' change of mind? When did you hear the gossip?"

"Oh…middle of June or so."

I jotted that.

Underlined it.

"About a month," I said, "before Montie confronted your husband, angry, about the property. Your husband gave him some excuse about a short fall in crop sales. Told Collins the deal was off. Collins felt like he was being cheated, or discriminated against, or both, and struck out, enraged. He admitted that. He grabbed a tool—a horseshoe puller, I believe—and swung at your husband, striking him above the left ear."

Mrs. Roberts had finished her cracker.

Lowered into her seat.

Listening.

"Collins says your husband dropped in the breezeway, unconscious, the instant he was hit. At which point he searched for Mr. Robert's wallet, to steal cash that he, in his anger felt he was owed. Now, Ginny, all this took place before you entered the barn, while you were driving up and parking, right?"

"Yes."

"The coroner's report confirms the blow was inflicted prior

to death, almost certainly prior to the shooting, and it was definitely inflicted by the shoe puller at the scene. Your husband's blood and hair were on it, together with Collins's fingerprints. The coroner also affirmed that the blow was hard enough to cause a concussion—but no fracturing, or intracranial hemorrhage."

"Excuse me?" she said.

"Pardon me, I was a nurse. Point is: there was insufficient head trauma to cause death or permanent disability. The blow struck by Montie Collins would not have killed your husband."

"So? The gunshots did."

"Precisely."

"You've...lost me, Mrs. Russell."

I set my pad and pen aside on the fainting couch then stood and entwined my arms, my steps soft on the Persian rug. "Sherry, please," I said. "Call me Sherry."

Mrs. Roberts' interested eyes tracked me.

"Very well—Sherry. You've lost me."

CHAPTER 29

DID MONTIE COLLINS KNOW WHERE to find your husband's gun in the tack room?" I shrugged, my arms still knotted, beneath the oil-painted gaze of Ginny Roberts' great grandfather. "Did he even know there was a gun in there?"

"Apparently he did."

"Not according to him."

"Per...perhaps...he was lying."

"Why didn't you run?"

"Pardon?"

"When you were walking from your car, heard eight gunshots, rapid succession. From a forty-five automatic. That's a lotta noise. You couldn't see inside. Been me, I'd've dove under my car. If not behind the wheel and been halfway back to Tennessee before my ears stopped ringing. You waltzed right in."

"I've lived on this farm fifty years, Sherry. I'm no stranger to gunfire. I assumed J.B. was excitedly shooting at some varmint or snake or something. Never—never—occurred to me what had really happened."

"Must've been a awful shock."

"Yes."

"To your knowledge, *was* Collins aware where your husband kept his gun?"

"No, not to my knowledge. Perhaps J.B. got the gun from the tack room during the argument, and Montie took it away."

"No physical evidence of a struggle, except the blow to your husband's head. Also no physical evidence your husband entered the tack room in any sort of rush. No evidence Collins did either, especially considering he'd have to have tossed the room to find it. The tack trunk, where you told Sheriff Turbeville the gun was stored, was still neatly arranged inside, lid closed."

Her right leg was crossed over her left knee. Right foot jumping. "Perhaps Montie did know where the gun was. He'd been around this farm all his life. Heck, he might've found it when he was a kid. Snooping where he didn't belong."

"Might've," I agreed.

"Perhaps he neatened up, shut the trunk after removing the gun, to throw off suspicion. After all, J.B. was unconscious by then. He would've had time."

"Also possible. Why?"

"Why what?" she rasped.

"Why shoot your husband?"

"To kill him."

"Why?"

"Because he was angry. Enraged. Felt cheated, discriminated against. Whatever his father was, Montie was no Uncle Tom."

"He'd already clubbed Mr. Roberts with the shoe puller. Why go get a gun, and shoot him? If he'd clubbed him, why shoot him? And if the coroner got it wrong, why club him *after* he'd shot him?"

"I certainly don't know, Sherry, what goes on inside the head of an angry colored man."

"Don't you think it's reasonable to assume the coroner was correct? Mr. Roberts was knocked out by the shoe puller before he was shot?"

"I suppose."

"Why was he shot eight times? Why was the trigger pulled repeatedly until the slide locked back? That's rage. Or terror. And I doubt Montie Collins, who was at least as big as your husband, and half his age, would have been terrified."

"Then he was enraged."

"He was enraged when he swung the shoe puller. Then what?

He walked calmly in the tack room. Found the gun, neatly removed it from the trunk, without disturbing anything, then *closed* the trunk, and walked out and—and then fired eight shots into your husband. Missing only once."

"Your point?"

"This rage. Would've been expended with the shoe puller. It certainly would not have burned on through the trip into the tack room. If he was simply trying not to leave a witness alive, then that was a thoughtful process, and he would've fired only once, maybe twice, not eight times. The noise alone would have added to his risk. And if that were the case, why run when he saw you? Why not silence you?"

She burst up.

Got in my face, roaring:

"What you want from me? All I can tell you is what I saw. Montie Collins kneeling over my murdered husband, stealing from his wallet, and when he saw me he seemed to panic, grabbed the gun and ran—that so hard to believe?"

She stalked away.

Catching her breath.

"Which raises two other questions."

She jerked around.

"There's more?"

"Why take cash from the wallet? You've killed a man. Take the wallet."

She shrugged... "What's it called? Incriminating evidence."

"Yes."

"Wouldn't the wallet be incriminating?"

"Sure."

"There you go."

"The gun was incriminating. Why take it? It was empty. And if you're going to take it, why hide it outside your own front door?"

"I hate to say this," Ginny argued, "but Montie Collins was not a towering intellect. He was under pressure. People under pressure do irrational things, don't they?"

"Yes ma'am, but not insanely illogical inconsistent things at every turn."

"How many psychology degrees do you have? How many

police departments have you worked for?"

"Zero," I said, "on both counts."

"You told Bobby Ray all this?"

"No, ma'am."

"Then have this discussion with him. What makes you think you're covering bases he didn't?"

"Easy. He had an eyewitness. You. He had evidence. And a quick arrest. Case closed. And I'll give Sheriff Turbeville—or at least the public defender—the benefit of the doubt, and assume these bases would've been covered once Collins's trial approached. But he was murdered. Lynched. Making further investigation of your husband's murder a moot point. Especially once they had a new quadruple murder on their hands."

"Again, Sherry, you're losing me."

"A fair trial would have either cleared up those loose ends, or Collins would have been acquitted. But with Collins dead—no trial, no compelling reason for Bobby Ray Turbeville to continue investigating what to him seemed open and shut. I can't help thinking..."

"What?" Ginny huffed.

"Whether by some chance, however remote, Mr. Roberts was killed by someone other than Montie Collins."

"Who?"

"I don't know," I said. "But to that person, Montie Collins's murder was gift. All wrapped up pretty in paper and shiny ribbons."

CHAPTER 30

I WAS HUMMING BACK TO Jasper when I had a thought.

Blondes do sometimes, I swear.

I pulled onto the shoulder to study my George Wallace map, Engelbert Humperdinck on the radio. A county road up on my left would start me back towards Lavonia. I took it, and thirty-two miles later I veered into a parking slot near The Mayflower Café. At almost four o'clock I was bustling the two blocks to the library, perspiring freely through my slip. I was being sneaky, avoiding having my car seen on the square. I didn't think Deputy Loftin could actually enforce my banishment from the county.

For now though a low profile seemed prudent.

My brilliant idea was to dig back, focusing on the *Lavonia County Broadcaster* and the *Tuscaloosa News*, figuring the area's rural and small-town folk would prioritize those over the Birmingham papers. Also, rather than working forward starting with the Roberts murder, I went backward. Asking the librarian for every issue of the two papers for June, which was when Ginny Roberts started to hear gossip about her husband holding out on Montie Collins.

The local paper fretted an awful lot about the lead content of Lavonia County moonshine, and June's big world news had been the U.S.S. Liberty attack, killing thirty-four Americans, by Israeli torpedo boats and planes. There, of course, was the Arab-Israeli war, and Vietnam, and the AMA favoring legalized abortion. I lit a cigarette, shook out the match. Huffing, I skimmed a piece, a New Mexico town raided by Mexican-American rebels, laying claim to 2500 square miles of northern New Mexico. LBJ was forming a committee.

Fascinating as all this was—none of it would've triggered anyone bothering J.B. Roberts about selling land to a Negro. I hadn't been led to believe there was any great objection to blacks buying property down here. Money, not skin color, according to Ruthie Mae's brother-in-law, was the barrier to black property ownership.

What changed in June?

I found nothing to suggest any violent racial unrest locally prior to mid July.

I scanned further back, Nashville's Fisk riot getting some press, but that was April. The only thing that subtly piqued my interest, before I got ushered out for the library's closing, was an editorial in the *Tuscaloosa News*, run on a Sunday—a big circulation edition—railing against trial preparations underway in Meridian, Mississippi, ninety miles from Tuscaloosa, which was a scant forty miles from Lavonia.

The Imperial Wizard of the Mississippi Klan—Sam Bacon—and seventeen others faced federal conspiracy charges stemming from the 1964 murders of three civil-rights workers in Philadelphia, Mississippi. The piece recounted the case's checkered history—no local grand jury, for example, had ever returned an indictment, and previous federal indictments had been thrown out on technicalities—including the fact that murder was not a federal crime. The U.S. Supreme Court, however, had green-lighted felony prosecutions on charges that the murdered youths had been deprived of their constitutional rights. The trial would begin in October.

Next month, I thought, crushing out my a cigarette.

The editorial was inflammatory.

Might be what I was looking for.

It accused the justice department of running roughshod over state sovereignty, and the rights of the accused to swift and fair trials, before juries of their peers. It cited the three years lapsed since the murders, and recent cases in Alabama and Georgia in which federal courts had convicted Klansmen, where state courts had refused. "With all these machinations," the rant concluded, "we fear justice for all may be swept aside in a riptide of national fervor for racial equality. True equality, after all, cuts both ways."

I placed a long-distance call from my motel room at 5:45 to catch Tom Miller at his desk in the newsroom of the *Nashville Banner*. He was still the police reporter, though my father expected him to be named city editor. He was also my former fiancé. We'd broken it off seven years ago after I'd caught him cheating with a Harvey's salesgirl.

"BannerMillerspeaking."

"Tom. Sherry."

"Well..." His chair swiveled and squeaked on the line, a nearby typewriter rapping. "Haven't heard from you in a month of Sundays—not since you got hitched to that mountain man."

"Fred, Tom. My husband's name is Fred."

"Just joshing, Sher. To what do I owe the enormous honor?"

"I'm on a case. I need a favor."

"A case? What's this? The feed store belly up? Bigfoot sending you out to work?"

"Stop the name-calling—and, no, *nobody* sends me anywhere."

"Ookaay. What can I do you for?"

"Know anybody on either Birmingham paper?"

"Birmingham...Sure, couple, three guys I was in school with."

"I need somebody," I said, tapping a cigarette ash, "who knows about the Klan down here."

"As in Ku Klux?"

"You know another?"

"You're in Birmingham?"

"Jasper, Alabama, close enough."

"Hafta make a couple calls, cookie. Gimme a number."

"Two-oh-five area code," I said, and read him the number off the dial. "Room one-seventeen. Don't give out my number or location please. Arrange it and I'll meet whoever it is—early tomorrow if possible."

He said he'd phone back within half an hour. I winched the curtains closed, then hung my jacket up, and thumbed down and stepped out of my skirt, which I spring-clipped to the same hanger. Up and over I partly unzipped my blouse, then fingered up behind me, finally got hold of the tab and unzipped the rest of the way. I fluttered the blouse, draped it over a chair. The straps I pinched off my shoulders and wriggled out of my damp slip. It got rinsed and hung over the shower rod. Same with my nylons. When the telephone rang I padded out in my bra and panty girdle, garters dangling, and picked up.

It was Tom Miller.

"Sher—talked to a reporter with the *Post-Herald* named Walter Biggs. My friend J.D. swears he's the guy to talk to about the Klan."

"Good enough," I said, bent over the nightstand, writing on a Holiday Inn pad. "B-I-G-G-S?"

"Yes."

"Got it."

"He'll meet you ten A.M. tomorrow. Lounge, basement of the Granada Hotel, Fourth and Twenty-third. Next door to the newspaper plant."

"Perfect. Thanks, Tom."

I straightened, grasping the phone cord.

"You okay?"

"Yes, Tom, I'm fine. Thank you."

"Great to hear your voice."

I pressed my lips.

Glanced away.

"Sher? *Hear* me? Good to, you know…"

I swallowed.

"Tom. I'm married. You're my ex-fiancé. Who, by the way, cheated on me. You blew it. I appreciate your help in a professional capacity, but I'm am not going to sit and have a friendly talk with you."

"You don't have to be like that. Thought you might be lonely."

"If I am, I'll call Fred. Anyway, you seem under the mistaken impression I've forgiven you."

"It *was* a long time ago."

His inflection screaming how intolerant and unreasonable I had always been about the whole matter. "I was in Harvey's picking out our china pattern, Tom, when I spotted you with *her!* Hundred years won't be long enough. When will you realize that? Again, thank you, but good night."

I broke the connection with a stab.

Then slowly, tightfistedly, I cradled the receiver. With a shaking head I turned for the dresser. Got a pale-blue double-knit out and pulled it on, careful about my hair. I donned some navy-blue capris, zipped up the side, and laced on a pair of tattersall Keds. I strolled to the motel coffee shop. Still early, two other tables were occupied, each by one man dining alone. I picked a spot well away from either. Along a side wall, papered with freakishly large Magnolia blossoms. I drank Sanka and had the chopped-sirloin steak with mushroom sauce, tossed salad, and potato. It was nearly dark when I signed the check for $2.55. I drove to a store and bought a six-pack of Schlitz. Back in Room 117, I crunched one beer into my ice bucket and pulled the tab on another and drank it watching Lucy and Andy on TV, and at eighty-thirty *Peyton Place*. I dozed during *The Big Valley*. Up preparing for bed, I heard some news. We were bombing a harbor called Haiphong, and a bridge seven miles from Red China.

Up at six.

By 7:15 I was getting breakfast and reading the paper. "My God," I exclaimed aloud, stirring two sugars and cream into my coffee. I tapped the spoon off without looking. About 10:40 Monday night—about when I'd fallen asleep—a bomb had destroyed the Temple Beth Israel synagogue in Jackson, Mississippi. Ripped through offices, a conference room, tore a hole in the ceiling, blew out windows, ruptured a water pipe, and buckled a wall. The FBI had found doors jimmied, and said the bomb—a boxful of dynamite—had been planted next to the Rabbi's study. No one had been inside, fortunately. The article quoted sources about a suspected link between the blast and preparations then underway in Jackson for a civil-rights murder trial to get underway in Meridian in three weeks.

123

CHAPTER 31

THE BIRMINGHAM NEWS-POST HERALD Building stood downtown on the corner of Fourth Avenue and Twenty-Second Street. To the east, belching black pollution, rose the ugly gray stacks of a steel plant, a pall of smoke and cinders shrouding the city. I knew little of Birmingham, aside from its racial infamy, earning it the nickname "Bombingham." It was a young city, founded by speculators, post-Civil War, eager to exploit the region's iron, limestone, and coal deposits—perfect for iron and steel production. Birmingham's blast furnaces were the largest south of Pittsburgh.

The plant housing, under a joint-operating agreement, both the morning and afternoon newspapers—the same situation existed in Nashville—was a six-story Jacobethan beauty of brown brick and beige stone. I was to meet Walter Biggs next door at the Granada Hotel, but was ninety minutes early, having raced over after learning of the Mississippi Klan bombing. I worried Biggs might be too busy for me, that he might've even left for Jackson. I found the *Post-Herald* newsroom—found it fairly tomb-like, in fact, at that hour, the managing editor's secretary holding the fort.

Biggs would've checked in before leaving town, she assured me, adding that Walter Biggs was rarely in bed before three. Thus, my ten-o'clock appointment was, for him, practically the crack of dawn.

I thanked her and asked to borrow a desk and phone book.

I located a home number for Dennis Roberts—Ginny and the late J.B. Roberts' son—who attended medical school in Birmingham. I assumed he wouldn't be snoring the morning away, but I cradled the black receiver on my shoulder anyway—setting aside a jar of rubber cement from the middle of the desk—punched an outside line, and rotated in the number.

No answer. I tapped the switch-hook. Keeping the receiver against my ear, I looked up the Medical College of Alabama, dialed a main number, and was eventually transferred to a Marjorie in Student Affairs. She talked like the magnolia wallpaper in my motel's coffee shop. For the third time I explained who I was, what I wanted, and she said Dennis Roberts, a third-year student, was on his internal-medicine clerkship at University Hospital. She would locate him and find out when he could see me. I told her anytime after noon would be lovely and I would call her back.

Fifty-five minutes before my meeting.

I returned the phone book, restored my borrowed desk to its prior chaos, thanked the secretary and left. On the street my eyes stung. I thumbed more change in the meter, traffic humming and growling, building with the heat. Birmingham's downtown seemed more vigorous than Nashville's—the might of its industrial economy bolstered by the hot war in Vietnam, and the cold one with Russia. It took much iron and steel to wage modern wars of all temperatures. I browsed Magic City Newsstand, then found a Glazy-Glazed shop and commiserated with coffee and a hot donut. At a quarter to ten I repaired my lipstick and pecked my heels over to the Granada. Down a flight of stairs I found the basement lounge, a sign beside the padded-leather door reading: MEMBERS/GUESTS ONLY.

I grinned—key for any self-respecting newspapermen's watering hole:

Circumvention of any and all draconian local liquor laws.

Dark, cocktail loungey, a piano, ringed by stools, ashtrays on top, an empty tip glass. I imagined Sinatra tickling the ivories. "Strangers in the Night..." Carpet a dingy burgundy and gold, small round black tables, one black plastic ashtray centered upon each. There was a full bar at one end, manned by a red-vested bartender. He cast me a nod while polishing a Martini glass, which he then raised toward a light and peered through. Along the wall before me were booths of reddish leather, or vinyl mimicking leather. The walls were dark wood below, red velvet above. There were British-Empire-motif oil paintings and other affectations—even a suit of medieval armor.

One customer.

Middle booth, below a foxhunt scene, hunched over a quarter-folded paper.

Had to be Walter Biggs.

Like a dozen newsmen I knew:

Weathered, callused, wearied.

Too much alcohol, tobacco, cynicism.

The world's H. L. Menckens.

Never-married, or frequently divorced, or if not, ought to be. My father was neither as hard-drinking, nor hard-bitten as this particular species of middle-age reporter, though all gentlemen of the press manifested the traits to a degree. My father was an idealist for one thing. For another he had a Vanderbilt law degree, and had been promoted out of the news department to editorial years ago, putting him on a slightly higher ethereal plane. In my paisley Ban-Lon shift dress of hot pink, gold, and various shades of green, I sashayed across. My goal—to be noticed, and the man obliged, lifting rummy eyes, marveling over me.

Fred called this my hippy dress.

"Mr. Biggs?" I said.

He wore a fedora older than my first training bra. He doffed it. "Mrs. Nates, a pleasure..." In fits and jerks, half-climbing from the booth, he gestured for me to slide in facing him. I told him to call me Sherry. Sherry Russell. I gave him a business card. The table was littered with his newspaper, a smoldering cigarette, half-drunk coffee, and a plate of scrambled eggs covered with ketchup, and home fries. He pocketed my card down the side of his rumpled coat. His striped tie, loose at the neck, was too narrow, and ketchup stained to boot. A small hole was burned by a cigarette ash in his lapel. "So," he graveled, settling, "you're Charlie Russell's little girl."

"You know my father?"

He coughed phlegmatically. Picked up his cigarette, letting its long snaky ash drop at a time and place of its own choosing. "Mostly by reputation. We had a drink at a press banquet, some years ago. The young man I spoke with was, I believe, your ex-fiancé. Smart not to marry a newspaperman."

"Probably. Especially since he didn't wait for the wedding to start cheating."

"Real go-getter."

"And I got up and left."

He nodded and smoked. Offered me a clean home fry off his plate, which I pinched and ate. The bartender came with a steaming pot, a mug hanging from his other hand, and asked would I like coffee. "Please," I said, then he warmed Biggs' up and while I added cream and sugar to mine, Biggs produced a silver flask. "Scotch," he said. "Want some?"

"Ah, no," I said, astounded. He shrugged, splashing some in his coffee.

"Your father writes for a good paper."

"I think so."

"Bit liberal."

"So's my father. And, I'm a chip off the old block."

He huffed. "So how can I help a sweet left-wing filly like you?"

I swallowed some coffee and let him light me a cigarette.

"I want a crash course. I'm looking into the Lavonia Massacre."

"Nasty piece of business."

"What's your opinion of the investigation?"

"Zealous," he said. "If unfruitful."

"Zealous, on the part of the FBI?"

"Always."

"Yet they pulled out?"

"Can't get blood out of a turnip. They felt their resources could be more gainfully deployed elsewhere. That's the public face." He shrugged. "I dunno anything different."

I nodded. "Somebody knows who killed four people. Or has a idea. They're just not talking."

"I think, my dear…your grasp is accurate."

"Is it the FBI's style, then, in the face of that, to retreat? In a parade of black government cars?"

"No. Not their style."

"Why then?"

"I don't know."

"You've asked?"

"Asking's my job."

"What do you think?"

"You don't go down easy, do you?"

"If you said I did—would it be a complement?"

He huffed.

"Touché."

Gave his ash a flick.

"I believe," I said, "a man like you would have a buddy or two over at the FBI field office, who would've talked off the record, and you would have maintained that confidence. I'm just asking for a crumb."

Biggs drank some laced coffee.

Snuffed out his filterless Camel and fired up another.

Then, both elbows on the table, he held the cigarette in front of him, one ropey-veined hand cupped over the other, and he shrugged. "They don't know. Which means they're either truly at a dead-end—unlikely—or there's some high-level stonewalling."

My brows knitted. "A cover up?"

"Didn't say that. Governments keep secrets for legitimate reasons."

I frowned. "Some other time I'll give you my left-wing position on that."

He chuckled gruffly. I opened my pad, jotted a note, then asked about Sheriff Turbeville.

"Wasn't one of Colonel Lingo's cronies, if that's what you mean."

"Lingo?"

"Wallace's Safety Commissioner."

I nodded. "So, he's okay?"

He shrugged. "Never heard him called friendly to the Klan."

"Good cop?"

"It's rural Alabama. He's as good as his peers, maybe better than most. There was a real mean, crooked, sonovabitch over there ten, fifteen years ago..." He shook his head. "Can't remember his name—Turbeville, though, seems to run a tight ship."

"I'm told he ran for election on having killed two Negroes."

The reporter's head shook.

Easy dismissal. "Rumors, spread by his opponent, to steal the black vote. This came right after the Voting Rights Act, when white candidates, all of a sudden, had to start taking the black voting bloc seriously. Lies were an easy solution. True, Turbeville killed the two, but he didn't brag about it. Never ran on it."

"He *did* kill two Negroes?"

"As a city police officer in Tuscaloosa, believe it was fifty-nine—we investigated all this—he shot and killed an armed man holding up a, think it was drug store. The robber happened to be black, but Turbeville killed him not because he was black, because he'd turned a gun on him."

I nodded.

"Second incident?"

"His first term as sheriff, Turbeville broke up a knife fight between two Negroes drunk on moonshine. One of'em charged him, Turbeville shot in self defense. Other kid ran off. Never found him."

"No witnesses?"

"Not in either case."

"So," I said, "no proof he wasn't trigger happy."

"No proof he was—and even down here, a man is innocent till proved guilty."

My eyelids flickered.

"If the man's white."

"That's northeast-liberal propaganda."

"Montie Collins' family believes Sheriff Turbeville to be a violent racist."

Biggs shrugged. "Enough blacks believed the rumors about Turbeville, they voted overwhelmingly for his crooked opponent, who would've robbed them blind, I guarantee you. Enough whites disbelieved them—or *believed*, as the case may be—that Turbeville was re-elected by a slim margin. For whatever it's worth, far my paper's concerned, he's a better sheriff than most. That said…"

I leaned back, fingering one of my earrings.

Pink-enameled glass balls.

Swinging by two-inch gold chains.

"The southern rural sheriff can be a virtual God," Biggs explained. "He determines whether the Klan can exist with any degree of strength. He hires and fires deputies. He's popularly elected. Now, the Klansman doesn't give a damn what community leaders think about race. Businessmen, local gentry, they send their brats to private schools, move to expensive neighborhoods, hang out inside walled country clubs—where they aren't going to see a black man, 'less he's a waiter or groundskeeper. But the sheriff and his deputies, they come out of the same world as the Klansman."

I bit my lower lip.

"Turbeville, I'll tell you, is no fan of civil rights, and his deputy called me a nigger lover to my face. Yet, I've been assured, by several sources, black and white, there was little to no overt Klan presence in Lavonia County until the Roberts killing blew the lid off everything."

"Which gives us three possibilities," Biggs said. "One, Turbeville is anti-Klan and kept them at bay until he couldn't anymore. Two, the rabble-rousers waltzed in from outside the county…"

"Three?"

"Maybe Turbeville's pro-Klan, maybe even a full initiated member—they call it *naturalized*—but has cunningly kept that hidden. You see, my dear, the Klan's greatest strength is its secrecy, its cloak."

I nodded. "The masks, robes, hoods…"

"If you don't know its members, how do you know who to elect? Who to seat on a jury? Who to have investigating a Klan massacre?"

"Turbeville's a wild card."

"Very wild"—his eyes flashed—"and, very dangerous."

I nodded. "I understand."

"Do you?"

I found him glaring straight into me, grave and grizzled.

Smoke coiling off the tip of his Camel. "There was a time, young lady, I would've said that you, as a white woman, were immune from Klan violence, notwithstanding Viola Liuzzo. But times have changed. Things have gone too far."

"The divide between white and black?"

"Yes, but even that's just a symptom of a wider cancer..."

Suddenly he began to stare upward. then lowered his look, quoting:

"It was the best of times, it was the worst of times, it was the age of wisdom, it was the age of foolishness, it was the epoch of belief, it was the epoch of incredulity"—getting louder—"it was the season of light, it was the—"

"Season of darkness," I cut in.

Recalling my Dickens. I'd once, after all, planned a teaching career. He smiled approvingly; there *was* hope for the younger generation...

"It was the spring of hope," he said.

"The winter of despair," I said.

"Everything before us."

"Nothing before us."

"All going direct to heaven."

"All going..."

Curling my lips.

"Direct the other way."

CHAPTER 32

THE KU KLUX KLAN WAS responsible for the Lavonia Massacre.

Several of Biggs' best tipsters, he told me, had independently corroborated the assembly of a so-called Special Violent Action Group to deal with the Montie Collins problem. A highly trained, highly secret hit squad, committed to the violent defense of segregation and white supremacy. These sources, however, denied knowing any names. I asked if he'd passed his sources along to the FBI.

I got the members-of-press-have-a-sacred-duty-to-protect-their-sources spiel. The bartender interrupted us, refilling coffee, and I leaned back in the booth, ate another cold home fry, smeared through a refreshed puddle of Heinz. Biggs covered his mug. "Nougha that filthy stuff. Dewar's and soda. Short one, though, lest the lady think me a reprobate."

Then he bulged me an endearingly crazed look:

"Anything stronger? My tab."

"Still early for me, I'm afraid."

"Balance is important. Most people don't appreciate that. Not too much, not too little, around the clock. That's the secret." Waggling a finger, like this was the unified field theory or something. "You should write a manual," I quipped.

"And so I shall."

I laughed.

"Know how long since I've had a cold, sugar? No self-respecting germ can live in this body."

I shook my head, amused.

"I was about to say, you seemed surprised, your sources didn't know more."

"Kluxers think they're right, and righteous, and to boot, they're an ignorant bunch of goddamned braggarts. For them to be this quiet, even amongst themselves, is odd, and, frankly, disturbing."

I had my mug, wisping steam, by the handle and pink-smudged rim.

"Secrecy, you said, was their strength."

"It's a strength the FBI can defeat, when they swarm an area, face down all threats—and believe me, they get them—and keep at it, and at it, till something gives, somebody talks: a scared Kluxer, maybe, or a citizen recalling a key detail, a certain pickup passing, a certain back street, a certain hour... Then another, then another, and eventually the conspiracy falls apart. What was different this time?" He spread his hands. "I dunno, for sure."

"You have a theory?"

The bartender brought Biggs' drink. He threw back half the glass in one gulp. I tapped an ash from my Kent, hooked my hair back with my left pinkie nail. After swallowing and smacking, he opined:

"The Klan is scared shitless. Pardon my vulgarity."

I nodded.

"Course, you heard it all, didn't you? Daughter of a newsman?"

"And Navy man—yeah, pretty much—that, and ward nursing at Nashville Receiving."

I gestured:

"They're scared..."

"Civil rights is winning, will win, and they know it. Blacks are voting. Getting better jobs, better education, higher salaries. Moving into white neighborhoods. All the laws and bigoted cops that formerly kept the black man down and shielded the Kluxer, they're falling like dominos. The Klan to its core is frightened to death—of these outside forces certainly—but it's also crumbling from within."

"How so?"

"There's always been financial corruption. That's bad enough. But my sources, both in law enforcement, and the Klan, tell me that at least one in five Klansmen, today, is an FBI informant."

I whistled.

"The Klan, young lady, is on shakier ground, yet more dangerous, than at any point in its history."

"The stereotype," I pondered, "of the wounded animal."

"The FBI failed in Lavonia because nobody's talking. Nobody's talking because they don't know. They don't know because a small hard core of Klansmen did those murders. Not your average weekend cross-burners. These are dedicated, vicious, cunning terrorists, who'll die before talking, to anybody, friend or foe."

"Who would run such thing? This core, this Special Violent Action Group, who would assemble and dispatch it?"

He shrugged. "We don't know."

"Guess. I'm not asking you to go to press."

John Riley Hobbs.

Deliverer of the *only-good-nigra-is-a-dead-nigra* speech.

"Imperial Wizard," Biggs elaborated, "of the Amalgamated Klans of America."

"Amalgamated Klans?"

"The new KKK is not the monolith most outsiders envision. Most Klaverns are autonomous local units answering to no central authority. Oh, there are overlapping loyalties, weak alliances, but for the most part the Klan landscape is like a jigsaw puzzle when it's first dumped from the box. There's really only one leader working to change all that, to consolidate what amounts to a loose rabble of violent tribes."

"John Riley Hobbs?" I said.

"Bingo. Hobbs is the most notorious, and most powerful bigot in America. He's not the most violent, but then, you see, that's what makes him so dangerous, so effective. A mix of violence and political savvy. I and others in the press estimate Hobbs wields control over some ten thousand Klansmen, all across Alabama, Georgia, the Carolinas"—he gestured—"your

Tennessee."

"Mississippi?"

"Some, though he has rivals there."

"That synagogue," I said. "Would Hobbs have sent a Special Violent Action Group to blow it up?"

"Very possible."

"Wasn't sure you'd see me this morning. I thought you might be in Jackson."

He drained his Scotch very suddenly. Then signaled the bartender, and studied his glass with its ice remnants, rotating it.

Silence stretching. I sensed emotionality; I'd drilled down, somehow, to Walter Biggs's center, however inadvertently, and knew instinctively to wait. Not push, and at long last he said:

"Last Klan bombing I attended personally was the Sixteenth Street Baptist Church."

I leaned in.

"September 15, 1963. Four years almost to the day. What do you know about that? Seven blocks from here. Congregation…bloody, torn, screaming, showered by stained glass and plaster. Mutilated bodies of those girls—one eleven-year-old, three fourteen-year-olds—killed dressing in their choir robes after Sunday school. Unaware some crazy bigoted lunatics had placed a bomb against the north wall of their church. From that point forward, Sherry my dear, I stopped going to Klan stories. People bring them to me now."

I waited till he had his new drink and hoped I never needed a drink that badly.

"Why a synagogue?" I asked finally.

"Don't you know?" he announced expansively.

Grew straighter. "Jews are trying to take over the government. They engineered the civil-rights movement to destroy and subjugate white, Anglo-Saxon, native-born Protestant American patriots. All a conspiracy between Jews, blacks, and communists against the Gentiles. For, as you know"—he was waving the red plastic stirrer from his drink—"the black ain't got the intelligence to manipulate the strides he's made. It's the Jews backing all this. Jews are dangerous people."

Biggs threw down his swizzle stick.

Shot his glass up in salute.

"So sayeth John Riley Hobbs."

"He's crazy," I said. "Surely everyone realizes that?"

Biggs tossed back.

Erupting in bitter delighted laughter.

"From your lips, sugar, to God's ears."

I asked, eyes narrowing: "What's *The Flaming Cross*?"

"The magazine? It's Hobbs. His mouthpiece. He publishes. Edits. Writes a lot of it. It's hate literature. And the most marvelous collection of prose unfettered by the rules of grammar and style in the history of the English language."

"You have copies?"

"Yes."

"You subscribe?"

"Yes."

"May I see them?"

"You got the stomach for it."

CHAPTER 33

BEFORE WE LEFT THE BAR—on a cocktail napkin—Biggs sketched me a tall isosceles triangle with two short legs and feet sticking out the base and two eyes near the point.

No coincidence it was a cartoon of a robed man wearing a pointy hat and mask.

He divided the triangle into four parts drawing horizontal lines such that the area of each part—representing subsets of Klan membership—became progressively smaller from bottom to top.

At the bottom were the rank and file, organized into *Klaverns*.

Each Klavern governed by an *Exalted Cyclops*.

The next higher level was the *Province*, all Klaverns within a congressional district. Provinces ruled over by *Great Titans*. The state-level Klan unit was the *Realm*, presided over by a *Grand Dragon*. Finally, the point at the top of the triangle was the *Imperial Wizard*, the national head of his faction of the Invisible Empire. The White Knights of the KKK was an example I was given.

Hobbs' Amalgamated Klans being another.

Any Klan official with *Grand* in his title was state level.

Imperial indicated a national office.

In the newsroom Biggs showed me two issues of *The Flaming*

Cross, one of which was the one I'd spied on the desk of Ginny Roberts' strange pastor, Horace Cothran.

Cothran, who had brokered my meeting with the widow, at the suggestion of Deputy Loftin, who had wanted me badly to believe that Sheriff Turbeville had had nothing to do with said suggestion.

Interesting, though, how a carload of Klansmen had found me at the church.

Who'd sent them?

Cothran?

Loftin?

Turbeville?

But if Cothran was Klan, why go through with brokering my parlor tea party with Ginny Roberts?

I told Biggs I'd be interested in all issues of the hate magazine for six months prior to the murder of J.B. Roberts. He had them at home and said he was glad to let me borrow them. "May I use your phone?" I replied, then dialed Marjorie at the medical college, covering one ear to hear over typewriters hammering, other phones ringing, vacuum of the tube system delivering edited news to the composing room.

Marjorie had arranged with Dennis Roberts' preceptor for me to meet the student after their noon conference. His time would be limited and I was instructed to be at the Ward 4A nurse's station just after one. I checked my watch.

"That'll be fine," I said, and told Biggs: "I have an appointment at one at University Hospital." He glanced up from reading some copy torn off a UPI teletype. "Plenty of time," he said. He lived three miles away in a shabby duplex off Airport Highway. He went back in the house, gathering the magazines, while I perused up front. Awards from the Alabama Press Association for "Best Reporting in Depth" and a plaque "In Recognition of Outstanding Contributions to the Southern Educational Reporting Service." Military regalia: he'd been a bomber pilot in World War II and Korea, retired from the Air Force Reserves as a full colonel. As with his suit coat, cigarette burns pockmarked the rugs and furniture. When he came out it was with a cardboard box—actually a liquor carton—holding a year's worth of *The Flaming Cross*. Keep them long as I needed, he told me, then fixed himself a highball, offering me something for the road.

"Still early for me, thanks all the same, but I do have one more question…"

"Shoot." He pocketed a hand, swallowing from his drink.

Making a sound like it refreshed him.

"Ever heard of Wesley Swift?"

"*Swift.*"

His frame swayed.

"Who is he?" I asked.

"Runs a church in California. Hate propagandist, extreme racist, anti-Semite."

I nodded.

"So anybody with a bunch of his tapes would be the same?"

"Safe assumption. Who?"

I lifted the box.

"Same person on whose desk I first saw one of these."

I drove through a tunnel and came up beside the huge Main Post Office. Then came a string of hotels, the Redmont, for example, where Hank Williams spent his last night. My windows were up, air-conditioner running, Biggs's racist propaganda in my trunk that I'd probably need special glasses to read, the ink probably treated to sear the retinae of ardent desegregationists, such as myself. At Fifth and Twentieth I wheeled south, a block over from a tall narrow white building close to thirty stories. A half-dozen others were in the twenty-story vicinity. Nashville's building boom, by contrast, was just sputteringly starting.

Another tunnel under a railroad yard cutting the city in half and six blocks later, the huge brick-and-concrete University of Alabama Hospital, sixteen or more stories, cupola on top, across from the VA hospital, and overlooked distantly by a fifty-foot cast-iron Vulcan, atop Red Mountain, the Roman god of fire and warmth, of the forge and of volcanic eruptions, raising his torch to light the Magic City.

I was early.

I went to the canteen.

Got an egg salad sandwich out of a machine, ate it quickly, and minutes before one I was at the designated nurses' station facing a woman with black hair, wearing a white uniform and origami hat. Besides the hair, she was how I might now look had I not been fired and/or blacklisted—along about the time of the British Invasion—by every hospital in greater Nashville.

She was taking a phone order from an arrogant-sounding doctor for Butiserpine and Esidrix for someone having a BP of 210 over 115. I waited, deciding I didn't miss that side of the desk. She hung up and peered at me. "Can I help you?" All the warmth of a giant squid. I told her I was there to meet Dennis Roberts, a medical student. Over her shoulder: "Where's that med student?"

"Dictation room," replied the ward secretary.

"Round the corner."

I thanked her and hooked a sheaf of hair back and found a clean-cut young man like one of the kids on *My Three Sons*, reading a patient's chart in a room the size of a phone booth.

"Dennis...?" I said.

"Yes *ma'am*," he reacted.

Jumping to his feet.

Tall. Soft brown eyes. Sheepish mouth. He'd make a doctor people would warm to and trust easily. If his training didn't chisel him into a sonovabitch first. He looked more like his mother's pictures of him than his sister the beatnik would. Neat sandy hair, short and thick. He closed the steel cover of the chart and gave me a damp eager handshake. Bowed awkwardly, like he was taking me to the prom, nervous about fastening on my corsage. "Sherry Russell," I said, and gave him a card. "Were you told what I wanted?"

"Yes ma'am."

"Forget the *ma'am*—I'm maybe four years older than you. Call me Sherry."

Brown slacks, brown wingtips, white shirt, brown necktie, largely a study in brown except for the shirt and short white clinic coat with the embroidered medical-college seal. Each pocket bulged and clattered with a plethora of manuals and instruments. Out of one breast pocket, for instance, protruded an eye chart, tuning fork, penlight, earwax loop, and several tongue depressors. Dennis needed no aids to exam me, however, just big brown eyes darting over loose-fitting paisley.

And what lay beneath, flowingly hinted at.

Should I be ashamed?

For plying, incentivizing him, to make time for me?

Just don't tell Fred.

"We can't sit and talk in here. We'll find the nurses' lounge. C'mon."

"Uhm…" He scurried after me. "We can't. Nurses don't allow med students or residents in there."

I grinned back. "You're with me." And I explained I used to be an RN—still was, officially. The lounge was where I thought it would be. We let the heavy door hydraulically shut behind us. A couple of gleamingly-uniformed women were there: one sipping coffee with a lot of milk, paging through *McCall's*, the other snuffing out a cigarette, then stretching her sweater back on to return to work. A radio played Percy Sledge. The walls were pea-green. There was a refrigerator, cabinets. A twenty-cup brushed-aluminum percolator. There were two battered round tables with folding metal chairs. We were between lunch and shift change and managed some privacy at the back table. "This won't take long," I said, crossing legs, stockings swishing. I took out a cigarette.

"Mind?"

"Oh, no," Dennis said, drying palms on his trousers. When I'd lit up and dropped the match in an ashtray, I rested back in the chair and offered my condolences.

He nodded.

"To hear your mother tell it," I said, "your sister wasn't too broken up about your father's murder."

He stiffened, flickered off. I waited through two puffs.

"My sister," he sneered at last, "is a flower child in California."

"So I heard. And saw. Anything to do with your father?"

"Huh?"

"Her rebellion. Whatever drove her to the land of free love, grass, and LSD."

He inhaled. "My sister had no feelings for our father I don't share. She just coped differently."

"Okay."

I paused, hoping for further spontaneity. You can sort of tell though when nothing's coming. "Interested in elaborating on what you two had feelings about?"

"My father was a pig. I don't mourn him."

I lifted my brows.

"Why was he a pig?"

"He cheated on my mother practically every day of their marriage. He wasn't there for any of us. He was either working, or off with some concubine, or torturing horses." He shrugged. "Which was a blessing, I guess, because when he was around everything was tense. There were lots of arguments and he'd slap her around sometimes."

"Your mother?"

"Yes. Threw hot coffee at her once."

I squinted.

"He hurt you or Sandra?"

"Physically, no." His head jerked. Rubbed the side of his nose. "I mean, there were spankings, but we usually deserved them. He didn't beat us or anything."

"Pardon me, but you said…"

I winced.

"Your father *tortured* horses…"

"Tennessee Walking Horses. They have to have this Big Lick gait to win ribbons. Last ten years or so they've been using kerosene, mustard oil, chains, modified shoes, whatever, to basically irritate the forelegs. Make them step higher—like if you stepped on a tack."

I nodded.

"They call it *fixing*. What it is, is torture."

"Your father win these shows?"

"Many times."

"He grow up a horseman?"

His head shook.

"Those horses cost a pretty penny, and my mother always told us, when she was upset with him, that he was just poor white trash from Walker County. That marrying well had been his leg up."

"So how"—two taps over the ashtray with my cigarette—"did he get into breeding and training Tennessee Walkers?"

"That wasn't my father; it was my great-grandfather."

"The portrait," I said, "over the mantle."

"Yes. They were war horses during the Civil War. After Reconstruction, Great Grandfather Seeley selectively bred them. Turned that land into one of the best stud farms in Alabama. Then my grandfather took over. He was a businessman, not a horseman. He kept the breeding operation, because my mother loved the horses. But he also expanded the farm, devoted more land to crops, to generate a steadier income, put more people to work."

"So it was your mother with the original passion for horses. What did she think of the fixing? As you call it, torture?"

"Oh, she stopped going to those awful shows long ago." He rubbed the side of his nose and sniffled. "Got shook up once when she saw blood shoveled out of the ring, after this one class."

I waited while the nurse who'd been at the front table, eavesdropping, washed out and hung her mug on a peg and left. I sighed. "Your mother told me nothing about these arguments," I said. "Your father slapping her. Of course, I didn't ask. I had no idea. Doubt the sheriff does either."

"Obviously she's proud," he said.

Pushed up. Rearranged gangly limbs.

"Why didn't they divorce? *My* parents did."

"Appearances. Sake of the children."

"If they had divorced," I said, "what would've happened to the farm?"

"Pardon me?"

"*Her* family farm. Which your father inherited outright."

He got a peevish look.

"You know a lot of personal stuff."

"More," I said, "now that we've talked."

He made a gruff sound, shuffled, knuckles white. Beginning to worry if he was hurting his mother. Right then the door flew open. A tall, thick-shouldered man, late twenties. "Denny!" he barked. "Yo!" The man had a crew cut, lots of angles to his face, wore a long white coat. "Rounds with Ol' Man Barrett, Radiology, one-thirty. Be there or be square."

And he was gone.

Door sinking closed.

I checked my watch. "We'll get this wrapped up, Dennis."

He rotated back.

Met my gaze.

"What would have happened to the farm if your parents had divorced?"

A short silence.

Then:

"Obviously, I don't know. I know my mother worried herself sick. But…"

I bent. "But…?"

"Not even he would do that. Would he?"

"Do what?" I said.

"Steal my mother's farm."

I unfolded. "Dennis…"

"Yes."

With a sudden quickness I flipped my pad to a clean sheet.

Rotated and slid it across.

"You grew up on that farm, right?"

"Sure," he said.

"Draw me a map."

CHAPTER 34

I ASKED DENNIS ROBERTS ONE last question at the stairwell door.

"Have you seen your sister since she left for California? Has she made any return trips, perhaps your mother didn't know about?"

"No," he said.

"I'm assuming if she did come back, she'd get in touch with her big brother, maybe crash with you."

"I haven't seen my sister," he said. "Far as I know she's still out there, shooting up, or tripping out, making a general tramp of herself. If she ever did come back, no crashing with me. More likely I'd belt her for what she's doing to our mother. I hate her."

I nodded slowly.

Swallowed.

Said, "Thank you."

I pulled in an Esso on the outskirts of Birmingham. The attendant checked under the hood while the gas pumped, and billed me $5.21. Driving back on Bankhead Highway I felt thoughts racing. I had ideas, and believed I knew what they added up to, but belief was not certainty. And still further removed was that elusive commodity: legally binding proof. I listened to music, hoping something might click. Tammy

Wynette, "I Don't Wanna Play House." Elvis doing gospel. Pauline Prescott's new duet with David Houston. The synagogue bombing led the two o'clock news. Mississippi FBI agents had made three arrests, following a two-A.M. armed confrontation in a church parking lot. All those arrested had links to the White Knights of the KKK.

Walter Biggs, I realized, that morning, had mentioned them. They were a different KKK faction from John Riley Hobbs' Amalgamated Klans.

By twenty to three I'd reached Jasper.

My left signal blinking to turn into the Holiday Inn—

When a newspaper photo flashed in my head.

The Lavonia library. First trip, scanning items about the killings.

I remembered the caption.

Something like: DISTRAUGHT WIDOW STANDS BY AS LAW INVESTIGATES HORSE BARN SHOOTING

In the breezeway door, Ginny Seeley Roberts clutching a Kleenex, and down by her right side, her handbag. Why I thought that might be important was almost fleeting. Like memories of a dream, slipping further off.

A car horn jarred me.

"Sorry," I called to the man idling on my bumper. I checked traffic and accelerated back onto westbound 78. Spurred the Impala to eighty. Again consulting my map, about sixteen miles ahead was Carbon Hill, and from there I worked my way into Lavonia, parked and walked up to the library, just as I had done the day before.

Page 1B, *Tuscaloosa News*, Wednesday, July 19.

Took me forty minutes to find it.

Grainy photo of the crime scene. Sheriff Bobby Ray Turbeville, hands racked on his gun belt, barking an order, pouch of Redman pocketed, bulge in his cheek. In the foreground, Ginny Roberts: big polka dots, poufed A-line skirt, white organdy collar covering her shoulders. The Kleenex was in her left hand, and as I'd remembered, purse down her right side. I reached for my cigarette and took in some smoke, rested my head back, eyes closed, and blew it all out through pursed lips.

With which hand, I was contemplating, had Ginny Roberts served me iced tea, and drank hers, and ate her crackers, cookies, petit fours?

Possibly her left.

Couldn't be sure. Some detective. I tapped ashes, flopped back. I could check with Dennis. He'd know whether his mother was a southpaw. I hadn't asked when we were together because I hadn't yet thought about it then. Something else to ask Dennis…

I bent forward.

Whether his mother wore summer gloves during the day. I often did, and women of her generation would be more likely to. But I'd always lived in the city, or bigger towns. Fashions no doubt differed in Lavonia County. In the news photo she was sans gloves. Either she hadn't worn them, or had, but ditched them between going shopping and getting her photo snapped. I took notes. To organize my thinking.

Ginny's purse was as I'd remembered:

Big tote-style. Gros-point embroidery, best I could estimate from the poor image. Some flowery, leafy pattern. Two large loop handles of light-colored leather or vinyl. Top open except where a flap of the same light-colored leather or vinyl brought the edges together in the center, between the handles. The flap fastened by some twist-lock-type brass hardware.

Sheriff Turbeville and Deputy Loftin were waiting at my car. They climbed out the unmarked Chrysler Loftin did his cruising in, and snugged on and tugged down their cattleman's hats, as I approached in my loud hippy dress. They hoofed out into the street to meet me, Loftin's metallic eyes probing, the sheriff's heavy arms knotting. "Gentlemen, how goes it?" I said as the khaki-clad pair separated. Loftin backing up actually, to thumb open my door.

"Allow me," he said.

I got in. Placed my pocketbook on the passenger seat.

And saw with a silent curse my motel key on the console, room number in big white numerals. The *if found please mail to…* message on the back of the green plastic tag. "Nice car," Loftin said, shutting my door. Leaning on the sill, pig-mouth grinning through the window, which I'd left rolled down to keep the seats cool.

"Shame if anythin' wasta happen to it."

I laid my hands on the wheel. "Why should anything happen?" Down in my face, tongue wetly manipulating a pink wad of gum he was talking around. "All sortsa hazards, these country roads round here. Get a tire blown, stranded miles from the nearest phone. Or piece a farm equipment, or loggin' truck surprises you, flyin' out a side road. You swerve. Hit a tree head on. Me and the sheriff, we see it all the time. Awful thing when a pretty face like yours goes through a windshield. Plum awful."

The corners of my mouth pulled. "Appreciate the safety lecture, Deputy." I faced forward and started my ignition. Loftin hauled upright, stalking back. "We'd all agreed you'd stay outta my county."

I curled a brow.

"It's a free country. Right Bobby Ray?"

Twisting over my shoulder.

"I'm here," the sheriff boomed, "'cause I tole you to leave Ginny Roberts be. Naturally, you can come and go as you please, Mrs. Russell, but I ain't standin' for you pesterin' that widow."

He spat splashingly onto the pavement.

Then to Loftin:

"Best get on out on prowl patrol, C.O." Turbeville then turned and began to saunter towards the sheriff's office, hand resting on his six-gun. "Sure thing, Bobby Ray." Loftin turned his metal-blue gaze, creepily luminescent, back down on me. "I was you," he said through gritted teeth, "I'd start thinkin'bout that husband of yours. He attacked them boys behind the church. ADW. Assault with a deadly weapon. Be real easy for the sheriff and me to resurrect them felony charges. Real easy."

I laughed a few bars.

"Surprises me," I said, "two strapping lawmen, scared of one smart-alecky blonde."

His eyes narrowed.

Blackened.

"We ain't scared, ma'am."

"Threatening my family?"

"We're the law here. We can usually make our threats stick."

I got out of the idling car and faced him pointblank. "Here," I fumed, "you're the law. You think you can do something to me, make it stick, go ahead try. As for my husband—he's in Tennessee. Good luck getting him extradited on some trumped-up ADW beef, because Governor Ellington and my father are like that. And Fred's family knows some bigwigs of their own. If you bring those charges, my story will change like the snapping of a rubber band. I'll insist Fred was protecting my honor. From a bunch of hooligans, tearing at my clothes. No telling what would've become of me if Fred hadn't shown up. Story like that from me, in Nashville," I said, with snarly teeth, "you won't get him out of Tennessee with a crowbar!"

The tail didn't show till I was well past the LEAVING THE BEAUTIFUL CITY OF LAVONIA sign. Out in the country. Country that might as well have been Botswana. He came up on my stern doing ninety, Loftin yanking the wheel of the big Chrysler in my mirror. The Newport cast a diabolical reflection: bat-like fins, four headlights arrayed angularly, upper lamps spaced wider than lower, between them a huge trapezoidal grill, like some grinning monster's gnashing teeth.

My heart went like a bass drum.

I wouldn't let him pull me over. Not if I could help it. He could shadow me to the next town if he wanted to and I'd find a police station to pull into. For now he seemed content to ride my backside. No siren. No flashing lights. I bypassed my turnoff at Big Oak Baptist Church—my shortest route to Jasper, but that involved twenty miles of desperately little before leaving Lavonia County, and I reasoned if Loftin was going to do anything bad to me—like run me into a tree, sending my pretty face through the windshield—he'd do it in his own county. So, I stuck with US 43 straight north. The roads were better and busier and Winfield, a decent-size town, was just over the county line.

Twelve miles ahead.

Twelve nerve-racking miles.

Did Loftin plan to dog me all the way to the Holiday Inn? Why bother? If he'd seen the key on my console where I'd left it like an idiot. On the outside chance he hadn't seen it, or bothered to read it, I didn't want to lead him there. I didn't know what I'd do if he made a serious effort to stop me before we were out of the county—or if he continued to trail me past the county line. But I decided to take a cue from Scarlett O'Hara.

Worry about it later.

If either thing happened.

It didn't.

Loftin broke it off, indeed, at the county line. A wide, sweeping U-turn, a plume of exhaust, and the finned rear of his cruiser shrank off in my mirror, and I blew through pursed lips, puffed cheeks.

CHAPTER 35

I PEELED MY DRESS OVER my head, at the motel about 5:40, and wadded it in a canvas laundry sack. My slip went in after it, and I rinsed and hung out my stockings. Shortly after, same light-blue pullover, navy capris as last evening, I got a fresh pack of Kents from my suitcase, crushed some beer into an ice bucket to chill, and strolled, swivel-hipping, to the coffee shop. I had a turkey salad bowl, and a parfait and chocolate-chip cookie.

Stopping by the car on the way back, I hauled, gritting teeth, the White Horse carton full of Walter Biggs' Klan magazines inside. I lugged out my old Royal portable. Got my spiral pad out, split open a pack of typing paper, and pried the tab off a Schlitz. I slurped some, swung back the typewriter-case lid, rolled some paper in and started typing, cigarette hanging from one side of my mouth. A fresh page began each interview: Ginny Seeley Roberts, Walter Biggs, Dennis Roberts. On another sheet I summarized my ruminations about the crime-scene photo of Ginny Roberts.

The telephone shot me three feet in the air while I was on my sixth cigarette and third beer, paging through a copy of *The Flaming Cross*. On TV was *The Red Skelton Show*. Hand patting my chest, I stepped over and snatched up the phone.

Fred's voice gave me a jolt.

He asked how my trip was going.

I beamed, and said, "Actually very well."

"Good. Terrific."

A stiffness. Like making an effort to sound happy, which I guessed, was not necessarily bad. One of my cheeks twitched. I moved my loose typewritten stack and sank with a leg folded under me onto the bed. "How," I asked, "was your day?"

"Good. Busy. But good. Got those backordered Farnam supplements."

"Oh good." I nodded, as if he were there in the room. We listened to each other's breathing after that. "I'm really glad," I finally said, "you called."

"Been hopin' you would, Sherry."

I bit, and released my lower lip.

"I know. I should have. Just busy."

"I miss you."

"Miss you, too. I really do. You finding yourself something to eat all right?"

"I won't starve."

"Hope not." I smiled.

"You said…said things were going well?"

"I really think," I burst excitedly, "I might be able to clear Montie Collins' name."

My shoulders rocked, a little swagger of pride.

"Well, good for you. You're wrapping it up then?"

My lips parted, but the words lodged.

"Fred—I said I might be able to clear a man of a murder charge."

"I heard. I ain't deaf. Now you're coming home where you belong, right?"

"I don't know when I'm coming home. I'm not done. I'm on track with something, I think, but I've got to finish. Then take what I have to the sheriff. I think I can—"

"Sheriff?"

"I think I can help him arrest the r—"

"Oh come on!"

Seconds lapsed.

My vocal cords recovering from paralysis.

"Fred…Fred what do you think I'm doing here?"

"I want my wife back, sweetheart."

"You don't believe a goddamn word I've said."

"Course I do."

"Not really. You don't."

"Talk sense Sherry."

"You think I'm down here on some female flight of fancy."

"Naw—"

"Yes!" I burst. "You think I'm puttering around to satisfy some vague curiosity, maybe for me, maybe for Ruthie Mae McNair. But you don't believe I'm doing anything of real consequence, do you?"

"Whadaya wan'me to say?"

"What you feel. Deep down, that nothing I'd be doing down here could possibly be of any interest, of any use to the sheriff, or FBI—"

"FBI!"

"Because I'm a woman, and we can't do anything on our own. Our only use is sex, and to help men by following orders, as long as it's men running the show."

"I didn't say any of that."

"You didn't have to. Look, if I take something to the sheriff and he doesn't buy it, it's my problem to convince him. I expect to have to do that. I don't expect to have to convince my own husband to respect my abilities."

"Who's not *respecting* you? I want you home."

"Where I belong?"

"Yes. In Murfreesboro. In our house. With me."

"Damn you Fred!"

Unfolding I rose off the bed.

"What?"

"Damn you!"

I flung the handset, bounced it off a wall. It struck the nightstand and spun to the carpet, twitching on the end of its cord. I heard Fred still on the line, repeating my name, saying: "What is it? What's wrong? Tell me."

I sighed.

Bent and pressed the receiver back to my ear.

"I've told you, Fred," I said exhaustedly. "You just don't hear."

"Say something makes sense!"

I clamped my eyes.

Slumped as if speared through the stomach.

And hung up.

Outside, key in my fist, I stalked the breezeway, through a cloying night raucous with frogs, cicadas, all manner of other noisy creature. Long strides, exaggerated arm swings, I planned to completely ring the motel, repeatedly, maybe all damn night. Back home I'd have set off on some far-flung hike, but here, venturing too far afield might make me a target for the Lavonia sheriff, or another carload of Klansmen, or—hell—why not some crazed lead-poisoned moonshiner hearing there was a nigger-lovin' blonde on the loose.

Stick close to the lighted areas.

Pace the courtyard, pool deck.

I never made it nearly that far.

Third room down the door stood open with flickery interior light splashed across the sidewalk. As I reached that point the room's occupant shambled out, one hand pocketed, other sloshing a whiskey it precariously grasped. "Hellooo honey bunny."

I staggered back.

Gasping, "What?"

Tall and lanky, loud sports coat, white polyester slacks. Attempting to be suave, dancing to a samba in his head, when all I heard were crocking frogs. Two nights running I'd seen him dining alone. We'd never spoken, but as I'd walked out the restaurant *that* evening, I now recalled, he'd hoisted his drink at me.

Grinning.

Winking.

Jesus Christ.

I tried shouldering around him with a polite, "Excuse me."

He skittered back and sideways.

Booze spattering. "Sonny Greene's my name, Electrolux is my game."

"What? Get outta my way!"

"You're lonely, honey bunny, and I'm lonely."

Both arms spread, one to corral me, the other to keep the dripping whiskey off his clothing. "Now, I got me most of a bottle of Jim Beam open inside." His long arm snaked back of my shoulders, grappling on. "Whyn't you and me make a dead soldier out of it, see where nature takes us."

"Damn you!"

I shoved into his ribs.

Teeth bared.

"Damn you, damn you, damn you!"

I flailed, stormed back the way I'd come, and made violent use of my key to get back inside. A furry bald man in an sleeveless undershirt looked out the room on the other side of mine. Asking was I okay, and I heard Sonny Greene: "Her time of the month I reckon, pal. Wanna drink?"

CHAPTER 36

I CHAINED THE DOOR, GRABBED my phone off the hook, and showered. When I came out, cleaner and calmer, *CBS Reports* was on, profiling the "New Left." Interviewing Stokely Carmichael. I wasn't in the mood, yanking my head out of my shower cap. I clicked over to *Hollywood Palace*. Beach Party episode, hosted by Phyllis Diller—I gave that a chuckle all on it's own—with Frankie Avalon, Annette Funicello, and The Fifth Dimension, who did their new, "Up, Up and Away." By the time Phyllis was thanking everybody in that voice of hers, I had on a pastel night gown, and my last beer open. The slogan was right: When you're out of Schlitz you really are out of beer. I stored away the typewriter, punched off the TV, and crossed my legs on top of the bed.

Chin in my hand.

Fred was right. too.

Sheriff Turbeville wasn't going to be inclined to believe anything I tried to tell him about J.B. Roberts' murder. Other issues aside, it was simply, to him, a closed matter. An important closed matter, which—if I was right—he'd botched.

Thus, handing off everything to Turbeville and just going back to being a housewife was not a viable option. I needed to ride herd on this.

Sorry Fred. I lit a Kent, sighed the smoke, and spent the rest of that night, before my eyelids refused further cooperation, trying to figure how to crack the nut that was Ginny Seeley Roberts.

The grieving widow.

I went back to Biggs' *Flaming Cross* magazines—the most insane amalgam of racism, anti-Semitism, anti-Catholicism, anti-LBJ-ism, conspiracyism, imaginable. Ironically, Imperial Wizard Hobbs' utter contempt extended to the American Nazi Party! Apparently Nazis lacked a Jesus-loving, God-fearing dimension to their hatred, rendering it unacceptable to Klansman. Equally ironic, J. Edgar Hoover was viewed to be the Klan's ally, various articles extolling him as the nation's top crime fighter, applauding FBI efforts against Martin Luther King, and their refusal to hire black agents. Reading on, I was stunned and embarrassed to come upon an article purporting to be a scientific examination of the Negro male libido. Which allegedly responded to phases of the moon.

Anyway, I found, I thought, in the midst of this utter trash, the particular piece of utter trash I was looking for. The February 1967 issue had a commentary by John Riley Hobbs lamenting the victories of the civil-rights movement. Espousing the grave danger further mongrelization meant for white, gentile, Protestant, native-born America. White men were being de-franchised, you see, and the mass raping of white women by black men was around the corner. He implored patriots to battle this rushing tide by any means. No act too small.

For example:

Denying Negroes property ownership.

CHAPTER 37

I PUT THE PHONE—REMARKABLY undamaged considering I'd bounced it off a wall (kudos to Western Electric)—back on the hook, and it woke me about one A.M. Strange time for Fred to call, but we had had a terrible argument. I clawed the receiver to my ear, groggily answering, "Hello."

It wasn't Fred.

Wasn't even Sonny Greene, three rooms down.

It was white. Over forty. Probably over fifty. A smoker.

Git out of Alabama, it said.

Else they'd show me.

Me, and my "nigra-lovin' cunt."

CHAPTER 38

I PRESSED GINNY ROBERTS' DOORBELL ten the next morning, a crystal-blue, bird-singing Wednesday on the farm. Eighty-eight was expected, down from yesterday's ninety. Autumn would begin that weekend. Both Ginny's station wagon and her late-husband's Buick were in the driveway. She wasn't off at the Piggly-Wiggly, footloose and fancy free with the checkbook, which she no longer had to beg and borrow.

Waiting for the door, I stepped, crossing arms, to the front edge of the porch. Negro pickers worked the large field, colorfully dressed and kerchiefed men, women, and children progressing along planted rows, plucking mature bolls of cotton. Each dragged a sack, clouding dust in the air. The sacks were emptied into bins towed behind a red Farmall tractor driven by a white man. Two small boys jumped atop the full load of a bin along the road past the house. Excluding the tractor it might've been a scene from a hundred years ago. Ginny came to the door in a plain housedress, and I turned.

"I wasn't expecting you," she exclaimed.

I asked could we talk.

I wore a copper-and-navy houndstooth dress, matching belt and black buttons. My handbag was quilted black vinyl with gold chain handles. My gloves black pigskin. She asked me in, provided I could excuse the housekeeping. I joked I shuddered to think what my house looked like, having left Fred bach'ing it.

Laughing like Minnie Pearl, Ginny offered to perk us coffee.

The breakfast table was green enamel. There was a napkin holder, a newspaper, a loose-leaf *Better Homes and Gardens Garden Book*. While Ginny fixed coffee I flipped pages. Eventually I glimpsed up at her: "I have a theory why your husband turned on Montie Collins."

"Pardon?" she said, plugging in the pot.

"Why Mr. Roberts wouldn't sell."

"Oh…why?"

She turned, hands back of her on the counter.

Jade eyes listening.

"I think the Ku Klux Klan got to him."

"The Klan," she gasped.

Pads of fingers pressing her chest.

"I think they threatened him. Don't sell to a black man. Or else."

The dark brows lifted. I don't think she'd known or suspected—which was in no way inconsistent with my hypothesis of J.B. Roberts' murder. "I told you," she drawled, "J.B. had nothin' to do with those people."

"I believe you."

"What kind of threat?" she asked.

I shrugged mildly. "Could be anything." My legs were crossed, forearms atop the garden book. "Do as we say or we'll…shoot one of your walking horses, or…burn a barn, or…field of crops."

"My…"

"You know anyone in the Klan?"

"No."

"How about Pastor Cothran?"

Her jaw sagged.

"I…I hardly think…man of the cloth?"

"Not aware the Klan excludes clergymen. And before he began preaching, he was a blue-collar steel-mill worker. Proves nothing, but it's fertile ground for Klan recruitment. Do you remember Cothran's sermon last Sunday?"

She blinked.

Flashed me strange eyes.

"Why on earth would I?"

"You go to church, don't you?"

"Every Sunday. Not that one."

"Horace Cothran isn't your pastor?"

"Heavens no. I'm Episcopalian. I go to Trinity downtown."

I nodded.

"I was misinformed."

The kitchen smelled of bacon and eggs, a dirty plate and silverware on the counter, cast-iron pan on the stove. The percolator gurgled. "I can tell you what it was," I said.

"What?"

"The sermon."

"Not sure why—"

"Sex Perverts, Beatniks, Pinkos, and Communists."

"Oh my."

"The article he drew it from," I said, "was about current entertainment—books, movies, TV, magazines like *Playboy*—undermining our morality, introducing debauchery in an attempt to ease the eventual takeover by Satan, in the guise of Communists, Jews, and Negroes. That title came straight from a KKK propaganda rag. I saw it and the half-typed sermon on Cothran's desk last Friday. Was he ever over here?"

"Horace?"

I nodded.

"Of course. He's a friend."

"Way back?"

"Yes, as a matter of fact."

"His father sharecropped for your father."

"Yes."

"He has a photograph of you on his desk."

"I wouldn't know."

I swallowed.

"Were you lovers?"

CHAPTER 39

H OW DARE—"

"Sorry for my bluntness, ma'am."

I hoped the quick apology would circumvent me being thrown out on my pretty derriere. I had a theory the only thing that would stop a Southern lady, such as Ginny Roberts, from throwing out of her house instantly the purveyor of such a crude suggestion, would be the subliminal effect of being confronted with the truth. And if I knew that deep dark secret, surely she'd be curious what else I knew. "I was only *sixteen*," she replied savagely, "when Horace left to find his fortune—railroad work it was going to be."

I said: "That doesn't answer my question."

"Yes, it does," she spat.

And turned, began preparing mugs for our coffee. She asked how I liked mine. I told her, watching her hands. "Did Pastor Cothran ever visit Mr. Roberts alone. Say, at the horse barn?"

"Yes." She brought our coffees.

She was left-handed.

She sat. I told her the coffee was good, though it was, in fact, weak for my taste. "I visited your son yesterday at the hospital."

"He told me," Ginny said evenly. "Called me worried he might've said too much. About our personal business."

"Don't blame him," I said.

"I don't. It's okay. J.B.'s affairs were legendary."

"Embarrassing for a lady."

She shrugged. Fingering the lip of her coffee mug.

"Did you kill your husband?"

Her face shot up in a rictus.

"N-no. Why ask such a thing?"

"Was he going to divorce you?"

Her jaw hinged open.

"Steal your family's farm?"

Her eyes, wild and green, slowly regained focus.

"Dennis didn't tell you that, did he?"

"Guess he wasn't," I said cruelly, "s'posed to know his parents' marriage was a sham."

"A mother doesn't want to worry her children."

"He knows you were scared, Ginny. Scared Mr. Roberts might one day force you off this land. Your birthright. It was happening wasn't it?"

"Huh?"

I swallowed coffee.

She was locking up.

"Kids were out of the house," I said, "one way or another. Sandra flaking out in California. Dennis, a soon-to-be doctor. Very nice, polite young man by the way. You're to be commended. Anyway, you no longer had to hold it together *for the children*." I gestured quote marks in the air. "Which was probably important to both of you."

She nodded. Exhaled spastically. "J.B. had a girlfriend. Serious one this time. Office manager of some furniture factory in Columbus. He planned to marry her and bring her here."

"My God," I said quietly.

"Yes," she agreed. "My God."

"What were you going to do?"

"Hire a lawyer."

She laced her fingers on the table. "Fight him tooth and nail."

"Could you win?"

"J.B. had all the money, political strings, friendships with every big lawyer. Even the ones too decent to help him against me, they'd refuse to represent *me* for the same reason."

I nodded.

"So you killed him."

Her face ticced.

"N-no."

"Only way to be sure. You couldn't lose this land. I might've done the same thing."

"No," she mewled.

"You were afraid. You planned to kill him."

"No! I never *planned* to kill my husband."

She enunciated each word precisely.

"I know you didn't," I said.

She paused.

Confused.

"It wasn't planned," I said. "But when you drove to the horse barn to return that checkbook. A demeaning thing. Anyway, you drove out and walked in on Montie Collins and your husband. Right after Montie brained him with a horseshoe puller. Probably while he was stealing from J.B.'s wallet, recovering a small sum of what he felt, correctly, your husband was stealing from him. He fled. You saw the chance of a lifetime. You went into the tack room and got your husband's gun and you shot him. You emptied the clip. Searing with anger and betrayal. You couldn't stop shooting until the slide locked, and the gun was empty. Then…"

"Then…?" she said.

Like she'd suffered some palsy of the face.

I removed from my purse Dennis Roberts'—her son's—hand-sketched map of their sixteen-hundred-plus acres. Unfolded, spread it onto the green table before her. The property was roughly the shape of Nebraska, less the panhandle. The north and south boundary lines ran parallel east to west, the west boundary straight north to south. The east property line was irregular, running northwest to southeast, bounded by Highway 43, a main route between Tuscaloosa and Lavonia.

The map, at my request, detailed the roads crisscrossing and running into and off the farm. The dirt drive in front of the house ran west from US 43 for a half-mile then dead-ended. South off 43 was the dirt road with the gate, leading to the horse barn. From there it curled sharply north then east to intersect the north boundary and run along it for a half-mile till it met up again with 43.

Where this loop came to the horse barn—site of J.B. Robert's murder—a narrower twistier dirt road spurred in a west-southwesterly direction, passing a number of sharecroppers' homesteads, then crossed the west property line. This was Rocky Branch Road and after it left the farm it tied up with Old Liberty Road. Old Liberty stretched from Adams Road to a county road intersecting US 43 south of the farm. Adams Road zigzagged roughly parallel with Old Liberty below the fork where they separated, eventually ending at the same county road Old Liberty did. But on the way Adams, a public road, cut across the southwest corner of the Seeley-Roberts Farm, effectively parsing out a 36-acre section.

That 36 acres was subdivided into two 18-acre plots, one of which was the contested land worked by the late Montie Collins. What had been the Collins' residence was located at a bend in Adams Road a third of a mile from where it crossed Rocky Branch.

All this meant that, by road, it was a two-and-a-half-mile round trip between the horse barn and the Collins' house. Taking the hypothetical vehicle past several houses and for a short distance onto a public road. There'd be a decent chance of being spotted. Which was only significant if anyone bothered to ask. But it didn't seem a risk even the most inexperienced, panicked murderer was likely to take.

Ginny Roberts focused silently upon the map.

I asked if she concurred with it. She did and I pointed with my long tapering nail at the starting point of a light pencil line that had been added by Dennis Roberts after he'd completed the rest of the map and I'd prompted him with some follow-up *what if? how would you, or your mother?* questions.

The line started along Rocky Branch Road a third of a mile from the horse barn and took a stair-stepping course southwest to join Adams Road almost directly across from Montie Collins' house. "According to your son," I told her, dragging my metallic-pink nail, "this is a tractor path used to transport equipment, workers, crops to and from various fields you have under cultivation."

"So?" she shrugged.

Her voice, though, carried a sickish undertow.

"Having lived here your entire life," I said, "you know these rabbit paths like the back of your hand. In fact, Dennis says you routinely drive them to get around the farm and as shortcuts to other places. For instance, he said you often make your way to Adams Road at the back of your property, and take that into Lavonia. He confirmed that was how you would've gone to the Piggly-Wiggly that day—the day your husband died—unless the tractor path happened to be particularly mucky, which it wouldn't have been. It didn't rain that day, nor had it for several days."

"What on earth are you blathering about?"

"About you," I said. "Scared. You'd just seen Montie Collins rob your unconscious husband, and run away. You'd just gotten his .45 out of a tack trunk, and emptied it into him. And there you stood, murder weapon in hand. Free of your husband. Your farm at long last safe and secure. You could rebuild your life, maybe get Sandra back from California, and straightened out. If only you could avoid the electric chair."

"This," she fumed, "is all wild speculation."

"You didn't know what else to do. You had to work fast. You knew Montie Collins was guilty of assault and robbery. You knew he had motive. Circumstances and racial stereotypes being what they are, you'd have no trouble convincing anyone Montie Collins was the shooter. Now, I don't think you relished shifting the blame. You liked Montie; you'd known him all his life. But"—I shrugged with hands and shoulders—"you didn't have much time. You were teetering off a cliff."

"Teetering?"

"Between losing and winning everything. You decided. To take that empty gun in your hand and plant it outside Montie Collins' home. Then tell the sheriff a lie only a couple of critical points away from the truth: One, that your husband had already been shot when you found Montie kneeling over him. And two, that Montie had the gun, and fled with it.

"Now—you couldn't be seen traveling to the Collins' place, nor planting the gun. We know from your statement and Collins's that he drove east away from the barn in his pickup. He turned north on 43. Away from his house. He said he didn't know where he was going. He was thinking of lighting out to

Birmingham. But to start he headed toward Bankston to try and find his wife, tell her what had happened, tell her goodbye. He got stopped by the train, and while he was sitting there, decided to just go home. Wait for her, wait for the sheriff.

"You didn't know any of that. You just knew he wasn't going directly home, and you'd have time if you hurried. There was the time factor, plus you didn't want anybody in these sharecroppers' cabins"—I tapped the map with my nail—"recognizing your car, or anybody happening to see you out on Adams Road. So you took the shortcut. Planted the gun and hightailed it back. Back to the horse barn where your husband was lying in a puddle of his own blood"—I saw Ginny's left eyelid twitch—"and you called the law from there. As if you'd just walked in and caught Montie hovering over Mr. Roberts with a smoking gun."

CHAPTER 40

BEFORE I CAME THIS MORNING, I trespassed. My apologies. You may call a cop if you like. I drove to the horse barn and from there to the Collins' house, via that tractor path. Using your son's map—please, don't hate him by the way. He had no earthly idea why I was asking. Anyway, I was able to navigate the tractor path to the Collins' house and back in my car, which proves you could have. I made the round trip in five minutes, including playacting rushing to the woodpile to hide a gun, and back to the car. That five minutes, plus a few more for getting the gun, the shooting itself, your uncertainty, hesitancy, wiping fingerprints, et cetera"—I shrugged—"easily accounts for a roughly thirteen-minute discrepancy in the homicide file between the official time the sheriff's office logged your call, and when Montie Collins claimed to have arrived home.

"You killed your husband, Mrs. Roberts," I declared. "And shifted the blame to an innocent man, who was killed as a result, along with his pregnant wife and two other people."

We were quiet for a time.

I drank my, by-then, lukewarm coffee. She might have become cataleptic. Eventually she moved her head, and asked: "Do the police think I killed J.B.?"

"Not that they indicated to me."

She nodded, lingering in a trance-like numbness.

"I think," I said, "they think you incapable of having done it."

Her head and eyes adjusted.

She was listening.

I added, "I don't."

She tipped back. Swallowed, then lowered the point of her chin.

Jade irises shifting rapidly.

I held tightly onto my breath.

"You cain't," she said, "prove any of that."

Shit.

I'd hoped for a confession, and that was the point I was going to get it, if I was going to get it.

Implement, therefore, Sherry Plan B:

"No, I can't and I have no intention of trying. I might've done the same in your shoes."

She swallowed.

Getting used to this strange turn, like wading into cold lake water.

She finally said, "I'm glad…you're a woman."

"Sugar and spice and everything nice."

She huffed. "Yes."

I held my lower lip in my teeth.

Waited a beat.

"Just one thing," I said, and giggled for effect. "It's a silly, bizarre, request you should feel perfectly free to refuse. Then I'll be out of your hair…"

"What?" She seemed intrigued.

And giddy.

"I was looking at a photo of you at the crime scene—your *handbag*, was just lovely."

She hunched.

Stunned.

I waved a hand, sudden embarrassment.

"Forget it. It's a ditzy thing to ask."

"Ask?"

"To see it."

"You're interested," she replied flabbergastedly, "in my purse?"

"I'd love to get one like it." I grimaced... "Could I see it, please, just to get a better idea what I'm looking for?"

"Not sure I remember…"

"A multicolored tote. Some kind of needlepoint."

Thick brows flickered. She seemed amused. "It's nothing special; I think I might've ordered it from Sears and Roebuck"— she shrugged—"few years back."

"Oh. Wonder if they even make them anymore."

I sounded crushed.

My lips pouted.

"I wouldn't know," she said, concerned for my plight, albeit at a low level appropriate to its triviality. She lifted her mug, careful at first, seeming surprised it didn't shake, and drank from it.

"Maybe I can make one. I'm good at that sort of thing."

"Well…" She strained to her feet, creaking the table, chair scraping back. "We can go upstairs if you really want to. I'll have to get it from the top of my closet." She grinned scoldingly. "Provided you promise to excuse the unmade bed."

I stood.

"Girl Scout's honor."

I followed her through a pantry, through the dining room to the parlor, into the entry hall. *Clop, clop, clop* up the grand staircase, stained-glass gleaming down sunlit and colorful. A right angle to the left, a second short flight to the upstairs hallway. Two rooms came off to the right, and ahead a door onto a second-story balcony, a typical Queen Anne feature. We followed the banister rail to a single door along the left side of the hall. "This is my bedroom," Ginny said. Turning, eager to share her life now, with another woman, a woman she could be honest with because we had already shared the greatest, dankest secret a woman could hold: that she'd murdered her husband.

Indicating the door opposite hers: "That was J.B.'s room. We'd slept apart for years."

"Sorry," I said.

"Don't be." She smiled bitterly. "That's marriage."

Sleeping apart, I thought.

One ruling the other through fear.

Violence.

Purse strings.

Culminating in murder.

I prayed that wasn't marriage. We were in her bedroom; she opened a narrow closet and climbed onto a step stool she'd dragged out. Couple dozen handbags on the shelf and she did a lot of shuffling, finally retrieving the one I'd gone gaga over. She dropped back onto the heel of her house slipper, shut the door and pivoted me the bag: "There it is, all its glory."

"Oh, that is so cute," I marveled.

I took it, twirled it. She must have thought me a real dingbat.

"I suppose, if you like it that much, you can have it."

"No, goodness, I'm not asking for charity." Loop handles between my thumb and forefinger, flat bottom cradled by my other hand, I pretended to study the embroidery. "I just want to remember everything so I can buy one, or copy it."

"Come to think of it," Ginny said, "doubt I'll be using anything associated with that day again. Whatever problems we had, I was still married to the man twenty-five years. And I do owe you: Please take it."

I placed the bag on a cedar chest across the foot of the unmade four-poster bed. A quilt was folded atop the chest. I looked down on the bag from above. Figure-eight, sort of: pinched closed in the middle by a bone-colored plastic flap, open at both ends. I unfastened the flap. "Do you mind?" I asked, having already stuck my hand inside. In nursing it was always easier to ask forgiveness than permission. "Whatever you like." Ginny shrugged. Resting the backs of her wrists on her hips, as I searched the bag, peering and probing. A single center partition formed two deep pockets. Neither were empty. "You know, Mrs. Roberts, I do the same thing…"

"What's that dear?"

"When I change purses," I explained, my digging, squinting intensifying. "I just move the big stuff…wallet, checkbook, mirror, keys, makeup case…leaving this permanent, thickening debris layer…like you have…compacts, Kleenex packages, pens, lipsticks, little peppermint candies."

I ran fingertips through every nook and cranny of the front compartment. Nothing. Butterflies prickling my gut as I switched to the rear compartment. "What *are* you doing?"

Ginny, harsh now, eyeing me. There was loose change. This was so much a long shot, yet it didn't feel that way. Like what I was looking for had to be there, decreed so by the sum total of all the physical laws of the universe. There was a wadded, wrinkly Kleenex. Ewww.

"Mrs. Russell?"

Next she'd snatch the bag away. Make me leave. Not because she suspected what I was doing but because she wouldn't want a lunatic in her bedroom. I thrust my writhing hand, elbow locked, deep in a far-flung corner. Steeling myself to look like an absolute fool—

The nail of one of my fingers jammed in something.

Tube like.

Cool. Hard. Metallic.

Cap of a pen, for instance, except shorter. Length of a thimble, not quite the girth. I slipped my eyes upward, darkly victorious, onto Ginny Roberts. "What is it?" she asked. I pulled my searching hand out, letting the purse capsize onto the quilt. I faced her, raising my hand for both of us to see, like a one-armed surgeon, after scrubbing, entering the operating room. Capping my right ring finger:

A small brass object.

"Bingo," I said savagely.

"What is that?"

Torrentially confused.

I took the object into my other hand, and scrutinized it, rolled it.

"Empty shell casing," I said.

She squinted.

Clawed at silver-flecked hair.

"Huh?"

"Spent bullet. Part that gets ejected when a pistol's fired."

I sounded impatient at her obtuseness. The inside was caked with soot, brass rim bent flat on one side, making the opening vaguely D-shaped. Deformation by the pistol's extractor. I fingered my treasure around, read the back side. A dent in the center, where it had been struck by the firing pin, and embossed around the outer edge:

45 AUTO.

"Same kind of gun that killed your husband."

Part fear, part incredulity gelled.

"How? Did that get there?"

Corners of her eyes crinkling.

"It's the empty shell casing," I said, "missing from the crime scene."

CHAPTER 41

Y OUR HUSBAND'S COLT WAS FIRED eight times," I explained. "Seven rounds hit him according to the autopsy. One missed and lodged in a wall inside the barn. Eight bullets equals eight shell casings. The sheriff found seven."

I indicated the object.

Closed my fist over it.

"Meet number eight."

"But...?"

"How?" I said, playful eyes.

"Yes."

She was deflating.

"You're left handed."

She took slow steps as through molasses, sagged onto the high mattress of the four-poster, half sitting, half leaning. Then looked at me like I'd read her a calculus problem. "What's that got to do with anything?"

Almost angry.

"My guess is you walked into that barn, in on Montie Collins rifling your unconscious husband's wallet, with this purse in the crook of your right arm." I lifted the bag by its handles, letting it scud down my forearm to demonstrate. "Once Collins fled you made a split-second decision to take advantage of situation, and shoot your husband to death."

174

"We've been over this."

"You knew the gun was in the tack room. You either placed this handbag on the ground by your right foot, then turned and went in the tack room, or you held onto it, still on your right arm, and went in, got the gun."

"Actually I hung it from a bridle hook," she offered.

She was either giving up, or still couldn't grasp how any of this possibly mattered.

"Go on," I said.

"On the wall. To the left outside the tack-room door."

My eyes rose. "To your right as you faced Mr. Roberts before shooting him."

"Yes."

"You walked out of the tack room, holding the gun in your left hand. But guns are designed for right-handed people. Spent shells are ejected to shooter's right. In your case, across the front of your body, over your right shoulder. Seven of them bounced off the wall behind you and fell to the concrete floor. The eighth, *this* one, hit the open top of your purse, and dropped inside. You carried it away unknowingly—and the police never found it."

I placed the shell casing back in the handbag, fastened the flap and held the bag alongside my thigh. "I'm taking this to Sheriff Turbeville. Care to accompany me?"

Nearly imperceptibly:

"I'll go. May I dress?"

"I'll wait in the parlor," I said.

In the entry hall I retrieved my keys from my own pocketbook, which lay, with my gloves, on an antique hallstand. Outside I locked Ginny's purse in my trunk. The spent casing I'd removed, wrapped in Kleenex, and buried inside the Impala's glove compartment. Then I let myself back in the house, hearing Ginny upstairs, a bath running. I thought about the layout, and didn't believe she could flee without taking the grand staircase. I snugged on my gloves and took my purse into the parlor and, tucking my skirt, lowered onto the end of the fainting couch. From my purse, I took out my nickel-finished Smith & Wesson.

Laid it upon my lap, loosely gripped.

Concealed by the black, quilted bag.

I sighed nervously. I'd never brought a murder to justice. I didn't think Ginny Seeley Roberts would come downstairs guns ablazing. Yet she had shot her husband seven times, eight counting the miss. That was her husband.

I wasn't.

I was, however, a threat...

I waited thirty-five minutes while she bathed, did her hair, dressed. Once, I clipped back through, and helped myself to coffee, unplugging the pot. My eyes thought, how sad the family this great old mansion had nurtured for generations had disintegrated.

I returned to the parlor, drinking my coffee. In time, she came down carrying an alligator clutch purse, wearing an emerald-green sheath dress with a large gold pin, and a pleated brown pillbox hat with attached veil. She had not brought down a .50-caliber machine gun. Draped over one arm, however— both hands in sight I confirmed—was, forgodsakes, a ranch-brown mink stole.

It was too hot for that but I was sure she was making some sort of statement.

Or committing suicide by heat prostration. "I'm ready," she said levelly.

I felt like shit. I slipped my revolver back inside my pocketbook.

"Don't suppose, Mrs. Russell, you'd permit me to drive my own car?"

"Not on your life," I said.

CHAPTER 42

C OUPLE HOURS LATER I WAS with Sheriff Turbeville in his
corner office with the high windows, watching the big
man in khaki chew his hot ham-and-cheese with cheeks
bursting. I had a BLT on toast, sliced in triangular halves. I bit
off a larger than ladylike corner, but maintained, I thought, some
decorum. My lunch had been tacked onto a standing delivery
from the Mayflower Café. We drank RC Colas from the bottle,
fringes of my hair whisked by the black oscillating fan.

A steno had taken down and typed up Ginny Seeley Roberts'
confession. The queen bee of Lavonia County had signed it, and
Loftin was off booking her into the county jail, the building
behind us. Had a mink ever had to be stored, I wondered, with a
prisoner's effects? Turbeville ran a wrinkled napkin around his
mouth, balled it up and bank-shot it into the cardboard delivery
box. Tipping back he thumped a black boot on the corner of his
desk. My eating seemed to interest him. Eventually he began to
rock with laughter, shaking his broad balding head. "The missing
cartridge case," he reflected, at the tin ceiling, "was in her purse."

Then, swiping a fly and swigging off his Royal Crown, he
looked at me.

Delightedly. "How the hell'dew find it? How the hell'dew
even think to look?"

I grinned. Smug, yet dainty. "I've dropped things into my
purse before, Sheriff. Lost things at the bottom, found them six

177

months later. My guess is, neither you nor your deputies have."

"True enough."

"Had to be somewhere. I looked the only place I could think. I mean, her dress had lots of pleats. A shell casing might've caught in one, but that could've dropped out anywhere. The bag was my best bet. Hadn't been there, I might've found a way to search her car. But, I admit, that would've been a long shot."

He howled.

"That's rich. Long shot, she says. Well maybe we just oughta hire ourselves a woman deputy one of these days."

I shrugged in a *just-what-I-was-thinking* way, chewing from the second half of my BLT. He hauled his boot off the desk and took a drink. "That explains how you found the cartridge case…"

"Why her?" I said. "You convinced me no one had been there, other than Montie Collins, J.B. Roberts, and Ginny Roberts. J.B. didn't shoot himself seven times. And there were too many things not making sense about Collins."

"Like…?"

Half chuckling.

"Like…" I said, "why Mrs. Roberts went inside after hearing eight shots, instead of jackrabbiting like any sensible human being. How'd Collins know where to find Roberts' gun? Why eight shots? And there were behaviors that just didn't seem rational. Crouched over the wrong side of the body, for starters, for somebody who'd opened fire from the tack-room doorway."

He gave a thoughtful nod.

"Why take an empty gun," I went on, "hide it in an incriminating location? Why not grab the wallet and go? Why go home, wait to be arrested, *then* lie? The real killer, seems to me, would've either confessed, racked with guilt—or gone on the lam. Would a black man with any lick of sense try to game the criminal-justice system, with a shaky lie? In *this* county?"

Creaking back, Turbeville palmed both sides of his gleaming forehead.

Smoothed the gray at his temples.

Then rested clasped hands across his belly. "Not ever'body acts rational under stress. I might say *most* don't."

"In that respect, also, I saw things differently. Not because

I'm a woman, because of inexperience. I saw irrationality as evidence of innocence. You accepted it." He was listening. "In another situation I might've been wrong. But in this case it helped to have a, shall we say, less cynical perspective. Plus, your investigation *was* prejudiced."

"I resent that, now—I swear, Montie Collins—"

"*Was* a black man who argued with, and assaulted, a white man. When that white man turned up dead, you did not hesitate to prejudge the black man to be the killer, did you?"

"We had evidence. And an eyewitness!"

"Let's discuss that eyewitness. A white woman. Prominent. Whose statement you accepted at face value. Every bit as *unwilling* to consider the possibility Ginny Roberts was lying—as you were *willing* to believe Montie Collins was."

He slumped.

Staring away.

Slowly began to nod.

"There were three people in that barn, Sheriff. One was killed. The killer had to be one of the other two, but instead of starting from that, you automatically dismissed Mrs. Roberts. Owing to her gender, and social status. Yet to me, a woman—once I asked the right questions, it was obvious Ginny Seeley—I use her maiden name deliberately—had motive and lots of it. Enough to make her a suspect at least: years of a bad marriage, physical abuse, emotional abuse, affairs. Finally, facing divorce, loss of her farm. Her *family's* farm. The man's wife—Ginny Roberts—perhaps couldn't have done it. But Ginny Seeley surely could've."

I took out a cigarette.

Struck a match to it harshly. Tossed the match in the glass ashtray. Blew a gray stream at the ceiling, which got washed around by the fan breeze. "Once I knew all that," I said, gesturing my cigarette, "I asked myself, how could she not have blasted him eight times?"

Turbeville's eyes sparked

"A wife, with a big house," I added, "nice clothes, prestige, money—is not automatically happy. Nor contented."

I took a draw off my Kent.

Wondering even to myself where that had come from.

Turbeville smiled, and excused himself to a private washroom behind me. Having unbuckled his gun belt, he slung it heavily off and onto a wooden peg on the wall. Then he took a wrinkled magazine, and shut himself inside. What transpired you can probably guess, but I won't stoop to detailing it. I was about to go for a walk, when Deputy Loftin snatched through, running sweat, carrying his hat by the rolled brims. Finished, I guessed, handing off Ginny Roberts to the jailer. He jerked me the pig-mouth grin, then noticed the gun belt on the peg.

"Twice a day," he remarked.

Head wagging, dipping. "Like clockwork: first cuppa coffee in the mornin'. Right after lunch."

"Guess I know when to plan a crime in Lavonia County."

Loftin roared laughing, going over and bumping his fat deltoid against the frame of one of the tall windows, gazing at the square. "I'll...wait in the outer office," I said, pivoting up. Then the flush came, that or the Hoover Dam had burst. Turbeville emerged at long last, and buckled back on the gun belt, shoving and jamming the holster down his thigh as he crossed the shag carpet to his desk. When seated he fished out some Red Man and wadded his right cheek full.

"Our guest comfy?" he asked Loftin.

"You bet, Bobby Ray."

"Arraignment tomorrow," he told me.

"You need me?"

"Naw."

"She'll make bail?"

"Sure."

I nodded.

"Can I see her?"

CHAPTER 43

U PSTAIRS IN THE JAIL WAS bleak and smelled of age, and occupancy, and disinfectant, not unlike Nashville Receiving where I'd cut my teeth as a registered nurse. Fluorescent lights flickered; a NO CUSSING OR SPITTING sign was affixed to otherwise bare gray-green walls. The floor was vinyl-asbestos tile, bolted in the center of which was a battered table. One stippled-glass window had prison bars on the outside. Metal chairs surrounded the table. I sat, legs crossed, facing Ginny Roberts. Quiet and still. The window behind her, raised to sustain oxygen-respiring life, looked out onto coiled concertina wire, the grim parking lot of the public-works department. I felt sorry for Ginny.

Then again, she had murdered her husband.

I clutched the outsides of my arms below the copper-and-blue short sleeves of my dress. The sheriff's chair was back from the table, ankle of his right boot atop the other knee. He spat into a trash pail. Violating the sign. Ginny wore ill-fitting, coarse-textured prison garb. Her eyes more gray than green in this sad place. She was breathing but you had to look close. No mink...maybe they'd let her wear it to court? She had turned down her right not to talk to us, nor did she want an attorney. A matron was there too, with orange hair and a face that would crash a train. She normally ran the kitchen. She stood against a wall, crossed arms swashing her gigantic bosom, black shoes

JAMES K. RONE

belonging on some old Russian peasant. "You were responsible, Ginny," I said, "however indirectly, for the murders of Montie and Dorothy Collins."

She stirred as if a rheostat had amped up some low current shocking her body. I was being as gruff and stone-faced as I could, being about two-parts Marlo Thomas, one-part Jayne Mansfield. "Montie and Dorothy and their unborn child and two others, you effectively killed five people, Ginny. Besides your husband. The Lavonia Massacre would not have happened if Montie had not been thought to be your husband's killer."

Her hand went to her hair, side of her head, urgently nervous. Dropped back to the table. "I know," she finally said, vaguely to the ether.

"What were you thinking?"

Vicious with contempt. Her head rose, focusing, as if she'd been underwater too long, remembering she needed air. "I felt plum awful Montie was…"

She sighed. "What's the term? Taking the rap? I *was* going to help him. Best lawyers. Plea for leniency. I woulda taken care of him. And his family. And if he'd gone to the electric chair, I woulda made sure Dorothy and that little baby never wanted for anything."

My eyes crinkled, astounded.

Feet stamping the floor, the sheriff said:

"You wanted to help Collins, Miss Ginny, you could've tole me the truth."

She blinked at him.

"Didn't have the courage."

"You had the courage," he said, "to shoot your husband, eight times, or was it only seven?"

Wished he'd shut up.

Ginny sniffled. "Only after Montie knocked him down for me."

"You sayin' Collins helped you? You two conspired?"

"No, no, no, Bobby Ray. All happened just like Mrs. Russell says. Like I already signed my name to. I walked in on them. J.B. was already stirring. Montie'd hardly touched him. Shoe pullers ain't that heavy you know. When he saw me, Montie ran like a cottontail bunny. I got the gun and I shot J.B. before he could get on his feet."

"Then planted the gun," I said, "framing Montie."

"Yes."

"Then called the sheriff and lied."

"Yes."

"Continued to lie and omit until Montie and the others got lynched!"

Her eyes bored in on mine.

Narrowing. "Don't you know I can barely live with myself."

"Anyone speak to you? Say something that didn't mean much? Sounded like *talk*? Don't worry Ginny we're gonna get those…" I flung a shrug. "Whatevers."

She shook her head.

"No…"

"What?"

"'Cept for, well…" she said looking up, "that Hobbs creature."

"John Riley Hobbs?"

She shrugged. "I guess."

I glimpsed the sheriff.

"Klan's Imperial Wizard," I said, and he nodded.

"When was this?"

"J.B.'s graveside. Horace introduced us."

"Horace?" Turbeville looked.

"Pastor Cothran," I said, then:

"You told me you didn't know Cothran was Klan."

"I didn't!"

"You knew Hobbs was Klan?"

"Horace said he came up outta the blue. I was leaning on Horace a lot that day, so it was natural. I mean, didn't seem like they had to have known each other…As you've discovered," she added quietly, as if privately to me, "we're close."

Turbeville boiling:

"What exactly did Hobbs say?"

"Basically what Mrs. Russell said: Don't worry, ma'am, if that…nigra…that was how he said it…if that nigra ever sees the light of day, won't be for long. Count on it.'"

"What," I asked, "did you tell him?"

"That I wanted nothing to do with him or his kind. Then I

walked on to the limousine where Dennis was, holding the door
for me."

"You tell anyone?"

"No."

"Head of the KKK," Turbeville blasted, "in several states
boasts he's gonna take care of the black man everybody thinks
killed your husband, and you don't tell me?"

Her eyes sheepish green darts.

"I thought, Bobby Ray, it was hot air."

"After Collins was murdered? Tell anybody then?"

"N-no."

"Not me! Not the FBI!"

"No."

In her first *no* there had been enough of a catch, I wondered
if she had told someone.

"Any idea," I said, "who did the lynching?"

"No."

"Ginny, did you ask, or pay anybody to silence Montie?"

"Nooo…"

A wounded moan.

"I don't believe for a minute," I told her pointblank, "you
cold-bloodedly tormented and shot four people, a pregnant
woman included. But…weren't you worried what would come
out if Montie made it to a courtroom? That Montie or his lawyer
would figure it out? Who could blame you for trying to silence
the only other human being alive who knew Montie Collins
hadn't fired those shots. Because keeping that secret meant
everything to you. It was worth the rest of your life."

"You're wrong," she growled.

"How'm I wrong?"

"I *wasn't* worried. I didn't need to silence a man nobody'd
believe…" She shrugged, dropping back, crossing her arms.
"Everybody'd say he was just tryin' to save his own skin making
up a story like that. And because it was directed at me, the
widow, they'd hate him all the more."

Nodding, I rearranged, lining of my dress swishing my slip.
"Ginny," I almost whispered, "I have just one more question,
very important. Did you tell your secret—the shooting and the
cover-up—to anyone, for any reason, before telling us today?"

That catch again—
Made my eyebrow tug.
Backs of my fingers graze some blonde hair back.

"No," she said, glimpsing Turbeville. Then slipping me a grim sly smile, a tiny upturn of red lips. If I read my black widows correctly, there was someone she had talked to—but not in front of the sheriff.

Who would she tell about committing murder?

Her son?

Hippy daughter in California?

The man she'd loved before J.B. Roberts?

CHAPTER 44

I SCUDDED BACK AND THE sheriff towered to his full six-foot-three. I took my pocketbook, and turned on my Corfam pumps and Turbeville followed, reaching ahead for the door. I was pausing, pinching a strap through my collar, when Ginny asked: "Can we talk, Sherry? Woman to woman."

I looked from her to Turbeville.

"With Bobby Ray's permission."

He gave it, but asked for my purse. "Cain't have you slipping her no contraband lipstick, now can I?" I handed it off by the gold chain handles, then gave the matron in the Russian shoes a hard eye. She had gone over to grab Ginny back into thrall, relishing the prospect—Ginny being one of her betters in the caste system still operating in the Deep South. "You too Liz," Turbeville ordered. "C'mon out." She was a big-boned woman who piled a dump-truck load of hateful glower on top of me as we passed.

To the effect of: *Who the hell do you think you are you skinny bitch?*

Ginny and I were alone.

I sat one buttocks onto a corner of the bolted-down table, and leaned onto the heel of one hand, looking down on top of her. "We're as alone as we'll ever likely be again, Ginny, if you got anything to say."

Coming to her feet, she turned. Looked down out the window at the barbwire and yellow county trucks and bulldozers. I stepped up behind her. "Sorry it had to be this way."

"It's okay," she sighed over a shoulder. "Now I don't hafta hide such a terrible secret; I can get what's coming to me, then try to salvage whatever is left of my life."

I nodded.

Didn't seem likely she'd walk out of the pen before she was an octogenarian, but—maybe one of those lawyers she'd planned to have represent Montie, try to save his bacon, could do something for her. "I did tell somebody," she said.

"That you killed Mr. Roberts?"

"Yes."

I waited. She swung around, eyes pleading.

"Think Horace Cothran really is a Ku Klux Klansman?"

"He reads Klan literature. Weaves it into Sunday sermons. He wears a Confederate-flag vest. I know—because you told us—he has some connection to John Riley Hobbs. They could have known each other before the funeral, and pretended they didn't for your benefit."

She nodded.

"Damn," she said.

I sighed.

"You told Pastor Cothran?"

She wrung out tearful eyes.

Nodded spastically.

"Why?"

"I got to worryin' what that Hobbs said. About gettin' Montie."

"Why tell Cothran, if you didn't know he was Klan? Why not go to Hobbs directly?" I stepped around, facing her from the side, lifting my chin. "It was risky, telling even one extra person."

She eyed me.

"Wouldn've been proper…"

I rolled my eyes. "Oh," I said.

Knotted my arms.

"Horace heard what Hobbs said at the funeral and I asked him, as a friend, to go on my behalf. Assure him I wanted nothing done. I told Horace why, because I knew Montie to be innocent."

"Because you'd done it. You told him that?"

"Yes."

"Trusted Cothran *that* much?"

"He's my friend, an old dear friend."

"More than an old dear friend," I said.

She nodded.

Eyes flickering.

"Ex-lover."

Nodding.

"Possibly future lover."

"Yes."

"What did he say?"

"He'd take care of it. And pray for me."

I nodded. "And?"

"Meantime, I wasn't to say—his words—nothing to nobody."

"You didn't?"

"No."

"He came to you with my interview request," I said. "Why didn't he just stonewall me, like the sheriff? Why, for that matter, did you agree?"

"Horace insisted. Said I should see you, not tell you anything, then we'd be rid of you."

She grinned sadly giving me a straight look in the eye.

"Guess he read you wrong."

CHAPTER 45

I REJOINED TURBEVILLE, YUKKING IT up with a gawking male jailer, twisting a billy stick in his hands. The orange-haired matron practically bowled me over to retake charge of her prisoner. As if Ginny Roberts were the most dangerous thing since John Dillinger. "Go git'er!" the jailer called after her, baring bad teeth. Again, I felt very sorry for Ginny, but it wasn't my fault. Not really. My pocketbook hung from Turbeville's fist alongside his thigh with the six shooter. "Looks good, Sheriff," I said, giving him the eye. "Matches your belt and boots beautifully."

The jailer roared out an evil laugh.

Turbeville acted good-humoredly.

"Very funny."

I took the bag, let the chain fall out to full length and slung it from my shoulder. "Heavier'n an average lady's handbag," he commented. "Then again, we've established I ain't no expert. Don't suppose you go' tell ol' Bobby Ray what she wanted?" He stabbed a chin at Ginny Roberts, being escorted off along the gray corridor. Big silver soda-acid fire extinguisher, the kind you turned upside-down to activate, mounted, near where Ginny and Orange Hair took a left, disappeared.

She'd said nothing about telling or not telling Turbeville about Horace Cothran. She'd waited to get me alone, but that might've been propriety. Embarrassed to talk to anyone but a woman—a woman warmer, that is, than Brünnhilde the jail marm. Anyway, my status vis-à-vis Ginny Roberts involved no obligations of confidentiality. I decided, nevertheless, to keep what I knew to myself. I needed to mull things over, fold the Ginny Roberts/Horace Cothran connection in with everything else.

Like nuts into cookie dough.

Bobby Ray Turbeville might be a decent lawman as Walter Biggs believed, but even good cops could be blunderbusses. And Turbeville would be under fire: For arresting the wrong man, a Negro, in a high-profile murder. For then making no arrests in a Klan massacre. Perhaps there was nothing sinister in that state of affairs.

Or perhaps it was the design of a Klan sheriff.

And I suddenly knew with a clammy shudder that I had to keep my mouth shut. Because if the Klan had murdered four people, and Ginny Roberts and I knew something about it no one else did, and I told the wrong person—like a Klan sheriff—I'd be jeopardizing the case, plus my own delicate hide.

And hers.

He gruffed, big brown sweat stain under an arm raised against the wall:

"Gonna play coy, huh?"

"Like the lady said"—I shrugged—"woman to woman."

Turbeville said no more about it.

Big press cameras flashed.

Reporters and photog's ambushed us exiting the alley behind the sheriff's office. After the dim gray of the jail the white blaze of sun made it almost impossible to see, the cameras making matters worse. Only the first wave. A fresh arrest in the Roberts murder would be big news—scathing in some camps. The sheriff tugged the brim of his cattleman's hat, pulling his politician's grin across his face. Jammed some guy a big smacking handshake. I shied, masking myself.

"This the lady detective?" came one titillated query. Turbeville—the biggest man out there by far—made short work of herding me clear. Across toward the square, halting traffic. A photo or two of our backs were snapped. He hollered back—

"no more, please, gentlemen"—promising a full press conference, three o'clock. Savvy, I thought. More regional reporters would get there, yet still time for the TV people to get footage for early evening. This story was going to be headlines— including in Nashville—even without the lady-detective angle. Naturally I didn't know what Turbeville was going to say— maybe he didn't either—but I credited him for not stifling coverage of what could only, for his office, for him personally, be a black eye.

I began to regret my recent suspicions.

Of course, I had no legitimate, non-emotional, factual reason to lift them.

Could I trust Turbeville? Or not?

And if I wasn't sure...

Wasn't that the same as not?

When we got to my car I grasped back some warm-breeze-blown hair, and over light traffic told Turbeville I was sorry. "For what?" he asked, pressing down the gun belt, wringing squeaks and rubs out of the old leather.

"For you being shown up by a woman."

He shook, near-silent laughter, darting observant eyes.

"Like I said, Miss Sherry, I give credit where credit's due. You showed me up 'cause I screwed up. You're one smart lady."

"Not sore?" I said. "No, *if this pushy broad had only...?*"

"Naw, I was thinkin', in fact, few more noses, good as yours—prettier than Dudley's—might be nice. Say, wanna stay for this press conference? You'll be famous. Helluva story."

"Yeah..." I smirked. "One that would distract them nicely from raking you over too many coals."

He huffed.

"Cain't blame a guy for trying."

"I'm the daughter, and ex-fiancée, of newspapermen. The glory of the press wore off for me long, long ago. Look I mean it... Keep my name out of it."

"They know."

"Downplay it. Take the credit. I was just helping, but you called the shots."

He sighed.

Stared off a few different directions.

"Scared, ain'tcha?"

"A little. Besides, my mother believes a lady should eschew the limelight. And my husband seeing my face plastered across the news won't do me any good patching up my marriage."

He nodded.

"Do the best I kin, but I ain't takin' credit for thinkin' of the handbag."

I smiled. "Don't look a gift horse in the mouth, Sheriff. Might need'n extra female vote or two one of these days."

"Might at that. Headed back up Tennessee way?"

"Haven't decided," I lied.

"Don't you go off on your own, now, tryin' to solve the Montie Collins killin'. Whoever killed them people was downright vicious—but I don't guess you take advice from men very well, do you?"

"Women either."

"Lemme know where you're staying, number to reach you. Case the solicitor does wanna talk to you, or Ginny Roberts gets in the mood for more girl talk."

I told him my motel and room number, and asked they not be shared with anyone. Wasn't sure it mattered. Somebody, somehow already knew. The obscene phone call. And my best—only—guess as to how my eloquent admirer got my number, was either Deputy Loftin or Sheriff Turbeville or both had provided it, from the key lying in the open, when they were hanging around my car yesterday. Maybe him asking now was just clever window dressing. Maybe they were all Klan: Bobby Ray Turbeville, C.O. Loftin, Horace Cothran, John Riley Hobbs.

Birds of a feather.

Who'd like nothing better than to pluck mine.

I was backing from my parking space when I stamped the brakes.

Threw my transmission into park, and flung open the door, calling the sheriff back.

We went around to examine the Impala's flat front passenger-side tire.

Sitting on boot heels, Turbeville stared up over his shoulder:

"Valve stem severed at the base," he said. "Woulda took

anybody five seconds to slip in, do it, slip away."

CHAPTER 46

TURBEVILLE GOT A SKINNY GUY with a tow truck to change my tire, and waited with me inside the library. I politely refused protection, and his offer to summon the police chief, since technically my car's vandalism was his jurisdiction. I said I'd prefer not to make a big deal of it. He said the best thing for me to do would be, go home, back to being a housewife, forget all about Alabama. I tried to pay, or at least tip the tow-truck driver, but he refused. "'Preciate it, Willy," Turbeville said and the skinny guy bowed and scrapped. "A'ytime, Sheriff, you just call."

Betwixt Lavonia and Jasper I heard Buck Owens, the Statler Brothers and, before the signal sank in static, most of "You Ain't Woman Enough." I'd met Loretta Lynn briefly, during the Pauline Prescott matter.

Back in Jasper, four-fifteen, I changed into a yellow pullover with short rolled sleeves, wide-wale corduroy stretch pants, a bright leprechaun green, and a pair of suede shoe boots. I took my cigarettes, key, some change, and got a Coke and sat by the pool. I smoked a half a pack of Kents while deciding to go the next morning, and have a nitty-gritty talk with Preacher Horace Cothran.

Turbeville's friendly suggestion I leave the state notwithstanding.

Heck, his deputy'd only banned me from the county!

I'd exonerated Montie Collins but hadn't solved his or his wife's or his unborn son's murder, which was what Ruthie Mae had roped me into this to do. I know, I know. I put my head back on the chaise lounge. I'd told her that was over my head, and the sheriff had just reminded me of the same, without really expecting me to listen. I just didn't feel right about dropping everything.

Not yet.

Especially since I'd withheld a key piece from the sheriff: That Ginny Roberts had confided her guilt to Horace Cothran, for the expressed purpose of heading off any vigilantism. If Cothran was Klan, or had connections in the Klan—like Hobbs—and if he had gotten the word out Collins had not in fact killed anybody, why had Collins been lynched?

Did Cothran fail to get the word out?

Or did he get it out, and it made no difference?

And if it made no difference...

What the hell did that mean?

CHAPTER 47

ALL WORK AND NO PLAY makes Jill a dull girl.

Sherry too. I'd eaten at the motel in spite of the hellish magnolia-blossom wallpaper, two nights running. Considering I'd solved a murder that day, like a real detective, I thought I deserved a celebratory feast.

And a real drink.

Trumping all else—there was the door-to-door vacuum-cleaner salesman who'd tried last night to lasso me into some mutual marital infidelity. For, you see, he'd worn a wedding band he hadn't even had the sense to twist off before his drunken flirtation. And he certainly knew I was married; my big sparkly diamond could not be missed. Maybe he figured it safe, and I would think it safe, to cheat with another married person. Mutually assured destruction, to use Cold War vernacular. Anyway, eating in the same restaurant a third evening would convince him I was on the make. I could say *no* till I was blue in the face, and he'd still think *yes* was in there somewhere till I shot him.

Close to five-thirty I crushed out my cigarette and strolled to my room. Sonny Greene's Oldsmobile was, indeed, in front of his.

I cut on the news while freshening, as they say, for dinner.

Ford strike.

LBJ calling for air-traffic-control fixes.

I picked out a sweater and changed pocketbooks.

And there came the body counts.

KILLED.

WOUNDED.

MISSING.

Separate for U.S., South Vietnamese, North Vietnamese. The American public was supposed to feel all cuddlesome, I guessed, about the fact the numbers always were highest in the North Vietnamese column, and lowest in ours.

Hey, hey, LBJ
How many kids
Did you kill today?

I put in a fresh pack of Kents, pushed the thumb release, breaking open the cylinder of my gun. I snapped the gun closed and stuffed it into the purse. Switched off the TV, and as an afterthought dialed Walter Biggs's home. No answer. I caught him at the paper typing madly at his desk—flailing incessantly his worn, long-abused city-room typewriter, even as we talked, as only a dyed-in-the-wool newspaperman could. I could hear in the background, knew from growing up around the business, he was surrounded by a passel of rewrite men, fighting deadline, fitting words to facts, snugger the fit, better the story. Speed was key, writing to measure, to the space mark branded by the city desk: ten lines, twenty lines, short spread, three-quarters of a column. I asked Biggs for a good steak-and-booze recommendation. He offered to take me out on the town, said it had been awhile since he'd "cut a rug."

I said I was married. Besides I didn't want to dress. My night. He told me to go to the Red Carriage Grill and gave me directions. He'd have them take care of me, whatever that meant. And truthfully, all my above reasons for refusing to let Biggs escort me were true. However, I was getting so paranoid about this invisible-empire crap, I wasn't even ruling out Biggs being a Klansman.

What better way to get scoops?

CHAPTER 48

FORTY MILES AWAY IN BIRMINGHAM I found the Red
Carriage Grill and Talley-Ho Lounge. They had a dim-lit
corner booth waiting for me thanks to Biggs' call. A
candle flickered inside a brandy snifter. The seats were brass-
studded leather. There were heavy beams and fieldstone, lots of
colonial affectations. I expected George Washington to thunder
up on back of his steed. I ordered a Dewar's and water, and their
most expensive, at $7.95, charcoal-broiled steer steak, the New
York Sirloin, plus French-style onion soup, and a trip to the
salad table. I had two more cocktails before my steak, losing
count after that. A couple. More than a couple. Strawberries
Jubilee for dessert. Coffee. When I brought my wallet out the
manager informed me Mr. Biggs had instructed them to charge
everything to his Diner's Club.

I huffed gigglingly.

Inflated princessly.

Biggs, my father too, would raise toasts to my booze
consumption, induct me into their club. I tapered my cigarette
thoughtfully, and took a draw. Fred would glower in
disappointment. Not that he had a thing in the world against
drinking—just my drinking. Which gave me more than enough
reason to vacuum the remnants from the melting ice of my last
empty. Scotch adhered so well to ice. I thunked down the heavy-
bottomed glass, and rubbed my face, which felt pretty numb. I

left a very-over-generous tip, and there was a full moon not quite straight overhead as I crossed the lot.

Swaying to my car, gorged and quite agreeably inebriated.

There were more music stations between Birmingham and Jasper than out Lavonia way and at night they came in clearer. I had the windows down, singing tops of my lungs: "The Ballad of the Green Berets," "Windy," "Love Potion Number Nine," "Wild Thing," "California Girls," "Light My Fire," and...

"Eve of Destruction."

CHAPTER 49

ABOUT THE TIME SHERRY RUSSELL Nates—*codenamed "Betty" by the Klan for the Archie comics blonde or, take your pick, the World War II Jap bomber known for its highly vulnerable fuel tanks and distinctive tail (leading to the U.S. Navy slang "Big Butt Betty")—was downing her first Scotch at the Red Carriage Grill—with her big butt and vulnerable tanks—a secret Klonkave was convened in a bachelor apartment over a garage elsewhere in Birmingham.*

Present:

—Exalted Cyclops (EC) of the Lavonia Klavern.

—Grand Kleagle of the Alabama Realm.

—Klokann of the Lavonia Klavern (aka, Lee David Autrey, who had punched, kicked, and gouged Fred Nates to a draw five days before behind the Free Will Baptist Church).

—Klarogo of Eastview Klavern 13 in northeast Birmingham, in whose home they were meeting.

—A half-stoned Klavern 13 member named Ben Jackson.

—Three canebreak rattlesnakes.

A fiery summons went out that afternoon. A fiery summons, to a Klansman, must not be ignored. Ben Jackson had to go even if it meant losing his truck-driving job. He was dispatched to Rattlesnake Mountain to bag as many of the area's namesake reptiles as possible, time permitting. He was last to arrive. "You're drunk, Ben," the Klarogo, or inner guard, roared, barring entry. "Goddamnit I'm entitled to drink—I been climbing rocks all afternoon to bring you these damn snakes."

"Enter Klansman," overruled the Grand Kleagle.
All suddenly washing back—
Jackson hauling through a big quivering burlap sack.

CHAPTER 50

I PARKED ASKEW FACING ROOM 117, engine tinkled down
while I sat listening to myself breathe, eventually fumbling
out, my sweater spilling off my shoulders. Headfirst I dove
back exaggeratedly, retrieving my purse—giggling—then shoved
the door, every action, of course, having that equal and opposite
reaction we learned about in school. I took in lungfuls of
oxygen, and finally, standing on my own, I hooked the purse in
one elbow, and shifted and crisscrossed my sweater sleeves in
front of me, and strode for my door. Walking was much tougher
than driving, as it turned out—and I chuckled aloud at that.

Color TV flickered in Electrolux Man's window. Door ajar.
Cozy cigarette smoking, ice tinkling. Sonny Greene counting on
me being drawn by these romantic enticements. I was drunk
enough that actually last night's Jim Beam offer was sounding
like a good chaser for the Scotch. Yeah, I was *that* drunk,
pressing one side of my helium-inflated skull. I was not,
however, insane.

And I wasn't only thinking about my pending hangover:

I liked where I was. Not wanting to go into that man's room,
but delighted it was my choice. That if I really wanted to try
getting away with something, there was no one there could stop
me...

What kind of goddamn wife did that make me?

I zipped the key clumsily in my lock. It stuck as keys are wont to do. One side of my mouth pulling, I worked it, and the knob, and eventually pitched through the flying open door.

Managing not to fall on my face.

The lights were on.

I'd left them on.

I re-locked the door, sealing out Sonny Greene's lechery, and my temptation, and I turned carefully around, and breathed air into the mix in my head, dropping my key and purse randomly. Managing more footsteps, I got the TV on, then dumped my ass on the end of the bed, and capsized backwards, arms sprawled. Brain like sorghum. I was no novice drinker but I hadn't consumed that much hard liquor in a while. On TV were the last few minutes of *Run For Your Life*—Ben Gazzara still dying of that same leukemia as last season, which had no debilitating symptoms.

Would that it were true.

I awoke after midnight with an exploding bladder. Flung up, stripping out of my clothes along the way. Completing my pee of Biblical proportions, my heart thudding like a pile driver, I reeled back into the searingly lit room, banking off a door jamb. I batted off all the lights and the TV and clawed back the bed covers.

Got in on my stomach.

Felt my heart beat against the mattress.

CHAPTER 51

T HE BIRMINGHAM KLAVERN 13 KLAROGO *thundered his own red-and-white Chevy Bel-Air up Bankhead Highway toward Jasper. Lee David Autrey, riding shotgun, could scarcely concentrate, and Ben Jackson was in the back—*

With his knotted-closed burlap sack.

The car was a rolling arsenal, typical of Klan cars, a two-way radio installed, meaning the Klarogo might be KBI, Klan Bureau of Investigation. Autrey didn't know the man's name, just "Big Bad John." Discovering a Klansman's true name, even for another Klansman, wasn't easy. Some were ex-cons with aliases, others businessmen concealing identities. Everybody knew Ben Jackson, though, as a tough man in a fray, insanely fearless about snakes. Autrey had been with him once, at a traffic light, downtown Birmingham, pulled up next to these Negroes—when Jackson pitched a rattlesnake in their car!

They carried a couple of fifths of Canadian whiskey, one already being passed man to man. It was plain to Autrey the Klarogo resented like hell his being along, and as the alcohol went, so the animosity came out. A profane argument had already erupted at the Klonkave, when Autrey tried to insist they take his car, which he was supposed to do whenever possible. Betty, however, would know his Plymouth, after that church fiasco. In fact, the whole reason Birmingham Klansmen were involved was the risk Betty might recognize, by physicality, or voice, the Grand Kleagle.

And the Exalted Cyclops.

In fact they'd left the Klonkave early, establishing airtight alibis at a

204

bar. Autrey was along because he knew Betty and her car, and knew Jasper and the surrounding countryside better than the Birmingham men did. All true, but it was mostly that Autrey was the Kleagle's man. The Kleagle had recruited him personally back in '54, and there weren't that many men left you could completely trust.

About eleven o'clock they reached the Jasper Holiday Inn. The gold Impala was there, the lights in room 117 ablaze. The room three to her left was up too. The Klarogo backed into a space from which to stake the rooms out, while smoking, bullshitting, and quaffing Canadian Club. They had a key to 117 pilfered by a Jasper city police officer—a Klansman—who had earlier distracted the clerk with a bluff about a Mercedes-Benz outside being on his hot sheet.

They had bolt cutters for the chain lock.

Betty's room went dark.

Betty, aka Sherry Russell Nates.

About 12:35.

Ten minutes later a male figure looked out the other room, as he had several times before. "Maybe he's a Fed guarding her," Autrey suggested. "I say split."

"If he's a Fed," the Klarogo said, "I'll kill the sonovabitch."

"Goddamn, you shoot an agent our operation's blown."

"Ain't gonna shoot him, Bro'," the Klarogo grinned.

And from under his seat he brought out a hunting knife.

Unsnapped the sheath.

"Just jab him in the back with this."

Then that room went dark.

CHAPTER 52

M Y BLANKETS FLUNG OFF, STIRRING me up, like mud
from a river bottom.
Left wrist clamped, up into the fleshy hollow of my
back. I might've gurgled, "No!" Second man, more rough-
handed, wrists crossed, first man binding them. I thrashed
peroxided hair, threw open my lipsticked mouth to scream.

An oily cotton rag staunched it.

My jaws snapped.

"Bitch bit me!"

"Shut the fuck up, Bro'." Winding, knotting. Something the
way he'd said *Bro'*. "Relax," he told me. Other voice, not
familiar, saying, "You nigger-lovin' bitch, you nigger-lovin'
bitch." Out of the semi-dark, dim lit by mercury-vapor lamps
leaking in from the parking lot, I saw ghost-white masks, eyes
gleaming down out scissored holes. I fought to spit out the gag,
wrenched by my elbows, riving pain. I'd locked the door, sure I
had—shellacked as I was.

Any little less shellacked, I might've shed, with the rest of my
clothes, the iron-maiden bra and lace briefs I was very glad to
still be wearing—kicking, wailing, hauled into the bathroom. The
figure on my right had a strong body odor; otherwise I could tell
little about him. The other hooded Klansman I knew, by voice,
by dime-store aftershave. He wore heavy lace-up ankle boots
under his robe. They sat me onto the toilet, backs of my thighs

206

smacking the seat. I shrugged their hands off, peering up wild-eyed. To my surprise the hooded pair withdrew. Putting on, in fact, a pretty fair Three-Stooges bit.

As if afraid of something.

The third Kluxer appeared and I shrank against the raised toilet lid, a bra strap dropping. He was lugging a tumbling sack, a fifty-pound-size grain sack like at Fred's mill. Grasped near the bottom, clutched closed at the top. Through the burlap something was alive. He taunted me, gave the bag violent shakes, laughing dementedly. Bending my head back, a complete nightmare, tears blurring my eyes. He repeated the nigger-loving-bitch epithet—darned cleaver these Klansmen—then yelled back of him:

"Git ready to haul ass, gentlemen!"

Which point he simply pitched the big sack—heavy, scratchy, and squirming—onto my half-naked lap; the crazed man ripping out of there himself, slamming the door, plunging me into pitch-darkness.

Whatever was in the bag was mad, savage muscular thrashing. I shot to my feet, catapulting whatever it was to the floor, leapt onto the toilet seat, balancing despite both hands tied behind my back. Shuddering out of all control, straining, listening over my own gaspings.

Stirrings—

I heard.

Dry rustlings.

Below, everywhere.

Ceaseless movement.

Unleashed.

Frantic.

Rats? all I could think of…

But didn't feel, or sound right.

Not rats.

Some deep throaty hiss issued up, followed, suddenly, by a different note.

Buzzing.

My flesh ran to ice.

Ears darted.

Same sound, different direction.

Not buzzing.

Rattling!

Rattling from at least three different locations in the tiny sealed-up room.

Rattlesnakes.

Inching back, thighs quavering. Sweat wringing out every pore, making my body slick, including the soles of my feet on the toilet seat. Think, Sherry! Rattlesnakes? I knew, as a nurse, they were killers. That was no myth, and they were powerfully aggressive when threatened.

When cornered.

Which is what we all were, wasn't it?

The rattle of course was a warning.

I am in fact threatened by you, my pretty, and I'm about to strike.

My chest heaved in the dark.

They could lunge half their length.

That was a fact.

Could they see?

See in the dark better than I could?

I didn't know, then something along those lines—they were deaf!

Sensed vibration.

Heat

Smell.

Not sound.

Lightheaded, I was bordering on some kind of breakdown. If I hadn't been so damn drunk I'm convinced I would have. As it was, my mind became seized by, behind me, an unexpected loosening.

So sudden, unexpected, I couldn't have been more surprised if there had been another person back there untying me. On a subconscious level I'd been struggling, naturally, against my restraints, and somehow had managed to work some slack into them. And, oddly, it turned out to not be very much of a knot.

The point being, I got my hands free!

And held onto the rope—not sure why—bringing my stiff sweat-running arms forward, kneading the muscles in both my slippery shoulders. I removed the rag from my mouth. Which gave me the option of screaming myself silly. But, truly, no joke, I didn't want anybody finding me this way.

I, literally, would have sooner died snakebit.

And anyway, how long would this hypothetical rescue take?

Wasn't sure I had that long before venom-dripping fangs began to sink into juicy USDA Prime Sherry meat. Quietly I opened a gap between the vinyl shower curtain, to my right, and the tile wall, and stepped over into the tub. It spanned the length of the room, to alongside the only door, only escape. I swallowed, fine hairs straight on end, and made my way. The shower curtain, I soon realized in horror—what flimsy protection it was—was tucked to the inside!

Desperately, carefully, I flipped the bottom edge.

Its little magnets.

To the outside.

Soft little *tick, tick, ticks*. Not much, but it gave the snakes an extra barrier to contemplate and circumvent before dropping over into the tub with me.

My heart thudded, pounding blood all through my body.

They were probing.

I clawed my hair on both sides. Some burst of nervous energy. Facing the foot of the tub—I breathed hard, smelling the sweat under my arms—the way out was to my left, other side of the shower curtain. Reaching I felt a clean bath towel hung from a rack.

That gave me an idea.

That length of braided nylon.

I looped it over the towel rod and, grasping it with both fists, tested if it would hold my weight. Then I wound my right hand with the free ends and pulled onto the ledge, brushing aside the curtain. Spurring of rattles, hisses. Gripping the rope I thrust a leg back, leaning out like one of the Flying Wallendas. Touched the opposite wall with my nails and grazed down till I felt the switch plate.

Snapped the switch.

The ceiling fixture blazed.

I dropped back into the relative safety of the tub.

Back slapped wetly against tile, white bra pumping in front of me. It was a translucent shower curtain. The light sparking a surge in the hue and cry of our serpentine friends, beyond that ridiculously insubstantial barrier. Then with a sharp intake, in utter horror, clutching my wet stomach, I spotted a triangular head.

Curved muscular neck.

Levitating.

Sweeping.

Elegant.

Outside the vinyl.

I even made out a darting forked tongue. In pure revulsion I kicked my foot. Curtain fluttering, magnets ticking. Half surprised no immediate reprisal organized against me. I had to remind myself there was no human intelligence out there.

Nor evil.

Only instinct. Dangerous determined survival instinct. As new a situation for them, as it was for me, and I at least had the brains, and somewhat, for once, the brawn. I grabbed the rope, remounting the tub rim.

Peering round, with a raw gnawing primal fear.

Three snakes.

Large ones, heavy-bodied.

Dark crossbands.

Grayish-pink.

Tails black.

The granddaddy was six feet, easily. The others, say, four. One coiled so only an angry head and quivering tail were up, tongue flickering, tasting me through the air. The remaining pair whipped in eerie elegant curves, gliding and traversing, yet it seemed they were struggling, a serpent version of fumbling around drunk, something I was acquainted with.

The tile floor!

No traction for their belly scales, which perhaps I had to thank for not having been envenomated so far, because by mere size these creatures easily dominated the room. I'd be in range of strikes from any and all, should I dare expose myself. No taking these fellows by surprise, leaping, and racing for the door.

And as if to prove my point—

Granddaddy, the bastard, gaped his jaws.

Erecting fangs.

I got down. Breathing through my teeth.

I ripped the shower curtain down. Popping grommets that held the metal hooks threaded on the rod. I bunched the whole thing in my arms, alert, flinching, my non-human adversaries reacting coilingly, sidewindingly. One hovered near the door, more interested in the gap beneath it, than me.

I gathered, cautiously, my shower-curtain bundle under one arm.

Yanked the towel off the rack.

Beat it at the snake.

Like I was beating out a brush fire.

Herding it back towards the toilet. The others undulating, heads up, rattling, hissing.

I dropped the towel and cast the shower curtain over all three snakes like a net.

Leapt out on top and—palms greased with sweat—fought the door open. Lunged through, swung round, and hammered it closed, hard with all my weight.

Yanking the knob, double-sure the latch had clicked.

I staggered back.

Raking hair, sopping.

Heaving lungs violently. Then I ran the room and twisted the door lock. Fumbled on the light. Had a key! The Klan got a key to my room! Shit! Shit! Shit! Gasping, quaking, I noticed, glimpsing up, the chain dangling loose.

I pulled it, snapped it taut.

Undamaged. I clasped my eyes shut.

Even a key couldn't have gotten them past that! I'd made it easy, being drunk and stupid.

Slapping the chain at the slot I got it latched, finally. Then lowered myself to the floor. My underclothes sweated through.

And was violently ill.

CHAPTER 53

UGGING MY STOMACH I STUMPED to the vanity, and rubbed beneath one wet arm. There was stubble and I sniffed, disgusting myself. I undressed and gave myself a sponge bath. Then gargled, and downed two glasses of water. Wiping my mouth, back of my hand—

My rings!

Missing!

(Specifically: a five-diamond, 1¼-carat total, 14K white gold wedding band, and a one-carat diamond engagement ring—total value $1345.)

Berserk searching.

All the while knowing I hadn't removed them, nor lost them in the bathroom playing funhouse with three snakes. I staggered, my head in a vise grip. Collapsed on the end of the bed, and sobbed racking sobs, equal parts anger and fear. One of those Klansmen had robbed me while I was too damned out of it to notice. God Almighty. I picked my head up, lowered it again.

Smacked my forehead.

Fred would kill me.

I beat the top of my own skull with my fists.

Stupid, stupid, stupid!

After several minutes, I made myself stand, and hook on a clean bra, and step, unsteadily, into some underpants. Still rocking my head in self-castigation, I gathered my top, slacks, and shoes, and finished dressing. It wasn't Sunday-go-to-meetin' garb but I wouldn't be arrested for indecent exposure. There was nothing of mine inside the bathroom other than a Lady Eversharp, which I could easily replace, so I gave it—the razor, and run of the bathroom—to the snakes. I packed haphazardly then hauled my bags, typewriter, and Biggs' box of hate literature to my car.

Then I took a sheet of typing paper and wrote boldly:

DO NOT ENTER

SNAKES!

I'M SERIOUS!!

Stuck that in the jamb of the bathroom door, then put out the DO NOT DISTURB sign and locked the room behind me. I drove away without checking out. Two-thirty A.M. I went 59 miles and registered at the Holiday Inn in Tuscaloosa under the alias, Dorothy Wilhoite. I didn't even telephone Fred to tell him I'd moved. I took a scalding hot shower then slept till past nine-thirty.

In a putrid mood, saggingly, in the restaurant, I soaked down a lot of coffee, and orange juice, and carefully ate half an order of pancakes and bacon. Less queasy than weak, and a little watery, I looked better than I felt. I wore a purple dress, black gloves, pumps, and an Orlon scarf hat of blue, green, and red. I was sick about my rings.

I skimmed the paper, frowning, until a Walter Biggs byline, caught my eye:

Across Mississippi, since Monday's synagogue bombing—it was Thursday—dynamiters had attacked a rabbi's house, a Negro church, and the home of a white beer tavern owner known to support Negro voter registration. Since July—two months—Biggs wrote on, between Mississippi and west-central Alabama, there had been burnings or bombings of eight Negro homes and four churches, besides that week's incidents.

If one didn't know better, I sighed…

Firing up a cigarette…

One might think the Klan was mobilizing.

For war.

CHAPTER 54

NOT UNTIL EARLY AFTERNOON, CLOUDS high and wispy, did I make it to the Free Will Assembly Baptist Church in Lavonia. Slogging, I mounted the portico of the wing off the back, finding the door open. I wafted though, shoulder first, and checked the office. No Cothran. Only thing added since my last visit, I noticed, glancing silently, was a new and interesting item of clothing, hung from that coat rack, joining the black tailcoat and rebel-flag vest.

A white robe.

I walked over to it and spread it in my hands.

Bridal satin with a red felt emblem affixed to the front.

The emblem showing a cross and a single drop of blood.

I swallowed.

Jolted by a bumping, heavy sliding noises—I twisted—let the robe billow back, and followed a passage to the chapel. Rows of crude bench pews were empty. Cothran was working alone, black trousers, dingy undershirt with suspenders. I made no effort to hide but he was half-deaf from years of steel-mill work so didn't hear my heel-taps, crossing the stage, gradually halting. He had dragged aside his pulpit and was muscling into place some kind of—altar? On top of that he stood a cross built out of plywood and light bulbs. He threaded the cord out, then crouched arthritically, to plug it into an outlet in the floor, testing the bulbs. They worked and he unplugged the cord and got himself up.

An open Bible was laid upon the altar.

Then a sword.

I advanced, circling, as he arranged crossed American flags behind the light-bulb cross. In his old T-shirt he appeared a rather wasted figure, a pitiful little potbelly. His eyes flashed quite a lot of surprise when finally they saw me. Apologizing, I explained I'd found the door ajar, and let myself in. "Hope that was okay?" I went before the altar.

Examined the laid-open Bible.

Romans 12.

I nodded, familiar from my research with the marked verses.

"I beseech you therefore, brethren," I read, glimpsing up, Cothran listening, rubbing the side of a bulbous nose. "By the mercies of God, that ye present your bodies a living sacrifice, holy, acceptable unto God, which is your reasonable service."

Cothran rattled a cough.

"And be not conformed to this world," I went on, preachily, "but be ye transformed by the renewing of your mind, that ye may prove what is that good—and acceptable—and perfect—will of God."

I stepped away.

Circling again.

Cothran's eyes tracking me.

"That's how the Klan justifies itself," I blistered. "The murder, the hatred. All some perverted interpretation of the will of God."

He drew back.

Mildly sneering.

"Don't bother denying you're Klan, sir. Tell me about you and Ginny Roberts."

CHAPTER 55

HALF-FACING ONE ANOTHER ON a front bench pew, Cothran clacked down on the stem of a pipe, and I took out a cigarette. "She's not your parishioner," I said. "Yet you and Deputy Loftin lied to me she was. Why?"

He took out a wooden match.

Struck it on the back edge of the bench.

Gave me a light.

Ever the gentlemen.

"Ask the C.O.," he said. "I didn' lie, just didn' correct a lady of quality. Didn' seem polite. Besides, Ginny and me were, and are, good friends. Didn' see it made no difference how we knew each another, long as I did you the favor you wanted, set you up a meeting, which I did."

"Fair enough," I said. "But you were, and are, more than friends. Might've even been some hanky-panky behind the proverbial woodshed"—my brows danced a jig—"when she was a mere sweet sixteen, or younger. That's her photo on your desk."

He rearranged.

Crags deepening. "She tell you 'bout us?"

"No specifics. She confided, woman to woman, you'd been lovers. Given the timeline of your departure to find fame and fortune on the railroad, she couldn't have been any older than that."

216

He shrugged, bowl of his pipe in hand. "Don't fault me for not being up front with you 'bout that. I was protecting her reputation."

I gave a nod.

"She was crushed when you left."

He was studying a thumbnail.

Picking at the cuticle. "Always intended," he said, inside himself, "to return, to marry her. Once I got decent steady work. Felt I could support her in the manner to which she'd became accustomed."

"Why didn't you?"

"Isn't it obvious? I'm the son of a sharecropper."

Embittered.

"She knew that," I said, "when she fell in love."

"She was a kid."

"Not a kid. Maybe not a woman, but to say she was a kid is to dismiss what you had. Still have. Not saying it would have been an easy row to hoe. Not saying her parents would've given their blessings. I am saying she was, and is in love with you, son of a sharecropper, or not."

"By the time I come to my senses…"

Grit in his voice. "She'd took up with J.B."

"Frustrating," I said, pulled some smoke off my cigarette. Tapped it over the beanbag ashtray between us, slid it closer. "Ever marry?"

"Nope."

"Her marriage to J.B. Roberts was a nightmare."

"Yes."

I flicked a brow.

"She told you?"

He steepled his fingers, cruel mouth set. "We talked. I was her friend, and I think, a spiritual advisor. Her faith was important to her. Something we always shared."

I nodded.

He huffed, grinning off. "Used to talk about church, God, Christ when we was kids."

"What did you advise? About her marital situation."

"I did not advise her to kill her husband."

"Did you offer…aid and comfort?"

"I did not. Ginny Seeley Roberts is a lady. I have not—*known* her, the way Adam knew Eve—since before I left home. Certainly not since she become another man's wife."

"What did you advise?"

"To remember her vows."

"Sounds spiteful. You made your bed, Ginny, my dear, sleep in it…"

"Not at all, it's biblical…"

Quoting in that Kentucky colonel drawl:

"They are no more twain, but one flesh. What therefore God hath joined together, let not man put asunder."

I held a defiant stare, then deflected it, dabbed a tear with my little finger. Then came back into that face, that damn-full-of-piety face. "You advised a woman," I began. Stamped out my cigarette. "A woman who was your first, perhaps only real love. Whose husband *hit* her. And notoriously carried on affairs with other women. You advised *her* to remain in that marriage?"

"If ye suffer for righteousness' sake, happy are ye: and be not afraid…'"

"If there's one thing I know, being a private detective in Nashville, the Buckle of the Bible Belt, it's the Bible's position on divorce. Jesus permits it where the spouse commits fornication, correct?"

"Woulda been self-serving of me to countenance divorce."

"After J.B.'s murder, did you talk about getting back together? She was free."

"After a respectable time, period of mourning, I woulda called on her."

"Ironic," I said. "J.B. Roberts' murder freed Ginny to pursue happiness. Yet it led her into a more literal bondage. Of course"—I shrugged—"never know how her trial will go. How sentencing will go."

"Your point?"

"Better for you, and Ginny, if I'd kept out of things."

"Ain't sure what you're askin'."

"Nothing really. An observation. When the world thought Montie Collins had killed J.B. Roberts, everything was coming up roses for you two. She was available—to you—after over three decades. Not many couples get second chances like that.

Then I come along and prove Montie Collins innocent. Largely, anyway. You must hate me."

"I don't hate."

"The Klan hates, Pastor Cothran, and you're Klan."

He drew rigid.

"We ain't gonna talk about that."

"Just talk about me, what I did to Ginny."

"Know the 'Serenity Prayer,' Mrs. Russell?"

I shook my head.

"God give us the grace to accept with serenity the things that cain't be changed, the courage to change the things which should be changed, and the wisdom to tell one from the other."

I nodded.

Thought.

"You failed to have the courage," I said, in a scathing tone, "both before and during Ginny's painful marriage, to try to change her life, lessen or prevent her suffering."

Like a tiny earth tremor going off in him. "Maybe," he said, throat full of gravel, "I had the grace to accept what was."

"I had surprisingly little difficulty getting her to confess."

"She was a gentle woman, no doubt racked with guilt. If we confess—"

"You don't need to speculate how racked with guilt Ginny was. You knew before I ever set foot in Lavonia. Before four people and an unborn child were murdered. Murdered by the Klan. You knew Collins was innocent. You knew Ginny killed her husband."

I shook myself out another cigarette.

Tapped the filter twice, put it between my lips. The stone-still pastor did not, that time, offer me a light. I struck my own Holiday Inn match and puffed and fanned it out. Cast it like a dart in the ashtray, then crossed my legs.

Lightly slapped, arranged black gloves atop my purple skirt.

"She came to you," I said. "Told you everything. And you told her not to say anything to anybody and she didn't. She told me all this at the jail yesterday. We were alone. I haven't told anyone, other than you—yet."

CHAPTER 56

I KNOW…

I'd set myself up.

I doubted Horace Cothran would kill me in his own church. I also doubted I'd be able to solve a quadruple murder. Not by conventional means, anyway. My best shot was to be the proverbial bull in a china shop. Make so much ruckus, somebody had to come out of the woodwork.

It was a dangerous game of chicken.

"Ginny Roberts told you she killed her husband," I said. "After you introduced her to John Riley Hobbs at J.B.'s funeral, and Hobbs promised reprisals. She asked you to stop him, assure him there was no need for any. Not against Collins, nor any other Negro."

Cothran's pipe had gone out.

He studied it, hammered the tobacco out of the bowl.

"Did you talk to Hobbs?"

He wheezed in and out.

"Cain't say. But do us both a favor and git outta this—go home, leave us be."

"Did you tell Hobbs?"

"Don't ask me that."

"If you didn't tell Hobbs, or somebody in his chain of command, then it forces me to think *you* might've killed four people. And I don't want to believe you'd do that, sir."

It was like I'd just woken him. "What on earth…"

"There are three possible reasons Montie Collins was killed, seems to me…"

The bowl of his pipe had cooled enough he slipped it in a hip pocket, then stood with slow effort, hands sliding in his pockets. My hazel gaze tracked him.

He looked around: "I'm listening."

"Possibility one: He was killed by you to protect Ginny from prosecution."

He huffed.

Shaking his head.

"I assure you, I didn't."

"Okay, two: Hobbs killed him, or had a Special Violent Action Group do it, for the sincere purpose of revenge. Unaware Collins was, in fact, innocent. Which would mean you didn't do what Ginny asked, and therefore you share responsibility for four murders. In fact, you might've not told, in hopes somebody would kill Collins, thus protecting Ginny. Third possibility…?"

"I'm fascinated. Go on."

"Hobbs and his minions killed the four in spite of knowing Collins was innocent."

A hand smoothed back the dyed black hair on his head.

Grasped the back of his neck. "Why would they do that?"

Genuine curiosity.

Perhaps, alarm?

"To advance the Klan's agenda…" I speculated, shrugging. "Damage the civil-rights movement by maintaining the public belief that J.B. Roberts was killed by a black man. And not just any black man, one who was practically a member of the family. Can't trust any of them, right?"

He massaged stubble on his face.

Paced slowly all around inside the church, eventually putting hands down the back pockets of his trousers, elbows bent behind. Completing his orbit, he stopped in front of me, looked straight down and asked softly but pleadingly:

"Cain't you just go home?"

"No."

"I don't wanna see nothin' happen to you. God's truth."

"I appreciate that."
"If you stay, I cain't promise nothin'."

CHAPTER 57

I WATCHED SMOKE COIL FROM my cigarette.
Looked up:
"Answer me one question. No Klan secrets, no names,
I'll swear on any Bible you bring me, I won't repeat your
answer." One skeptical nod. I stood, squaring my shoulders.
"Do you know who killed Montie and the others? Have personal
knowledge of anyone directly involved?"

"No."

"I think I believe you," I said.

I described my rattlesnake incident. "There were three. Two I
didn't recognize. One, I did, despite his robe, hood, and mask.
He was one of them who accosted me out back here, last week.
First name, Lee. Drives a beige Fury"—I shrugged—"late fifties
model. Tell me his name. Might as well. If I ask around,
somebody'll ID him."

"Lee Autrey," Cothran relented. "And he's a real rough-and-
tough sonovabitch. Just what I was talkin'bout. Please leave
town, ma'am. If you don't, I mean it, I cain't be responsible. So
far, believe it or not, you been gettin' real friendly warnings."

"Yeah…I guess…compared to what Montie Collins got,
they're friendly. Now my guess is, the man you told Ginny
Robert's secret to, is the same man who ordered those lovely
snakes for me. I just want to thank him personally. A girl gets so
weary of roses. Three snakes and three Kluxers for delivery men:

223

In the room, where I was in bed, sleeping!

"Who did you tell? I wanna *know*, and I wanna *know* goddamn now!"

"Sorry, truly, for any indignity—"

"*Indignity.* If you're the least bit sorry—"

"I cain't."

"Why so much loyalty, you of all people, to a group standing for hatred, bigotry—"

"The Klansman does not hate. The Klan stands for white Christian American values. For the sanctity of this country, a God-given gift to the white race."

"The Klan stands for the beating and shooting of a pregnant woman, far as I'm concerned, bombings and burnings of churches, people's homes, businesses. Children blown up in Birmingham."

"War is hell, Mrs. Russell, to quote a Yankee."

"What war?"

"A people fighting for their very existence, very way of life. I abhor violence. The Klan abhors violence." He paused, catching his breath. "Maybe I can explain—you got horses and cattle up'n Tennessee, right? Most farmers would kill you, you put a Jersey bull among their white-faced Herefords. They'd shoot you. But, I—"

"Don't compare human beings to cattle!"

He halted.

Sighed.

"Mrs. Russell, I'm going to reveal something I shouldn't. Because I respect you, respect women. Because the Klan respects women. Do you know what an EC is?"

"*Exalted Cyclops?*"

I half rolled my eyes. "Head of a local Klan chapter. Klaverns, you call them."

"A-plus, Mrs. Russell."

He stepped back toward the chancel.

Facing me alongside the altar he'd set up. Crisscrossed his arms: "I stand before you, His Excellency, the Exalted Cyclops of the Lavonia County Klavern of the Amalgamated Klans of America."

He was dead serious.

I managed not to laugh.

"I'm honored."

"I doubt that. I'm telling you so you'll accept the rest of what I'm about to say. After which I pray we never lay eyes upon each other again. I swear to God I don't know who murdered those people."

I nodded.

"If my Klavern had done it, I'd know, and I don't."

"All right."

I waited.

Swallowed.

"What I do know, is you, young lady, have been given every inch of slack you're gonna get. I am not threatening you. I wouldn' do that. I'm stating an inalienable fact. Go home. I cain't protect you. Go home to your husband. *And the Lord God said it is not good that the man should be alone.* Go home, Mrs. Russell. Forgodsakes go home!"

CHAPTER 58

Horace Cothran—retired steelworker, Baptist preacher, Ginny Roberts' one-time lover—ran the local Klan. Ginny Roberts had confessed to Cothran. Thus Ginny had unwittingly confessed to the Klan, confessed her guilt, and by inference Montie's innocence. Cothran had probably told someone else in the Klan, and that person, or others up the chain, failed to stop—or deliberately proceeded with in any case—the lynching of Montie Collins.

Who?

Why?

Who had Cothran told?

And who had given my motel and room number, first, to the obscene caller, then to Lee Autrey, and two others, who'd invaded my room, robed and hooded, carrying a sack tumbling with pit vipers?

Besides knowing my motel and room, the snake trio had somehow obtained a key. And while that was a frightening proposition all on its own, I was sure there were many ways for quasi-criminals to get keys. So, I shrugged, I wasn't sure the key really mattered. Who had passed my room number along? I didn't think I'd been tailed. And I'd told only three people in the entire world where I was staying—even in what town!

And two of them were in the clear.

Admittedly neither Fred nor my ex-fiancé Tom Miller were

totally happy with me just then, but I doubted either would arrange to have me cast half-naked into a room full of poisonous snakes!

That left the third:

Sheriff Bobby Ray Turbeville.

Who might be a Klan sheriff.

I'd told him on the street following Ginny Roberts' interrogation. Twelve-odd hours after the obscene middle-of-the-night phone call. Meaning *the* leak, or *another* leak, had sprung before I'd voluntarily told Turbeville. That didn't mean Turbeville couldn't have been involved with the snake night-ride, but if the same leak had led to both the phone call and the snakes (consistent with Occam's razor, taught me by a doctor back when I was a full-time nurse—meaning basically, the simplest explanation for anything is probably the correct one) the only time I could imagine *that* occurring was when I'd left my key on the console of my car in front of the Mayflower Café on Tuesday. Leading me back to Turbeville.

Or his deputy.

Turbeville or Loftin or both were Klan.

Possibly quadruple murders.

According to Walter Biggs the sheriff set the tone, whether or not the Klan could operate, in the county, as well as within his department. So, again based on Occam's razor, it was looking like Turbeville was my man.

The only vehicle besides mine outside the church was an early-fifties black Chevy 3100 pickup. Exercising my Holmesian skills, I deduced the old black Chevy likely belonged to Cothran. I got a screwdriver from my trunk, then pranced over and knelt back of it. My devious intent: to stab out a corner of one of Cothran's taillights. That spot of white gleaming through red would give me something easy to track at night. Trick I'd learned tailing wayward husbands all over Nashville at unspeakable hours. Vandalism, however, proved unnecessary with this particular vehicle, which had only had one taillight—driver's side, above the license plate—which should make things easy, I thought, as I rose, retreated furtively.

Returning to Tuscaloosa I used the dashboard lighter to get a Kent going, and began to think—or try to, exhausted as I was. Any progress in this thing was contingent upon me discovering who Cothran had told Ginny's secret to. Made sense to me it was either John Riley Hobbs or somebody else further up the Klan ladder than Cothran was. Now, whoever he'd told was either responsible for the massacre, or had told someone else, who was. Cothran had gone out on a limb to convince me the Lavonia Klavern had had nothing to do with the massacre. The massacre's ring leader, therefore, was somebody between Cothran and Imperial Wizard Hobbs, if not Hobbs himself, though I doubted imperial wizards did their own dirty work.

And no I wasn't being naïve:

Cothran might've lied.

About his being EC.

About his Klavern's complicity.

Cothran's story did, however, make a certain amount of sense. For example, if Montie and the others had been killed by some rabble of low-rent Klansmen from Lavonia, then the FBI likely would've cracked the case locally. Cothran's story was also consistent with what informants had told Walter Biggs. That the Lavonia Massacre had been carried out by an elite, exceptionally violent, exceptionally secretive cell—a Special Violent Action Group—and that such a group would only take orders from the highest of Klan officials.

Like a John Riley Hobbs.

Once I was well down in Tuscaloosa County, I put on my blinker, and swung a U-turn. Retraced my steps for a mile, then repeated the U, and continued southeast. No one was following. Why would they? Nobody knew I'd fled Jasper, moved my base of operations to Tuscaloosa, which was part of the reason I'd stayed registered in Jasper, why I was racking up bills at two motels.

Fred was going to be furious.

And with the heel of a fist suddenly I was hammering my steering wheel, then clamped my temples. Plowing a black-gloved hand up into my hairline. Hot tears sprang in my eyes and I spat angry sobs. Look at me!—doubling back, playing shell games with motels—yet I'd gotten blistering drunk, virtually thrown my door open for three Klansmen with a sack full of snakes! And if they could do what they did, they could've done more. Raped me. Stabbed me. Carried me off to some farm in the night to string a noose around my neck.

Stupid, stupid, stupid, Sherry.

I was a nurse forgodsakes. I knew life and death, knew conscientiousness, knew I was dealing with dangerous characters. I wasn't some amateur incompetent nincompoop, yet I'd acted like one and on top of everything lost my rings and Fred would never forgive me, and I wouldn't blame him.

Who had benefited from the Lavonia Massacre?

(1) The Klan.

Punishment, by especially heinous means, of the suspected murderer of a white man. And, if they knew before the fact the guilty party was Ginny Roberts, the murders facilitated concealment of that truth from the general public. Sowing amongst moderate whites a more-terrible fear, fomenting racial violence, and a more generalized anti-Negro sentiment. Seizing upon the Roberts murder to further hobble the civil-rights movement, which at that point was being seen as moving too fast by many—with all the busing, open-housing laws, lawless urban rioting.

(2) Ginny Roberts.

Freed from having her guilt revealed, or at least openly contemplated, during Montie's murder trial.

(3) Her children.

Same reason—except, as far as I knew, neither Dennis nor Sandra knew their mother killed their father.

(4) Horace Cothran.

Along with Ginny, he had benefited because the killings fostered her continued freedom, and the possibility the couple might at long last enjoy a future together. I took it as obvious that Ginny Roberts hadn't slaughtered four people. And for the time being I was trusting Cothran's claim he had no personal connection to the massacre. But just because he hadn't done it, did not mean he hadn't suggested it—perhaps unintentionally, perhaps not—to whomever he'd told Ginny's secret to.

A notion appealing to the twisted romantic in me.

Cothran had set into motion a hideous act that had nevertheless rescued the only woman he'd ever loved. And with her husband and any pesky murder charges gone, they would be free to marry. Erasing what Cothran saw to be *the* great mistake of his youth.

I needed to know who he'd gone to.

I'd laid my cards on the table.

I'd told him what I, and I alone knew. At least suspected. If he was, in the end, a loyal Klansman—and I doubted one got to be an Exalted Cyclops otherwise—surely he'd feel compelled to report our meeting. Likely to the same figure he'd reported Ginny's secret to.

I just needed to be at that meeting.

Simple.

Right?

CHAPTER 59

AFTER A DOUBLE CHEESEBURGER AT a Tuscaloosa McDonald's I found a phone booth and let my fingers do the walking. I found what I wanted in a shopping plaza on Fifteenth Street. I went in THE COIFFURE CLOSET: HAIR GOODS & SUPPLIES, emerging twenty minutes later swinging a candy-striped box, containing a Styrofoam head wearing a poufed dark-auburn wig, which cost me $72.28 including tax. I'd brought $200 of my own money to Alabama and had $87 and change left—plus, rolling up bills at two motels.

Back at the Tuscaloosa one, on Holiday Inn stationary, I typed a letter to *Walter Biggs, c/o The Birmingham News, 4th & 22nd, Birmingham, Ala.* It outlined all I knew and suspected about the Lavonia Massacre, and concluded, if anything should happen to me, he should use the information to expose the conspiracy and bring those responsible to justice. I sealed a carbon copy inside a second envelope addressed to Tom Miller at the *Nashville Banner.* I fished two five-cent stamps out of my wallet and drove out searching for one of those red-and-blue U.S. MAIL boxes.

Back in the room *The Edge of Night* was on as I brushed my teeth and changed. A private detective never knows what she'll get into—especially at night, when a lot of the "action" went down on my divorce cases. I'd need a flashlight—two, actually, a heavy-duty three-cell, plus a penlight—camera, film, binoculars, jackknife, simple tools, and proper attire. This was not a frilly job, one reason my mother had never cottoned to me doing it. Most surveillance involved sitting in a car or watching across a restaurant or bar. I'd had occasion, though, to scale fences, crouch in bushes, crawl in dirt. Be chased by an enraged German shepherd. Without expecting to need them, I'd just sort of automatically packed my trusty old stalking clothes, which I was now looking at myself wearing in the vanity mirror.

All black: knee-highs, long-sleeve turtleneck zipping up the back of the neck, knit pants with stirrups, rubber-soled, flat-heel, soft leather ankle-boots. I pinned and clipped my hair, then fitted my new wig over the blonde morass. Voilà, instant brunette. Add some big Foster Grants and, guaranteed, no one would ever recognize me.

I ran a Thermos full of water and ice. Checked that my revolver was loaded and flashlights worked. A small handbag held my gun, licenses, cash, fresh pack of Kents, a matchbook, and five extra .38 Special cartridges from a box of ammo in my suitcase. I took everything to the car, got a Coke and bag of Fritos, and thought about calling Fred but didn't think I should delay any longer. The Impala had a third of a tank of gas. I filled up then drove forty miles to Lavonia.

Horace Cothran's Chevy was, I breathed a sigh, still parked behind the church. I drove along Tenth, U-turned, and approached to within a hundred yards to begin my stakeout. I drank my soda, ate my chips. Staticky news on the radio: Navy jets pounding Haiphong, Romney dropping to last among GOP White House hopefuls—having mortally wounded his campaign saying he'd been "brainwashed" during his Vietnam visit. Jesus Christ, that meant the Republicans would run Tricky Dick again! If not him, that actor-turned-Goldwater-conservative running California. LBJ had to go, of course. I only prayed Bobby Kennedy or Gene McCarthy could somehow wrest the nomination from him. Top of everything—George freaking Wallace had enough support—even in the north!—to get on the ballot in every state. In local news: Destruction of three stills in two days in Tuscaloosa and Pickens Counties, seizure of a thousand gallons of mash. Nothing, though, about snake-wielding Klansmen...

Men arrived at the church.

One driving that beige Fury.

Lee Autrey.

By seven o'clock, sundown, I'd counted seven men, besides Pastor Cothran, those seven including two of the three others who'd harassed me with Autrey outside that very church, six evenings before. Might be some men's-only religious function, or meeting of the county bass-fishing club. I was pretty sure, though, I was witnessing a gathering of the Lavonia Klavern of the KKK.

No Turbeville.

Nor Loftin.

Some formidable pack of terrorists. Eight counting the EC, and the official meeting broke up after only forty minutes. Everybody still milling and carousing outside when I saw Cothran lock up and rush to the Chevy, wearing a blue windbreaker. I followed, tracking easily that single red taillight. We drove out of town south on Route 159. Soon deep in the country. The moon wasn't up and out there the mercury lamps, the cumulative lighting from homes and businesses, you get used to in town, were scarce. To keep that single crimson glow in sight I had to foot my accelerator past sixty, sometimes seventy. After two miles a white clapboard church flashed past, then nothing, the Impala's quad-headlights boring a safe white tunnel between walls of night and heavy timber. Their onrushing glare would show in Cothran's mirror, of course, but this was a state highway. One car, well back, shouldn't rouse suspicion. Nevertheless, I felt my heart.

I'd tailed men many times, all hours.

But on familiar turf. Blending was easy in Nashville, and were I caught, my prey weren't generally dangerous men—merely immoral, unfaithful ones. Once I'd had a wife beater draw a knife on me in a parking lot. No sooner had he done it, though, than he ran and I happily let him. It was after that I started to carry a gun in my purse.

Tonight, every roll of the odometer took me further from civilization—tracking a probable accomplice to a quadruple murder, to a meeting with, perhaps, the murders themselves. I had to take care not to blunder into anything. Follow Cothran to the middle of a cross-burning or something.

The red glow curled left, then a jog to the right. The spot vanished.

I pushed the V-8. Easing off as I steered. The taillight came back in view, a distant shaft of the pickup's headlights. The Chevy stayed in sight through the next wobble in the road. Slowing. I gave my brakes gentle pressure. A rise in terrain on my right. The pickup rounded a bend and I entered the same turn. We were three and a third miles south of the fork onto 159, by my odometer. Nothing was down this corner of Lavonia County, nothing, that is, worthy of notation on the George Wallace map. I came out of the hairpin leaning right. The ribbon of highway straightened.

No red spot.

I sped the Impala, saw the road sink and veer left. Probably sight Cothran once I was through that. I dropped, left leaning this time, wheeling hand over hand.

A long straightaway.

No lights!

Eyes darting.

Teeth gritting.

"Damn!" I screamed.

Slammed the brakes full on, slewed to the left, screaming Goodyears, and rubber smoke, and I twisted back. I was alone. All quiet. Just the grumble of my idling motor and squeak of my body in the vinyl seat. There'd been a glimpse of a signpost where the straightaway began.

A side road?

He'd turned off.

I maneuvered violently around and revved back to a barely paved county road going up into the trees. I took it, headlights fanning and jarring as I pulled the wheel. Craggy timber country. I stopped where there was a dirt spur to the right. The paved road angled left, continuing into the hills. I cranked down the window, but couldn't hear. I killed the motor.

Couldn't hear past the curtain of insect-and-frog noise.

What am I doing? I felt incompetent. Stay on the county road, I told myself, because it's paved, meaning it's safer, which was not a goddamn valid reason. However, in the absence of evidence to the contrary, the paved road would be Cothran's more likely route—right?—because bigger roads went more places. Besides, dust would be lingering—wouldn't it?—drifting through my light beams, swirled by the old truck taking the dirt road.

At last I overcame my paralysis of indecision—convinced I was using logic, not just playing it safe, or worse, following feminine intuition or some other such voodoo—and continued higher, even considered cutting my lights, groping along by parking lights. I didn't want to be caught. There'd be no explaining. I'd either blow the tail, or be in serious trouble, and probably both.

But the *very* last thing I needed was to bury my grillwork into a tree up here.

Hey, Fred, guess what? Lost two diamond rings *and* wrecked the car.

Miss me?

The road angled.

Long slope down a hollow, the forest narrowing, closing over in spots, forming cavern-like tunnels. Felt like a Grimm Fairy Tale, a black wood rife with wolves and witches and lady-PI-eating ogres. My knuckles were white on the steering; I began entertaining the notion of tucking tail, backtracking out of there. A dirt road declined on my left—I slowed—a hand-painted sign, shape of an arrow:

GRINER BROS. CAMP.

No dust.

Cothran must be well ahead by now, enough his dust might clear by the time I reached his turn off. I might have no hope of finding him out here, and wound some dark hairs of my wig round a finger, as I contemplated things. Logging roads, I decided, for hauling timber out, crews and equipment in. I went on, growingly pessimistic. Couple hundred yards further another uphill track, another sign. I didn't stop, nor slow, nor obsess over floating particles. I couldn't check each of these damn roads, and I couldn't lollygag. If Cothran was going to a Klan meeting, others would be too. What if a carload roared up on me? Klansmen were so conditioned to distrust, suspicion coming so easily, they wouldn't ignore my presence, even if it were plausible. And not a lot of blondes go gallivanting in the Alabama boondocks at night. Unless they're looking to be raped by a bear. I sped, still descending, another bend.

Tiny red glow.

I braked.

Hammered off my lights.

Silenced the V-8.

Hundred yards ahead, maybe less. Figure moving, vaguely I heard a door squeak, then slam gruffly like doors on rusty old pickups. The engine revved, headlights raked as the Chevy swung down a slope.

Slowly I started up and rolled crackingly, almost silently, to where I'd seen the black pickup disappear. Same general category of road as the others webbing through these hills, and a sign like the others, this one saying VENABLE CAMP. The woods were thick; straddling where the road plunged through were two heavy posts. A chain secured to each lay in the dirt across the road.

That's why Cothran had stopped—to unlock and drop the chains, granting access to the logging camp to whoever was meeting him.

I drove on and after a short distance a hollow dropped away steeply from the very edge of the asphalt. Then came a split in the road where the left fork followed the lip of the hollow, while the right climbed away and was marked by an official sign.

I flashed my brights.

CR6, it said, indicating the Belk community was three miles that direction. Belk, I recalled, to be seven or eight miles southwest of Lavonia. There was a third spur, another logging road, perpendicular to the county road opposite the hollow, a dozen yards back. I reversed, twisted my body, and gunned backwards up that road, parking nose down.

Ratcheting the emergency brake.

I got out, stiffened by three and a half hours of either staking out or tailing Horace Cothran. I touched my toes, bent sideways both ways, bent ninety degrees at the waist, arms stretched in front, then pulled up behind my back. Those ballet classes my mother made me take, the dreaded warm-ups Madame Stalin, as we girls called her, put us through. I locked the car, my handbag in the trunk. On foot I'd have to travel light: penlight, jackknife, revolver. I lifted my turtleneck, tucked the folding knife down between the cups of my white bra. Stretched the black top back down. Then I went to the edge of the woods and thumbed my pants down and squatted to urinate. Bottoms back up, I donned a pair of old black capeskins, grabbed my gun and penlight off the car, and set off. The penlight had a clip, which I secured in the small of my back.

Eight-thirty.

Bright three-quarter moon rising.

CHAPTER 60

I T WAS A FIVE-MINUTE jog back to Venable Camp Road. I dropped my hands to my knees, puffing, sweat running. Were I a complainer, though, I wouldn't be out in the pitch dark, playing Daniel Boone with a bunch of Ku Kluxers, would I? I saw a NO TRESPASSING sign, in the dirt, attached to one of the chains Cothran had let drop. Behind me, the terrain elevated to a high craggy tree line, sharp against the less solid darkness of the night sky.

I decided to cross to that side of the road and wait, crouched in a ditch full of thistles and burdocks and other things pricking and jabbing me through my clothes, at the base of the escarpment.

Almost immediately white spears fingered through the pinewoods. Sifting and picking in the night like antennae, then the escalating growl of a big car. Twin pairs of high beams slashed like a scythe over my head and laid bare everything. My wig snagged as I periscoped up and watched the car swerve in, and plunge down the logging road, tires crackling. No hesitation. Somebody knew these backest of back roads of Lavonia County—knew them like the back of his hand.

Like a sheriff might?

The car was a Crown Imperial judging by the unmistakable spare-tire bulge in the trunk. Not many Klansman, I ventured to guess, rode fancy wheels like that, which gave me hope I might have a big fish hooked. I crossed back over, gun tight in my fist, and dropped on one knee—red horizontal taillights bottoming out and throttling uphill, flickering off into the trees. There was a concrete-slab bridge at the bottom. I ran to it, spanning a creek babbling off into the hollow. I crossed over and began to climb, laboring, feeling my way in the thick dark.

Sheena, Queen of the Jungle.

All I needed were leopard skins.

And to perhaps cut down on my smoking.

After two hundred yards I saw floodlights filtering down out of the wilderness and a compound of some sort—the logging camp—took shape, broken up through the timber like a disassembled jigsaw puzzle. There were men's voices and I picked up whiffs of tobacco smoke, and where the road widened into a tire-gouged red-clay clearing, I shrank back, into the vines and underbrush. The land dropped away ahead on the left, sloping to the creek. To my right it rose, gentle to start, then becoming quite steep, reaching for a saw-toothed, tree-studded crest.

A single war-surplus Quonset hut and a couple of wood-frame sheds comprised the logging camp on the down-slope side of the clearing, while built into the hillside was a larger building of galvanized-tin construction. The big corrugated structure was the source of all the light that had led me there like a luna moth to flame. Spotlights burned at either end, and there was interior lighting, a pale brilliance seeping out seams and gaps in the metal siding, glowing under the eaves.

On careful inspection—for which I stalked haltingly nearer—all those leakages grew dimmer, to the point of disappearing, toward the end of the building I was nearest. Perhaps, I pondered, an interior wall separated the dark part of the big shed from the lit-up part at the far end. It was in the latter part that I assumed, for obvious reasons, the Klan was holding its meeting.

All of which meant, I might be able to spy on said meeting.

I'd set out merely to ID to whom, in the Klan, Cothran was reporting, but to actually hear what was said, seemed incredible, a wild stroke of luck, which I'd be foolish to squander ruminating further, so, I rushed in fits and starts, head low like in the infantry, till I'd reached a half-grass-and-red-dirt yard, lit by flood lamps blazing from the roof peak. Below, down the corrugated wall, was painted, barely readable through years of weathering:

J A VENABLE LUMBER.

The yard was strewn with heavy equipment in stages of disrepair and disassembly, grasses and weeds and vines grown over and around, in some cases masking the mechanical thing's original identity, in some cases sprouting completely up through the middle of the thing. I crept alongside a bulldozer missing an engine block. Like the rotting carcass of a triceratops on some Mesozoic plain. At the blade end, my black glove against mud-crusted caterpillar track, I lowered and listened. Voices inside, the meeting was underway, and I was missing it. I tramped the remaining few yards to the rust-streaked wall and flattened against it, lungs pumping. The flood lamps straight over my head, I was actually in relative shadow, inside the big circles of light they cast. I sidestepped to the corner, hugging the building, pinching through my turtleneck a bra strap.

Across the clearing, peering, I was close enough to one of the sheds to read:

KEEP OUT.

HI-EXPLOSIVE.

I craned further; at the far end, parked on uneven ground, were side by side the Crown Imperial and Cothran's Chevy 3100. Then a man, a guard, appeared in the light—I ducked back—light from no doubt an array of flood lamps at that end matching those above me. I didn't know the man, but he looked like Jackie Gleason, and wore a dark suit and necktie. I saw him sweep his jacket back to get a handkerchief to mop his brow, exposing a holstered pistol—a .45, I thought—on his belt; he also carried a small rifle.

I knew a little about guns.

For a blonde, in fact, I knew a lot about them, and this one was an M1 Carbine, a military weapon with a box magazine that could riddle my pert figure full of a great many .30-caliber holes, were I careless enough to make a target of it.

I kept watching and he soon placed the Carbine on the roof of the Crown Imperial and reached in for a pack of smokes. He lit one. Sweat was soaking my neck, leaking down from the headband of my wig. He took the gun then, and propped it against a fender. Then rested back, facing the trees, belching up smoke, like one of those Birmingham steel mills.

My end of the building was locked with a big chain and padlock. One half of the double door, however, was bent outward near the ground. Pried that way, probably, by juvenile delinquents plotting theft or vandalism. They must've been pint-sized though, because crawling through would be a tight squeeze even for me.

But I got an idea, and returned, crunching lightly, to the corner. Ralph Kramden firing up another smoke, seated on the hood of the Imperial, seemed not to be paying attention. So I craned further, squinting through dark, along the base of the side wall…

There…

Few yards along, above a crumbling foundation, a vaguely evident opening. Cut in the metal siding, I reasoned, to drain water when it flooded through from the hillside.

I spurted along the corrugated wall.

Dropped on my belly. Face to face with the hole. I transferred my gun to my left hand and reached behind my back for my penlight. I lay the gun against the foundation where I could find it again in the dark, and used that gloved hand to shield the light, which I clicked and ran quickly around the opening, then through it.

Strands of barbwire crisscrossed to prevent incursions such as mine. Others, though, had obligingly come this way before—more trailblazing delinquents?—and had snipped the wires, which had then been loosely bent back in place. If I got out of this alive I'd find some home for wayward boys and donate to it, or maybe spring them, meld them into my gang. Biting down, I quietly displaced the wires. Muffled voices broadcast out the opening, which was plenty dark, reassuring me I could—with luck—sneak inside, and do a little spying, and not get caught.

I groped for my gun, then reached it inside, tapping and scraping it to the left. Beside it went the penlight, then with a breathy, "Here goes nothing," I hoisted my bosom over the ragged, eroded lip of the foundation and softly grunted and sidewindered through. Like Alice down the rabbit hole.

CHAPTER 61

DARK.

         Oil- and iron-smelling.

         I rose, peering. Muffled men's voices came from the far end. I crouched to retrieve my gun. Penlight too, which I clipped away, there being sufficient light to navigate. My heart ran like a locomotive. It felt sick and heavy, and the only part of me I could make move was my thumb, nervously rubbing the back of my revolver, where a hammer would be if it hadn't been hammerless, which was what made it a good purse gun.

I found myself in a quite unfeminine maintenance shed where burly men repaired and rebuilt anything and everything needed to fell timber, and get it hauled to a sawmill. There was arguing from the direction of the light, reverberating unintelligibly off everything. Sections of tin siding up to the rafters partitioned off my area into what seemed to be a machine shop.

The front, where the Klansmen were, judging from how sounds carried, was a large garage space. Where I was there were workbenches, and a lathe, and a hub of some monstrous wheel atop one of the benches.

I prowled, making myself move, toward the column of light dividing the halves of the partition, my gun at hip level. Anvils stood about, lay sideways. Yes, anvils—don't think I'd ever seen one in my life, except on *Road Runner* cartoons. Chains hung like jungle vines, pulleys and hoists, a coarse deep grease, I ducked and edged past. Batteries stood on benches or had to be gingerly sidestepped. I could make out more what was being argued, threading my wig hair back.

Horace Cothran spewing his Foghorn Leghorn oratory.

The others spoke little, and still too low for me, but I was pretty sure there were two besides the eight-fingered pastor, who'd swallowed the bait I'd thrown like raw meat to a blue-tick coonhound. He was reporting, as intended, what I knew and postulated about the Lavonia Massacre. I slinked half on tiptoe. Steadied a hand lightly to metal, bending toward where the light shone through. About to risk peeking, one-eyed, past the metal edge, when—

"Dammit, Johnny, she knows!"

"Knows what?"

"You was at Roberts' funeral—"

I blinked.

"—talkin' to Miss Ginny."

The third man: "It does link you, Johnny, if only circumstantially."

I could narrow that voice down to two men—but that second man!

Johnny?

John Riley Hobbs?

Imperial Wizard.

And not just any Imperial Wizard: Grand Imperial Wizard of the Amalgamated Klans of America, publisher and editor of *The Flaming Cross*, warrior general to ten thousand Klansmen over five states.

America's bigot in chief.

Who'd ranted on the steps of the Lavonia courthouse days before the massacre that the only good "nigra" was a dead "nigra."

I looked upon the conclave of evil men.

One, Cothran, not so evil as the others, but nor could he be given a pass, facing them with a lot of cock and bluster. They were seated in metal chairs. The one I was sure was Hobbs had his back to me, a lean brooding man, Brylcreemed hair, an oily sheen in the gray light. He ground a cigarette under his shoe.

When he turned I saw sharp features in profile. I'd seen many a photo of Hobbs's smug face of dull intellect. Flattened at the sides as if by some birthing accident, tiny protruding ears. It was him. Sure as shootin', my mother would quip.

The third man was Chief Deputy Cecil Orval Loftin.

I shrank back.

Inhaled a lot of machinery-laden air.

Turbeville's deputy was Klan.

High enough in the Klan to have the Exalted Cyclops of the local Klavern bowing and scraping, alongside the Grand Imperial Wizard himself. Turbeville might be a lower-ranking Klansmen than his deputy. Could that happen? Maybe I'd ask Biggs. Or perhaps Turbeville himself was very high. "Back to your little church, Horace," Loftin was ranting disgustedly. "So damn cunt-struck, yew obviously ain't thinkin' straight."

"I'm thinkin' plenty damn straight, perhaps the first time in a long time. Is what she says right? I want answers. I got no problem killin' a nigger who's got it comin'. Eye for eye, tooth for tooth. Biblical. But murder? Four people? Some conniving scheme? Well, gen'lemen, that leaves a bitter damn taste in my mouth. What're we turnin' into, buncha damn Jews?"

Loftin flung his chair.

Clashing against the interior of the building.

I flinched.

"Shut your damn mouth you old bastard!"

"Or what?"

"Or I'll knock your damn brains out and bounce your eyeballs off every wall in here."

"Try it you poor-white-trash sonovabitch! Better men'n you've tried. Including your father, who I never liked, and he was a holy saint compared to you. I come here—a loyal Klansman—to help you people, warn you."

"Stop it, both you!"

John Riley Hobbs' chair squawking back.

Pocketing his hands he stalked, short and skeletal, limbs insectoid. He wore a houndstooth jacket, enormous diamond on the little finger of the hand he plowed his greased hair with. "Both you know how bound and determined I am to *stop* all this bickerin' amongst ourselves. Ol' Martin Luther Coon, gotta give that big gorilla credit for havin' the nigras under better control, better organized'n we have ourselves." He pivoted. "Well now's our last chance. Last hope. And so help me I ain't gonna have it blown by Klansman fightin' Klansman. Clear? You two cain't work together, I want it settled."

"Will be, Johnny," Loftin gruffed.

"Tonight," Hobbs added. "After I'm done. Now, this woman. Who's helping her? She's a misfit degenerate Com'unist."

"Who wouldn've got to first base," Cothran blasted, "if *he* hadn't said: set her up a meetin' with Ginny Roberts. Oughta kick your teeth in jus' for that, C.O."

"My error in judgment," Loftin said, apologizing to the Wizard, not to Cothran. "But now I agree with you, Johnny, she must be gettin' help. Jews maybe. Sounds like a damn good theory."

Misfit degenerate Communist?

Jews?

Jesus!

Cothran, exasperatedly: "What if she goes to the Feds?"

"Course she's going to go to the Feds," Hobbs hissed.

Plugged a cigarette in his mouth. Fired up a Zippo two-handed, clapped it shut, then waved the cigarette spastically. "And when she does she's going to implicate you, Preacher, and me, in four murders, but all she's got's a crazy theory—no proof."

"Ride it out?"

Cothran, with what sounded like relief.

"Any other time," Hobbs replied. "But I'm sorry, Preacher. We gotta nip this Betty problem in the bud. Now, 'fore she has any more chance to tell her tale to the Feds."

CHAPTER 62

"Kill her?" Cothran advancing. "This ain't no nigger."

"She's a married woman," Hobbs countered, "away from home, involved in immoral—"

"Ain't gonna have nothin' to do with killin' no woman, white or black. Wanna know the truth, Johnny, I'm glad I dunno who killed them four, 'cause I dunno for once if I'd be able to keep silent: Collins' wife, pregnant, that teacher, they shoulda never been touched! By God, that ain't what we're about."

"The ends, Preacher, justify the means."

"He that justifieth the wicked is an abomination to the Lord."

Loftin grasped his leather gun belt beneath his overhung belly. He wore civvies, out of uniform, but was armed with the six gun as usual, like his boss's. He looked eager to tear into Cothran, like a bulldog snapping tight his chain.

Hobbs was placing his hand wearing the pinkie ring on Cothran's shoulder. Shook it, genuinely, like men who respected, liked each other. "Shouldn't be telling you this, Preacher," he said, "but you're a good Klansman and deserve to know. There's a mission underway to save this nation from itself. It's the beginning of the end, the beginning of victory. I truly wish I could tell you more. It'll be soon, though, and it'll answer all questions. But things are...*delicate* right now. We can't afford this

Betty's meddling."

Who the hell was Betty?

Twice he'd said that name.

Loftin said: "We'll handle her, Johnny, don't you worry."

Hobbs craned.

"*I'll* handle her. Personally. Tonight."

Loftin deflated.

Low and angry, throwing Cothran a poisonous scowl.

"Whatever you say Johnny."

"Gotta mind to send the KBI up here, clean house."

"Johnny…"

"Relax—something else we can't afford now—but for damn sure, come next week, there's gonna be a house cleanin' in all the Klaverns, everywhere. Gonna be some squeamishness, I reckon, when we've done what we have to do. We'll know then who the real Klansmen are. Who we can count on—"

Darting a condemning look at Cothran.

Which Loftin registered.

Nodded at.

"—to save this great land of the white race."

"Amen, Johnny," Loftin said.

And with a hawkish, mirthless face that ran me cold, the Wizard darted his cigarette, and left spiderlike through a half double door sagging open. Loftin and Cothran, abruptly facing the opening, stiffening to military attention—

Thrusting out two straight-arm Nazi salutes.

CHAPTER 63

I WAS STILL WATCHING FROM the darker half of the building when Deputy Cecil Loftin drew and cocked that Colt Frontier revolver.

And shot Cothran.

The gunshot came through the sides and high roof of the tin shed, a blinding deafening concussion that knocked me on my knees and I was still bent up, arms wrapping my head, eyelids clamped—when the second shot boomed.

And the third.

And fourth.

All wracking down on me. Jolting me each time they came. And when they stopped my first thought was how cold-bloodedly deliberate, lazy, they had been. Not angry, not a rabidly pulled trigger flinging hot lead. Something particularly ruthless about that, cruel.

Cock, squeeze, fire...

Cock, squeeze, fire...

Still jangling my ears, my ribs shaking, when I lifted my head, staggered upright.

Loftin's big back was, that instant, plunging through the sagging-door exit, holstering the smoking six-shooter. It was after I'd heard him slam the door of the Crown Imperial, the ignition firing, that I dashed to where Horace Cothran lay, his hands fumbling at his body. Burnt gunpowder stung the air. I dropped beside him, placed my gun on oil-spotted concrete, and grasped my hand out of one glove. Two manicured fingertips stabbed the artery in his neck.

Thready pulse.

His gasping filled the shed.

Alive, but after four to the abdomen from a .45, at close range…

I swiveled.

No phone. Wouldn't matter, but seemed like I should try. There was a funny bulge in his powder-stippled blue windbreaker, seeming to bother him. I got the jacket unzipped. Laid it open—

Saw a glistening heap of intestine flop from beneath his gray-white T-shirt. An agonized cough spurt more bowel through the wound. I jerked away, willing the pressure up the back of my throat, to dissipate, back of my hand against my mouth. He squirmed, hugged onto the loops like dirty laundry. His eyelids flickered, face poured sweat, and only then seemed to perceive another human presence. He struggled at picking his head up, to see me. Like it was important to him. I slid higher alongside him, and cradled one gloved and one ungloved hand beneath his head, helping to lift it, smiling.

But he wasn't recognizing me. I thought for a second, and dragged my wig off.

He nodded.

Twitched his own smile.

Said fadingly:

"Feds… my dear… only chance… kill you… sorry…"

Fighting for breath.

"Who the hell is Betty?"

One of those instants I would regret in my life, that I hadn't said something more noble at that juncture. "You're Betty… kill you… Tell Ginny… I…"

He died.

Swallowing, I lowered his head.

It sagged to one side.

I clawed my gun up, and my wig, and staggered dizzily back, with a curl of lips:

And of the Cannibals that each other eat…

I was outside dead running, climbing in the cab of Cothran's black pickup. Squealing shut the door, keys in the ignition. Clutching the three-spoke wheel I started the cranky dinosaur. It growled out exhaust. Then, grunting I employed my rudimentary skills with a clutch and stick—which my father, bless him, had insisted I learn. I managed to grind the rattly beast, engine moaning, as if keening for its dead master, back to where I'd concealed my car up a logging road.

I floored the gold Impala.

A 385-horsepower scream of pain through the night.

First chance I'd call somebody about Cothran. For now a flaming something drove me in pursuit of Hobbs and Loftin. If I hadn't blown it already, lost them in the night, they were my next link to Montie's killers and—something else suddenly felt dreadfully important—to learning more about this cataclysmic event on for next week.

Plus, on top of everything, I'd overheard John Riley Hobbs vowing to arrange for my own death.

Betty's actually.

And, strangely enough, I was Betty.

Making arrangements, personally, tonight. Which suggested wherever the Crown Imperial was going might relate to my aforementioned death. It seemed, therefore, prudent to keep tabs. If I had them under surveillance—right?—I could see what they were up to and couldn't be taken by surprise. And when the time came—which I assumed I'd instinctively know—I would break it off and go to the FBI.

To whom I would report everything and be out of it.

Braking at the stop sign I hadn't seen another soul, much less three Klansmen in a Crown Imperial. I contemplated with a huntress's eyes the sign pointing left for Lavonia—7mi—and right for Tuscaloosa—46mi.

Hobbs hailed from Tuscaloosa and was the high-muckety-muck, so I peeled off to the south, spurring the speedometer above a hundred. Halfway to the county line I hit a straightaway and thought I had them. I gained enough to confirm the taillight array, then settled back. At US 82 in Pickens County we turned east—still looking like Tuscaloosa. They pulled off at a closed-for-the-night filling station in a town called Gordo. I sailed past—not too slow, not too fast—and ducked down a side street. I three-point-turned and rolled back to the corner, then sat while I pulled my wig back on and contemplated the situation. I didn't like it one iota, to tell the truth. Loftin knew my car. But I hadn't expected to run into Loftin, had I? He got out of the Imperial, made a routine-looking scan of the area, then put two calls through from a phone booth.

We were off again in under five minutes. It occurred to me he might've spotted me and phoned to arrange my reception committee. Well—that was why I had a .38 on the seat, wasn't it? About 9:45 we crossed into Tuscaloosa County, eventually turning down a road skirting the municipal airport. We passed a reeking, blazingly lit paper mill, and a brick yard, before being stopped by a strung-out train of empty freight cars.

I idled, feeling my heart's drumbeat.

Bumper-to-bumper with a carload of Kluxers wanting me dead.

As the train trundled agonizingly through the night—flatbeds, tankers, boxcars, on and on—my clothing soaking up Miss Dior-scented sweat by the bucket—I couldn't stop thinking of Viola Liuzzo:

White homemaker.

Klan-labeled nigger lover.

Sound familiar?

Shot dead behind the wheel of her car one night by Alabama Klansmen. I blew out through puffed cheeks, verging on U-turning the hell out of there.

But when we finally got going I stayed with it—something more to do with inertia, than any easing of my anxiety—the airport off to my right. Chain-link fencing, warehousing, illuminated sign saying DRUID CITY PIPE CO. Then thick woods, penetrated by small dark side roads, with small sad houses. The Imperial signaled, slowed, and trailed dust down one of them. I drove on. Hundred yards farther a dead-end barricade loomed. Beyond it impenetrable forest, the Black Warrior River back in there somewhere. I backed and steered my way, reversing course, half expecting to be boxed in by robed, hooded night riders, hoisting torches, swinging a noose.

The road, however, was dark and unobstructed.

I trolled back to the street sign where the Imperial had turned. I flashed my penlight:

D RUSSELL RD.

I chuckled over the irony, and gingerly turned in. Knowing it would be ridiculously easy to get trapped down a one-lane blue-collar goat path like this. Why not go to the FBI? Guess I was clinging to the hope I might somehow finger the perpetrators of the Lavonia Massacre if I stuck with this just a little longer. Plus I had a vested interest in learning how they planned to kill me.

I still had a heavy car and a gun.

Not invincible, but if I avoided stupidity and carelessness like last night, there was still a lot I could extricate myself from.

CHAPTER 64

RUSSELL ROAD WAS THICK with evergreens obscuring all moonlight. Dogs, the bane of sneaky detectives, barked as my tires softly crunched over the road surface to the end, less than a quarter mile, and I looped around and sat idling, in the still night. Seven dwellings, a mix of mobile homes and frame houses, yards strewn with junk, strung with clotheslines. The working white poor. Low-wage labor for area factories—cast-iron, tires, munitions, chemicals—spurred to easy racist paranoia by John Riley Hobbs, himself a former B.F. Goodrich worker.

Middle house on the left, the Imperial pulled onto the lawn, no mistaking it—not being a neighborhood flush with nice cars of recent vintage. *Money and luxuries most of them could never hope for,* Walter Biggs had waxed philosophic. Somewhat as poor blacks wanted the best for their ministers, Klanspeople wanted their leaders to make an impression, to lead the life they coveted for themselves.

I killed my engine. The dogs quieted. I lit a cigarette, watching the house. No sentry. I used binoculars. I checked my watch. Nearly ten-thirty. No exterior lights, a dreary board-and-batten saltbox. Three cars besides the Imperial, Loftin's unmarked Chrysler being one. There was a dark Buick Electra, and a lighter Comet. I was starved, achy deep in my joints. Spying on an important Klan hideout.

Debating.

Staying put, I was relatively safe, but my brain wasn't being overburdened with new information. I couldn't be sure they didn't have a detective-eating Doberman out back, but I'd not seen nor heard evidence of one. Which didn't mean the neighbor dogs wouldn't raise a ruckus. I finished my cigarette, and climbed out and eased the door shut. I carried my small flashlight, my gun, plus a pad and pen. I needed hard data for the FBI, to get them to take me at all seriously. When the dogs bellowed—I heard a chain snap tight—I ignored them. Didn't even flinch. Convincing them there really wasn't anything there. Mind over matter. And it sort of worked. No unceasing tirades, no teeth and claws dragging me to the ground. And no one opened up on me like I was the Viet Cong, despite me being dressed all in black.

Coming to the mailbox of the Klan house, I paused. Windows glowed, heavy curtains pulled. Shielding it, I clicked my light, and read the number. Then, head low, I crept to the bumper of the Imperial. Kneeling, I laid down my revolver, in weeds, patchy grass. Couple dogs alternated barking. I drew my leather-bound pad. Blinked my light, then jotted the Alabama license number. If that car was registered to Hobbs, or could otherwise be linked to him, it would be harder for anyone to dispute my identification of him as one of the parties Cothran had met with, fatally, at the logging camp.

Re-surveying, I tucked away the pad, and picked up, shook debris from the revolver, then moved off like Judy the Chimp. The Buick, dark green, had Mississippi plates. I copied that number, and for good measure copied the plate numbers of the Comet and Loftin's patrol cruiser. Loftin was a murderer—of Horace Cothran, at least—and Hobbs was an accomplice. That was something, even if we never got the massacre pinned on them. I was feeling my own heart throughout my body, and knew the best thing was to beat a hasty retreat, not get greedy. Except that ol' curiosity—which kills cats, and nosy private eyes—got hold of me. I withdrew, but as I went I shone my light in every car. Loftin's first: shotgun, billy club, military-style ammo canisters, boxes labeled .00 BUCKSHOT. Moved off to the Comet. Nothing too exotic there.

Next the Buick.

A heavy piston-engine job, a DC-3, or the like, roared overhead. Treetop level, shaking the neighborhood, its deafening growl in the night slowly fading. I cowered till the dogs stopped yelping.

Then I rose.

Black-gloved fingers on the sill of the Buick's front passenger door. I wanted to whistle aloud. Starting with toolboxes, maps, ball of twine, rolls of electrical tape—moving on to a gleaming black German-looking submachine gun, with spare high-capacity clips (the weapon indeed was German, I would later learn, called a *Schmeisser*). There was also a Walther semi-automatic, a pair of handcuffs, and hundreds of rounds of ammo. I was mesmerized, eventually crawling to the driver's side, exposing myself to the house, and made out the titles of two books inside the car:

Anatomy of Spying.

Gray Ghosts of the Confederacy.

I hit the dirt, face-first.

Car steering onto D Russell Road!

And, of course, this being freaking Grand Central Station, it pulled onto that lawn, by which point, I had snagged up my gun, and slithered, snug as a bug in a rug, beneath the Imperial. A single figure ran up to the house—

Hammered the door. "It's Lee, open up."

Lee Autrey?

He was let in through a screen door that rattle-banged. I clambered from under Hobbs' car, my black clothes stuck all over with dirt and debris, and scurried over and hunkered, peering, against the rear fender of the Buick—and sure enough there it was, swerved in—the beige two-tone Fury, all whitewalls and chrome, and big engine tinkling down.

Sonovabitch!

CHAPTER 65

I WAS IN MY CAR, a little smarter and a lot dirtier. I could do an ad for Tide—hey, ladies, filthy night of detective work? Launder with Tide! Hubby will never know you've been out of the house.

'Less you lose your wedding set.

The trio from the logging camp emerged just past eleven-thirty. Hobbs and his driver took the Imperial, Loftin his own car. I rubbed my face, and shook my head to bounce my brain awake. My body craved sleep in every muscle and joint and in every way. I stayed put. Electing not to follow Hobbs and Loftin. D Russell Road, the little saltbox house, seemed to be the epicenter of current interest. I could get the FBI and they would raid it, see what was going on, confiscate at least that German-looking machine gun. Except—I massaged my eyeballs in circles—I'd have to break contact to find a phone. Take me some time, perhaps hours, to convince anybody. Twice as long as a man. The house could be empty by then, and I would have frittered away the slim advantage I now enjoyed over a bunch of Klansmen plotting to kill me.

I stayed.

Watched.

Yawned. Blinked, then unhooked the back of my bra, sighing in relief, rubbing under both breasts. I was exhausted. Had to pack it in soon—I mean, these loons couldn't know where I was staying now, right? And my new motel, by coincidence, was only five miles away. Beckoning. Few hours shuteye, go right back to Klanbusting—all bright-eyed and bushytailed.

Except…Lee Autrey.

Getting pretty damned tired of him, that cocksure Kluxer Fred duked it out with, who last night broke and entered my boudoir—such as it was—and strong-armed me, half-dressed, into a roomful of live reptiles. That just about stuck Mr. Autrey at the bottom of my list of favorite people.

There were at least two others in the house:

Owner of the Buick with Mississippi plates—a mobile arsenal.

Owner of the uninteresting little Comet, who was probably some loyal Klansman offering up…

I startled awake after midnight.

Flurry of confusion.

Then curses.

I rolled up the window, the night having grown damp, penetrating. Scratching through my wig I wondered how long I could keep this up. Twelve-thirty, I decided, and I would go get some sleep and have a shower and a good breakfast and dress up real nice and go to the FBI.

Then home to Fred.

Chalk that one up to mice and men.

As in, best laid schemes, because at twelve-fifteen—fifteen minutes short of me packing it in—circumstances dictated otherwise. In fact, I was quite astounded, as I heaved erect behind the wheel, a two-car caravan driving away from the Klan house. Lee Autrey's Plymouth, and two people I didn't know in the green Buick. I set off in pursuit, rolling my shoulders to get the kinks out. My lights stayed dark till their red ones turned at the main highway.

Toward Tuscaloosa.

But within ten minutes all of us were suddenly speeding north on Route 69.

Away from the city.

I thrashed open my George Wallace map to get the "lay of the land" as my father said. The lay of the land was it was a long way to the next big town—

A good fifty miles!

Which I dreaded considering how tired I was, but more importantly, I had a queasy feeling I knew why we were going there.

To kill me.

Only, I wouldn't be there.

So I assumed everything would be okay. Right? And if I and my half tank of gas managed to stick this out I just might be rewarded with some very damning evidence for my report to the FBI.

As it turned out, everything would not be okay.

It would go ghastly wrong.

CHAPTER 66

RACING THE ELECTRA UP THROUGH west-central Alabama was a tall, thin, older man, wearing plaid with tightly rolled sleeves. He'd emerged seconds after Autrey with a cardboard box beneath one arm. This box had been placed inside the Buick's trunk, much attention paid to positioning, other items shifted to secure it, before the trunk was closed. Softly. After which the man hooked fingernails under the edge, double-checking the trunk was securely latched. Last out of the Klan house—flouncing lithely off the porch, twisting to toss a wave goodbye—had come the Buick's current front-seat passenger.

A woman.

It was her presence, I confess, which had astonished me. She was my age or younger, small and buxom. Tight high-cut shorts. Low-cut jersey top. Carrying a wicker handbag and a small wrapped package which she gave to the tall man. He placed it on the middle of the front seat between them.

A woman involved in a Ku Klux Klan operation...

Ironic, I of all people being so flabbergasted by that...

CHAPTER 67

RRIVING AT THE ADDRESS ON *the outskirts of Tuscaloosa,
Lee David Autrey was alarmed to find a girl, a hot little number
actually, partnered with the infamous James Chambers. To an
ordinary Klansman like Autrey, involving a woman in Klan violence was
unthinkable. The times they were indeed a' changin', and this was yet
another fiery summons. Not in all his years in the Klan had Autrey seen
anything like it—*

*Loftin had reached him at the VFW where he tended bar. He'd
debated calling in, but by the time he'd gotten his shift covered, any further
delay reporting would've led to suspicious questions, which Klansmen always
had set on a hair trigger. Autrey, an Air Force veteran, was confident he'd
taken the initiative correctly, based on what he'd known at the time. But
upon finding himself introduced to—by Imperial Wizard Hobbs himself—
and shaking hands with Jim Chambers, known to all Klandom, and all
southern law enforcement, as "Dynamite Jim," he silently cursed all that
had conspired to bring him to that inauspicious point in his life.*

*Chambers was a rangy, uneducated, former quarryman, who had split
off from Hobbs years ago, ran a splinter organization called the Locust
Fork Group. Specializing in racial bombings. He and Hobbs were
supposed to hate each other. Grasping at straws, Autrey protested the plan
as it was being laid out to him, as too dangerous for a broad to go.
Chambers, though, dismissed all objections, insisting Patty Thurston was
one of Sam Bacon's best.*

Bacon!

Imperial Wizard of the Mississippi-based White Knights.

Another ultraviolent splinter group. Another powerful archrival of John Riley Hobbs. Dynamite Jim was working for, or at least with Sam Bacon...

And Hobbs was involved...

Something was very wrong...

And Autrey had stepped in the middle of it.

Chambers launched his own objections—to taking along some sonovabitch he'd never met—that would be Autrey—and Hobbs interjected: "I'll be responsible for Lee. Dammit, we hafta work together, trust each other. Or we might as well give up, let our rights be negotiated away by Jewish priests, and bluegum black savages, and mongrelized money worshippers."

Autrey burst:

"Amen Johnny."

Autrey knew the target and location; Chambers and the girl didn't, so grudgingly Chambers relented. As for Hobbs and Loftin, they didn't trust Chambers, and wanted an AKA man, Autrey, riding herd. Not that Chambers might be a Fed, quite the opposite—he was a self-styled "guerrilla for God," who didn't need the high ordinary Klansmen got from all the bluff and bluster. Dynamite Jim, never wore a sheet, never went to a rally. Mixing, after all, might expose him to FBI infiltrators and informants. Chambers was a loose cannon. And Hobbs was about to loose him in the middle of Alabama.

With the plan nailed down and Hobbs and Loftin gone off, Chambers and Thurston kept to themselves, while Autrey and the homeowner, a quiet Klansman he knew only as Lew, watched TV, swilling Vodka. The girl, who had lovely brown eyes, in Autrey's wolfish estimation, busied herself cleaning and reloading a .25 Beretta, which went into her basket-weave purse. Along with a goddamn hand grenade! And he was supposed to contain things if they went all to hell!?

About 11:50 Autrey announced: "Guess I better take me a leak!" He swaggered to the back of the house. He had a revolver on his hip. He had a permit to carry it signed by the Lavonia sheriff, and sometime he patrolled with them. He bypassed the bathroom.

Continued to the bedroom and direct-dialed a woman named Barbara in Lavonia. She was a Klan wife and valuable asset going back years. She slept with Autrey on a regular basis, and was a wellspring of gossip. "Don't talk, listen," he half-whispered. "Use that special number. Tell'em the Jasper Holiday Inn—"

Footfalls stormed along the hallway.

"Sorry as hell, darling, cain't be helped, something's come—"

Jim Chambers tore through the door.

"Who you calling?"

Autrey turned, lowering the receiver.

Barbara would know what to do.

"A girl expectin' me after work. Just tellin' her I cain't make it."

Chambers seized the phone and listened, hearing an angry female blistering Autrey about breaking their date.

He hammered it down.

"I don't appreciate that worth a damn."

"Nobody makes phone calls after we gather."

"Who's goddamn rule is that?"

"Mine—I don't trust you one inch pretty boy."

"Fuck you. I don't take orders from you." Autrey long ago learned the only way to deal with Klansmen was to show you weren't afraid. "Maybe I'll just make another goddamn call."

Chambers drew his gun, back-stepping.

Jerking his wrist.

"Come way from that phone," he said, "or I'll blow your brains all over these-here walls." Behind Chambers, Patty Thurston—Autrey thinking those bare sexy legs and those big tits in that tight little top, and that aimed Beretta all combined to make just about the sexiest goddamn thing he'd ever seen in his life, a life that saw more sex than most. "Fine—but Hobbs'll damn-well hear about this."

"Not if I shoot you first."

"You and who the fuck else, ol' man?"

And he shouldered Chambers out of the way, and squeezed by Thurston—leering long and hard down the neck of her shirt, saying, "Pardon me ma'am."

CHAPTER 68

THE PLYMOUTH AND THE BUICK pulled off in a wooded area east of Jasper, and I drew to a stop along the highway, dousing my headlights, the tall man unlocking the Buick's trunk. He lifted the box out, placed it gingerly on the ground. The girl held a bright flashlight while he worked on the contents, like a surgeon operating. I caught myself striking a match to light a cigarette. Cursed, shaking it out, then jammed the Kent back in its pack. Cigarettes could be seen and smelled over quite a distance. I raised my binoculars back up, and watched the box be placed on the front seat this time, between the driver and the girl.

Twenty after one we were northbound on a dark Jasper street. Not twenty-four hours since I'd fled that same town, a Klan rattlesnake party having been thrown in my honor. Pretty sure I knew where we were going, I broke off my tail, and stair-stepped west and north, soon careening onto Bankhead Highway. I glided into a closed filling station, swung round the pumps, and jammed to a stop facing my old Holiday Inn.

West of the big, iconic, neon-lit sign, I had a view of the west side of the motel, along the ground floor of which was my old room. If I thought I could get a cop in time, I'd find a phone. Surely that submachine gun was illegal, even if driving around with a box in one's car wasn't.

But I didn't know if I could get anybody in time, and I didn't

263

want to miss being an eyewitnesses to my own attempted murder. Besides, knowing how heavily armed these Klansmen were, any hastily arranged police interference might trigger a bloodbath.

Better to sit tight, let the Klan discover I wasn't there, then drive off.

I wouldn't follow.

I was done.

I was in over my head and was a big enough girl to admit that. The FBI could trace down the Electra using the license number I'd recorded. And with that I glimpsed over at my leather-bound pad on the seat. I stuffed it, for safekeeping, in the glove compartment.

Two minutes later I was getting my bra refastened in back as the Plymouth and Buick came from the east. They steered slowly around the green-and-yellow motel sign, over the hump, and I watched both cars thread to the right, Upon reaching the back they hairpinned—I got the binoculars off the seat—headlights flashing as they started back my way. Parading before the rows of rooms, blue tubular balcony rails upstairs. The glasses had a sharp focus and my old breezeway was well lit. The Fury crossed before Room 117, Lee Autrey's muscle-bound arm stuck out his window, balling up a sheet of paper.

He dropped it.

Directly in front of 117, and drove on.

A signal.

I was chewing my lip.

The DO NOT DISBURB sign.

Still hung from my old doorknob.

The binoculars tore from my face.

I gave a horrified gasp.

Autrey wheeling back onto Bankhead, east toward town. I jerked the Electra back into view, the binoculars, jumping with the beat of my heart. It muttered past 117 and I entertained the vain hope it would follow Autrey on out. Instead it U-turned, nosed into a slot facing 117, in the outermost row of parking. The lot was under half full—Jasper, Alabama, thankfully, not the tourism Mecca of the western hemisphere. Most rooms stood dark, this late, vacant or not. A notable exception being the vacuum-cleaner salesman's. This side of 117. Milky luminescence seeped out the edges of his drapes, and his door was cracked, his familiar habit, as he commiserated with Jim Beam.

In lieu of Sherry Russell.

The driver of the Electra climbed out. My binoculars up, he got out a pistol, tucked it down his waistband. Next he took the cardboard box, scanned, and shut the car door. The young woman remained, looking out. The tall man, cradling the box, gripping the pistol, moved cautiously. I hadn't imagined they'd act without confirming I was actually in the room! That damn DO NOT DISTURB placard. It was making everybody—the Klan, Sonny Greene, the motel staff—all assume I was still inside, a happily registered guest, which is what I'd wanted twenty-four hours ago. I just hadn't imagined by now someone wouldn't have discovered my ruse.

I had to warn somebody, but the girl in the hot pants might spot me, and I had to assume she was armed. I sat vacillating like a lab rat in an electric-shock experiment, as the man placed the box directly under the window near the bed in which he thought I was sleeping. He knelt over it, pulling up cardboard flaps, then opened and thumbed a cigarette lighter.

Spewing.

Like Fourth-of-July sparklers.

A fuse?

A simple flame fuse...

Like in a Bugs Bunny cartoon.

Couldn't believe it.

He folded the flaps back, manhandling the last under the first. Then like an artist perfecting his work, he repositioned the box, dead-centering it beneath the window. My window, far as he knew, and with that I felt a sudden flush in the face, and nausea in the belly. White smoke seeped up as if alive, fuming up through cardboard crevices, and the man backed away, watching for a few seconds, then he hurried to the Buick. The girl swung his door open. He jumped behind the wheel.

And sped off.

I was crossing the highway, as if shot out a cannon, before their growl had faded from earshot and red taillights from view. I vaulted a drainage ditch and ran weaving through the lot, bounding to a halt twenty feet back from the box with smoke pouring out it. A Clorox logo. Beneath the diamond design it said 10 QUART BOTTLES, and ice shimmied along my spine. I sidestepped nervously. As if I'd encountered a lion on a romp through the Serengeti, and was trying to sneak away without rousing it. As if the slightest sound might set off the bomb. As if my being quiet might prevent its blowing.

Both propositions were, of course, equally absurd and since I ranked bomb disposal right up there with nuclear physics on my list of strong suits, I decided I would do nobody any good hovering there like a mother hen. That would just get me blown up like the Klan wanted. So I spun and ran hell-bent for the office. Maybe we could get a fire alarm pulled, people out, police called. Hardly seemed likely there'd be time for all that but I did have this Pollyannaish streak.

"What the *hail* is this?"

I stormed to a stop—horrorstruck. Lashed around. "No!" I screamed hard enough to shred my vocal cords. Sonny Greene the vacuum-cleaner man, tall and lanky, out of his room in a T-shirt and plaid slacks. Shambling up to the smoke-sputtering Klan package, staring straight down on it, dumbfounded. He rapped hard on 117's door. Thought I was still in there! He bent over and lifted the box.

Studied it, listened to it, shook it like a Christmas present.

"Sonny!"

I sprinted.

"Put that down! Run!"

He pivoted, glassy-eyed at me.

Cradling the fuming carton. To this day I question whether he thought was being heroic, or if he was merely imbecilic. But something primal gave me the presence of mind to stop running and dart sideways behind Greene's own Vista Cruiser station wagon. "Drop it! Run! Sonny run!"

He began to walk my way.

"It's a bomb!" was my next shout.

He never heard me.

I didn't hear myself.

Later I swore I could recall seeing Sonny Greene's arms separate at the shoulders from his torso as the yellow explosion consumed him and ripped open the night. The blast wave blew out the Oldsmobile's windows. Knocked me tumbling and somersaulting twenty feet. Tornadic forces stripped off my brunette wig and the air felt hot and thick in my concussed lungs, and for a time there were only deafening bells howling in my head. Then stinging bitter smoke, and a hard rain of glass, plaster, and wood splinters. Screams and cries began to emerge. Flames leapt skyward out of demolished cars, and from the motel, a hole gored out where 117 and the room above had been. If there was a window left in the county unshattered, you couldn't have proved it by me. Someone told me later I'd been lucky to have had my mouth open screaming at Sonny Greene the instant the bomb detonated, because that probably had saved my eardrums. Artillerymen in the Army opened their mouths along with covering their ears, when they pulled their lanyards.

One of Sonny Greene's arms was found across the backseat of a Dodge, blown through the rear windshield.

CHAPTER 69

LEE DAVID AUTREY DOUBLED BACK, *killing his lights. Returned to the motel in the wrong lane, and steered against the arrow marking the exit, figuring the giant sign with its big lit yellow star would mask his return from Patty Thurston's lovely brown watchful eyes. And once he'd pulled through where registering guests idled, he'd be well out of their line of sight.*

Autrey wondered if Chambers would go through with the plan. He had overheard him, in fact, dripping with perspiration, telling the girl—during that stop outside town to insert into the bomb the blasting cap and fuse they'd carried separately on the front seat—that he had half a mind to go off looking for a target of opportunity.

That he'd much prefer blowing up some niggers or Jews to some white woman.

Autrey decided, then and there, he wasn't going to try and stop Chambers, either by force or subterfuge, not single handed. Better to get the bomb left there, let the chips fall, he'd figured, than have it wandering about town, Chambers searching for something else to use it on. He supposed he could have just shot Chambers and the girl when he'd had the chance. Too late for that now, and anyway he sure didn't have permission for anything like that, not from anybody, Klan or otherwise.

He parked alongside the restaurant and crept up on a black U.S. Government Chevrolet grumbling at the northeast corner of the lot. Chambers and the girl were hotfooting it by then, proof positive the bomb had been planted: Chambers would be driving much more gingerly were the device still in the car. Autrey rapped on a rear window of the black Chevy—then dove in the backseat. "What the devil is going on?" barked FBI Special Agent Alan Legate.

"That Buick…"

"Yes?"

"Dynamite Jim."

"A bomb? You should've warned us."

"I tried! Any harder, I'd be dead."

Legate maneuvered out the exit and whipped back through the entrance, shortcutting around the neon sign, then accelerated, coolly professional, to northwest corner. "There it is!" Perry, the other dark-suited FBI man, leaning, pointing out Legate's window. "Box pouring smoke!"

"He cut the fuse to three minutes," Autrey reported.

"Look!"

Perry again.

A male guest walking, drunk it seemed, toward the box!

Then Autrey:

"Holy shit it's her!"

Clad all in black, dark-haired, not blonde, but Autrey was certain.

She'd spun, racing toward the drunk man screaming.

The dumb-ass picking up the box! Facing her with it as if presenting her a present—a love offering of nineteen sticks of dynamite, wrapped with electrical tape, a blasting cap wedged inside a primer charge at the center, and attached to that a burning fuse, cotton and jute fibers impregnated with black powder.

"C'mon!" Legate threw open his door—

The shock of the enormous explosion shook the FBI car on its springs.

Legate fell back inside, agape. "Holy mother," he said catatonically. Straightening eyeglasses, knocked askew. Lee Autrey watched Sherry Russell Nates blown violently backwards, and for horrified seconds, thought her head had been taken off, the woman decapitated. Then he saw her rolling, dazed, possibly hurt—but with blonde tresses, at least, fully attached.

A wig, he realized.

Legate still only managing curses, flying debris settling, flames licking up at the night. Scores in pajamas and bathrobes beginning to emerge, helping those staggering out of rooms closer to the detonation. Agent Marion Perry reaching tremoring for the radio under the dash.

CHAPTER 70

NINETY MINUTES SINCE ALAN LEGATE—*paid-informant Lee David Autrey's Boston College-educated FBI handler—took the emergency call from that concubine. Not much to go on but she'd insisted Lee would not have involved her if the situation weren't dire...*

Now this...

No way for Legate, pulling his gaunt face, smoothing Vitalis'ed hair, to have prevented this utter disaster. No excuse, though, would cut mustard with the Director, should the Bureau get egg on its face. Hoover would destroy everybody. Up to and including his golden-boy. "Who you calling?" Legate snapped at Perry, about to key the mike. "Don't think every yokel with a tin star in six counties isn't already burning rubber?"

Indeed the night was becoming alive with wailing sirens.

"Then an APB—"

"You want to explain why we're out here? Washington doesn't want you to, I assure you!"

For this was a COINTELPRO operation.

Internal Security Counterintelligence Program—the first version of which opened in 1956 to sow chaos and disruption within the American Communist party. Ironically one of its ongoing targets was Dr. Martin Luther King Jr., whom J. Edgar Hoover considered a debauched Communist. Then, 2 September 1964, Hoover dispatched a memo to seventeen Special Agents in Charge across the South launching the second

COINTELPRO.

To expose, disrupt, and neutralize the various Klans, their leadership, and adherents; to frustrate Klan efforts to consolidate and recruit; to exploit any and all organizational and personal conflicts in the leadership. The memo added: Under no circumstances was the program's existence to be acknowledged, and even "appropriate within-office security" was ordered. For you see, not a criminal investigation per se—COINTELPRO-White Hate Groups was a proactive, arguably illegal, campaign to destroy the Ku Klux Klan.

A staunch northeast liberal—people even said he talked like a Kennedy—Alan Legate had been Hoover's devoted acolyte in this anti-KKK effort. His devotion extending to the point of neither harboring nor expressing puzzlement over the running of this COINTELPRO at a time when the FBI was also actively monitoring and disrupting the very civil rights groups the Klan opposed.

Then again, even Legate acknowledged:

They were all working for a insane lunatic.

CHAPTER 71

MY SHIRT WAS MISSING MUCH of one sleeve, a bra strap flopping out, and my arm bled. I was hacking on smoke and burned TNT. A frail man in leather slippers and a plaid bathrobe helped me to sit upright on the ground. Repeating was I okay, was I okay. I'd about mustered in my ringing head a few coherent words—when he was shoved aside, rather gruffly, I thought, by a larger man. "I got her," he barked, gathering me, pulling me to my feet. "I'll get her to the ambulance."

Had ambulances arrived? my fleeting thought as he began scuffling me away from the flame-generated heat, a woman screaming, a baby crying. "Get you outta here," I heard him say from what sounded far off; I was watching our feet skitter across glass-and-debris-strewn pavement. Immense amount of glass. "Where's your car?"

Violent shaking.

"Where's your car?"

"Across…"

I coughed.

Throat raw.

"'Cross Bankhead."

"Keys in it?"

"Yes. Who…?"

Then the voice—

It registered, somewhere back in my half-concussed brain. The shoes!

Lace-up ankle boots which I'd last seen worn under a white robe by a man who'd just thrown me half-naked onto a toilet seat.

"You're Autrey," I gasped, and began a weak struggling. "Lee Autrey."

"At your service, ma'am." He clutched harder tugging me along in brutish fits and starts. Versus his superior strength and brawn I was impotent. "You're one of them," I managed.

A frustrated desperate half-scream. "Relax!" He held me tighter, a tightness of security though, not violence. "I know what you're thinking, honey, but right now trust me. You're among friends, and I've got to get you outta here." And what came through all of a sudden, was a voice not so much mean, or harsh, but a taking-the-reins voice. I twisted my buzzing head, up at the squarish, night-shadowed, flame-lit figure. A man, a complete man, sweeping me along. "You hurt bad anywhere? You need me to carry you?"

"No," I said and we were nearly across the four-lane when the first fire engine, splashing everything glowing red, was arriving, siren burring down—while all though it, out of the night, legions of deafening howls and shrills, descending like invaders from Mars. My gun was on the black-vinyl, red-light-swept seat when Autrey pulled open the Impala's passenger door. He got it and my binoculars, and deposited me in their place. I was robotic. He snatched my keys and locked the items in the trunk, then fell behind the wheel. "Off we go," he said musically, like we were going on a picnic.

A man was dead.

I was still half numb.

The annoyingly lecherous Sonny Green blown to small bits. I clawed my hair. Nasty flyspecks of him smattered in there, probably, I'd never get washed out. A man had died, utterly destroyed, a consequence of his infatuation, however unwanted, with me. Jesus God. Lee Autrey was tearing us off down the highway. Emergency vehicles of all variety, I looked back, lighting the night satanically, fires dancing ugly twists and lurches. The Klan had bombed again. People—one person anyway, I knew for sure—dead.

Innocent people.

I could have stopped it.

I faced front.

Stiff, blank.

Police car flashed by.

Doing ninety.

"Lord God," I said. "I could have stopped it."

"Huh?" Autrey said.

"Nothing," I said, unable to cry.

Like my tear ducts had been seared.

Maybe two miles west out of Jasper toward Lavonia I looked over at Autrey's profile, saddle-nose, wavy hair, in the low light from the dashboard, and asked:

"Where you taking me?"

He darted looks. "Relax, Mrs. Russell, or is it Nates?"

"Russell will do."

"Nobody's gonna hurt you, ma'am, my personal guarantee."

"What your personal guarantee is worth to me"—I cleared my throat—"is a subject for later discussion; I want to know where I'm being taken."

"To start, my apartment."

"Like hell," I said.

He tossed me a grin.

"No monkey business. You can freshen up there, then there's a man wanting to meet you."

"Who?"

"Don't reckon I can say."

I slowly nodded.

"Where'm I meeting Mystery Man?"

"Motel near Millport, halfway to the state line."

"No," I said.

"Sorry, ma'am, I got instructions."

"I don't give a rat's behind about your instructions. Mine are, take me to my motel in Tuscaloosa. I'll freshen up there, then we can talk about Mystery Man." Jaws bunching, Autrey twisted the wheel as we rushed through the night. My refusal seemed to be a problem. One he wasn't quite sure how to deal with. Which meant disobeying Mystery Man worried him. Mystery Man held some kind of power.

Who could put fear into a man like Lee Autrey?

Hobbs?

I shrugged.

Neither John Riley Hobbs, nor any other big-wheel Klansman, nor anybody acting on their orders, would care whether I cooperated or not. Club the nigger-lover over the head, toss her in the trunk. Problem solved.

If not the Klan, who?

"Take me," I said, "to goddamn Tuscaloosa."

"Relax, okay?"

He grinned out one side of his mouth. Relax, my Aunt Petunia. In Biloxi everybody and their cousin were driving me places I didn't want to go. Places not in my best interest to go. So I sat tight, feigning acquiescence, as Autrey flung us up Bankhead Highway surpassing eighty, even ninety. Every cop in the area, of course, was tied up with the Klan bombing of a major motel chain. No speeding tickets tonight. Jesus Christ, what must they've been thinking? What could make them so desperate? So frightened by little ol' Sherry Russell from Tennessee?

Autrey eased off, approaching the turn that hooked up with State 102 that came out north of Lavonia. When we'd slowed to what I estimated to be a sane speed—

For doing the insane—

I jumped out of the car.

CHAPTER 72

AUTREY YOWLED TO A STOP. Leaving the car idling, he doubled back.

When I'd leapt, I'd twisted to face the back of the car, tucking my head and limbs, and I'd hit pretty hard, and tumbled into prickly roadside grass that was at least more forgiving than the gravel shoulder. I came through with what would be a badly bruised hip, abrasions, knees ripped out of my pants, and the surviving sleeve of my turtleneck in tatters. My gloves saved my hands. All in all, compared to a Klan dynamite bomb, bailing out of a moving car was duck soup.

That side of the highway sloped steeply downhill. I was twenty feet below Autrey, low in some tall grass and weeds, when he reached where he thought I had to be. Twisting, lurching, when he didn't hear running feet, or find my bleeding body, he yelled:

"You win, okay? I'll take you to Tuscaloosa."

I made him toss my gun down before I scaled up to the road. "No stops," I said, winded, as he gave me a hand up the last little bit, under the strange light of the moon. "No detours. Do not pass Go, do not collect two hundred dollars."

He shook his head.

Grinning.

"You are one *crazy* broad."

"Don't *you* forget it."

CHAPTER 73

THE IMPALA GOT US TO Tuscaloosa on fumes. By 3:15 A.M. we were in my room at the Holiday Inn nobody knew about or had blown up. Autrey collect-called the Pine Crest Motel, person to person to a "Mr. Jones." Mr. Jones scorched up the line, Autrey launching gleefully into the tale of my leap from a speeding car along a US highway. The man—whose name was Jones as much as mine was Elizabeth Taylor—fell silent on the line, then said he'd join us within the hour. I locked myself in the bathroom with a change of clothes and my gun. Examining myself in the mirror, the full-flourishing of black-and-blue marks still to come, there was a repeating filmstrip in my head of Sonny Greene's arms flying from his body. After a shower I liberally applied Neosporin and Band Aids, did damage control on my hair, then presented myself with a bit of fuss and feathers, in a tight red turtleneck, and blue side-zippered slacks.

Low in the chair, dirty-white sock feet on my bedspread, the big Klansman leered me up and down. I smirked, cradled a hand on one hip, and waggled the other forefinger. "Eh, eh, eh… married woman. Remember?"

I needed to know, now, how much control I had.

My experience: A woman alone with a man (or men) held either all the cards.

Or zilch.

Seldom was there a middle ground.

Autrey began to theatrically massage his jawline.

"Hell yeah…I remember you're married."

"To a jealous man," I said, and came up, both my hands on my hips, glaring straight down on top of him. He wore a tan Poplin zip-front jacket and a navy mock-turtleneck that was skintight. His brownish eyes seemed to lick up me.

Then sighing, he dropped them.

"Cain't say I blame him."

"Fred? He's got no cause to be jealous."

"Ain't sure I see it that way. Or he would, but I'll keep in mind you said so." Leaning away, he lifted by the neck a six-and-a-half-ounce Coke. "Got this for you—if you promise not to tell Mr. Jealous."

I took the cold bottle, dripping. "Thanks." I lowered tiredly onto the end of my bed, folding a leg under. I swallowed some. Autrey had one too, and was smoking Winstons. My newspaper open on his lap. He was looking at me. "Your husband's a big guy."

"Yes."

"Knows a thing or two about boxing."

"Yep," I said. "Strong as an ox, too."

"Seems strange—him letting you do what you do."

I made a noise out my nose. I stood my Coke on the floor, reached and dragged my pocketbook across the bedspread. I got my Kents and matches out and lit one. I got the glass motel ashtray off the nightstand and put it beside me on the bed. I pursed my lips, blew gray smoke at the ceiling.

"No one *lets* me do anything," I said, finding myself suddenly unable to argue that subject. Sick about Sonny Greene getting blown to pieces over a silly crush. Over me. Sonny Greene who had a wife somewhere. Kids? I didn't know. I wondered if she was crying now. If there had been other women, other motels. I wondered if she knew. I wanted to tell her I was sorry, and I had done nothing. That *we* had done nothing. Why'd I feel so damn guilty? My head sagged, eyes clasped.

Then I shook off my grief, and swiped back my hair. I took a puff, flaring the tip bright orange, then ran the ash around the ashtray.

Looked up.

Fumed at Autrey: "You were at the house on D Russell Road."

As if I was Jack Webb on the rag.

CHAPTER 74

I WATCHED YOU LEAD THE bomb car. Spot my old my room for them. Proving you to be a full participant in a Klan bombing in which a man was killed. One at least!"

"That death was not planned."

"Killing *me* was."

"Yes," he said.

Glancing off.

Harsh drag off his smoke. "I'm sorry."

"*Sorry*... Say that like you forgot to mail me a birthday card."

"I didn't plan nothin'bout that. I got called 'cause I knew you, knew the town"—he shrugged—"layout of the motel."

"Because you helped two other Kluxers, the previous night, lock me in a damn bathroom with three rattlesnakes. When do you find time to sleep Mr. Autrey?"

His eyes dipped.

Sighing he folded the newspaper, laid it aside.

Looked up.

"Sorry about that too. Truly, I am."

"You're not forgiven."

"Both those times, I swear, I did my level best to protect you. I don't hurt women, Mrs. Russell. Ever."

"And we appreciate that," I said, "but try harder next time— if I'd been in that room tonight, I'd have been killed. Despite your noble efforts on womankind's behalf. As for the snakes..."

I took a breath. "Suppose I have you to thank, then, for being able to work my wrists free—thank you—but it was still pure luck I didn't get bit!"

"Look, you got every right to be mad—and, you're right, goddamn miracle you weren't killed by those snakes." He toasted me with his Coke. "I congratulate you, Mrs. Russell, you're a remarkable woman. But, if you was watching that house, you know I was last to arrive. I knew nothing before that point. My part in that bombing was just what I said, and I did try to stop it."

"Who else was there?"

"Don't reckon I oughta say."

"John Riley Hobbs was," I said. "Chief Deputy Loftin. What's he to the Klan, by the way?"

"State's Grand Kleagle."

"Let's see… Recruiting, right? Takes a cut from all initiation fees. Very lucrative."

"Dunno nothin'bout that."

"The two in the car, with the bomb? The girl?"

"Never saw her before. Patty Thurston. Out of state. Mississippi."

I glimpsed my cigarette. "How do you know if you never saw her before?"

"I got told, when I got to the house. Got told she was Sam Bacon's best."

"Bacon…"

I narrowed in the eyes. "Runs a Klan in Mississippi. Facing Federal charges."

"That's him."

"Who drove the Buick?"

"Jim Chambers. Dynamite Jim."

"He work for Bacon?"

"He's a…free agent. Partners with anybody, anywhere, long as they hate niggers."

"And needs one blown up. Or the odd pesky blonde."

I finished my cigarette.

Lit another. "You part of Hobbs inner circle?"

He glanced up. "Me? Naw."

"You were called *tonight*. You were involved *last night*. Who ordered the snake thing by the way? Horace Cothran? I know he's your Exalted Cyclops."

"Him and Loftin."

I nodded.

Unsurprised.

"They cooked it up. Cothran just wanted sort of a prank—you know, dropping a snake down a little girl's back. Scare you off. It was Loftin ordered us to go all the way—brung in the Birmingham people, who had no compunction whatsoever against killing you. It was a crazy scheme. And criticize me if you want, ma'am, but you are alive."

"My point being, Mr. Autrey, you seem unusually involved in local Klan mischief, leastwise when it comes to me. Tonight. Last night. Behind the church. Whose pet mastiff are you? If not Hobbs's."

I waited.

Smoked.

"Loftin's?" I said.

"You could say…"

"You're loyal to Loftin?"

He shrugged.

"What about Cothran? EC of your own Klavern?"

"Small potatoes. The Preacher's a mouthpiece. Brings in members, money. But he ain't big on skinnin' heads."

"Skinning heads?"

"Violence."

I nodded.

"He's dead."

Autrey's face snapped.

"Who's *dead*?"

"Horace Cothran," I said. "C.O. Loftin shot him, tonight, repeatedly, at point-blank range. I was there."

Focusing elsewhere, dull with ignorance and fatigue, Autrey muttered: "Don't surprise me none. Him and the Preacher hated each others' guts."

"So, you're Loftin's go-to strong-arm?"

"Suppose."

"And Loftin is inside Hobbs' inner circle, being a state official and all?"

"Yes."

"So you aren't very far outside?"

"I guess."

He tapped out a Winston and struck a Holiday Inn match to it. Puckering around the cigarette, he watched me like a blunt instrument, through whitish streamers of smoke about his florid face.

"Who's this Mr. Jones," I asked, "who's on his way?"

"Don't reckon I can say."

"Can't or won't."

"Okay—won't."

"You'd say if he was Hobbs, wouldn't you? Or someone in that inner circle? Coming to finish the job botched by Dynamite Jim and the Ku-Klux-Girl."

He huffed.

Amused.

"It ain't," he said.

I blew smoke.

Licked my lips.

"And I believe you because you're my…guardian angel? What do you think about the Montie Collins killings?"

A flash of disturbance.

He stiffened.

Shrugged. "He attacked a white man; he brung it on himself."

"He *attacked* a white man," I said. "He didn't kill one."

"We— That weren't known."

I pulled my lower lip from my teeth.

"Did you know Horace Cothran was in love with Ginny Roberts?"

"Naw."

"Ginny Roberts confessed to him—to Cothran, in the days between her husband's murder and Collins's—that she had in fact shot J.B. Roberts to death. That she wanted no acts of vengeance."

The heavy head rocked back.

"Yeah…?"

"I don't know who Cothran passed this information to," I continued, "but my hunch is it was the same pair he ran out and told, last night, after I let it be known, I knew more about the

Lavonia Massacre than was good for me."

"I don't..."

"I followed Cothran—after the Klavern meeting at the church—to a secret meeting with Deputy C.O. Loftin and Wizard John Riley Hobbs. Cothran was killed, and from there I trailed Loftin and Hobbs to D. Russell Road, where you appeared, and where my attempted murder by dynamite was planned, assembled, and put into immediate effect. My point being—I strongly suspect it was Loftin and Hobbs that Cothran went to with Ginny Roberts' confession. I submit that this information was ignored and suppressed by Loftin and Hobbs, who then ordered the deaths of Collins and three others, including a pregnant woman and a school teacher."

My gaze narrowed.

Focused onto Lee Autrey's hand tremoring.

As he took his cigarette from his mouth.

"Why would Loftin and Hobbs sanction a quadruple murder they knew couldn't be justified? Add to that, those murders were especially heinous, even for the Klan, a pregnant woman, a school teacher. Stripped, beaten, shot!"

I spurted to my feet.

Paced.

"Some kind of shock tactic. Some motive so big they couldn't afford to let the public outrage over the murder of J.B. Roberts—a rich white man allegedly at the hands of a Negro—go to waste." I faced him, folding my arms up under my bustline. "What would be such a motive?"

"I don't know!"

Agitated.

"Truly," he added.

A spastic little snit.

The territory into which I was about to venture could, I knew, goad a violent response out of a—to quote Pastor Cothran, of Lee Autrey—*a real rough-and-tough sonovabitch*. It was my sneaking suspicion, however, Lee Autrey would be on his best behavior given the impending arrival of Mr. Jones. I doubted he would, for instance, want to explain to Mr. Jones how I'd broken my jaw, or managed to get shot in the stomach. "If Loftin were planning a quadruple murder," I said, knotting my arms tighter, and padding near the foot of the bed. "Wouldn't he include his go-to strong-arm? A man I know he heavily depends upon to perform head-skinning tasks."

He ground out his Winston.

Then lay back his head.

"You accusing me?"

"Yes, I guess I am. I think you were there that night, down by that river."

Unblinkingly he stood.

Loomed tall over me. Seconds lapsed, us silently looking inside each other, then he rubbed the stubble on the side of his face, and massaged the meat at the back of his neck, then stalked away, uncomfortable in his skin. I felt—saw really—that I had struck a serious, very deep cord inside Mr. Lee Autrey. I decided to pluck it.

Demanding quietly:

"Who else was there?"

I thought for a moment he might use his fists, not on me, but the wall.

With splayed open hands though, he twisted with a jerk.

A constricted pink-faced howl asking:

"Whada you want me to *say*? If I was there—not sayin' I was—but how long you think I'd live if I start fingering the kind of people capable of what happened out there?"

He faced me squarely.

I picked up my gun. Taking no chances with a man I was almost sure *was* capable of what had happened out there. "You'd last, I imagine, about as long as you would if those same people found out about Mr. Jones."

"What?" he expelled.

"Special Agent Jones?"

There was a gush out of his throat. "What do you think you know?"

"I think you're one of those one-in-five Klansmen who's an FBI informant."

He dragged one arm up like the Mummy.

Pointing.

"Unfounded shit like that—true or not—could easily get me shot. The Klan is three-hundred-percent fucking paranoid about the Feds, so you better goddamn keep that yammer-mouth shut."

"Tell me what I wanna know."

"Not fucking likely," he said.

"Then I'll tell Mr. Jones I have reason to believe one of his private Kluxers is, in fact, one of the perpetrators of the Lavonia Massacre. I'll detail why I believe it, and if he's not the most flaming chauvinist in the country, he'll listen at least enough to start asking you some very uncomfortable questions, Mr. Autrey."

Till then, I'd felt pretty much in control. Like I had Lee Autrey wrapped around my little feminine pinkie.

Then he threw back, roaring out a great eruptive belly laugh.

And when he finally got it reined in, composure reestablished, he glowered at me sideways. My face, I'm sure, looked quite sourly back. I hated being left out of the joke—as women so often were.

"Special Agent Jones," he declared, "knows all the hell about it."

CHAPTER 75

THERE WAS A HARD KNOCK on my door at ten after four in the morning.

I opened up onto a tall, thin, fit man. He was crisp, clean, starched—and considering the hour, downright fastidious. Past him, along the exterior breezeway, waited a second man. Stockier, feet splayed, hands like catcher's mitts, loose in front of him, jacket unbuttoned.

I brought my harshest scowl back up into the sharp-featured face of the thinner man, as I drew the door wider, taking backward steps. He replied with this animatedly insincere grin, like some evil, demented clown—eyes fervent, and daggering down from above the crazed smile, through horn-rimmed spectacles. Mid-thirties, five-nine, give or take. Supremely confident, wearing a plain dark suit.

French-cuffed white shirt.

Thin plain tie.

"Mr. Jones?" I said, curl of tweezed brow.

"Mrs. Russell?"

He had a scholarly voice, like a northeast prep-school history teacher. Northeast, I say, because of a thick New England brogue, that was quite shocking, really, this far south. "Nates, actually. Russell is my maiden name, but I'll answer to either."

He drew a black leather badge case.

Unsnapping it open as he sidled inside, observantly.

"My name is Alan Legate, ma'am. I'm with the FBI."

Re-pocketing the Federal star, he gave the length and breath of me a fox-like once over, then took himself on a tour. I heard my shower curtain racked aside.

The second man removed his hat, entering, nodding with a round pink face. I closed and locked the door. Legate rejoined us. "This is Special Agent Perry."

Irritably I said, "How do you do."

Legate told me how impressive my bringing in Ginny Roberts was.

"You're to be congratulated."

"Impressive—for a woman?"

"No. Just impressive. But especially—"

"For a woman. Let's not beat around the bush, Special Agent Legate. This is your man? Your man inside the Klan."

I was gesturing at Autrey.

"The FBI's man," I blasted, "yet all the while he's been busy as a one-armed paperhanger trying to scare me off. I've been threatened with chains and baseball bats. A brutal fistfight with my husband. Rattlesnakes! Then! A bombing! That killed at least one man. And targeted me!"

"Mrs. Russell—"

"And you knew *everything?* All along."

"I didn't know about the bombing, ma'am," he explained, coldly analytical, "until little more than a minute before it detonated. My own ears are still ringing. Unfortunate we couldn't have prevented that. As for the rest"—he shrugged— "Mr. Autrey was under strict orders to do his utmost to protect you from serious harm."

"I was thrown half-naked in a roomful of rattlesnakes! Case you've forgotten—or maybe you don't know these things up north—rattlesnakes are quite capable of killing people!"

"Loftin's first idea, ma'am," Autrey said, sideways from the chair—a raised reluctant voice, as if he hadn't wanted to tell me—"was for you to be kidnapped, driven into some woods, where you'd have been stripped, flogged, then chained behind a pickup truck and dragged around a pasture. It was the Preacher and me who talked him into snakes."

"Well zip-a-dee-doo-dah. So lucky my government was

looking out for me. You sonsabitches."

Then to Legate: "Cothran your man too?"

"No."

"Preacher'd sooner shoot a Fed, as look at one," Autrey explained, "but he wouldn't cotton to hurtin' no white woman. He mighta killed Loftin sooner than go along with what he wanted to do to you."

"Speaking of that," I told Legate, "last night…"

"Yes?"

"I saw Loftin shoot Pastor Cothran to death, logging camp south of Lavonia."

"You're an eyewitness?"

"He died in my arms. I'll have to show you on a map."

He nodded.

"Shot him with what?" he asked very suddenly.

That detail seemed startlingly important to him.

"That Colt Peacemaker. I don't believe the bunch of you," I groaned.

"Mrs. Russell…"

It was Agent Perry.

Who cut himself off.

A warning glare from Legate.

"Mrs. Russell," Legate said, "the bureau apologies, I assure you, for any responsibility it shares regarding your difficulties. But I insist that you acknowledge you chose to involve yourself, a civilian, in these matters. And recognize that I could not risk compromising Mr. Autrey, or our operation, to completely protect you, from what you subjected yourself to. It was a calculated risk. I'm sure you unduhstand."

"What I understand," I said, "is you condone crimes your informants commit on the FBI's dole—"

"Of course we don't. Don't be ridiculous. But there is a greater good. Informants like Mr. Autrey would be of little value, were they not trusted by their fellow Klansman, if they were not made part of their illegal activities?"

"Some Klansmen," Autrey explained, "in years of membership, never witness any violence. They hand out pamphlets, go to rallies. Wives run bake sales."

"Bully for them," I said. "Others blow up churches with

children inside, synagogues—"

"You're correct," Legate said gravely. "The Klan comprises many factions, and it's that faction you describe that we must stop. At all cost."

I dropped my arms.

Swagged up, and jammed my index fingernail below the neat tight little knot of Legate's damn necktie. *"That's* what you're trying to do? *Stop* them?"

He lifted his glasses from the bridge of a blade-sharp nose.

Repositioned them.

"Of course."

"Funny way to go about it."

"Pardon?"

"The Lavonia Massacre."

Ice in my voice: "The FBI knows who tortured and murdered those people."

He huffed.

Smirked.

Shuffled.

"Him for one…" I pointed.

Legate's black eyes followed.

"Told her? Dumb, Mr. Autrey."

"Didn't tell her much…" Autrey looking away, head shaking. "Mostly she figured it out."

Legate regarded me.

Rocking on his heels.

"She wanted names, Alan. I didn't give her none."

"I want those names," I snarled. "From you, Legate."

"You have no standing to make demands, Mrs. Russell, with all due respect."

"With all due respect, Mr. Legate, the hell I don't."

Evil-clown grin.

"I want names, I want arrests." I breathed. "I want justice; I want the families to know our system works, for them, and us alike. And if I don't get those things, I'll go to the newspapers. Helluva story. It'll be the scandal of the century."

"They won't go to press on your word alone," he said, "and the Bureau will say it's poppycock. I'm warning you out of respect, ma'am."

He paced away.

Rotated.

"We'll quash the story, Mrs. Russell. And anybody who did print it would end up at the very top of Mr. Hoover's enemies list. And"—he shook his head—"nobody, not even presidents, want to be there."

"You have the power and the gall, I'm sure, to cause a lot of trouble," I said. "But I can cause trouble too. The men you're going to have to make squirm to kill *my* story, aren't just any editors and reporters. My father. My ex-fiancé. A retired Air Force Colonel, who was at the Sixteenth Street Baptist Church in Birmingham that Sunday. Witnessed those dead girls pulled from the rubble. Still carrying that horror inside him. You *so* sure you can silence everybody? Or'm I maybe somebody you need to deal with."

"What is it, Mrs. Russell, you think you know?"

The soft ivy-league voice scathingly harsh.

"The FBI made a show of pulling out of Lavonia County," I said, "having to all outward appearances failed to solve the Lavonia Massacre. When all along they had a paid informant, an eyewitness, a participant. The ignoble Mr. Lee David Autrey. Who called you the night of the killings from a payphone. The FBI's own pet Kluxer, who could have, any time since, fingered five white men who kidnapped and brutalized and murdered four blacks...two of them women...one pregnant!"

Legate's mouth became a thin pale line.

"You're wrong, Mrs. Russell."

I curled a brow.

"Am I?"

The exaggerated, V-shaped clown smile returned, the agent huffing, nodding to something inside himself. "Those FBI men pulled out under orders. Orders from the Director. They pulled out with no idea who those five killers were"—he stabbed his chin at his informant—"six, including Mr. Autrey. Their investigation did fail. The FBI, as an organization, does not, nor does the justice department, know who killed those Negroes. On the other hand..."

CHAPTER 76

Y OU KNOW," I SAID.

One hand pocketed, Legate paced loose-jointedly.

"I and Agent Perry. Handful of others here and in Washington. My SAC for example in Birmingham. Sorry, Special Agent in Charge. I tell you that so you don't think we're a pack of renegades. We are doing a job here."

"You're all FBI."

"The FBI is large, and complex, Mrs. Russell, many divisions, many varied responsibilities."

"Not unlike the Klan."

A huff, seeming to acknowledge the irony.

"General criminal investigation is only part of that. The men who pulled out of Lavonia were criminal investigators. But the FBI didn't leave. I'm here. Agent Perry is here."

"So? What are you, and your merry band?"

I twisted to Autrey.

Elaborate shrug: "Don't look at me, Fed's a Fed in my world."

I glowered back at Legate.

Eventually:

"Domestic intelligence."

"Intelligence?"

He took out a cigarette, fired it up with a Zippo.

Smoked it for a time.

"We deal in espionage," he said thoughtfully, "other subversive activities; we correlate information on internal security, develop counterintelligence to combat internal enemies. It's that which has brought us all together at this early hour."

"Counterintelligence?"

Couldn't believe I was saying it.

Like a Fleming or Le Carré novel.

"Yes, Mrs. Russell. Not the solving of a crime." He spread spiderlike fingers. "But the *interruption*, perhaps *destruction* of grave threats to domestic national security and stability."

I raked my hair, then parted my lips—

He interrupted: "So far I've told you little more than you could have learned looking up the Bureau in, say, *World Book*. However, I have a proposition…"

"For moi?"

He smiled.

"You might be able to help us. And, to be frank, I don't have time to find a better candidate. I won't lie—your life could be put in danger, but…" He sighed. "If you agree to give serious consideration to my proposal, I will seriously consider giving you what you want."

"Meaning…?"

"Names. The Klan killers of the Collinses, Wesley, the Malcolm woman."

I blinked. Swallowed, then approached, closer than Mr. Clean-Cut was copacetic with. What'd he think? I was going to swing my tassels at him? "Names are good. But—"

I stabbed Alan Legate with my forefinger. "What I really want are arrests and prosecutions."

"Surely you realize those are not entirely within my power to promise. Take the names, Mrs. Russell; I shouldn't be offering that, but I respect you, and I need you. Besides…"

He extricated himself.

I rotated, listening.

"Stick with me little longer and you'll unduhstand, I think, the wisdom of a tactical retreat on the Lavonia matter, in favor of more strategic concerns."

I was intrigued.

"I sort of figure," I told him after a time, "my life's been in danger most of the time I've spent in Alabama. So what's the difference?"

Tuscaloosa's Holiday Inn advertised meeting facilities for up to 150. Agent Legate threw some Federal weight and money around and, despite the predawn hour, secured us a conference room. There was a phone on a back wall, on which he placed a call after I'd told him where to find Horace Cothran's body. "I want those bullets recovered, on the Jetstar to Washington no later than ten A.M., clear!...Yes...I'll call Frazier myself...No, I'll take care of that. He'll know what to do. Just move it." He broke the connection, then got the kitchen to rustle us up some bacon, scrambled eggs, pastries, juice, coffee. A tall steel urn full of coffee. I was starting to feel my bruises.

Lee David Autrey and I sat side-by-side, facing Legate, pacing before a chalkboard. "Intelligence is, simply, information," Legate lectured like a professor. "Counterintelligence is any activity designed to keep the enemy from getting his intelligence against us. It's goal is also to deceive the enemy through deviousness, deception, and disinformation."

"Enemy?" I asked.

He faced me.

Tossed his chalk.

Caught it with a snatch.

"Most obvious example, Mrs. Russell, would be the Communist Party."

"We're not here about communists."

"No."

"The KKK?"

"Officially," he admitted, "since a short time after the murders of the civil-right workers in Neshoba County, Mississippi, in 1964, my division has been tasked with disrupting and neutralizing the Ku Klux Klan. To put it simply, cause it to rot and collapse from within. Every dirty trick: fake calls, letters, planted stories, harassing interviews, IRS audits. Using our network of informants—Mr. Autrey, for example—to report information, stir up dissension."

Narrowing eyes, I asked:

"Is this legal?"

He shrugged. "Ordered by Mr. Hoover himself."

"That's...not what I asked."

"Considering the compelling national interest, the despicable agenda of the Klan organizations, other hate groups—Alabama States Rights Party, American Nazi Party, Council for Statehood, National States Rights Party, White Youth Corps, there's a whole list—I think all intelligent, forward-thinking Americans would accept that the ends justify the means, don't you?"

Lest I show myself to be ignorant and backward thinking, I nodded. Adding a mental note to ask my father which article or amendment of the U.S. Constitution limited the scope of constitutional protections to only the intelligent and forward thinking. "Too bad," I said, swallowing coffee, tapping my cup onto its saucer, "this mighty counterintelligence apparatus couldn't stop a Holiday Inn from being bombed and a vacuum-cleaner man killed."

I know.

But seeing a man's arms blown off his body gives you a one-track mind.

Evil-clown grin.

Toss the chalk.

"If I could have prevented that, Mrs. Russell, I would have. But, given the unfortunate reality, I consider tonight, if not a victory, at least a step closer to the accomplishment of my mission. A point for us, minus a point for the Klan."

"A man died," I accused.

Sighed.

Miraculously—there had been no other deaths, or serious injuries. "Yes," Legate said. "An innocent man. A white man. And when other innocent white men across the nation, especially the South, hear Hugh Downs report the Ku Klux Klan blew up a Holiday Inn. Like the one they and their wives and kids slept nights on recent summer vacations. A bunch of them, I bet, will suddenly decide to stop tolerating Klan bigotry, begin to identify the Klan as the evil that it is, the evil that it does. I believe, tonight—without us making a single arrest—the Klan put one more nail into its own coffin. And I'm sorry if it disgusts you, Mrs. Russell, but I'm glad of it."

CHAPTER 77

SPECIAL AGENT LEGATE PRESENTED IN tabular and graphic form a spike in race-related violence beginning with five bomb blasts in Salisbury, North Carolina on July 1. Three weeks later, in Alabama, the Lavonia Massacre climaxed a spate of reprisal attacks following the J.B. Roberts killing. Subsequently, in Natchez, Mississippi, an NAACP officer was killed by a car bomb, and in Jackson, a real-estate office was blown up for selling homes to black families. That very week had seen attacks against the Jackson synagogue, of course, and a rabbi's house, and several black churches across Mississippi—all destroyed.

Now the Jasper Holiday Inn.

Scattered in and amongst these *major* incidents, the FBI had additionally recorded a number they were labeling as *minor*: the mayor's mailbox bombed in Macon, Georgia; a black-owned taxicab in Lake City, South Carolina; two bombings in Milwaukee; there had been shootings and beatings in Montgomery and Bessemer, in Alabama, New Bern in North Carolina, and Pine Bluff in Arkansas.

Particularly disturbing Legate was a reckless-driving stop by a night marshal outside Hattiesburg, Mississippi. Two Klansmen arrested. On the front seat of the stolen 1966 Chevelle, under a sweater, had lain a fully loaded World War II-vintage Thompson submachine gun—discovered to be from a 1958 National Guard

296

armory heist in Mobile, Alabama.

"So," I said, "the Klan may be in possession of other weapons from that heist."

"That is an ominous possibility, yes," Legate replied, after which the discussion came round to the Klan's cold-blooded murder of one of their own:

Horace Cothran.

It fit the bizarre recent pattern, especially since it was relatively inexplicable. Cothran was after all, an Exalted Cyclops, fiercely loyal to the cause, even if he and his Imperial Wizard did not see eye to eye on everything. No questions of, for example, financial corruption in the Lavonia Klavern, or of FBI infiltration—at least none Cothran knew about.

"I can tellya I ain't never seen nothin' like this madness," Lee Autrey said, shrugging, looking at me, then Legate, "all these fiery summons's, the Preacher killed…"

Legate approached the table's front edge. "They're sending a clear signal," he said, "that they're no longer limiting the violence to Negro homes and churches."

"The Jewish targets," I said.

"The anti-Semitism is a new dimension."

I swallowed some coffee.

"Could it be about this trial," I asked, "coming up in Meridian?"

He looked at the floor and back up.

"That trial is next month. I'd say you might be right except, we think we know the explanation, in general terms. What we lack are specifics…"

"I don't understand," I said.

Sweeping his jacket, pocketing both hands. "Mrs. Russell, the FBI has developed approximately two thousand informants, within fourteen different Klan organizations."

"I see."

"At least a quarter of those resources," he went on, "report that something big is set for next week: we've codenamed it, *The Big Event*."

"But you don't know what it is?"

"No."

I had an abrupt thought:

JAMES K. RONE

"At the logging camp Hobbs said—what was it?—there was a mission to save the nation from itself. Beginning of the end, he called it. Beginning of victory. Then he said—*after next week*—they would know who the real Klansmen were. Some Klansmen would be squeamish, about what had to be done. Like Cothran, no doubt, because it was right after that—I'm sure I saw this—he gave Loftin a *look*, a signal. Shortly after which, Loftin drew that big Colt of his—and shot Cothran."

Legate walked.

Shoes squeaking.

Looked back: "Didn't happen to say *what* was going to happen?"

"No. He made the point, in fact, that he couldn't reveal more."

"You think he knew?"

"Seemed like it," I said.

"We need to."

His tone grave.

"You're worried, I said, "it's something serious? More serious than everything else we've been discussing?"

"There's hardly a thing not serious these days, Mrs. Russell. We're at war. Multiple wars: a cold one with the Russians, a hot one in Vietnam. And we're about to have a real hot one on our doorsteps, if we're not careful."

"A race war," I said.

"If not started by the Klan," Legate added fiercely, "then by the Black Muslims, or the Black Panthers, or…"

His fingertips met in front of him, then he spread hands…

"You see our problem…"

"What is it you need me to do?"

CHAPTER 78

C HIEF DEPUTY CECIL ORVAL LOFTIN:
       Ringleader, not too shockingly, of what Alan Legate
       called *The Lavonia Six.*
Loftin was Klan born and raised—Autrey and Legate tag-teaming, relating me his history—his late father, dating back to the Depression, had been a brutal Frontier Colt-packing Lavonia County lawman, and moonshiner. *His* father and uncle—C.O.'s grandfather and great uncle—had co-founded the tiny, feisty, backwoods Lavonia Klavern of the Ku Klux Klan in 1915. The brothers having stood with fellow-Alabamian William J. Simmons, burning a cross atop Stone Mountain in full view of downtown Atlanta, Thanksgiving night that same year. Sometime around 1925, one Loftin brother murdered the other in a money dispute, and the survivor got fried in Alabama's electric chair, leaving the Klavern to limp along through the thirties and forties, a loose gathering of hate-mongering hillbillies, denizens of the deep woods and swamps, getting drunk and disorderly, occasionally shot or stabbed, or hatchet maimed.

In 1958, Bessemer steel-mill-worker, self-made Baptist preacher, Horace Cothran got his fingers crushed by that pig iron, and retired. He'd joined the powerful Bessemer Klan in 1954 and upon moving back home, grew, organized, and tamed—however slightly on all counts—the Lavonia Klavern.

As Exalted Cyclops, he embraced the strength-in-numbers wisdom of Ecclesiastes ("And if one prevail against him, two shall withstand him; and a threefold cord is not quickly broken") and delivered his small rabble of bigots into the fold of the Alabama Krusaders of the Ku Klux Klan.

Which merged in 1961 with the AKA.

John Riley Hobbs anointed Imperial Wizard by acclamation.

Cothran became a thorn in Hobbs' paw from the beginning, yet both men agreed with the general goal of uniting the disparate Klans. Cothran, however, championed moderation and morality, resulting in him being marginalized in favor of Hobbs' more violence-prone stance. Amongst Lavonians, it was Cecil Orval Loftin, scion of a Klavern founder, and natural adherent to Hobbs' views on calculated ultraviolence, who rose through the ranks, becoming Hobbs' right-hand man, and a state-level Klan official in his own right.

Loftin, with Hobbs' blessing, had engineered the Lavonia Massacre—machinating Montie Collins' delayed release from jail, till nightfall, and so forth...

The scene that flame-engulfed-Ford-lit July night, on the Spanish-moss-hung banks of the Sipsey River, had to have been nightmarish. Loftin had pulled on heavy pigskin gloves, personally standing before a sobbing Montie Collins, his face bloody and swollen, with one eye bulging, the Negro's arms wrenched behind a tree, bindings cutting into his wrists, while nearby his similarly restrained wife screamed, begging for their lives, for the life at least of their unborn child. Loftin punched Collins mercilessly, before drawing and cocking that Colt .45—inflicting several non-lethal wounds, before the coup de grâce. All the while, nearby, George Wesley was being castrated alive.

Horace Cothran, the man Autrey called the Preacher, had not been present—he had told me the truth—nor, to Autrey's knowledge, had he been involved on any level.

Lee David Autrey had been there.

And knowing that made me almost physically ill to be seated so close beside him. Autrey was a Lavonia Klavern Klokann—responsible for investigating prospective members, and conducting financial audits. He was also Loftin's childhood friend, and therefore trusted ally. Autrey had not personally pulled a trigger that night—so he claimed—nor struck more than a blow or two, and then only to protect his cover, and only against the NAACP man, as if that made it all right. He had managed to be the driver, in order to keep himself out of the thick of it, to the murder scene of Wesley's Ford, always under the watchful eye, he claimed, of other Klansmen. No opportunity to get word to his FBI handlers. At the riverbank he had busied himself mostly with torching the car.

So he claimed.

Legate gave me all six names.

After Loftin's and Autrey's, however, the remaining four meant absolutely nothing to me. I was disappointed.

What had I been expecting?

Naturally, they would not all hail from Lavonia—the limit of my Klan experience. These men, these monsters, were highly trusted, with proven records of violence, culled by John Riley Hobbs from all over his multi-state domain. Only one other entry on the list had I had any contact with:

Calvin Dixon Harwood.

He was the Klarogo, or inner security guard, of Palace 13, a notorious Birmingham Klavern. Autrey had ID'ed him only as "Big Bad John," but the FBI had determined his true name. He was a participant in my snake attack. The creep, I quickly surmised, who'd stolen my rings!

I made Legate promise to try to recover them as a final condition of my signing on as a semi-official operative in J. Edgar Hoover's dirty little war against the Ku Klux Klan.

CHAPTER 79

SHERIFF TURBEVILLE WAS NOT ON the list, which I only mention because it pleased me. I liked Turbeville; he seemed a gentleman—even if somewhat Neanderthaloid on matters of race and gender.

"You think for a blasted minute," Special Agent Legate fired back, when I commented about Turbeville, suddenly quite savage, "that shit-ass sheriff doesn't know his own deputy is one of the top Klansmen in this whole godforsaken state?"

I took a hard pull from a Kent.

Pink-stained filter.

I shrugged.

"Unlikely, I guess."

"His jail, that Collins was released, late, from. Where they all were last seen alive. Turbeville didn't have to be there anymore than Hobbs to be guilty, and I'm going nail that backwoods bastard"—might've been Bobby Kennedy ranting at me—"if it's the last thing I do on earth."

"You seem certain?"

"I am."

As for what little ol' me could do for Uncle Sam, there was to be a big Klan rally in Mississippi over the weekend.

"We suspect it's a cover," Legate explained, "that it's primarily a gathering to launch next week's Big Event."

"Are there other rallies? Other states?"

"No." Legate paced. "But representatives are attending this one, our intelligence has determined, from nearly every state with significant Klan membership. Plus every cheap motel in a forty-mile radius of Raleigh—nearest town to the rally—is booked solid. It's clearly more than a local affair."

"Is that unusual?"

"It is," Autrey offered. "Partic'larly since the White Knights are hosting and organizing."

Plowing hair back from my left brow, I squinted.

"Sam Bacon's group?"

I was terribly exhausted.

"The White Knights," Legate said, forebodingly theatrical, "of the Ku Klux Klan of Mississippi." My eyes cranked up, listening. "The most violent, secretive Klan spawned in the Deep South this century. And they don't generally cross-pollinate, so to speak, with other Klans."

"Even Hobbs?"

"Especially Hobbs."

He lifted his coffee by the handle, and tried to drink before realizing the cup was empty. He clicked it back on its saucer. "We want you to go to the rally, Mrs. Russell, as Mr. Autrey's companion. Wearing a wire."

"A wire," I burst.

"Yes."

"Some of these people know me, want me dead! Loftin, for sure."

"We believe you'll be safe from recognition, Mrs. Russell. With Sam Bacon running the show, all our intelligence assures us there's no way Hobbs or *any* of his top people would attend."

"Be like," Autrey said, "the Hatfields and the McCoys having a party together."

"More ways than one," I quipped grimly.

"Hobbs and Bacon have never appeared in public together," Legate added, "not in three years since the White Knights severed ties, very contentiously, with the AKA. There should not be anybody there who would recognize you."

"That Thurston woman," I said, darting between them. "With Dynamite Jim."

"Dynamite Jim never goes to rallies," Autrey said, shaking his head. "And he wouldn't partner with nobody that would."

"No, what I mean is—she was one of Bacon's people."

"That's what I was told," Autrey confirmed with a shrug.

I turned to Legate.

"Yet Hobbs, Loftin, and Autrey were there."

"Yes?"

"Cross-pollination?"

"Could be," he said, cocking his head. "But that's behind the scenes; a rally is a whole different ballgame. Any appearance of the two Klans together—so big a gathering—would constitute a major public policy shift between the two Klan factions, and we've not caught wind of any such shift."

I nodded.

Skeptical.

In fact, a big lump of skeptical was log-jammed in the middle of my chest.

Finally I asked, "Why me?"

"You're a woman. An attractive young woman. You can go places a man can't. Get close to people a man couldn't."

"And," Autrey joked, "you sure ain't no shrinking violet."

I shot him a look, then Legate.

"By *getting close*, you don't think—"

"I don't think a thing, Mrs. Russell—"

"What are you expecting?"

"Not expecting you to do a single solitary thing, Mrs. Russell, to get a man to talk to you you wouldn't on one of your own cases. I'd be foolish, after all, to ask a skilled operative to change her methods."

"What methods? I'm a nurse, by training. We talk and listen to people. And as far as *his* shrinking-violent jab—we, nurses, learn to deal with crises."

"Fair enough."

"Anyway—I've never done anything, remotely, like what you're talking about."

"Undercover work?"

"Yes."

"You're smart, you're cunning, you've got brass. That's all it takes. How many women could've eavesdropped on a secret

Klan rendezvous? How many would've even thought of trying? For that matter *how many men?* Then you witness a murder, tail an Imperial Wizard to one of his bomb factories, then the bomber to his target." He pointed a finger at me, shades of the *I Want You* recruiting poster. "Let's be frank—not one lady in a million, could or would have done what you have, just tonight!"

"You flatter me, Mr. Legate," I said, lifting my chin, "and I appreciate the vote of confidence, I really do. But, truthfully, I follow cheating husbands and boyfriends, when I'm not ironing my husband's shirts, or passing pills in a hospital. Surely you have real-life Mata Hari's at your beck and call?"

"Actually," he said.

Shuffling feet.

"We don't."

"Mean to tell me, in 1967—there isn't a single female FBI agent?"

"No. Fact, Mrs. Russell, Mr. Hoover considers the women's liberation movement to be a dangerous left-wing conspiracy. Perhaps," he goaded, "you might convince the Director otherwise."

CHAPTER 80

I TOLD LEGATE I HAD to talk to my husband first. Probably gave him emotional security to learn I wasn't after all some wild Amazonian creature. I was indeed tethered to a man. I checked my watch. Fred would be up before long. I should reach him anyway, before he heard the news bulletins—because as far as he knew, I was still staying at the Jasper Holiday Inn.

I phoned from my room with Agent Perry, outside in the pre-dawn mist, standing guard. On the walk over, I'd commented, angrily, that I thought Legate had some pretty bawdy notions of how I did my job. Like I had to be using my body—sex!—to accomplish what they used their brains for. Perry proffered a quite sincere-sounding apology for Legate's chauvinism—Perry's term—then told me he admired me for all I'd accomplished and for how I'd stood up to Legate.

I'd thanked him, and now was placing a station-to-station call to Murfreesboro.

Fred's day to get the feed mill open by seven. I was fingering the black coil of phone cord. We hadn't spoken since Tuesday night when we'd argued; it was Friday morning. Time flew when you were dodging snakes and watching men be shot and blown up.

My rusty-bearded giant picked up, grunted a hello.

"Fred!" Eager and happy. "It's Sherry."

306

"Sherry," he replied.

Thickly. "What's wrong?"

Heard him groan. Our bed creaking. "Nothing's wrong, darling. I'm fine and I'm sorry I haven't called. I've been busy." Salivating all over myself with contrite apology. I wasn't being a good wife, and he was a great husband, and it was killing me; I prayed he would understand.

"Uh huh."

I sighed. Okay, *uh huh* wasn't exactly hostile.

"I love you," I told him. "I've missed talking to you."

"Not my fault."

"I know. You're right."

"Coming home?"

"That's…what I'm calling about, but first—"

"First what?"

My head hung.

Temples clasped tight.

"I have to tell you."

"Tell me what?"

"Calm down Fred. There's been an incident."

"You hurt?"

"I'm fine. That's what I'm calling to tell you. Not to worry."

"About what?"

"There was an explosion, the motel—"

"Explosion. What're you goddamn talking about?"

How do you tell your husband, who thinks you should be home knitting doilies and incubating a fetus, the Ku Klux Klan has you marked for murder? They tried to blow you up in your sleep? Put it that way and I wouldn't be able to control him. I'd be forced to drop everything. Or he'd be down here interfering—dangerously for us all. "You'll hear about it, Fred. Just don't worry, okay. I wasn't there. I moved to a motel in Tuscaloosa."

Proof—right?—that I was competent, that I knew what I was doing.

"Moved?"

"Want to jot down," I said, "the room number and phone?"

"I want you home."

"I know."

"Today."

"Fred… That's the other reason I'm calling—"

"What?!" he screamed.

I jerked. "Fred calm down. Please. Hard enough without you yelling. I'm not yelling."

"What?" he repeated.

Less volume. Not sure any less raw emotion.

"I'm pretty sure I can be home Monday; I promise I'll—"

"Monday, aw hell, Sherry."

"Fred, listen a second. Please. The FBI is involved, and they've asked me to help."

"Stop being ridiculous. What'm I going to do with you, Sherry?"

"What do you mean, *what are you going to do with me?*"

"This craziness. I want you home."

"What are we talking about here?"

"You coming home."

"Fred?"

"Now. End of discussion."

"We talking about you missing me? I miss you too. We talking about you wanting me there to cook and clean? I want to be doing those things."

"Then dammit, woman, get in the car—"

"Or are we"—I shouted, knotting up—"talking about you not believing what I'm telling you?"

"Whada you want me to say Sherry?"

I leapt from the edge of my bed. "That you don't believe your wife is lying to you!"

Hand clapped to my blood-flushed forehead.

"I don't think you're lying; I do think you're a little deluded."

My hand closed into a fist. Mangled the hair on top of my head. My eyes shut, bottom bounced the mattress. "Fred, *think* what you're saying. You saying you think I'm…crazy, or something?"

My lower lip quivered.

"I dunno. This situation is crazy."

"Fred…"

"I dunno what to believe."

Horribly, he sounded rational. Not angry or raging. Seriously, with a lot of thought and concern, questioning my sanity. "I'm putting my foot down Sherry. Get home now, or I'll come get you and drag you back. Sorry it's come to this, but you leave me no choice. None whatsoever."

That was the last thing I remembered.

I hung up sometime after, how long I would never recall. I wept for a long time and wasn't sure for how long I did that. Special Agent Perry—who I guess was a figment of my psychotic mind—knocked softly, after awhile. I found myself on the floor, knees hugging my breasts. Head between my knees. I dragged my head erect. Sniffled. Wiped swollen eyes. I called to Perry through the door: I was sorry; I'd be right there.

"You okay?" he yelled kindly.

I washed my face, brushed my hair, and peed, and then I went and told Alan Legate I'd help.

I'd sure as goddamn help.

Not my only monumental decision in those predawn hours of Friday the twenty-second of September.

The last day of summer.

The Summer of Love.

The...record of the Federal Government...has not been encouraging. No President has really done very much for the American Negro, though the past two...have received much undeserved credit...

Many white people...perceive the justice of the Negro struggle for human dignity. Many of them joined our struggle and displayed heroism no less inspiring than that of black people. More than a few died by our side...

—Martin Luther King Jr.

CHAPTER 81

THE FEDS PAID MY VARIOUS motel tabs and we found a beauty salon open early and got me overhauled: cut and color, shampoo and set, manicure, anything and everything to make me alluring for my Klan-rally debut, plus we'd discussed the disguise value of a change in coiffure, just in case.

Case of…?

The unlikely event—Legate insisted upon its virtual impossibility—I ran into a Klansman who knew me by sight. Something was making me think, though, of chum tossed in the water amid circling sharks. Anyway, I was actually quite pleased to go back to short, and curly, and mousy brown—back to Sherry before she'd changed to please Fred.

We low-browed up my wardrobe at Woolworth's, after which, driving my own car, I followed Legate out of Tuscaloosa, through Pickens County, north into Lamar County. Forty-five minutes later, off a main road linking Lavonia, Alabama, and Columbus, Mississippi, we pulled in at the Pine Crest Motel. The dozen rooms had red doors, little front porches, green-and-white metal awnings. A sign neoned NO VACANCY. The FBI had taken over lock, stock, and barrel. I was given a room, not as nice as a Holiday Inn's, but courtesy of Uncle Sam, and ringed by tough, dark-suited G-men. One of these Hoover Boys brought me a three-decker chicken-salad sandwich and vanilla milk shake.

Legate also sent along a strutting clucking silver-haired doctor with an old-fashioned black-leather bag, who examined me, and proceeded, as I grimaced, to extract from my upper arm a shard of glass.

I was advised to sleep.

Which I did, easily, and deeply—making no effort to inform Fred where I was. I made a mental note, however, to warn Legate of Fred's threat to come down, try to drag me home. I supposed it was possible Fred might make enough racket in Lavonia or Jasper to jeopardize the undercover job.

I drove, I thought, a pretty hard bargain for my services.

Which, I'd made clear, were for the weekend, no longer.

After that, I had to go back, deal with Fred.

Anyway, besides the Lavonia Six names, and some effort put into recovering my stolen rings, I demanded payment of all my expenses for the entire case, amounting to $125.31, plus my going rate of $75 per day for the entire period. Alan Legate agreed, more than happy to spread taxpayers' money around like confetti.

The agent woke me knocking on my door at six o'clock, and told me he'd wait on the porch while I got really to go to supper. His U.S. Weather Bureau report, he added, called for an evening in the high-fifties. He was smoking when I came out wearing plaid wool slacks, and a bright copper-gold sweater. He stood, grinding out his cigarette. Asked if we could have a word inside. "Sure," I said, and he followed, closing the door. Not locking it. I sat on the bed with a leg folded under, offering Legate the green-vinyl armchair by the window. "Rather stand," he said. "You're absolutely sure, Mrs. Russell—considering the lighting, the distance, the fact you were in hiding, trying assiduously, I'm sure, to avoid detection—the man you saw shoot Horace Cothran was Deputy Loftin?"

"Yes. Absolutely."

He nodded.

Paced.

Twisting sharply back. "Because, you know"—he was kneading muscles behind his neck—"he and the sheriff *are* built very much alike."

I scowled.

"I've spent quite 'nough time with both men," I said, "I can certainly tell them apart. And I got a good long look, heard his voice. Cecil Loftin shot Horace Cothran four times. Period. What's this about?"

He dropped the spindly arm. Pocketed the hand that had been pulling his neck. "Mr. Autrey—as you know, ma'am—reported Deputy Loftin shot Montie Collins. He has also insisted, in a sworn deposition, and under polygraph, that Sheriff Turbeville was not there. At least, not to his knowledge."

"So?"

"I have to ask you to not discuss this…"

I gave an askance nod.

"Mr. Autrey's statement doesn't reconcile with the physical evidence."

"How so?"

"Naturally, we ran a sweep of ballistics tests in the wake of the so-called 'Lavonia Massacre.' Including two Colt Single Action Army Revolvers, superficially identical, except of course for the serial numbers."

"Those Frontier Six-Shooters," I said, "Loftin and Turbeville both carry."

"Correct, and they *are* virtually identical. Five-and-a-half-inch barrels, chambered for the .45 Colt cartridge. So-called 'First Generation' models, of which over 350,000 were manufactured between 1873 and 1940. There's only one tiny difference between the two weapons, other than serial numbers. Turbeville's is newer and incorporates a modification introduced, according to our experts, beginning in 1896. It has a spring-loaded catch rather than a cylinder-pin retaining screw." My nod was small and confused. "They tell me," he went on in that Bostonian brogue, "it's something no one, not even the owner, would likely notice, unless they were disassembling the weapon for a thorough cleaning. Then, of course, they couldn't help noticing."

My tongue crossed my lipsticked lower lip. "What did Autrey tell you that didn't match?"

"Same thing you did."

He approached, bumping his knee against the foot of bed.

Sighed. "Autrey said Turbeville wasn't the shooter, that he wasn't out there, or if he was, at any rate, he didn't shoot Montie Collins. Except—our ballistics people say the gun that fired the fatal shots into Montie Collins was, in fact, Turbeville's Single Action Army Colt."

"I see."

"And I got off the phone an hour ago with our Firearms Identification Unit in Washington. They've examined the projectiles extracted from Horace Cothran's body, and bullets and fragments found at the logging-camp crime scene. They were fired from the same gun that killed Montie Collins in July."

"Turbeville's Colt," I said.

"Yes."

"I know what I saw, Agent. Loftin cocked that gun. Pulled the trigger. Repeatedly. Whose gun it was…" I shrugged. "Obviously I can't say. But, sounds to me like Loftin pulled a switcheroo—frame Turbeville, throw suspicion off himself. If the guns are that identical, Turbeville might not've noticed."

Legate rocked his weight onto one leg. "Or perhaps they're working together. Conflicting eyewitness testimony and physical evidence. Confuse the jury, give them an easy excuse to acquit; they often aren't eager to convict Klansmen anyway."

"You're grasping at straws."

"Yes."

"If they were working together," I said, "why use either of their personal—easily recognized—weapons? Why point any fingers at the sheriff's department if you didn't have to?"

"There is another scenario: You, and Mr. Autrey, could be working together."

"You gotta be kidding."

I glowered.

"To frame Loftin," he said, "for Turbeville."

"You believe that, then arrest me, or pay me what I'm owed, and I'll be going, and you can figure out some other way to infiltrate this Klan super-rally of yours. As for me: I've gotten what I came for essentially. I've cleared Montie Collins; I know who killed him, and why. As for this rally, I've got better, safer things I could be doing up home, plus—"

"Relax," he said.

Raising a hand.

"Relax? The FBI just accused me of being an accomplice to murder, or was it two murders, or more?"

"Relax. I trust you."

I blinked.

"You confronted me. I appreciate that. You haven't, I gather, given Autrey the same courtesy?"

"I admit. I assumed he was lying—in spite of passing our polygraph—until this morning when you told me the same thing he did. That Loftin was stupid enough to commit cold-blooded murder with his own, as you say, highly recognizable firearm. I haven't confronted Autrey because I didn't know what it all meant, and until I did, or until I had to, didn't want to taint him as a reliable eye-witness to one of the crimes of the century. Besides...as I told you, my job, my assignment here, is not to pursue convictions."

"No, you're in the dirty-tricks department."

"Whatever you label it, my job is to, once and for all, destroy the Ku Klux Klan, and I'm dedicated to that, ma'am, I assure you."

He took me to a spaghetti joint in Columbus, Mississippi, a military town of 25,000. As I sipped Chianti from a little round glass with green and white and red rings, I asked: "Other than ballistics, any other evidence against Turbeville? That he was involved in murder, or that he's, at all, a Kluxer?"

Legate swallowed some of his wine, placed the glass carefully, and looked me at length in the eye. "No. Only circumstantial, and lukewarm at that. There is the assumption that Klan violence flourishes only where popular and/or police sentiment permits it immunity."

"It *hasn't* flourished in Lavonia County," I said, "not until J.B. Roberts' murder stirred up the cauldron." I tore some bread and buttered it. Crustier than I was used to, but it was supposed to be that way, I knew. Fred would've accused it of being stale, and would be making blusterous demands of the waiter for something fresher, meaning softer. "He hired a chief deputy," Legate asserted, passionately, across the table at me, "who we know to be a major Klan figure."

"Anybody ask why?"

"No…" he admitted.

"Wait a minute," I said, thinking hard, staring through the checkered tablecloth. Then I looked up: "Had Turbeville's revolver been cleaned, when received by your lab?"

"I believe so. I can check."

"That means…"

I dropped my bread onto its small plate, and carefully laced my fingers.

"For what it's worth, assuming you do believe me…"

"I do."

"Then my report, supports Autrey's report—and clears Turbeville—especially if we also assume Loftin and Turbeville weren't both involved, reasoning if they both were, then to use either of their own guns would be beyond stupid, right?"

"Right."

"How do we know," I asked, "which man went with which set of ballistics tests?"

He shook his head dismissively and quickly. "Each provided a record of the serial number of his sidearm, which was matched against the number stamped on the weapon. And, yes, it was confirmed the actual weapon stamped with that number was physically taken from the man it was supposed to belong to. The FBI does not make Mickey-Mouse mistakes like that, Mrs. Russell."

"I believe you," I said, smiling.

And thought… "The shooter, Loftin, would have, probably, cleaned and oiled the murder weapon after the massacre. Both as a natural thing for a gun owner to do, and to eliminate any outward signs the gun had been discharged, when it wasn't supposed to have been."

"That follows."

"When he cleaned it, he would've run into that spring-catch/cylinder-pin thing. That told him he had to re-exchange the guns quickly, before Turbeville disassembled the one in his holster, and discovered the switch."

"Yes, but he must have been planning a switch-back from the beginning," Legate said, shrugging. "We'd have to find the proven murder weapon in Turbeville's possession."

"Could take weeks for an investigation to get to that point—and as an official involved, he'd have a certain amount of control, or at least warning. Loftin had the luxury of time. He must've been pretty sure, to have pulled this slight of hand in the first place, those Colts were so superficially identical, even Turbeville wouldn't notice. But when he discovered the spring-catch, he had to get that gun back where it belonged—pronto."

"With you so far," he said with a nod. "What are you getting at?"

"For Deputy Loftin to have tried this gag *again*, anticipating the logging-camp meeting, the premeditated murder of Pastor Cothran, he must've been sure he had a reliable way to obtain Turbeville's gun, and get it switched back in a hurry. On the front end, couldn't have been more than a few hours notice of the meeting. And…"

Suddenly I beamed Legate a smile—a smug, almost-Miss-America-worthy smile. "I know," I announced, "how they were switched!"

I twisted my wine glass, and began telling of the day in the sheriff's office, the day I'd brought Ginny Roberts in to answer for her crimes. How Turbeville and I ate lunch, after which he excused himself. Hanging his gun belt on a peg outside the washroom. How Loftin had come in, and begun laughing hysterically, relating how Turbeville moved his bowels like clockwork. After morning coffee…

And right after lunch.

"All he'd have to do was walk in the sheriff's office, like he did that day, on some routine business, be waiting on Turbeville to come out. All perfectly natural—except, during the wait he could quickly and quietly exchange the gun on his hip for the one in the holster on the wall. Then switch back, next morning's post-coffee trip to the john."

Legate nodded.

"You could be right."

The waitress brought us bowls of spaghetti. I had meat sauce, Legate Marinara, which he declared decent, but paling in comparison to Boston's North End. I'd been to Boston once, I told him, as a teenager, my father having taken me along on an NCEW—National Conference of Editorial Writers—trip. "Even if Turbeville knew nothing about the murders"—Legate resumed, as the girl went to fetch me more Federally-paid-for wine—"doesn't prove he isn't Klan."

I grimaced. "What do you have against him?"

I was twirling my spaghetti with a fork and big spoon.

"I assume law-enforcement complicity in Klan violence until proven otherwise."

"You mean," I said, mouth stuffed full, "Southern law-enforcement complicity?"

"That's a given."

"Why? Klan doesn't only exist in the South. You cited two bombings in Milwaukee." I pointed my fork. "This is about bigotry, Mr. Legate, and I'm right alongside you trying to stamp that out, but you're a bigot too. A Yankee bigoted against white Southerners."

"Perhaps."

He ate some.

"But there's more, I admit, with Turbeville," he said. "You've been in his office, he show you that FBI Academy certificate?"

I nodded.

"There's your answer, Mrs. Russell."

"Anybody associating him-, or her-, self with the great big beautiful shiny bureau must be above suspicion, above reproach. On some higher ethereal plane?"

He was wiping sauce from his mouth.

Spread the napkin back on his lap. "Something like that."

"Not like I'm the next Saint Bernadette," I said.

"Someone, Mrs. Russell, must stand up for what is right."

"You just damn-well better do the same."

CHAPTER 82

AFTER SUPPER I HAD A session at the motel with Legate and some other FBI people briefing me on *The Man From UNCLE* wizardry they had lined up. We even staged a little fashion show, me trying on my dime-store outfits—laundered repeatedly during the afternoon to wash their newness out—while concealing a white box, taped to my skin inside my bra, a quarter-inch thick, size of a commemorative postage stamp. It was called—I'm absolutely serious—a Micro 007, a totally self-contained transmitter powered by a hearing-aid battery. Its range, unfortunately, wasn't much over two hundred feet.

Insurance in case I got separated from my purse, which would carry Micro 007's big brother, a Clifton Mark VI Pocket Transmitter, inside a king-size cigarette pack. They asked me my brand, and said they'd have a pack of Kents prepared by the next afternoon. The range of the larger unit was a whopping quarter mile.

The Pine Crest Motel backed up to the Luxapallila Creek whose bordering swampland of moss-strewn cypresses rose and undulated close behind the secret FBI compound. Legate walked me to my room, the night teeming with sounds out of the swamp, punctuated by horrific prehistoric scrawks from, I presumed, a great blue heron. At my door, Legate said goodnight, and handed me a thick yellow envelope. My cover, he explained, false ID, biographical information. Study it, learn it—like my life depended on it—and, oh, purge everything from my own wallet and purse showing my real name, including initials.

Then he asked for my gun.

I refused.

He didn't think the Director would approve arming a female operative, adding they'd barely gotten approval for using me at all—and only then because ol' J. Edgar had been persuaded as to the urgency surrounding the Klan-rally operation, justifying drastic measures.

That was me, all right...

Miss Drastic Measures.

I assured him I would never in a million years go to Mississippi or anywhere else with Lee David Autrey—FBI informant or not—without my gun. He relented, but under no circumstances could I take it to the rally. Autrey would go armed because guns were part of the Klansman's world, plentiful at such gatherings. As for me—I'd have limited time to gain trust and Legate wanted nothing, like a gun, interfering with me being accepted as a harmless, pleasant-to-look-at-and-have-around, likeminded camp follower. I saw his point, and raised the envelope, between thumb and forefinger:

"So who am I?"

"Sue Williams," the agent said. "You're a Birmingham schoolteacher. You met Autrey six months ago through your brother. You hate the idea of"—he put on a fake hillbilly accent—"these coloreds goin' to the same schools as our little children."

I gave a flat smile.

"Got it," I said.

Saluting.

I listened to the Bell Telephone Orchestra on TV while dumping out my pocketbook onto the bed. I left a snapshot of Fred in my wallet, figuring he could be my brother. The one who'd introduced me to Autrey, after beating the snot out of him. I chuckled to myself. In the packet Legate had prepared was an Alabama driver's license showing a Birmingham apartment address. I memorized that. There was a membership card for the Ladies' Auxiliary of the Americans for the Preservation of the White Race. I wasn't yet supposed to be a Klanswoman. I was thinking about joining. That way they couldn't trip me up on any secret codes, or handshakes, or anything. Just had to bone up on my racist rhetoric, and I'd have the guys in the white robes eating out of my hand.

CHAPTER 83

LEE DAVID AUTREY PICKED ME up Saturday, ten o'clock sharp, driving the grumbling two-tone chrome-bedecked '58 Fury. I wore a light sweater, brown tank top, and beige Jamaica shorts with tiny brown flowers. Autrey complemented how tight-fitting they were on me, and I scolded him to get no ideas about anything. Folded neatly, pressed and pleated, across the backseat was Autrey's white Klan robe and pointed hat. None of my electronics went with us. Legate, Perry, and an FBI team from Jackson would meet us later to get me wired up for the nighttime rally.

The car was a war wagon. A member of his Klavern's security detail, Autrey was expected to travel well armed. Besides my revolver, and the one riding his hip, the Fury hauled a gas mask, tear gas canisters, chains, two extra handguns, a sawed-off shotgun, and what the Klan called a head-knocker: a child's twelve-inch baseball bat with the large end bored out, filled with molten lead, and sealed over with putty. Sanded and re-varnished the thing looked ordinary—yet those extra ounces transformed a toy into a weapon far deadlier than any ordinary police billy stick.

Forest was an aptly named town of four thousand 50 miles east of Jackson, nearly midway between the state capitol and Meridian, where in a few weeks Sam Bacon—John Riley Hobbs' chief rival—would face a Federal jury in a celebrated murder case. We checked into the Bon-Air Motel south of town. Legate had finagled us a reservation for one double room, Autrey registering us as husband and wife. I wasn't happy and—let me make this perfectly clear—Fred must never, ever know. However, if the weekend went as planned, we wouldn't be spending that much time in the room anyway. We got moved in, then I stood by while Autrey phoned a special number at the Jackson Field Office. We got instructions to meet a Klansman named Jesse Vance at the local VFW. One of Autrey's counterparts in the White Knights. We were supposed to put on a show.

Be noticed.

Autrey went in the bathroom to change and when he emerged I gasped, cupping my mouth.

Kind of a military uniform:

--White shirt, red silk lanyard, Confederate-flag shoulder patch.

--Italian tank corps helmet with ear flaps and yet another Confederate-flag emblem on one side, on the other a red SG (for *security guard*).

--White GI-type belt with a brass buckle.

--White pants

--Paratrooper jump boots, black with white leather laces.

I snorted a laugh.

Stifled it. He was taking all of this quite seriously, after all, and I knew I'd better, insane as it all seemed. On his left he carried a first-aid pouch and a whistle, on his right a Carbine clip and the head-knocker. He tucked a Colt .22 automatic in his left rear pocket, that in addition to the holstered .38, and a Bowie knife in a scabbard tucked down his right boot.

Well...

We *had* been told to be noticed...

I told him I wanted something to eat before we left, and I assumed in that get up he'd wait in the room, but he went along, much to my astonished embarrassment. Turned out, others in the restaurant were sporting similarly bizarre paramilitary garb, they and Autrey exchanging grave nods. I got some looks too, having shed the sweater. I wasn't really a tank-top-and-tight-shorts kind of girl.

I was, however, undercover.

We got to the VFW about 2:15, Jesse Vance at the bar swigging Vodka. He was a huge creature and he and Autrey greeted one other like best old army buddies, though my knowledge, they'd never actually met. Vance's job was to vouch for us with the local bigwigs. He was drunk, and reeking of it, which meant I was already taking a dim view of this whole operation.

Autrey introduced me as his girl, Sue. "Sue Williams," I said, trying to sound bewitching, as Vance began to ogle me. One of those guys whose eyes don't focus the same angle, so you never know which one to talk to. He was at least six-foot-five, and if not three hundred pounds, he was getting there. He wore black from head to foot, steel-toed cowboy boots, and a mangy gunmetal beard. He looked like an aging member of some psychedelic drug band. Loudly Vance ordered another round, and whatever we wanted put on his tab, and brought to our table. Linoleum-floored and low-ceilinged the room was choking with smoke. There was a pool table, some pinball, and lots of military and patriotic paraphernalia. Mounted behind the bar, for instance, like a fish trophy, was a World War II-era airplane propeller blade. I got a Coke, and Autrey a CC and Seven—boozing de rigueur, apparently, at Klan gatherings, at least as much as cussing was.

The club wasn't segregated.

When I commented on this Vance explained the VFW was neutral ground. Therefore, ideal for us. I asked what that meant, and got told: "You'll see, little lady, you'll see."

He added that Mississippi's population was 42% Negro—half again as much as Alabama's black population, and three times Tennessee's. "You, little lady"—he paused to slurp down a great draft of Vodka—"are smack in the goddamn thick of things here, ground zero, right goddamn here."

A jukebox played Rosemary Clooney. Vance had a curved furrow of a scar gouged in the right side of his head, his skull fractured and ribs bayoneted in hand-to-hand combat with two Chinese in Korea, 1951, the Iron Triangle. "Slew both them gooks 'fore I went down," he bragged, grinning with ragged gaps where teeth should be. "Woke up'n an evac hospital week later." He hated Communists worse than he hated blacks. Bending low, I asked, whispering, why he was helping us?

Strangely his eyes glazed over, focused off in a distance, as he pulled smoke from a butt pinched between tar-stained fingers. He drained his glass, then rapped the thick base of it. A cocktail waitress with a haggard look and skimpy outfit said she'd get him another. "Do that baby doll." Then he flipped a wild spinning eye at me: "Nobody ever the fuck asked me *Why?* Lemme see. Patriotism. That's a good one. Morality. Revenge. Protect my ass from the U.S. attorney. Money. Money most of all, but, little a' all that."

I faced Autrey: "You?"

"Money."

"How much?" I was accepting a light from Vance.

He clapped out his Zippo, Autrey answering:

"Say, twelve thousand bucks, over the years."

I whistled.

"Why else?"

"I love to fight," Autrey said lightly. "Even when I lose, I love it. And this's the biggest fucking fight of my life."

My companions kept evading the all-important question of how and when we were going to "get noticed," and by the time we'd been there an hour and a half, I was thoroughly fed up. I didn't know what we were doing, other than my two escorts into inner Klandom were drinking nonstop, and our real mission, at the rally, was hours off. They refused tell me what was going on; they were obviously keeping me in the dark, deliberately, and I had a scary feeling it was on Legate's instructions.

My car was back in Alabama; I was stuck there, unless I wanted to call Fred. I sighed. I'd made a deal, plus I couldn't stomach going back to Fred, tail tucked. I wanted to go back, don't misunderstand, but on my terms. I'd just have to trust Legate was watching my back, and prudence demanded I do some watching of my own. About then a group of white men in suits entered and filled up a big table at the center of the room. "*Show*time, boys and girls," Vance whispered, rotating back.

The loudest of the arrivals was short, piggish, and wearing dark glasses and a hat. Several others stood out because of solid blood-red neckties: "Klan security guards," Autrey explained, watching warily. "The ties signal they have special orders to shoot anyone interfering with them." Vance tossed back his latest drink, then eyed me, nodding confirmation.

"Fat cat's the Grand Klexter," he graveled.

"Klexter?"

"Sam Bacon's chief of security."

Then he knocked Autrey's arm, chin-gestured at two Negroes, backs to us, sitting at the bar. Autrey looked—shrugged a nod. "What?" I insisted, only to be ignored. My heart began to beat more perceptibly. The blacks had been there, keeping to themselves, drinking beers, watching the Twins and Senators. I couldn't imagine what they had done. The answer of course was, they had done absolutely nothing. "Ain't likely," Vance said, low and serious, "to get a better set up than this, Bro'."

Autrey grunted.

Slurped down the last of his CC.

"What?" I whispered through my teeth.

Vance leaned. "Time, little lady, to get noticed."

And he told me what to do.

Jesus Christ Almighty...

My lungs filling full of dread...

"Legate know about this?" I panted.

"Abso-damn-lutely," Autrey said.

And cracked an ice cube in his teeth.

CHAPTER 84

Oddly, I did not, for a single second, disbelieve him; the absurd ghastly thing was, of course, exactly what the FBI wanted. Only, I was cynically certain it was by design I was not receiving these instructions directly out of the mouth of anyone having any official standing. It would be a number of years before the term *plausible deniability* entered the public lexicon—coming out of the Church Committee, the Pentagon Papers, Iran-Contra—but I was finding myself, whether I knew what to call it or not, ensnared in, victimized by, a classic example. I shook my head, thinking of what was going to happen. "Go on!" Autrey scolded, whisperingly, and I blasted him back a big hazel-eyed burst.

However, overcome with revulsion, and weak with frustration, I turned, and scraped back, and crossed toward the bar like a robot, on flat-heel sandals, flaunting my tight shorts and top. Somebody behind me whistled, perhaps in the Klexter's party—noticing!—but it might've been in another room, another county, I was so unplugged from everything.

Except what I was boring in on like a heat-seeking goddamn missile.

The bar.

The blacks.

Watching baseball.

No idea how I, literally, was about to blindside them. Made

me sick to imagine; nevertheless, I did my duty for Uncle Sam, thinking: *Was this how the kids in Vietnam felt?* I got into the spirit, lobbing a little swing and sway into my hips. Sleazing myself up on the outside was easy, as I felt plenty dirty already on the inside.

Onto that empty barstool, to their left, I hoisted, eschewing choices more prudent, definitely more proper—no one, besides the three of us bellied up along the bar, that moment. I crossed a half-bare thigh over its mate and smoothed clammy hands down my brown-and-beige shorts. I asked the barman for Spanish peanuts. "Sure thing," he said, flicking eyes. "Bring'em to your table."

"I'll wait."

The Negro beside me was young, tall and sleek. Through the knit of his sports shirt I could trace the ridge of his spinal column. He glimpsed over and when he saw me, registered nothing. No polite nod, nor even smile, because either, at a white woman, could be dangerous for him in the rural and small-town South of 1967.

I felt like vomiting.

The man's attention slipped easily, unconcernedly, back to his game. Bottom of the eighth, two outs, two runners on. To his companion, he observed something about the rookie Carew's batting average. The second man looked forty, heavier than the first and quite strong-armed. Neither were a match for Vance, however, much less both Vance and Autrey. They were neatly attired and, this being the VFW, figured to be honorably discharged war veterans of Vietnam and/or Korea.

I did it.

What had to be done.

I sprang off my stool.

Gave a piercing squeal.

Like a housewife spotting a rat in my kitchen.

"You black bastard get your hand off my leg!"

No taking it back.

Out there, out of my mouth, the whole barroom heard it. And the poor man I'd unloaded a ton of bricks on whipped around glaring at me through a hard grimace, utterly stunned.

Horrified.

Uncomprehending.

I got tossed aside by Autrey wearing that crazy white uniform and rebel-flag-emblazoned tanker's helmet. And by Vance, all in black. And after that there was no controlling anything. I was outside looking in. Like the trigger of a gun—instigator of the shot, yet of no importance to the subsequent devastation. "You black sonovabitch," Autrey roared, pulling the younger man by his shirt, slamming him against the side of a pinball machine. Vance brought the other Negro down swinging a blackjack, then kicked him between the eyes, then the stomach. I staggered backward, hand over my mouth. Unable to see the face of the first man for the blood, beaten to his knees by Autrey wearing brass knuckles and whaling that horrible lead-weighted bat. The man blindly punching back. Autrey kicked him in the back and side, tore his clothes. "Bro'!" Vance was yelling, dragging Autrey off. "Gotta get outta here! Go, go, go!"

I stood mesmerized.

"You too, little lady. Go, go, go!"

I shook loose my brain.

Slowly, snatched my purse from the table. And followed. By then my escorts had been stopped by the Grand Klexter and his party, who were up and out of their seats, spoiling for a fight. But there were no takers, rest of the room, black and white, having either fled or ducked into hiding. "Don't look like you boys need'ny help"—the Klexter, booming, bloodthirsty with delight—"but, by God, you can let us buy y'all a round of drinks!"

"Much obliged, but I think we best be movin' along, don't you?" Vance puffed, wiping his flushed face, raking back gunmetal ribbons of hair. "'Fore the local constabulary busts down the door."

"Ain't that the truth," the Klexter mused, taking out a cigarette. "Cain't tell like you used to, how the wind's go' blow with them, can you? Time was you could count on a handshake, and a back-slap, at worst"—he grinned, reminiscently—"a friendly warnin' the Feds was on the way."

"Damn shame," Autrey said, "how times is changing."

"That it is, son, surely is."

"We'll watch your back," promised one of the Red Ties. "You get own outta here."

"Do I know you?" the Klexter queried Vance. "I do, don't I?"

"I been around."

"Y'all be at the rally tonight? Figger it'll be a big one," he said, puffing up, "close to fifteen thousand." He mined a calling card from inside his jacket, thrust it at Vance. "Show that to the guards at the speaker stand. Like to talk to you, and your friend, and—naturally—this brave patriotic American girl."

"*Yes* sir!" Vance said.

Then gave and was returned the Nazi salute.

Legate and his tech people were waiting, to wire me for sound, when Autrey and I got back to the motel. Vance would pick us up in an hour, and drive us to the rally. I bared my teeth at Legate. An agent I didn't know sidestepped me like I was a rabid badger. "You goddamn give me your word those innocent men will be taken care of. Top-notch medicine, all expenses paid. By you, you bastard."

"Mrs. Russell—"

"No discussion! If I find you haven't, I'll tell the press that whole episode"—I pointed back, vaguely in the direction of the VFW—"and when I get good and warmed up, I'll tell 'em about the Freedom Riders."

Legate's jaw muscles knotted.

Adam's apple bumped. "Your point is made, Mrs. Russell. Please relax."

Driving back Autrey had tried to mollify my aghast rage by telling me he and Loftin had been with the Klansmen in Birmingham in 1961 who'd beaten the Freedom Riders.

That the FBI had known all about it then.

And done nothing to stop it, nor prosecute the offenders.

CHAPTER 85

I T WAS TWENTY-FIVE MILES to the farm off Route 18 west
of Raleigh where the big Klan rally was. I was given to
understand these things were like carnivals, or religious
revival meetings, staged for outsiders as much as for members,
to spread the message, sign up fresh dues-paying meat. Autrey
and Vance and I, and the FBI, were figuring on the serious
business being conducted well behind the scenes somewhere—
perhaps late, perhaps very late, after the public show—and we
had to do our damnedest to be part of that business.

Or near enough to spy on it.

We arrived before sunset. Three miles north of the state
highway, a dirt road, towering pines, a cardboard sign scrawled
KKKK (for *Knight's of the Ku Klux Klan*). An arrow on the sign
toward an open gate, which we were motioned through by a
man with a walkie-talkie to his ear, and a .45 automatic on his
hip. Vance's car was a black '59 Lincoln, looking like it belonged
in a Mob funeral procession. We edged onto a large field,
encased in hills, with maybe two dozen people there so far,
clustered about a speaker's platform, and a shed turned
concession stand.

The far end of the hollow, a small frame house stood on
neighboring property, separated from the rally grounds by post-
and-wire fencing. Legate, Perry, and a Jackson Field Office
tactical team were inside. I'd gotten a stern lecture about keeping

within a quarter mile of that house, or they wouldn't be able to monitor my transmitters. Or if I had to move, give as much information as possible (direction, destination, vehicle description) before traveling out of range. On the rally grounds proper there were two house trailers on concrete blocks. Outside them were clotheslines from which hung work shirts and khakis and brassieres. Vance let the car idle as German marching music blared from speakers. Someone directed us where to park, next to the shed where women were setting out cupcakes, filling a coffee urn, icing down Cokes and 7-Ups, and grilling hot dogs.

I surveyed, glad to be able to get my bearings while still daylight. I'd changed into blue side-zipper jeans with saddle stitching, and a checked polyester shirt of turquoise, lavender, and pink. It was long-sleeved—it would dip into the forties by late—and I'd knotted it to flash some midriff, like Pauline Prescott did, and she was the sexiest woman I knew. I carried a leather shoulder bag, my cigarette-pack transmitter inside, and taped medial to my left nipple was the Micro 007. They operated on separate frequencies, Legate's team having an attaché case jammed-packed with an FM receiver and voice-activated tape recorder. Two Piper Cubs circled overhead, talking to men on the ground. I counted six armed men on horseback. I commented casually about these things for Legate's benefit.

Red-white-and-blue bedsheets wrapped the speaker's stand and flags bedecked it. Under a tree stood three oil drums holding torches soaking in kerosene. We got soft drinks and hot dogs, and milled about. One at a time, never in great numbers, a car or pickup or camper would rattle over the dirt road into the hollow. Gatherings of men and women against fenders talking, children playing tag and rolling in the grass—but the numbers never topped out at more than a hundred—even if it was twice that, it sure was no fifteen thousand predicted by that idiot Klexter.

Who were these people?

These *War of the Worlds* Martians I'd dropped in the midst of?

That they were poor was clear—poor in possessions, in education, in hope—but they also seemed proud, in a screwwormy way. Desperate to be better than somebody.

Anybody.

By any despicable means.

I found myself watching with fascination, I admit, a cross under construction.

That icon of Klandom.

It would be thirty-or-forty-feet tall. A smaller one, say, five feet, was already erected, and some men were struggling with the big one, wrapping two tree trunks with rags and burlap. They wired the trunks together, then paused to inspect their work, before dousing on thirty gallons of an oil-kerosene mixture. A half-gallon of kerosene—gasoline would do, either one—and five pounds of oil per foot of cross. That recipe was explained to me by a cretin in the audience staring at my breasts, trying to be my boyfriend. The men in the field grunted and gasped, sweated their shirts dark. As they stood back, wiped faces with arms, they accepted a round of applause from the rest of us. Including a slim figure in his forties, who suddenly broke through to the front.

Clapping and nodding.

Jesse Vance eased up one side of me, a foot taller and 150-pounds heavier than I was, and the cretin shrank away, scared, as Vance bent low to my ear: "That's Sam Bacon."

"Well, hello there, Sam."

There goes a man, I was thinking, Sue Williams would love to get up close and personal with.

CHAPTER 86

S AM BACON WOULD BE CONVICTED *less than a month later on Federal civil rights charges stemming from a 1964 triple murder. He would enter the Federal prison at McNeil Island, Washington, in April 1970 and be paroled in March 1976. Mississippi officials would report a small hardcore unit of the White Knights was revived within two days of his release.*

CHAPTER 87

I T WAS AN HOUR AFTER sunset and a few of the men and women—incredibly, even some of the children—had donned satin robes and high-peaked hats. Some wore masks but most made no effort to hide. Colors matched offices:

White—Klavern members and officers.

Red—provincial and state officers.

Green—Grand Dragons.

Purple—Imperial Wizard Sam Bacon.

Autrey's costume was white, Vance not having yet bothered. Except for colors, though, and stripes edging the hems and sleeves, the robes were largely identical, with the same emblem covering the right breast.

A red circle with a white Maltese cross.

At the center of the cross, a single red "comma," representing a drop of blood.

The blood-drop cross.

Or MIOAK:

Mystic Insignia of a Klansman.

Whose blood was symbolized was a point of debate: Christ's, or the white race's, or the Confederate soldier's, or that of some unnamed white female victim of lust-crazed freed slaves. Such as depicted in that epic silent film *The Birth of a Nation* about the founding of the Klan. Autrey told me officials used that film as propaganda still; he'd seen it over a hundred times in his years of

Kluxing.

Loudspeakers blared a conglomeration of Beethoven's Ninth, "The Old Rugged Cross"—a favorite hymn of my father's, though I'd never hear it again in quite the same way—and "Stars and Stripes Forever." Then a sinister recorded voice related Klan history. Their version, which insisted slavery was a political excuse, that the Civil War was in fact ignited by European Jewish bankers to usurp the manufacture and control of American currency, which they maintain to the present under the Federal Reserve system. Oh, and by the way—Lincoln was assassinated by Jews!

I was seeing more headlights, a trickle of late arrivals, which I wondered about. The recording continued hyperbolically, often absurdly, about the horrors of Reconstruction (though I confess to having been teethed myself on similar tales). The PA system told how white men were imprisoned, women raped. The "braaavest of the brave" then forming the Invisible Empire, and the Negro was disarmed, troublemakers chased north, the ravagers hanged; the Klan restored law and order, saved the virtue of white womanhood, and the honor of the disgraced United States Government.

Easy to laugh...

But these people took themselves seriously, scary seriously. A clergyman from Jackson took the podium and droned on about the symbolism of the burning cross—a hole being dug out in the field, as he did, for the large cross. A pickup was backed in, a rope tied between the bumper and the cross. The truck growled forward, drawing the cross upright, men pushing and guiding. It dumped into its hole, listing badly, the men and the truck shoving and tugging trying to straighten it, without success. They gave up. The sinister voice returned. Lambasting the Catholic church, then again lashing its wrath at blacks. So unspeakably, it was all I could do not to storm away, or strike back with some dose of Liberal sanity. The musical hodgepodge returned.

It seemed a very black night out there, beyond the lights. A German shepherd sniffed the soaking torches. A vehicle or two at a time still passing through the gate. One late arrival was the Grand Klexter with his red-tied entourage. I watched him shake hands around the speaker's platform. By then Sam Bacon, sporting a shiny purple robe, was at the podium, microphone in hand. Whistles and applause. After a few words, he turned the mike over to the Kludd, who prayed: "Lord bless all Klan members and non-Klan members at this party."

"Amen," I said under my breath.

The Mississippi Grand Dragon spoke. An enlarging circle of men and women clotted around the podium. One robed woman, against the tree, beside the oil drums, howled: "Aaaaa-men, brother!" The Grand Dragon screaming: "Now—let's get to the niggers!"

Autrey, Vance, and I decided it was time to make ourselves known to the Klexter, who had mounted the stand by then in a flowing red robe and pointed hat. "What if your daughter," the Dragon was ranting, "come home with a big black buck?" Vance approached some Red Ties, flashing the Klexter's calling card, but the stocky piggish man saw us first, shouting down my alias "Miss Williams" over the speaker's oration. He waved us to the end. "You'd have mulatto children," the Dragon had gotten to, then talked about ruining the greatest creation ever—the white man, which, he declared, not even God had the right to do.

Claps.

The lone "Aaaaa-men!"

The Grand Klexter came down wood-plank steps. Behind him, I realized with a shock, came Sam Bacon himself. "This here, Sam, is that brave young lady I told you 'bout. And her rescuers." Red and white and blue and gold stripes encircled the sleeves of Bacon's robe. "A great honor, meelady." He grasped my hand, shook it with slow reverence. "Just so sorry, I'm sick—sick—a fair young maiden, in the modern South, still must endure such indignities as being laid hands upon by a dirty nigra."

My eyes stung.

Throat dry.

I managed, my heart going wild:

"Well, sir, that's why we're all here I reckon."

"Indeed it is, young lady, indeed. Well said. Excellently said."

"Protest days are over," the Grand Dragon at the mike shouted. "We are committed to force, and to force only!"

"Aaaaaa-men, brother!"

"I was wondering, Miss Williams," asked Bacon, "if we might impose upon you?" I shrugged my shoulders, looking up at the tall slim figure, made absurdly taller by his pointed hat. "Anything I can do," I replied. The Dragon bashing by that point all the bickering and infighting within Klan ranks. "I'd like you to speak," Bacon said. "At the podium."

I blinked.

"Speak?"

"About your ordeal. A true, immediate, first-hand account of a ravager, his virtuous victim, her white knights. True, great, white Americans all. Why, when they hear your story, every man and woman out there with red blood in their veins—if they ain't already members—will be lining up, guaranteed."

The Dragon was banging his fist. Something about a "Universal Klan." One mighty unstoppable white force. The Imperial Wizard's request was, of course, far better than Agent Legate or I or anyone else could have hoped for. I was supposed to be working myself close to somebody who might get me close to some other people who might eventually say something interesting for the FBI mikes to pick up.

As it turned out, I wasn't just getting close. I was being sucked in, right up to the top. "The Klan!" boomed the sweating wild-eyed Grand Dragon. "Will again, like it did gloriously a hundred years ago! A century ago! It will ride! Ride! To save America! God bless her!" The crowd spurred to whoops and cheers. The robed woman: "Aaaaa-men!"

"Well of course…" I said meekly to Bacon.

Demurely placing my hand upon my heart.

Fingering the Micro 007.

"Anything I can do to help…"

The Mississippi Grand Dragon introduced a small man named Morgan, a fellow Grand Dragon from South Carolina, as I was being led onto the stand, with Autrey and Vance, thank God, on my heels. Morgan wore the green robe of his office, gesturing wildly, railing about "jiggaboos," and about the Klan of old, swinging niggers and carpetbaggers out the "winders" of the State House in "Columbier." Behind and to the right of the podium, I was given a seat of honor, from where I couldn't help but lower my head, clasp my brow, absolutely at that moment, utterly, mortally embarrassed to be white. "Ladies an' gentlemen," he preached, "today is the day to join!" Then he lashed at the Johnson Administration, at Congress, at the NAACP—which he said stood for "Niggers, Apes, Alligators, Coons, and Possums!" The crowd laughed like he was Bob Hope.

The Mississippi Grand Dragon returned to the podium when Morgan was done, to introduce his skeletal-faced wife. "We need more women," she urged, angelically. "We need the men, but we also need the women behind the men, to do like we done this evenin', and stand over there and cook an' take money." Then that ignorant cow fucking read a poem.

Which opened:

> When a white girl marries a Negro,
> Her sun of light goes down
> And glaring spots of sin
> Appear on her wedding gown.

And, truthfully, I can't bear the rest; I really can't. I wish to God I hadn't heard it. "Thank you," the Lady Dragon said at the end, and galloped down straightening her peaked hat, amid applause and cheers. I wanted out. It was like I was drowning in a sewer and it was a particularly vile sewer at that. Unfortunately Sam Bacon, that very moment, took to the microphone and introduced me—alias, Sue Williams—I, that virtuous victim of a black ravager, and of course, great American.

CHAPTER 88

REMARKABLY, SOMEHOW, MY KNEES GOT me up. Blearingly spotlit, I told my story in as interesting and overblown a way as I could fabricate. Petrified of course. I'd have been petrified even if I weren't an undercover Fed—marked for death to boot—thrust center stage at the Klan's big rally. I covered, by apologizing, my first time speaking in public, outside my classroom of course, remembering suddenly I was supposed to be a teacher.

I got encouraging claps.

Few wolf whistles.

When I'd finished, and Autrey and Vance, my rescuers, had taken their bows, Sam Bacon remounted the platform. The moon was up. It was nearly ten o'clock. The Klexter escorted us off and Bacon began to verbally lynch big business and big government, fluoridation, the UN, taxes, Jews, and Martin Luther King. The Klexter told me somebody was eager to meet me and, with his fat hand at the back of my arm, guided me, high-stepping, in the dark and grass behind the speaker's stand.

Autrey and Vance stayed with me.

Even so I ground my molars in fear, then out of the depths emerged—

Shocking me like electric voltage—

John Riley Hobbs.

***

340

He stopped, leaned forward, giving one the impression he might bound over your head, like a giant grasshopper. "Sue Williams," he said with thought.

Taking my hand.

"Yes," I said, cotton-mouthed.

Sick with terror.

"I've not heard your name, nor seen you around any Klan affairs."

"I'm not a member yet, sir."

I gestured back of me. "I came with my friends to get me a better idea, what it's"—I cleared my throat—"what it's all about."

"Oh?" And he went around and slowly, strangely, I thought, shook hands with Autrey. Odd to be so close, yet not have Hobbs recognize me—Hobbs, who I recognized so clearly from photos, and from the logging camp. He hadn't seen me then, of course. Had he, I wouldn't have gotten away any more alive than Horace Cothran. Then I thought, with a chill up my spine—

Those press photos…Turbeville and me…

"Lee…" he was saying.

Dark with suspicion, I could tell.

"Johnny," Autrey replied.

"You didn't say you was comin'. I'd've thought you'd've mentioned it. We only saw each other, couple nights ago."

"Spur-of-the-moment decision, Excellency. Sue was real interested."

Hobbs swung back, looking at me. I had a hard time swallowing. "Where might you be from, miss?"

"Oh…B-Birmingham, sir."

He nodded. "Well, y'all enjoy the rally."

"I will, sir."

He knew.

He said nothing more.

To me.

Autrey either, just a look.

He knew.

Strangely then, he strutted away, taking his purple robe and hat, and donning them as he went to the steps at the end of the platform and mounted them.

Why was he there?

Hobbs and Bacon.

Bitter rivals.

Something was very wrong. I dragged Autrey by the sleeve. "He knows," I gnashed, spinning around, when we were off in the crowd. Talking as much to Autrey as to Agent Legate, hopefully hearing all this. "He suspects," Autrey spat. "Don't panic."

"I'm not panicked."

"Yes you are!"

He yanked my arm.

"Fine, I'm panicked—I'll pit my judgment against yours any day, the snoot-full you've had."

"Best thing for you to do, baby, is relax, 'cause if you're right, they'll be watching."

Grinding my teeth.

Thrashing my head. "Why is he here?"

"I think, baby, we're 'bout to find out." I looked, Sam Bacon on the platform, introducing John Riley Hobbs. Hobbs crossing, like some little god, festooned in his purple robe and hat, a costume largely identical to Bacon's.

The men met.

Embraced. Slappingly.

Faced the crowd.

Raised clenched hands high overhead.

Then, Hobbs took the mike from Bacon, who shrank back, and Hobbs' harangue was more of the same drivel. Klan rallies, while not exactly boring, I decided, did suffer relentless redundancy. Autrey, grinning, told me Hobbs was usually good for forty-five minutes to an hour. "Terrific," I replied.

And, eventually, he got around to what I'd long before that point guessed:

That Bacon's White Knights:

Were rejoining Hobbs' Amalgamated Klans of America.

The AKA's most radical, violent splinter group was returning to the fold.

Return of the prodigal son. First step, Hobbs howled, in the forging, of a unified Klan.

A invincible Klan!
A Universal Klan!
Cheers.
Applause.
Some *Aaaaa-men, brother's.*
Bacon took the mike back:
"Klansmen! Report to the cross!"

CHAPTER 89

V ANCE THREW A ROBE ON over his shirt and trousers, then he and Autrey left me—
Left me!
—to join forty or so others with Bacon near the tall, leaning cross. The smaller one, ablaze, cast an eerie glow, the loudspeakers alive with a terrifying organ-and-choral rendition of "The Old Rugged Cross." I pressed my hand over my stomach muscles, which tightened concavely, as I watched Klansmen file past the small cross, igniting torches, then encircle the dark larger cross. They stopped, turned, in military fashion, touched flames to the ground, then raised them in salute. All at Bacon's stern command. Torchlight distorting the reds, greens, and whites of their robes and hats. On command they advanced.

Laid their flares.

Whoosh!

Flames leapt skyward.

Up kerosene-soaked burlap.

The air filled with crackles and sparks. Past eleven, sleepy grownups and children alike closing in, watching, reverently, the robed inner ring of Klansman marching round and round. Bacon eventually ordered a return to the speaker's platform. "The Old Rugged Cross" spun to a slow ending on the turntable. I saw a confab. An urgent temper about it. The Klexter. His Red Ties.

And Hobbs.

Fingers pointed.

My way!

Autrey and Vance's, too, though they, still with the robed men, tramping back, would not have seen. On the platform, Bacon was now joining the pointing and arguing. "Legate, if you can hear me," I said, "we might've been made. If you can get me help, do it. If you can't I may have to pull the plug. Sorry."

My eyes thrashed through a night smelling of burning burlap and kerosene.

Sparks sputtering and popping. Flames licking gently up the sides of the cross. On the platform they had walkie-talkies, in communication, I guessed, with those patrols on horseback, out in the dark. Sparks floating off, dying. I broke into a zigzag trot, fought the current of the dispersing crowd—finally reaching Autrey and Vance.

"We have to get out of here!" And when I explained what I'd seen, the bastards finally allowed that I might, possibly, be right, and we, all three of us, set off toward Lincoln. Others were leaving too. By mingling I hoped we might manage to slip away. Most of the vehicles were bumping, not surprisingly, toward the gate at the east edge of the property. The one we'd entered.

Others, though, I saw, were heading diagonally opposite.

Northwestward. None had arrived from that way, I was sure.

Where were they going?

"Some cars leaving northwest," I said conversationally. "Copy that? Northwest."

Our march, then—

Jerked to a halt—

Out of the dark materializing two Klan security guards, uniformed the same ludicrous way Autrey was, down to the jump boots, and tank-crew helmets. Then through the air cut a sharp, inhuman snort. I smelled horsehide, and looked up, peering out, and realized, the pair of guards on foot had backup—one of those mounted patrols, a burly black gleaming—like stars in the sky—draught horse barely visible, rider tall in the saddle, communicating by radio with the Klexter. He carried a Carbine. Aimed skyward, butt against his thigh. The two on foot carried Thompsons.

Both muzzles leveled.

At us.

The mounted man got off the radio.

Shouted down:

"Wait here, Klansmen. They're sendin' a truck over." Then he tossed me a nod, the horse dancing, fighting the bit, reacting to the burning cross. "You too, if you please ma'am."

"What the hell?" Vance boomed.

"Wiz wants to have a talk with your group."

To the detail:

"Get their weapons."

He reined the horse, moving in a half-circle, neck bowed, the rider lowering the Carbine. The guards brushed by either side of me. "Watch where you point those Tommy guns," I scolded. For Legate's benefit.

I turned, watching, with dread, the frisking of Autrey then Vance. Frisking with the skill and thoroughness of police officers. They might've been police officers for all I knew. They took from the men, dropped into a growing pile, the Bowie knife, Autrey's revolver, his Colt .22, the head-knocker—from Vance, a Browning pistol, another hunting knife, the blackjack he'd used at the bar.

Unbelievably, they ignored me!

And there my purse was, teeming full of Fed electronics.

I'd obeyed Legate, unfortunately.

Wasn't carrying my gun.

A rattly mud-caked late-1940s half-ton Ford—the same which had erected, and failed in the attempt to straighten, the large cross—came, and the men with the Thompsons got into the wood-plank bed with Autrey and Vance, while I rode in relative luxury, in the cab, still carrying my purse. The man on horseback cantered alongside as we pitched and rocked cantankerously, taking that same interesting northwest track. "Road's back there," I nagged the driver, who was about seventy, wearing overalls, cut-down army boots, and a train-engineer's cap. "What's up this way?"

"Yew'll see." Twisting the wheel the old man seemed engaged in an epic struggle for the vehicle's very soul. The

Ford's headlights only dimly piercing the dense wilderness night. Behind us the cross had dwindled to glowing coals. I asked if I could smoke. The driver shrugged, still overworking his steering. "Dunno why not."

I got out my real pack, some matches, and lit up. Upon returning these items, I palmed my jackknife, and thumbed it down my right front jeans pocket. I blew a stream of smoke through loosely pursed lips. And sat thrashing and jarring inside a rattletrap Ford making its way to God knows where.

CHAPTER 90

W E EXITED VIA A SECOND guarded gate, northwest corner, right-turning onto a dirt road. "How the heck far you taking us?" I complained. "All the way north to Tennessee?"

"Ain't that far," gruffed the crusty driver. "Just you relax, miss."

Disastrously, if we hadn't already exceeded the range of the Mark VI, we soon would. Severing our radio umbilical to Legate. Of course, the tiny bug taped to my breast was no good beyond the length of a football field, less than that even. We steered left, and after another hundred dirt yards were stopped by guards brandishing shotguns and flashlights. They waved us on. Us and the man on horseback, who I knew from the thudding of hooves was following. "Wait with the truck," one guard called out, "we was told to tell you, once you're up to the church."

"The church!" I exclaimed.

"Huh?" the old man said.

"Been a long time since I've been to church."

Another full mile up into the piney woods, by which point there was no chance of either transmitter being picked up, the deep-rutted track petered out into a clearing atop a sandy knoll. In the center of the knoll stood the aforementioned church— gaunt, weathered, of hand-hewn timbers, and sawn pine boards. Abandoned, I later learned, built in 1845, by a John Bixby. Bixby

348

and his wife Regan were buried next to the church. From the Ford, I made out weather-worn gravestones, and Klansmen strolling with flashlights, curiously reading names and dates. Many more milled in the clearing. Some drank from mason jars of moonshine.

All armed.

Perhaps thirty, ferried up from the rally grounds in four pickups, and a World War II Jeep, all parked, spoking out from the front of the church. Besides flashlights and kerosene lanterns, the area was lit almost exclusively by torches, mounted or carried. Like some creepy scene out of a Frankenstein movie. Villagers on the rampage. Faces glistening, the glow of licking flames. At gunpoint the three of us were taken down, marched close to the church. We began to be surrounded by a rabble of anger and hate, hoisted torches. The doors at the front and rear of the sturdy ancient building stood open, permitting me a view through the shadowy, flickery interior. Rough wooden benches, a pulpit at the far end above an altar. Outside, a barely legible sign:

BIXBY METHODIST CHURCH.

And just then, below that sign, Sam Bacon emerged.

Down warped steps, he wore dirty khaki trousers and a cardigan sweater. The circle allowed him to shoulder through, followed by the fat Grand Klexter, then John Riley Hobbs, stooped and puffing hard on a cigarette.

Then two others.

The first I had never seen.

He was, turned out, the Exalted Cyclops of Jesse Vance's Mississippi-based Klavern. My purse I held clutched beneath an elbow, my thumb hooking the shoulder strap. The transmitter inside I was sure was useless, but if the Klan found it there…

The torches warmed the autumn night air. "What's all this, John?" Vance to his EC.

"Bro' we wanna know *exactly* who the hell you work for."

"Fuck," Vance said, "you know, Page Trucking."

"Other'n that."

"Nobody."

"Sam's gettin' word down in Laurel, you're working for the Feds."

The circle of gunmen and torches tightened like a noose. Sam Bacon pushed close, ignoring Vance's extension of a hand to shake. "What have you got to say for yourself Klansman?"

It was *Vance*, I thought, dazed.

Vance who'd been recognized.

Not me.

"I dunno," Vance was answering savagely, "what've you got on your mind?"

"Ain't it a fact you're a Federal agent?" Bacon said.

"That's a damn lie."

"Watch your mouth," barked the Klexter, "or we'll put a bullet in it." Bacon waved forward the last man out of the church. Thick around the belt, this one moved with a swagger, and kept his identity concealed with a mask. He still wore the white bridal-stain robe, which hung open in front revealing some city police officer's uniform: dark tie, badge, whistle on a chain. "That's him," the moving mouth behind the mask confirmed with law-enforcement authority. "I seen him yesterday, black car, with two known FBI agents, outta Jackson."

"If he thinks he saw me he must be blind as a goddamn bat."

Bacon blistered Vance:

How many FBI agents he knew.

What their names were.

Where they lived.

What their wives' and children's names were.

"You're talking stupid man! Lemme outta here!"

The Klexter drove him an uppercut to the belly. I jerked, gasped.

Vance slumped forward, staggered.

Then lunged.

Took the Klexter by his fat neck. Shaking his hat off—the man, face gorging full of purple blood, clawing onto Vance's wrists. The tank-helmeted men waled onto the back of Vance's skull with billy sticks until he released the Klexter—the exposed informant's big hands like mechanized devices suddenly seized up by short-circuited controls. I was horribly sure I'd heard a wet crunching, like a large eggshell smashing through. Vance falling hard and heavy. A brief twitching of his left leg shaking down to stillness. Clutching his own neck, struggling to get wind back into himself, the Klexter hauled off and kicked Vance on the ground. "Fucking damn Fed!" A breathy high-pitched rasp. He kicked him again, then staggered back, fumbling toward the church.

Coughing.

Wheezing.

John Riley Hobbs strode forward, taking Bacon's place.

His stalk-like arm gestured forward another Klansman, out of the kerosene-smoke-laden dark. And unfortunately I did know this one. And he knew Autrey and me. He had a real shiner, and his arm in a sling.

Both courtesy of Fred.

My Fred.

Don't misunderstand, whatever my frustrations with Fred, I didn't blame him for this disaster. Even without Fred's help, this man, named Townsend, would have ID'ed me. That hippopotamus-looking grease monkey, whose clavicle Fred shattered with a big wrench a week ago. Someone lifted a Coleman lantern next to my face. "That's her. Done changed her hairdo, I think, but that's her, the bitch."

Adding, deflecting onto Autrey:

"And he damn-sure knows it."

"Very well," Hobbs said. "Dismissed, Klansman."

Townsend, a minor Alabama Klansman, had not, I learned later, been slated to even attend the Mississippi rally. Of course, if he hadn't come, he would not have recognized, on the speaker's stand, Klan heroine Sue Williams, brave American, as in reality Sherry Russell, notorious Negro lover.

But he was there.

Dispatched urgently to alert Imperial Wizard Hobbs in person to a stunning setback—the arrest for murder, by Lavonia Sheriff Turbeville, of Grand Kleagle, Chief Deputy C.O. Loftin.

CHAPTER 91

HOBBS CAME UP CLOSE, SEEMING to me rather scrawny for a terrorist leader. Given his gnarled posture, we stood almost eye to eye. I supposed, to his thinking, I was smallish for a Fed.

"So, you're the girl from Tennessee."

"Well," I said, swallowing, a twitchy smile, "Ain't the one from Ipanema."

Head cocking back, he wrinkled a large nostril, seemed to be sniffing me, judging me. "A married woman, out of her rightful place," he said. "You have been designated a public enemy of the Klan."

"Kill the bitch!" someone roared.

"What have you to say?"

I thrust out my chin, over-aware of my breathing. "Tell you what I have to say"—not feeling I was getting enough oxygen—"It is a far, far better thing that—"

He cuffed his hand across my cheek. Staggered me, reeling into the mob—which, cursing me, shoved me back. Autrey caught me under the arms, steadied me. Tears leaping up from where my face stung, from where my hand was rising.

Then I closed the hand.

Dropped it by my denim-clad thigh.

Some principle involved, not giving Hobbs the satisfaction.

If only I wasn't standing there crying and blubbering.

The Wizard stalked to Autrey. I watched, my left eye squinting: Hobbs was a pipsqueak; he wouldn't be so brave and cocky against Autrey, without these reinforcements. The muzzles of both Tommy guns, in fact, were buried hard in the small of the informant's back. "Mind explaining Lee…"

Voice low.

Menacing.

He lit a new cigarette. Blew the smoke, diamond pinkie ring flashing torchlight. "Why you brought a degenerate enemy, amongst your fellow Klansmen, under a false identity? Isn't it a fact you personally participated in three separate schemes for neutralizing this woman's threat. Schemes which obviously"—he swung a look at me, then back—"failed." He brought the pinched cigarette to his lips, drew from it, lowered it, smoke billowing off. "One might conclude from that alone, you was working for the Feds—in violation of your oath of allegiance, sworn in the presence of God and man."

"You accusing me, Johnny, of bein' a goddamn Fed?"

"Always have been rumors 'bout you, Lee, you know that."

"You took responsibility for me once Johnny. Till I got cleared, by your own damn KBI. Then there was that hooker in Atlanta—paid to make me admit to bein' a Fed. Well, she didn't did she?"

"I was informed," Hobbs continued, "upon my arrival that the White Knights had a Fed dead to rights." He darted the cigarette-holding hand, at the comatose Vance. "Imagine my surprise when that very infiltrator got introduced, on the platform, with you, Lee—C.O. Loftin's good buddy—we'll get to him in a minute—and this girl. Got me to thinking 'bout those old rumors. About Betty, your codename, for the lady private eye. Got me to thinking whether she, this heroine Sam's people dug up, sleazing it up in some bar, might be one and the same girl."

"This is bullshit, Johnny."

"I looked for somebody, any loyal Klansman, who could eyeball this Sue Williams, tell me if she was really Betty. Mr. Loftin seemed obvious. Problem was—I was late coming to the rally—did you know that?—because I was informed early this evening Mr. Loftin never left Alabama."

"So?"

"He's under arrest. Tell me about that?"

"I dunno nuthin', and that's the truth, Johnny."

"You're a Fed, and you're working with *that* Fed, and you're working with *her.*"

"And by God," roared some angry voice, back in the mob, "you *all* gonna get killed tonight!"

I wondered was there any possibility Legate was hearing this?

And knew I'd have to be a naïve little fool to believe he was.

Suddenly Autrey reared around like a grizzly and attacked both men with the Tommy guns. Nobody opened up, thank God, but it took about three seconds for ten men to mob up on Autrey and beat and kick him horrifically to the ground. At the end of which I was standing, an avowed Klan public enemy, surrounded by a Klan mob, deep in the Mississippi backwoods, flickered over by torchlight—both my assigned protectors laid out in bloody heaps at my feet.

CHAPTER 92

INSIDE THE FRAME HOUSE AT the far end of the hollow—the family put up in a nice hotel in Jackson, getting a nice fat government check for their trouble—Special Agent Alan Legate listened to a scratchy recording of "The Old Rugged Cross." It came through slightly garbled over the FM receiver, tuned to the 88.5 MHz frequency of the cigarette-pack transmitter. Inside the same attaché case, wedged in next to the receiver, a tape recorder spun away.

So far so good, Legate thought:

The Russell girl being invited to speak from the podium was a lightning stroke, and she'd pulled it off, he had to admit, brilliantly, for an amateur, a female amateur at that. She was getting herself to top in a way he hadn't dreamed possible. Legate, swigging from his Coca-Cola, found himself hoping against hope she wouldn't end up screwing anybody. He should have been clearer. He could just see the Director, narrowing eyes, pursing lips, studying the surveillance reports. Ironic, how many Klan informants, like Autrey, had been instructed to screw as many Klan wives as possible—for the expressed purposing of sowing distrust and discontent.

Yet they were men.

A woman was totally different. She would be a whore in the employ of the FBI...

Legate heard Sam Bacon bark "Report to the cross!" and walked through, pine floors snapping, with a child-like curiosity to a back window. He watched the flames burst skyward through his horned-rim glasses, across a few hundred yards of trees and pasture.

***

A radio call came from the agents Legate had posted south along the county road.

He listened.

Said, "Blast!"—then keyed the walkie-talkie:

"Roger, send them through."

He released the button with a jerk. He wanted no turf battles, not now.

Already he'd been privy to a huge piece of intelligence—directly, not through the questionably reliable braggadocio of some paid betrayer.

The melding of the White Knights and the AKA.

Bacon plus Hobbs.

If somehow Hobbs managed a snowballing of one Klan after another into this Universal Klan of his, it could be a savagely potent enemy. And while reunifying the White Knights and the AKA was a surprise, was extraordinary, it was nevertheless natural. Given that one had originally spun off from the other. Bringing together all the other Klans, across the country, would still be a tall order. That would take something big.

A call to arms.

Some inspirational success.

That was what "next week" was.

The inspiration, the galvanizing event!

The Big Event!

If it succeeded.

Legate had to make sure it didn't.

There was a knock. He turned from his picture-window view of the flaming cross, and reached the foyer as Agent Perry was ushering in Sheriff Bobby Ray Turbeville from Alabama, and Sheriff Grady Pickens and two deputies from Smith County, Mississippi. Pickens was touchy as an alligator about not being informed of an FBI operation in his jurisdiction. Before the arguing got too hot and heavy, though, one of the Jackson Field Office people, yanking off earphones, interrupted: "Sir—you'll want to hear this." And Legate and the two khaki-clad sheriffs gathered over the high-tech attaché case.

A crackly distant Sherry Russell speaking to them.

To them!

Directly through the mike.

"…been made. If you can get me help, do it. If you can't I may have to pull the plug. Sorry."

CHAPTER 93

W E WERE SEVERAL YARDS DEEP in the pinewoods to the left of the abandoned church. Uphill, through trees and bushes, I could see one heavy-weathered sidewall of the building. The road we'd taken to get up here, to the top of the knoll, on my right, was the only approach, as far as I'd seen. Back of the church, there had been built a red-earthen dome—activity back there, and light, and what might be camouflage netting, like in the war movies, over the top.

Jesse Vance was bleeding profusely, half-conscious, if at all, and a bunch of angry Klansmen had managed to stand him against the biggest tree around, and tie enough rope around him to hold him upright. Autrey, half beaten to death as well, was at least awake, talking—cussing mostly—his arms yanked backwards, wrists bound behind a pine tree. They were taking no chances, his biceps like cannonballs. More rope bound his ankles, thighs, chest, and neck, all double wrapped, knotted securely, blood thoroughly soaking the front of his white Klan security-guard shirt.

My turn.

Bacon and Hobbs were looking on. I'd heard them talk. They were going to have their meeting, after which a few select Klansmen would remain behind and kill us.

Wouldn't do, I guessed, to have excess witnesses to murder, even Klan witnesses. Murder was murder, and the two Imperial

Wizards were too prudent not to acknowledge the possibility of another informant in their midst. A Klansmen ordered me, "Back up to that little'n." Vaguely pointing a finger. I picked out a sapling pine, half-raised my hands, and stepped through some big bushes. I was helpless, backed up into the tree I'd selected. Thin needled branches, smell of sap closing around my head, my shoulders. My hands were pulled backwards through and tied behind the tree. Unlike with the men, they didn't bother to wrap me in rope like a mummy. Either they were out of rope, or assumed they'd done enough to secure me. Which, I admit, they had. Hobbs ordered:

"Get her purse."

My heart thumped.

A hunting knife was drawn, its glint of steel, even in the dark of night, the intense shadow, showed a murderous edge. The leather strap was sawn through, the bag passed off to Hobbs. With a bored look he opened it. Peered inside, tilting it and his head to catch what little dim light reached him from the church.

I didn't panic.

I was already in, I figured, as much trouble as I could be. Discovery of an FBI transmitter might even give me some leverage. I could foresee advantages, as well, in keeping the bug operating. So, I let nature take its course. Trust in the Lord, or fate, or whatever, and as it happened, remarkably, Hobbs registered nothing more incriminating than, apparently, a wallet, a few feminine doodads, and two white-striped packs of Kents. He turned and hiked uphill, swinging my bag by its cut strap. Sprang up the steps, into the front of the church—

Pine needles snagged at my hair, prickled my scalp, and sides of my face. The frayed ski rope and tree bark began to rub my wrists raw, and below where my blouse was knotted, night air ruffled tiny fine hairs on my stomach. I looked straight up through branches and trees, unable to make out a single star.

Nor the moon.

Then down.

I was sobbing again.

Trying to make myself stop.

A man yelled, "Come inside! Ready to begin!"

Klansmen meandered into the flame-lit glow and wavering

shadows, using both rear and front doors. Two guards remained outside. Enough shutters hung open or were missing I could hear a little, see the taking of seats. A man stepped to the lectern, up on the pulpit. "Oh God, our Heavenly Guide," I heard the Kludd pray, continuing at length, at last finishing with: "…in the name of Christ our blessed Savior. Amen."

The way my arms were strained backward made my breasts jut forward, rather obscenely, if you ask me. Not that I was ever what anyone would call busty. Even now, no one would mistake me for Pauline Prescott. The point being, my shirt was stretched, buttons straining, across my boobs. And the little postage-stamp Micro 007.

The shape and thickness of it I could see profiled, even here in the dark, through my bra and blouse. "Bixby Methodist Church," I said, distinctly, but quietly, talking oddly to my own left breast. "We're tied up in the trees, to the left as you approach. Vance and Autrey are in a bad way. Perhaps thirty men inside, heavily armed. Some kind of meeting. Two guards outside. Shotgun and a Carbine, couple pistols, I think, between them. Hand grenade maybe. Oh, there are guards at a checkpoint, mile before you get here. We're to be killed after the meeting."

I repeated this message every few minutes, variations to break up the monotony. Maybe I'd perform an interlude of "Moon River" in between. Radio Free Boondocks. I eventually dropped the warning about the checkpoint. Anybody close enough to pick up my transmission would've already encountered them.

CHAPTER 94

Y OUR MEN'RE STILL PLAYIN' TAG *team interrogatin' Loftin,"*
Sheriff Turbeville told Agent Legate contemptuously across the
farmhouse's map-layered dining table. "Twixt me and them, that's
near-twelve hours of grillin'. But he ain't talked; hell, he don't even want no
lawyer."

Legate smoothed his tie.

Adjusted the gold-plate clip. "I hear you roughed him up," he said.

"Mean I beat the shit outta his fat ass, hell yes I did."

"Can't you unduhstand that might have made him more resolute, harder
to crack, through more subtle means, gentle building psychological pressure."

"Shit..."

Turbeville gave his half-bald head a wag. "You may have the college
degrees, Miss-ter Legate, and I may be a backwoods sheriff, unfit to shine
your oxfords—but, I've known hard-assed shitkickers like Cecil Loftin my
whole life. And I guaran-damn-tee you his type eats your subtle gentle
building psychological pressure for breakfast."

"Perhaps—"

"That's one! Two—I got me a dep'ty made a jackass of me. You and
your boys thought I was a Ku Kluxer jus 'cause he was—when hell, I just
kept him on 'cause seemed he did an okay job for the last sheriff, and he
grew up in the county, and I didn', and I fig'red he knew where all the stills
was and who did all the bootleggin'."

"I see."

"Maybe he led a secret life, was some pooh-bah in the Klan." Turbeville *shrugged beefy shoulders. "Maybe that's bad; maybe it ain't. But he committed murder in my county. I'm told you got him dead to rights on the Collins killin's—dunno why I'm just hearin' that—but on top of everything—he used my gun, on Collins, then Horace Cothran, hopin' to frame me. Well, Miss-ter Legate, I dunno what you'd think about a shit pile like that in the FBI, but while I'm sheriff, any dep'ty does all that will be putting a few dents in the walls of my jail. That I promise, and do not apologize for."*

"You are one big dumb ape, Sheriff Turbeville. High time—"

"Gentlemen!"

Smith County Sheriff Pickens, marching in, having hung up the kitchen phone. He was tall, silver-haired, hard-bodied—ex-Army—wearing a green windbreaker. "That man Loftin had a panel truck loaded down with dynamite, blasting caps, fifteen .303 Enfield rifles, case of NATO M-14s, and a few thousand rounds of ammo. Far as we know he was transporting all that into my county. Which begs the question when you Hoover Boys—"

Agent Perry barked Legate's name.

Waved them all back to the open attaché case, picking up Sherry Russell's mike.

Legate checked his watch—11:18 PM.

She was in the middle of convincing Autrey and Vance to bug out.

"Dammit, no," muttered Legate.

"That girl is no pantywaist," Turbeville declared, hands heavy on his belt, handle of his gun. "It's thanks to her, I gather, you Feds don't have me halfway to the gallows for all Loftin's doin'. Well, if she says she needs out, then goddamnit you get her out."

"She's got to stay, don't you unduhstand? We don't know what their plan is. We do know, Sheriff Pickens, that Loftin's truckload was not the only shipment of arms and explosives bound for this meeting. We cannot, gentlemen, lose this trail."

"Some cars leaving northwest," came Sherry over the speaker. "Copy that? Northwest."

"No way to communicate back?" Turbeville asked.

"No. It's one way."

To Pickens: "Sheriff, help us out, if you please. Klan vehicles leaving northwest from the rally grounds. Where might they be going?"

A USGS map and a county highway map and some tax-office plat maps were spread open in the dining room, weighed down with ashtrays and coffee mugs. Perry, Pickens, and a Smith County deputy leaned over them—

pointing, tracing, brainstorming. From the receiver sounds of the trio tramping across the field.

Then what sounded like a horse.

A man talking.

"Wait here, Klansmen. They're sendin' a truck over. You too, if you please ma'am."

Vance: "What the hell?"

"Wiz wants to have a talk with your group…Get their weapons."

"Watch where you point those Tommy guns."

"Tommy guns!" burst Turbeville.

"Good girl," Legate urged. "She is a very cool lady."

"She wants out!" Turbeville blasted.

"No! You numbskull. They haven't taken her purse. We can monitor. If this truck takes them northwest there's a chance they're going the same place the rest of those vehicles did. They might led us right to the front door of their operation, and all that ordinance."

"There's a gate 'long this west property line," Pickens was saying to his deputy, "lets out on this farm road, right, boy?"

"That's right Sheriff."

Pickens straightened, took in a bird's-eye view of the maps. The engine grind and rattles of an old pickup came over the little speaker. The FBI men and sheriffs heard Autrey and Vance ordered into the truck bed, and Sherry into the cab. Doors slamming, gears shifting, engine growling. "Still got her purse!" Legate slapped one of the tech men atop the shoulder. "Be ready to move!"

"Road's back there," they heard Sherry say. "What's up this way?"

"Northwest!" Legate actually jumped.

Fist in the air. Then he took a breath. Smoothed Vitalis'ed hair, and clamped onto the nape of his neck. Sherry asking if she could smoke, her transmission ever more staticky.

"Dunno…not."

"…anks."

"What's she doing?" Turbeville grimaced.

"I don't know," Legate said.

"She's heading out of range."

One of the tech people, looking up.

Shaking his head.

"Hold on, hold on. Just want to know which way they turn. C'mon, c'mon."

"You're risking that girl's life!" Turbeville thundered.

"Shut up! Nobody made her do this. She volunteered."

"How the heck.........taking us......way north to Tennessee?"

"That's it!"

Legate punching the air. "North. Right turn."

He joined Perry and Pickens at the maps, Turbeville following heavily. "Still receiving her," the tech guy was saying, "real weak and intermittent."

"Stay on it," Legate ordered.

"Gain's up full. If we went mobile, sir, we'd have a better—"

"Groping around out there, we might run headlong into dozens of trigger-happy Klansmen."

Legate hard-eyed Turbeville.

Then Pickens.

"Agreed gentlemen?"

Pickens nodded. "Agreed."

Turbeville spat into a cup.

"Agreed," he added, disgustedly.

Four minutes passed before they picked up Sherry Russell again.

Somehow.

The tech guy was flabbergasted. The truck had braked; they heard the squeak. "...with the truck......told to tell...once you're......

"The church," Sherry practically shouted through her mike.

Loud and clear.

"Been a long......been to church."

"A church!" Legate shouted.

Started scouring the maps.

"What churches up that way, Sheriff?"

But Pickens threw his head back.

Paced away...

"Sheriff?"

"I be damned."

CHAPTER 95

I WAS SHIVERING. NERVES AND night-air. My mother was famously convinced there was something sinister and illness inducing about night-air. "Careful Sherry Louise—don't stay out in the night-air too long." The Klan meeting had been going on close to an hour. Hobbs was speaking. "The military and political situation with the enemy has reached crisis stage. Events this fall may well decide the fate of Christian civilization for centuries to come."

No signs of the man winding down, which was fine— because when he did, Vance, Autrey, and I would be shot. Probably while still tied to these very trees. Not unlike Montie Collins and the others. I continued my broadcasting, maintaining a vain thread of hope the FBI, my government, might be closing in, might pick it up.

I thought about Fred.

Began to cry again.

"Where we find corrupt and cowardly mayors and police, obviously, our members cannot submit..."

Jesse Vance hadn't made a sound. I twisted my head his way. He might be dead. I blinked tears that burned in my eyes like salt, and I breathed unevenly. Autrey had spoken a few times, in a bad way, but he was alive. The men were tied to larger trees, deeper in the woods than me, so I couldn't look around far enough to see either.

"...Must move swiftly and vigorously to attack the local headquarters of the enemy, destroy and disrupt his leadership and communication, and any news communication equipment in the area..."

"Bixby Methodist Church," I repeated.

"Tied in the trees, left of the church. Vance and Autrey—"

I clipped my words.

Licked my dry lips.

One of the Klan guards, the one with the shotgun, was at the tree line, wading through fringe bushes, swiping and whapping. The guard with the Carbine moved closer too. The first man angled past me in Autrey's direction. I craned over my shoulder, turned my body far as I could.

"...very swift, very forceful, no holes barred. The attack on the enemy..."

I strained to hear.

"You damn dirty Fed," the guard was saying to Autrey.

Who replied, ever eloquent, and diplomatic:

"Go fuck yourself."

What came next could only be the butt of the shotgun striking Autrey's face. An utterance of agony—distorted, gurgly—then my breath came faster as I heard a sickening nightmare, the helpless Autrey beaten, with fists and perhaps with a pistol, or blackjack. "Stoppit!" I finally shrieked over my shoulder when I couldn't help myself. "Goddamnit, can't you see he's half dead?"

The violence halted, only to be replaced by a sudden dread seeping all through me out of my quavering belly. I rotated forward, my eyes huge, flickering. I waited, swallowing, breathing quiet, as if by some magical way I could remain in hiding, despite being tied up, right out there in front. Tramping came through the forest from behind and right of me, through the dark. My heart quailing as the trees moved, and there he was, the shotgun coming up. The Klansman was a silhouette, moving indistinctly, featurelessly, between me and the light from the church, except for a faint glint from his eyes. I smelled moonshine on his breath, made out gaps where teeth should be. "I don't take orders"—I felt saliva spray my face as he spoke— "not from no bitch nigger lover?"

My chest rose and fell. "I'm no nigger lover, you imbecile," I said between my teeth. "I'm just no hater; can't you comprehend the difference?" He leveled the sawed-off into my sternum, and began to sniff aloud over me, spreading using the gun barrels as fingers my shirt collar,. "You got some nice lungs, ain'tcha?" he said, grinning in front of me, missing teeth, and not caring.

I jerked. Face ticced.

"...we as Christians have a responsibility, have taken an oath..."

Lowering, still holding the gun on me one-handed, he ran the other up the curve of my hip. The other guard ducked and bent, stalking closer. Then hesitated, worried about leaving his post, looking round at the church. He was twenty feet or more back, and he couldn't see much through the heavy shadow. I swallowed and thought, debating whether to cry out. I came back to Toothless, looking me over with his mouth open. If I involved the other man, I might be left alone, or I might end up dealing with both of them, or Toothless might just beat me to shut me up. He bent to stand his gun against the tree next to my leg. As he rose he said, "What the hail..." Half-turning to the other man, having made up his syphilitic mind.

"Thought you Kluxers," I said, gasping for oxygen, "respected Southern women? Took oaths about...about protecting our honor?"

"Don't reckon ol' Sam Bacon thinks that way 'bout you no more."

"Maybe...you ought to ask, be sure, before doing anything?"

"Shut up, bitch," said the Klansman; he yanked the neck of my blouse, popping buttons down to where I'd knotted the shirttails, as though tearing me open. I bit down on my rear molars, dug my heels in, withdrawing deeper into the needles and branches of the sapling. The sawed-off came up under my jaw. I made a small inhuman sound. Shutting my eyes, feeling him through my bra. My teeth set against darts of pain.

Suddenly he froze—

My eyes burst open—

He'd found the Micro 007, smallest bug in existence. A 1 x ¾ x ¼ inch box sold for $149.95 by the Continental Telephone Supply Co., Inc. Known in some circles as the sugar-cube mike.

"That's right," I managed hoarsely, "everything's been heard...so you'd better untie me, let me go, and when the Feds move in, I'll tell them how you saved me."

There was a tug—

The bra cup tore—

And Toothless rocked back, holding up the transmitter and the ripped-away crisscross of adhesive tape.

"Take your filthy hands off the lady!"

I heard a gun cocked.

Suddenly in profile, hovered before me like a religious apparition was a large-caliber revolver, drilled into the Klansman's temple. "On the ground, shit ass, and don't make a sound doin' it. 'Less you want your brains all over these-here woods."

Turbeville.

He followed the Klansman to the forest floor.

The second guard reacted.

A cocked head, eyes narrowing, Carbine pointing, through the darkness and trees and brush.

"Look out Bobby Ray!" I said out of a rictus. Then I heard a sound I will never forget if I live a hundred years—a snap-whip from the area of the cemetery, like a rubber band, or a sickle blade slashing. I was thinking the other guard heard it too, because he lurched around, backlit by yellow-orange flickers of lanterns and torches. A foot and a half of bright-wet arrow shoved out the center of his chest.

I gasped.

The Carbine fell, rotating out of his hands. I almost vomited watching him take hold of the solid-set arrow, all the way through him, feather vanes coming out his back. His knees hit, and he fell on his side, making a bubbling sound, then amazingly he rose again. I was mesmerized.

Horrified.

The shot man took a couple strides towards Bobby Ray and me, ghastly hand stretching out. Bobby Ray raised his gun, aiming it. The man opened his mouth. My teeth chattered, and he toppled forward. I heard a trembling in the leaves and sticks—like a rattlesnake—then he became still. Then, beyond his dying, I saw a whippet-thin deputy emerge, sideways, out of the weathered gravestones, far side of the clearing in front of the church. He carried a five-foot hunt bow, another arrow on the string of it.

I then made a savage sense of everything. He stood the bow against the spare tire, back of a parked Jeep. Drew his revolver. Agent Legate rushed ahead through the forest from behind me, between Autrey's tree and my sapling. I shook the dizziness out of myself. Legate crouched at the edge of the clearing, white-knuckled on a shotgun. Scanning.

Turbeville had Toothless cuffed and gagged.

He rose like a giant. Got out a knife, and sawed on the rope binding my wrists until it gave way. "Flat on the ground and stay there," he whispered, sounding angry with me. I got down in stages like into cold water, fixing my bra as much as it could be, and clutching the front of my shirt. Turbeville extended me the Klansman's sawed-off, his lower teeth bared: "Use this if you have to."

"Yes." I clasped it.

He moved off low.

"The leaders, of course, are not innocent," I heard Hobbs still speechmaking, "and they should be our prime targets…"

CHAPTER 96

I BE DAMNED..."
    Then:
    "Sonovabitch..."

That had been Sheriff Pickens' reactions to Sherry Russell's comment over the speaker about the Klan taking her to a church.

"Bixby Methodist Church," he declared, thumping one of the spread-out maps, indicating a location approximately a mile and a half, as the crow flew, from the farmhouse. "June, 1964, Agent Legate. Mean anything to you?"

"What?" Turbeville demanded.

Pickens glanced his way. "That church is where the White Knights originally met to organize and, effectively, declare war on the, so-called, communist authorities in charge of the national government. To launch the most violent campaign of terror in the history of American civil rights. Kluxers are nothing if not traditionalists. They began it there..."

"And they'll end it there." A tone of dread in Legate's words as they all began to pore over the maps and since—by some miracle of radiofrequency physics—Sherry's wire had also alerted them to a checkpoint of armed Klansmen, Pickens gave his estimate of where that checkpoint would be.

Legate dispatched two agents—if they thought they could neutralize the guard post when they encountered it, they were to do so. They did, without a shot fired. The Klansmen taken away by a Highway Patrol unit called in for backup. A small arsenal was confiscated: one Garand rifle, two twelve-gauge pump shotguns, three pistols, boxes of .00 buckshot, bayonets, half *dozen fragmentation grenades, four tear gas grenades, brass knuckles, bandoliers. Their car had a two-way radio installed. Neutralization of the checkpoint meant two things:*

Bixby Church was the meeting site. And, if they acted fast they could infiltrate close, surround the church, then raid the Klonvokation in progress.

Shattering the Klan's violent core.

They approached in four cars—four special agents, Sheriff Pickens and two deputies, Sheriff Turbeville, and the FBI technical men. More agents and the Highway Patrol were speeding to the scene. They kept monitoring, on the move, both of Sherry Russell's frequencies, eventually re-establishing contact as the caravan crept deeper and higher in the piney woods. The FM receiver tuned to the purse mike, naturally, actuated first. Not long after, fostered by the church's high-ground position, the tech people got a signal on a second receiver from the body mike.

They got a surprise though.

Two different signals: The cigarette-pack mike and the body mike were in different locations!

"They took her purse," Legate reasoned, the men huddling over the surveillance gear, on the hood of one of the black government Chevys. Near the top of the knoll, but still down in the trees, cars parked to blockade of the only access to and away from Bixby Church.

Sherry was talking to them.

Via the body mike.

Damn she was good, Turbeville thought, and he wanted her out of there more than he could stand, especially after he realized she had no way of knowing how close they were. That anyone was within range of her voice, as it pressed bravely on.

And it set his blood to boiling.

That pop-in-jay Legate was just using her. Her physical assets, her eager morality, her great inferiority-complex need to prove her worthiness to men. If Legate was too holier-than-thou to recognize most Southern white men weren't Klan at heart—fine—but Sherry Russell deserved better than to be treated like an attractive pack mule for five-hundred-bucks worth of transistors and printed circuits. In fact, to all outward appearances, Legate may have forgotten Sherry Russell existed. He was so enraptured by the other transmission, from the purse mike.

From inside the church!

Broadcasting live:

Imperial Wizard Hobbs reading his Imperial Executive Order to the joint White Knights-Amalgamated Klans. Little suspecting he had a small audience of FBI men and sheriffs listening as well, a few hundred feet away.

"I want all this on tape," Legate declared.

"Bullshit," Turbeville said.

"We have to be patient, sit tight. We've got the only egress blocked. They can't escape. Not in vehicles. Now, listen, my plan is, we wait for more manpower, then infiltrate through the forest and throw a noose around that church, surround and capture—"

"We don't get up there now," Turbeville argued, "take them by surprise—you heard the Russell woman—your three operatives are gonna be murdered when this meeting ends."

"We'll move in time to circumvent that."

"You're gambling with three lives, including that girl's."

"A calculated risk. And may I remind you, Sheriff Turbeville, you're here as a courtesy."

Turbeville spat an angry stream of tobacco juice onto the dirt road. "To hell with you," he said, rotating straight, "and to hell with your courtesies, and to hell with the goddamn FBI."

He began to hike uphill, grit under-boot, up the dark road. Taking out his Frontier Colt, actually the one confiscated from Loftin after FBI agents secured Turbeville's as evidence in the Cothran murder. "Sheriff Turbeville! Where the devil you think you're going? Get back here!"

Turbeville half twisted back:

"I'll be up here saving them people, Hoover Boy. Just try not to shoot me, when you finally do waltz in. All I ask."

"Halt!" replied Legate.

Jerking out his snub-nosed.

"Halt or I'll arrest you."

"Try!"

"That's enough!" Pickens roaring like he was still a colonel in Korea.

"Bobby Ray git back down here, and you Agent, put that goddamn gun away. This is my county and we're going up that hill." His eyes flashed as if crazed. "And we're goin' now. To save those people. But just as important—I don't wanna be chasing a few dozen Kluxers through these woods at night. Not to mention that man Loftin's van load of munitions could just be the tip of an iceberg. No sir, Agent, I want a lid on this. And I want it tight, and want it now, and the FBI can either assist, or stay outta the goddamn way."

CHAPTER 97

I DIDN'T KNOW WHAT WOULD happen next as I lay prone in the chill and dark, one hand clutching my blouse closed, the other hugging a sawed-off shotgun like a beloved child. I didn't know, but feared something reminiscent of Iwo Jima. So, flat on my bust and belly, I crawled. After a few yards I raised my head like a periscope, above the kudzu. Proceeded in a new direction, flopping and lurching to the large tree where Autrey was tied.

There was a charging behind me. I rose, half-aiming the shotgun, then lowered the dual-maw of the vicious weapon, seeing the rushing man was in uniform. Holstered pistol jumping on his belt, and he too lugged a shotgun. Lean, angular, silvery. He dropped in the vines and underbrush. Talking close into Turbeville's ear, looking and gesturing behind the church. Then silently he slapped Turbeville on the meat of the arm, pivoted and moved away, bent in that peculiar infantryman fashion, until he reached Legate.

I focused on Autrey, bleeding from the mouth, large head sagging from the broad shoulders, like a boulder. "Lee!" I whispered. I stood the sawed-off against the next tree, came round and pressed his temples, cradled his head back. "Lee can you hear me?" I grimaced; his jaw hung loose and funny. I sensed him give me a nod, responding to my voice. Holding his head, laying it against my shoulder, I hooked one of my fingers in his mouth, swept out the loose broken teeth. Then, carefully, mournfully, I let his head sag back the way I'd found it. Eased back. Alert, ready to catch it, like it might not hold. Then I plowed behind him through the groundcover. "I'm cutting you free, Lee, okay?"

He groaned.

"Sorry," I said, "this is going to hurt."

I didn't know his injuries' extent or severity and the RN in me preferred keeping him very still. There were other considerations, however, not covered in the curriculum of the Mid-State Baptist Hospital School of Nursing. I figured, for example, he'd be less likely to get a gunshot wound adding to his troubles if he weren't tied upright to a tree when lead began to fly. So, I got my jackknife from my pocket, and started sawing loops of rope, working upward from the bottom. I hoped if his legs were free he might manage some kind of controlled descent.

He outweighed me by a hundred pounds; I wasn't about to try to catch him. As I worked, running sweat, I glimpsed toward the clearing—saw Legate getting a call on a radio, tuned to a very low volume, grabbed from his jacket pocket.

"Here goes," I warned.

I had Autrey's wrists free, and neck, and was about the slice the rope strapped tight across his chest and shoulders. Legate was pressing the radio to his ear. Pressing the pads of his fingers over the free ear.

"Ready?" I said, and I think Lee Autrey grunted.

Legate was off the radio and suddenly he and the silver-haired lawman were practically at one another's throats. *Jesus Christ!* I thought. Turbeville saw what I saw, and went over with his head low, and dropped next to the silver-haired man. I cut the last rope and Autrey's knees hit the ground.

I heard pain, then he keeled over massively like the *U.S.S. Arizona*. I followed him down trying at least to protect his cervical spine. I felt for the pulse beat in his wrist which was regular, and fairly strong. Then I eyeballed, frowning, the now-three-way brouhaha between Legate, Turbeville and the other lawman. I resisted the urge to see what was so important it couldn't wait till we all weren't a few yards from thirty Klansmen who'd love to open up on us with Thompsons.

Instead I snagged up my stubby shotgun and, with my open clasp knife, left Autrey, and tramped downhill to where Vance was tied, his face bloody like something out of a cheap horror movie. More blood, very thick and sticky, matted the hair on the back of his head. My examining fingers palpated an obviously depressed skull fracture.

I felt his chest.

Funny breathing…

Heavy a few cycles…

Shallow a few…

Cheyne-Stoking, it was called. Severe brain damage was all I could recall about it. Weak pulse to boot. I cut him down as I had Autrey, for his own good—to keep him from getting shot—and he thundered to earth with nowhere near the grace Autrey had.

Enough patience. The debate between my gallant rescuers showed no signs of abating, and since my pretty derriere was on the line too, I decided to find out what was happening. Knife pocketed and shotgun tipped up and back, I approached from the right and behind and crouched onto one knee. "What is going on? What are you waiting for?"

CHAPTER 98

L EGATE'S RADIO CALL CAME FROM *one of the tech guys still recording everything said inside the church. He was relaying a priority message received on the car radio from the Special Agent in Charge of the Jackson Field Office. "Abort," it said. "Do not interfere with church meeting. Repeat. Do not interfere with church meeting. Extract personnel and withdraw. Orders from Directorate. Repeat. Orders from Directorate."*

Why wouldn't Hoover, who'd authorized the anti-Klan COINTELPRO, even opened just over three years ago, the Jackson Field Office, specifically in response to the Klan threat, not want this meeting broken up? Why wouldn't he revel in the Klan equivalent of the Mafia fiasco in Apalachin, N.Y.? Then again—that raid by New York State troopers on a 1957 underworld conference had proven oddly and profoundly embarrassing for Hoover. Who had for three decades denied the existence of both the Mafia and anything called organized crime!

Alan Legate knew not what to make of the order.

But worse—he had mutiny on his hands. The sheriffs wouldn't withdraw; they and probably the Mississippi Highway Patrol were going to do their level best to disrupt the meeting anyway. If Legate disobeyed, or failed to stop the locals—either way, he'd bring down upon himself the Director's famous wrath. Avoidance of which by fearful agents was described by a former agent in 1962 as a "burlesque comedy of a kindergarten class."

CHAPTER 99

EYEGLASSES REFLECTING TORCHLIGHT, LEGATE TOLD me over his shoulder he had orders from Washington to abort the operation. Quickly insisting he knew no more than I did. "I don't care what you know," I blasted. "Not pretending to tell any of you gentlemen your jobs, and I don't care right now if you abort, or blow that church to kingdom come. But! Those men back there will be dead soon. So make up your minds. Setting up camp here is no damn option."

The silver-haired lawman twisted.

Grinning very white dentures.

"Quite little spitfire ain't you?"

It seemed to be a complement.

"Sheriff Pickens, young lady…"

We shook. "Sherry Russell," I said, morosely.

"Genuine honor, ma'am. Damn fine job." Then his focus stabbed back at Legate. "There's a cache of weapons back there big enough to fight World War III that I ain't leaving here without. Clear!"

Turbeville crawled beside me:

"Sheriff Pickens and Agent Perry found a bomb shelter back of the church."

The earthen dome, I realized.

"Chockfull," he said, "of weapons and explosives."

***

All hell broke loose.

Submachine gunfire behind the church.

A handgun returned it, four rounds, fast.

Silencing the machine gun with a frightful scream through the fiery night. Turbeville tackled me flat. Yelled me to stay down. I had a strange sensation he'd done the same before—say, twenty-some years ago. Battle of the Bulge or something equally intense and historic. As his weight lifted off I heard more blistering gunfire. Dirt spouted around us. Whirrings. Legate and Sheriff Pickens opened up and Turbeville fell beside me wounded, maybe dead.

I jerked with a spear of pain through the back of my right thigh.

I cried out and writhed and grabbed my leg. Scrabbled like a whipped dog behind the nearest big tree. Love to report I was brave or stoic or some noble thing—but I wasn't. I was hurting and screaming. Dropped with my back against the bark of the pine trunk, amongst a gnarl of woody roots, both my legs out before me. My right hand clamped onto the top of the tremoring right leg. Holding it like I was having to keep it down with all the strength in my arm and the rest of my body.

Lips drawn against my teeth.

I saw nothing of what transpired behind me.

Again, I lay no claims to gallantry here. I smelled a smoky cloying sweetness of burnt gunpowder. I heard perhaps thirty seconds of shattering noise. It rang in my skull, throbbed my eardrums. Wangs and splinters in the air. Booms of shotguns, night-splitting cracks of pistols and rifles, two more short bursts from a Thompson.

Then a loud, ringing, half-muffled explosion.

A yellow bright flash.

Swroomph!

That shook the ground.

Coming from behind the church.

Two soft pops towards the end, which I eventually learned were two of the Klan's own tear-gas grenades deployed against then. Taken from the Klan car at the checkpoint, lobbed through open windows of the church by the same Smith County deputy who'd center-shot the Klan sentry with a hunting arrow.

Tear gas billowed out windows and doors. The Klan's brutal elite—gathered from many states to south-central Mississippi—fled the building hacking and vomiting.

Some still shooting.

They were cut down.

Some tossed weapons out ahead of them or out windows or dropped them inside the church, emerging with hands raised. Overeager adrenaline-spurred deputies and agents shot some of them as well. The remainder ordered to the ground, face in the dirt, spread eagle.

The shooting seemed to have stopped.

I rolled carefully onto my elbows. My heart beating against the pine-needle floor of the forest, my head lifting. A deputy wearing a gas mask and Sheriff Pickens with a handkerchief over his nose and mouth entered the church, guns leading. A single shot followed, yellow-flashing in the windows, a haunting chemical mist gathered all round, drifting fog-like through trees. My eyes began to burn and water. Men were moaning.

"God I'm shot," somebody wept.

I managed to stand. My leg wasn't too bad. Some bleeding, not much, and it didn't hurt much either, now that I thought about it. Stiffly I advanced uphill to where Turbeville went down. I didn't see anything. Felt relief, he must be all right, off arresting Kluxers. The whole clearing and the fringes of the forest were well lit now by the headlights of arriving cars, and flashlights sweeping.

I saw the big sheriff half buried in kudzu.

I moved through small trees and tangles, sidestepped over a rotting log. He was flat on his back, legs splayed out. Wet glint in his open eyes. Might have been stargazing but for the shotgun still gripped in the fist formed by his right hand. Laying across his hip and the lower portion of his large belly. His signature pouch of Red Man knocked half out his breast pocket by the fall.

Squeezing the wound in my leg, I gritted teeth, and knelt.

"Bobby Ray," I said softly.

As if not to disturb him, exhaling.

"Where you hurt?"

I shifted to cradle his head. Lift it out of the brown, pine-needle clutter. Surveying his length and breadth, no obvious wound, no blood staining the khaki. All I saw was a smaller-than-dime-sized spot touching the upper fringe of his heavy left eyebrow.

I stabilized his head.

Began to ease my right hand underneath, between it and the forest floor. That hand suddenly plunged into a gummy warm pool. Chunks were in the pool. Like stew beef in sauce. Three of my fingertips, curling to cup and lift the man's head, fell inside a fist-size cavity in the back of Bobby Ray Turbeville's skull.

My heart sickishly pounded.

A numbness overtaking the rest of me.

Splintery bone rimmed the cavity. Torn scalp. I withdrew my hand—gaped at it, rotating it. There was a detachment. Like it wasn't my own hand that looked as if I had just, for some incalculable reason, plunged it to the wrist in a can of dark red paint.

"Mrs. Russell!"

I heard.

Didn't register.

"Mrs. Russell…Mrs. Russell…"

I twisted at last. Looking up blankly. Legate, jacket flapping, tripping in some roots. "You hurt?" he asked, puffing, reaching me.

I swallowed.

"I'm okay."

As if he'd asked if I'd wanted a Kleenex.

"Please hurry."

"What?"

"Come with me."

Reaching out a needful, pleading hand.

"Yes," I said numbly. "All right."

I stared back at my hand. Wiped it through kudzu, smeared it on my pants leg. I stood, pressing my own wound against the bone in my thigh. Intense pain loosening the grip on me of whatever trancelike state had taken hold.

"C'mon."

Legate urged.

"Hurry."

One shoe between the dead sheriff's knees, I lifted and placed the other on the other side, and trailed after Legate. Sirens began to wail through the night. Legate never mentioned Turbeville. I was moving stiff-legged, trying to keep up. Rounding the rear corner of the church—

Jolted to a halt.

Something at my feet, blocking my way, something I'm convinced to this day no human being was ever meant to lay eyes upon. Not in Mississippi, nor the Mekong Delta. I took it in, because it was there and shouldn't have been and I couldn't help but absorb it. For all time. Till death do us part. I remembered the explosion behind the church and knew, instinctively, what had caused it. Saw it all, in fact, like a little gory movie in my mind.

A Klansman lay in a strangely grotesque posture, his entire right buttock and part of his back blown away. Internal organs visible in the cavity. Still holding the ring and safety pin of a hand grenade in his hand. He was dead. Legate's voice cut through:

"Mrs. Russell. Please."

Waving me forward. I looked at him slackly. He was paying as little attention to the blown-up man—who'd obviously fallen, perhaps shot, on top of his own grenade—as he had to Bobby Ray Turbeville. I wanted to cuff him across that smug face, say *look around!* But didn't. I followed him like I had that grenade ring through my nose.

Legate led me down cinderblock steps, then crawling on hands and knees—I was still in a daze—through a short tunnel underground, beneath the red-earth mound, which indeed was shrouded over by military-surplus camouflage netting, concealing the excavation from nosy aircraft. Once through the tunnel we could stand upright, inside a dome fashioned out of corrugated steel, partially buried, and covered over with earth. A generator was operating, powering electric lights, which reflected off the silvery dome, intensifying the retina-hurting brightness of the chamber.

I knew what it was—what it was intended to be—a steel-igloo-type fallout shelter. They were sold as a prefab kits to bury in backyards or set up in basements. All ready for doomsday. Spacious, too, designed to house an entire suburban family in the aftermath of a Soviet ICBM attack for days or weeks. "It's Agent Perry," Legate pled. "He's badly wounded, dragged himself back in here. You were a nurse right? Please help him."

Fuzzily I nodded.

"I'll try."

CHAPTER 100

THERE WAS BARELY ENOUGH PLYWOOD-over-dirt floor under the dome for me and Legate to stand, with Special Agent Perry on his back, and the one other agent, at Perry's side, rendering first aid. The shelter was, as I've said, spacious, but the Klan had it stacked high, all around with crates of heavy weapons, grenades, dynamite. There were steel ammo boxes. I got Legate to lug one over, and turn it on its side, lift Perry's feet onto it. I, of course, had more critical concerns than taking inventory—but even I found it impossible to ignore two particular items the Klan had stockpiled:

A bazooka.

Complete with six rockets.

And a flame thrower!

"Jesus Christ," I muttered, then knelt stiff and slow beside the wounded Perry, careful with my leg. "My name's Sherry," I said, through a grimace, across to the freckled young agent, scared to death, mashing a blood-sodden handkerchief over Perry's left shoulder. "Ma'am..." he gasped. He looked pale, was breathing unevenly, which was the way it was with medical emergencies. A wise doctor, back when I was a full-time nurse, once told me:

First, take your own pulse.

Legate ordered the kid to take charge topside. "Yes sir," and I took over pressing the shoulder, the source of Perry's most obvious hemorrhage. I only half registered Legate removing some mimeographed papers and folded maps from an open foot locker, passing them to the departing agent. "Nobody sees these. Unduhstand? Lock them in your trunk—first priority."

"Yes sir."

Legate rotated back, punched his glasses up the bridge of his nose, and told me:

"He was shot with a Thompson."

"Shit," I said, peeling up the blood-saturated handkerchief. A welling of dark blood inferior to the clavicle—and some spurting. Subclavian artery injury. "Press hard on this like he was. If you have another handkerchief stack it on top."

Perry's suit jacket was off, folded like a pillow under his sweat-riveted head. He was awake, dull-eyed, but fixed on my face, which seemed to reassure him, or comfort him, or something. Whether a function of femininity or if I emanated some caregiving competence, I didn't know. His white shirt was laid open, tie loosened, right shirtsleeve cut, torn up to the shoulder. The fabric blood-splotched and spattered by a bullet wound through the right upper extremity. The young agent had formed a tourniquet out of his own necktie and applied it above the wound. He'd knotted a ballpoint pen into the necktie and used that to twist the tourniquet tight and secure. I would loosen it later to prevent ischemia. For now, though, my predecessor had done well. I got out my own jackknife and sliced, then ripped from the bottom up, the wounded man's undershirt.

Darting at Legate: "What caliber?"

"Forty-five."

"Goddamn," I said, rubbing my forehead with the back of my wrist. The vicious weapon had stitched across Legate's partner's body, right to left, at an upward angle. First the arm, then a nearly bloodless, perfectly round, half-inch-diameter hole abutting the right nipple. Then left edge of the sternum, second intercostal space, oozing somewhat more than the previously described, otherwise similar wound.

The bleeding from those wounds, second and third in line, was not impressive. That was the thing with trauma—important structures of the extremities were superficial, their injuries tending to be rather obvious. Great body cavities though—the chest and abdomen—had a lot going on deep, injuries to which might manifest little or nothing externally. Lastly Perry had been shot clean through the left shoulder. With Legate holding pressure, controlling that hemorrhage, the two chest wounds worried me most. I brought myself back to cope with them, ignoring all the rest. Pleural cavities could flood full of blood with no exterior bleeding. It was therefore of no small consequence that Perry's breathing seemed to have grown more labored in just my short time with him. I fingered the carotid pulse, my own leg having begun to throb rather badly. I bowed my head, squeezing shut my lids. Legate was impatient: "Do something!"

My face expanded. "I am!"

Perry's neck diaphoretic, stubbly.

Felt along his trachea.

Deviated? I laid my ear upon a mat of chest hair, listened. His heartbeat pulsed away, though the *lub-dub*s sounded distant, muffled. I dug nails into his groin, through his trousers.

Thready femoral pulse. He was clammy.

Cold, and drenching. Perry spoke: "Can't breathe..."

Like a drowning man. I stroked his temple. "Going to try to help you, I promise."

My eyes twitched around. "Do something!" Legate again.

"Shut up!"

I thumped over Perry's ribs.

Sounds on the left dull, flat, solid.

Hollow on the right.

"He's dying!" Legate chided.

"I know that!"

Clamping my temples. "Ballpoint pen," I exploded.

Stabbing a look across.

"Do you have one?"

Still mashing down on the bloody shoulder he mined the pen out of his jacket with the other hand. Retractable type. Good. I unscrewed the tube. Flung away the guts, ink cartridge and spring. I groped around, found on the floor my own knife.

Clean and sharp as anything down there. I wiped the blade, both sides, on my shirt sleeve. I doubted the Klan had stocked their underground munitions bunker with an autoclave. Then I thought—

"No whiskey down here is there? To use as disinfectant?"

Legate lashed around.

"Don't see any; I can—"

"Forget it."

"What are you doing?"

Ignoring him, through Perry's fatty sallow skin, I pressed for a spot. Between two ribs, inferior to the midpoint of the right collar bone. Side of the hollow percussion sounds, and the nipple wound. Which, depending on the bullet's trajectory, probably had done only one thing—blown a hole in his right lung. Which I'd seen enough gunshot wounds to know might not be as bad as it sounded. I stood the blade tip of my knife over the point I'd mapped out, upper edge of the lower rib bordering that intercostal space. Oriented the blade parallel to that rib.

Gritting teeth.

I covered my fist with my other hand.

And stabbed the blade down though. Forcing my weight into the effort.

"What are you doing?"

"Saving your buddy's life, I hope!"

A spewing of air.

I pulled the knife out, quarter turned it, and drilled again down into flesh, muscle, and gristle. With the blade still embedded, I stood the tapered end of the disassembled plastic pen tube over the wound, directly in contact with, alongside the blade. Wishing I'd used the knife first to enlarge the hole at the tip of the pen tube. One of those times you could wish for a lot to be different, instead of just doing what the situation called for. I forced the pen tube down through the wound.

Simultaneously withdrawing the knife.

The bloody cut skin edges self-sealed, the man's body seeming to welcome and embrace the tube, air hissing up out of it.

Stopped.

I pushed.

Pulled.

Angled.

Nothing—I finally lowered and put my mouth to the end of the tube and blew into it to dislodge whatever was gumming up the narrow internal opening.

Another gush.

Then a sucking, Perry's lungs gaining a great rush of breath. "My God," Legate said, as if strangling on his own tongue, "you got him breathing."

"For now." Clawing my scalp, pulling my own hair. "Switch sides," I said. My leg had stiffened a lot and I bared my teeth and groaned, grasping my thigh as I straddled Perry. Trickles like small cockroaches skittered down my leg, and my hand covered a circle of denim grown warm and sticky as if with maple syrup. "What about the shoulder?" Legate asked as he squatted where I had been. I scanned, grit under my feet. There was a low barrier of sandbags across the bomb-shelter entrance to keep out rainwater. I told Legate to lay one on top of the wound and folded handkerchiefs. "First though give me that pen," I said. "One your other man used."

I indicated Perry's arm. "Loosen the tourniquet. If there's much bleeding, knot it snug, but not over-tight. If there isn't, just bandage it with material from his shirt sleeve."

After a few seconds he extended me the other pen across a still-half-suffocating Perry. He literally *was* still half suffocating, if I'd diagnosed correctly. The pen was one of those clear Bics. I used my knife to cut the ends off, discarding the guts like before. I punctured the same X between two ribs that I had on the other side, except this time it was Perry's side, below his armpit. I forced the hexagonal pen barrel through the wound, then withdrew the blade. The clear lumen flushed dark purple, which spurt out the end. Spattered the floor and my shoes—a bloody, bubbly side-shooting fountain. Less or none during inhalations, which rapidly strengthened. Mere seconds later Perry became magically alert—as if kissed by Princess Charming—and he muttered me a grateful, "Thank you." Smiling upward, prayerful, as if reborn. "You did it.," Legate puffed.

Full of awe.

"Don't get excited," I whispered gravely.

Then I glimpsed down at Perry, got up and crept, limping, a couple of steps away, so he might not hear us. I pulled Legate around. "It's not going to last. He had a tension pneumothorax. On one side. Hemothorax on the other. Air flooding one side of his chest"—I gestured, illustrating with my hands— "compressing the lung, and blood doing the same on the other, see? I've released that built-up pressure, but it isn't going to last. If nothing else I've just given him two open pneumothoraces. He needs real chest tubes hooked up to wall suction in a real goddamn hospital; on top of that, he needs his chest cracked."

"Can you do that?"

"Don't be silly," I shrieked, then glimpsed around at the wounded man. Back to Legate, leaning, whispering: "I think he's been shot through the heart."

"What? How…?"

"Or darn close."

I shrugged. "He's alive, so there's a chance. There's always a chance. Or maybe I'm wrong. Anyway he needs a hospital." Legate's jaw muscles bunched under the harsh light. "Should be an ambulance soon," he said, looking back, and up, toward where a number of sirens had been winding to a stop. "I'll check, get a stretcher down here PDQ."

"Go," I said, swiping my hair, exhaustedly.

He hesitated. "You're okay?" He glimpsed, indicating my blouse—which frankly I'd forgotten about—half-ripped bra cup hanging out, and red gouge marks where Toothless had clawed up the bug. "Yes, I'm fine, thank you for asking." And I turned away, and lowered back beside Perry, clasping my leg, reacting to the pain, then after a grunting exhale, I rolled back the sandbag, curling lips with the effort. The bleeding had slowed, which was either good or bad—either we were getting hemostasis established, or he was slipping deeper into shock. Legate was on hands and knees scrapping back along in the tunnel. He craned around. "No matter what, Mrs. Russell…"

I looked. "Yes?"

"Thank you."

"It's my job, I'm a nurse. Go."

I came back into Perry's eyes.

Staring up into mine. I cradled his head and beamed him my everything-is-coming-up-roses, nurse smile I held in reserve for only my most ill patients. "Ditto," he said, voice crisp, but weak.

He shivered, slick with perspiration. I smiled some more.

Then sighed.

"You deserve to know…" I swallowed. "Sorry, I've never known your first name."

"Cal. Calvin."

I blinked.

Nodded.

"Cal. You're badly hurt. I've bought you a little time. That's all."

He nodded. Sweat trickling, diffusing into his hairline at his temples. "Maybe a few minutes," I said emotionally. "Maybe enough to get you to a hospital." My lips quavered. "I don't know…I don't know…"

He coughed a slight deep rattle I didn't like, then managed:

"Got something for you…"

"Why don't you wait," I said coquettishly. "Send me a dozen big roses when you're all better?" I swept my hair back. "I love getting roses. Redder the better. I challenge you to make them so big and red my husband will be green with envy."

"No," he said.

Catching some breath.

"Paper…" His eyelids sank.

Mine narrowed; his rolled open again. "Inside coat pocket…Legate…good man…but he would never let…never give it to you…and…you deserve…to…to know…"

I nodded, squinting.

"Know what…?"

I heard scrambling. Over my shoulder, Legate appeared through the tunnel.

"Stretcher's coming; how is he?" He got to his feet, brushing off.

I looked down at Perry.

His eyes were shut.

CHAPTER 101

I SUPERVISED CAL PERRY'S LOADING onto a gurney they'd somehow managed to get down into the bomb shelter, the grunt work done by the funeral director, who owned the ambulance, and a cooperative Klansman, who'd neither been shot nor blown up, and who had been a stretcher-bearer in the army. I obsessed over my improvised thoracostomy tubes, being sure they weren't dislodged. I also carried out Perry's jacket, not having yet had time to look at the paper in the inside pocket. The paper he'd said, with what he had to have known might be one of his dying breaths, that Legate would've kept from me, that I deserved to know…?

Know what?

What the paper contained?

What all this was about?

Legate, if I had to guess, had told everybody to obey the hell out of me, on threat of Federal indictment, because never in my whole professional life had I enjoyed so much unquestioning, unhesitating cooperation from a bunch of men.

Outside was nightmarish.

The scream of sirens.

Spotlights.

Uniformed law officers and plainclothes FBI swarming over the knoll. Wounded men everywhere, and the same number of puking men, effect of the tear gas. There was a veritable traffic jam, vehicles of all types, but somehow they'd managed room for a sleek state-of-the-art Pontiac ambulance to maneuver in, get wheeled around. It was a modified hearse, of course—they all were—all white with a giant red rotating roof beacon and four alternating red bullet lights on the four roof corners.

Painted on the door:

PHELPS MORTUARY EMERGENCY AMBULANCE SERVICE.

I broke away in search of Autrey and Vance. I'd laid Perry's jacket across his legs on the stretcher, after having slipped the mysterious paper out, and tucked it down the back pocket of my jeans. Legate shouted after me, as I hobbled off, telling me he wanted me riding to the hospital with Perry. He was right, of course—ambulances in those days, the pre-paramedic era, were strictly "load and go." For Perry to have a ghost of a chance I did need to stay by his side. My finger-pointing reply though was to the funeral director, not Legate: "You got two more stretchers in that thing, right?"

"Yes, ma'am."

"Bring one."

"Mrs. Russell!"

"They're your men too," I blistered at Legate, then turned, wading off into the trees. Coming close to tripping in the pitch dark beyond the lights, I veered left of where I estimated I'd been tied, pine-needled branches sideswiping me, and I stumbled almost literally upon Autrey—crumpled, face-first, where I'd left him. I knelt to the forest floor. "Lee," I said, and gave his big shoulder a gentle shake. Warm to the touch, which was a good sign. "Lee, it's Sherry." I frisked his flanks and thick back, came across no stray-bullet wounds. "Oh God, Lee," I exhaled, bending over him. He gurgled, and I was beginning to be able to see better in the dark. One of his contused eyes came open barely, registering recognition, and I smiled. "Hey cutie," he managed, garbled, out of the shattered mouth, full of glistening blood, a bubble forming on his lips, and popping. "How'bout we go back to our motel…you patch me up, an' I'll show how grateful I am."

"Some other time," I smirked, "you big palooka," as the funeral director joined us, with his assistant, and a folding stretcher. "Load him up," I said, and stood.

Staggered, backward and sideways.

Dizzy.

"Y'okay?"

I grabbed my forehead.

Two handed.

Waited for my brain to gel.

"Ma'am?"

"I'm fine!" I said, rocking my head, still holding it, guessing I was more exhausted than I'd thought. Carefully lowering my hands. "Give me your light," I said, and the director extended me the small flashlight from his belt. I took it, and as they worked I stumbled over, tripping and lurching, grasping my shirt closed, to where I knew I'd find Vance.

Unresponsive, as I'd expected, and I thumbed open one of his eyes, then the other, flicking the borrowed light, documenting bilateral dilated fixed pupils.

For the record, he was breathing, and had a pulse. I didn't, however, think he'd live. What I did think was, his brain was squashed, oozing like Silly Putty out the bottom of his skull, destroying his brainstem as it went. Maybe prompt treatment, by a neurosurgeon, a big, well-equipped, well-staffed hospital, could save him. Maybe, but I doubted it—nor were we exactly on the doorstep of such a place. I leaned straight, breathed heavy. This kind of decision was beyond the pale of my qualifications; however, I was the closest out there to being qualified, that night, in the cordite-smelling, blood-soaked woods surrounding Bixby Methodist Church.

Autrey was bad off, but could be saved.

And the delay to load a third stretcher, especially one holding a man of Vance's proportions, would condemn Agent Perry's very slim chances to nil.

I'd seen what I came to. Clicked off the mortician's flashlight.

And rose.

Quickly.

Too quickly.

It felt like something knocking against me, sending me reeling. Washed over with nausea, and waning strength, I broke out in an icy sweat all over my body. My vision grayed, and went double. I clawed onto the bark of some large pine, there for me, floating in the India-ink woods. My heart beat wild, but my eyes cleared, slowly, by the blink. And like through quicksand, I slogged, my pants' leg feeling wet, steering toward blinking ambulance reds, I could see floating out there, swirling ahead of me. As I got closer I saw they almost had Autrey loaded, and I sped up, trying to run, but it was like I couldn't get traction, no matter how I tried.

Damn—I couldn't let Perry's transport to the hospital be any further delayed.

Not by me.

Certainly not by any absurdly girlish fainting spell.

I don't faint!

Dammit.

I was a licensed nurse.

A licensed detective.

Did Mike Hammer goddamn faint?

I managed past a deputy, clutching his sleeve, and was halfway to the ambulance.

Legate waving me forward.

All of him in fact looked wavy…

Watery…

Gray…

I was coming to, muttering, "I'm okay, I'm okay," Legate and the funeral director facing one another, lifting me, sort of a cradle carry, with their arms slung under my back, behind my bent knees. I felt my thigh hurting, and remembered being shot. The white-clad attendant had their third stretcher deployed, suspended from the ceiling, ready and waiting for me. I was arguing I could manage—but they were having none of it, hoisting me to chest level, as the deputy who'd arrow-killed the Klan guard, rushed to help, and the foursome threaded me headfirst onto the slung stretcher. When I was inside enough I could grasp the frame and had begun to worm and drag and grunt myself the rest of the way, I said, "All right, all right—quit mothering me! Let's go!"

Staring down the full-slabbed-out length of myself I saw Legate swing and slam the long side-hinged tailgate, then hammer the glass with the palm of his hand, the funeral director jumping under the wheel—his and the attendant's doors clashing shut in rapid succession. The engine gunned, siren cranking up to a deafening wail, and my stretcher pitched and yawed, forcing me to hold my stomach in my hands, as I bent my head, crimson beacons sweeping the black façade of the old church, which shrank away through the tailgate windshield.

They raced us to Scott County Hospital, west of Forest, on the way to Jackson, a difficult twenty-three-mile run of twisting dark country roads—the screeching Federal Q-2 splitting open my head like an ax the entire wretched trip. Standard-issue, I later learned, fire-engine siren of the day, and the funeral director was ever-so proud of his ambulance being equipped with so superlative a device. I was shivering, listening through it and my thoughts of Turbeville, and the blown-up man, and the throbbing in my leg to the sounds of Autrey, below me, half strangling, and Perry dying. I rolled onto my stomach to do what I could—there being no space, with three stretcher patients in the back, for an attendant too—punching with my fist, gnashing my teeth, tugged Autrey's white shirt with the Confederate-flag patch on it, screaming at him, through his own delirium and pain, to keep off his back. Cursing him—he seemed to respond to that—so that all that blood and mucous from his smashed-to-pulp face would drain out, rather than puddle in his lungs and airways, drowning him. Had we not scooped him up when we did off that forest floor, I was convinced, with all those secretions, and swelling, and hematomas, and fractures, he would have suffocated.

As for Perry…

He died.

Stretching, I was trying to find his pulse

But I'd lost it, somewhere in all that dark.

Somewhere in the middle of the run.

Nothing to do.

Not even oxygen aboard.

I rolled back, up at the ceiling, pressed my face with the palms of both hands, then I pulled my blouse closed and folded my arms—caught whiffs of sweat and perfume from myself—and turned to the outside, toward nothing, and wept.

CHAPTER 102

ABOUT THREE THAT MORNING I was in a back-hallway green-tiled treatment room that might've been in any small-to-medium-sized hospital anywhere in the United States. This one happened to be in Morton, Mississippi, overworked and overrun by the wounded, dead, and curious, teeming out of the tepid night from what the press was already calling the Battle of Bixby Church.

The police and deputies had orders to keep reporters away from me. I was thinking about that, my head on pillows, the bed's head cranked up at sixty degrees. Five-percent dextrose was running into a big vein in my arm, on a board, plastered over with tape, tubing, and gauze. The fluid was a chaser for a unit of whole blood, ordered by a doctor with a Mennonite beard, who seemed remarkably competent, by the way, for an emergency-ward night man.

(This was still the era when emergency practice was not a real occupation for any self-respecting physician—hospitals resorting to troubled, transient, or aged doctors, alcoholics, drug abusers, criminals. Perhaps they forced shifts on their radiologists or dermatologists, men with little skill or interest in trauma care. It was a little known fact that an American wounded in a jungle or rice paddy of Vietnam had a far better chance of rapid, definitive surgical care, by board-certified specialists, than one injured in an interstate accident in the continental United States, or struck on the curb outside most U.S hospitals.)

My wounded leg, according to the Mennonite, had hemorrhaged just enough to cause my humiliating fainting spell, in combination with a general degree of dehydration, and the stress of everything I'd been through.

I sighed, and looked over, studying the top of a Mayo stand.

Down at my leg.

Shot with a .30-caliber rifle bullet.

An M-1 Carbine.

Same Carbine, same spray of gunfire, that had killed instantly Sheriff Bobby Ray Turbeville.

The Klan gunman, who had shot both of us, was critical.

Ripped open by double-ought buckshot in the right leg, and two loads in the right arm, nearly severed. Left upper thigh chewed by a slug from a .357 Magnum. Still in surgery, police outside the OR, patrolling the corridors and grounds. Part of the Klan code, it seemed, was to kill a fellow Klansman who might talk, who had significant knowledge of Klan operations…

Klan operations…

I sighed.

My foot dangled, tapping the floor.

My left leg, the injured one, stretched the length of the bed. Pants leg cut by a nurse's scissors to my groin. The gunshot had entered the back of my thigh nine inches below the hip joint, and exited anteriorly, a couple inches superior, ripping the lateral quadriceps. I'd be fine, the Mennonite promised, cleansing the wound with hexachlorophene, performing a little debridement, applying a temporary dressing. I was awaiting his return to finish the patch job, then give me a tetanus shot and some antibiotics. I pulled the paper, again, out of my back pocket.

Unfolded it one-handedly.

The bloodstained paper out of Agent Cal Perry's jacket.

An itinerary.

It started 10:55 the following Tuesday morning with the arrival at the Jackson airport, from Atlanta, of an Eastern Airlines jet.

A jet carrying: The Reverend Martin Luther King Jr.

By motorcade, King would travel to Meridian for meetings with the local NAACP, related to the upcoming trial. He would leave at three, again by motorcade, and travel to Lavonia County, to speak that night, at the Barbee Creek Primitive Baptist Church.

Where I'd been accused of not contributing enough to the cause of freedom.

Was a chunk of meat out of my leg enough?

A haggard Special Agent Legate timidly opened my door.

"Not the girl's dorm," I said, with some amusement. "C'mon in." I refolded the bloody paper, slipped it away, in the sheets. "Sorry," I told him, contritely, as he stepped alongside, the door hissing closed.

He pocketed hands.

"For what?"

"Had I not delayed us…"

I shrugged. Sadly.

Difficult to meet his look.

"No," he said.

He shook and lowered his head. "Not your fault. You performed magnificently, Mrs. Russell. I'm going to make personally sure the Director knows everything, how far you went to save one of his men"—he glanced an old-maidish look off my bandaged, but otherwise naked, Radio City Music Hall leg— "despite yourself being wounded. I'm sorry; I didn't even know, before. The Bureau is in your debt, Mrs. Russell."

I shrugged again, sighing.

"Perry's dead."

"I spoke to the doctor." Legate shoved his chin. "An autopsy is pending, of course, but he believes the bullet severed the pulmonary artery, above the heart. Might've even, he said, punctured the heart itself."

I flickered eyes.

"It appears," he said, "you were correct."

"I take no pleasure in that."

Legate grinned bitterly. "No way Agent Perry could have survived. Maybe if a surgeon could have gotten him open, a few minutes. Nobody's fault. Least of all yours. So, those few minutes delay, for good purpose"—he gave a reassuring nod— "they made no difference."

I nodded.

Swallowed. Hauled my good leg up, carefully atop rumbled sheets.

I brushed some red clay from the blue denim, and Legate brought out an envelope.

"What's this?"

"Payment, for services rendered, plus expenses. There's a bonus too. Call it combat pay. We'll take care of this, too, of course." Gesturing the hospital.

"And Autrey's treatment?"

"Yes. And, also, in accordance with our agreement…"

"Yes?"

"We got'em all. The Lavonia Six."

Intrigued, I stretched back, and he told me about Grand Kleagle Cecil Orval Loftin's arrest in Lavonia. Thanks to me, the Feds had worked with Turbeville Saturday morning, and caught Loftin red-handed switching the .45 Colts. Turbeville had been at the logging-camp crime scene Friday morning, blowing Loftin's first opportunity. Something else happened in the afternoon to blow the second. He finally managed, early Saturday to take the Cothran—and Collins—murder weapon from his holster, and slip it back into Turbeville's gun belt, on the peg, on the wall outside the private washroom of the High Sheriff of Lavonia County. The FBI then tailed Loftin, arresting him Saturday afternoon as he approached the Alabama-Mississippi line at the wheel of a 1961 Ford Falcon Econoline, laden with military ordinance. Beside him was Calvin Dixon Harwood, Klarogo of the Palace 13 Klavern in Birmingham— third of the Lavonia Six to be accounted for.

"The bastard who stole my rings," I muttered.

Legate seemed suddenly smug.

"He had a claim ticket when he was booked," he said, with the clown grin, "a Birmingham pawn shop. Seems he'd recently hocked two diamond rings for $472. I told an agent from my office to go over and scare the pants off that pawnbroker."

I flickered a brow.

"The rings'll be," he said, "waiting at the Pine Crest."

I smiled.

Weakly.

Felt inappropriate to be happy about something so material, after all we'd been through. Legate went on to tell me the remaining three members of the Lavonia Six had been in attendance at the Bixby Church meeting. One dead, two under arrest. "You'll press for murder indictments? In the deaths of the blacks, not just whites?"

"We'll get them. Maybe Federal court, maybe state, but we'll get'em."

"Autrey will testify?"

"If he wants immunity. He was there; he's technically guilty of murder."

"You'll protect him?"

"Soon as he's off the critical list we'll put him on ice at Maxwell Air Force Base, outside Montgomery. Nobody can get to him there."

I nodded.

"They admitting you?"

"I refused," I told him.

"I think—"

"I'll take care of my own leg, thank you."

"Suit yourself."

"They're busy enough here."

"If you're sure…"

"I am."

"I'll see somebody drives you back to the motel in Forest, get your belongings, then to the Pine Crest. You can rest there, long as you want, but I suppose you're anxious to get back, to your husband."

CHAPTER 103

"WHAT WAS IT ALL ABOUT?" I asked.

A corner of his mouth twitched.

"Hobbs," he said, "conspiring to formulate a Universal Klan."

"You got Hobbs?"

"We will. He was seen fleeing south, through the woods on horseback. We think he bolted, second the shooting started. But he's got to emerge somewhere. When he does, we'll get him."

I nodded.

"What was next week? The Big Event?"

Shrug. "Might never know."

"Then…?"

I took out, opened the mimeographed paper stained with Cal Perry's blood.

"It had nothing to do…"

Gave my head a little shake. "With this?"

Legate's jaw sagged. Black eyes briefly unfocused, behind the horn-rimmed glasses.

"I'll…have to ask you for that."

Tipping, he began to reach—

I whipped it away, let it refold itself.

"Mrs. Russell…"

I tucked it through my collar, snugged it safe and warm down between my safety-pin-closed shirt and right bra cup. Legate seemed prudishly scandalized, me brazenly patting over where the paper showed vaguely through. "Not on your life," I said. "I owe that to your partner."

He rocked back a step—I think, a tiny bit scared of me.

"What is it, ma'am, you think you have there?"

"Insurance," I said. "Take it, if you dare—because it will involve strong-arming, molesting, a woman in a hospital bed—and I'll be forced to reveal what I know. And you know I can do you damage, embarrassment, the very least. Let me keep it, and I'll squirrel it away; nobody will ever see it—unless of course, something, anything, should happen to me."

He grinned the deep V grin.

Chin long, pointed.

Nodding…

"You're being melodramatic."

"Am I?"

Hands pocketed deep. "I mean: Who? What do you think we are?"

"I don't know *what* you are."

"We're not monsters."

"You got orders from Washington," I accused, "to let the Klan have their meeting. Possibly get away with some or all of those weapons and explosives."

"They would have changed their minds, trust me—"

"Trust you?"

"Over the bazooka and flame thrower, they would have changed their minds. My SAC practically stood on his head when I told him on the phone."

"Why would Washington, that is, Hoover, want us pulling back?"

"I told you…"

"I know. You're as in the dark as I am. Would you have obeyed, had the shooting not decided for you?"

"What would you have had me do, Mrs. Russell?"

"Destroy the Klan—a goal you swore devotion to, to my face."

"And that was sincere. I don't always agree with my superiors, ma'am, but I do obey them."

"It's common knowledge the FBI is investigating Martin

Luther King. Trying to discredit him as a communist. But you haven't been able to, have you?"

His head tipped back.

"How did the Ku Klux Klan," I pressed, "get hold of Reverend King's detailed travel arrangements?"

My lips curled. "Detailed to the minute?"

His head shook side to side, slightly, and shruggingly.

"I have no idea, truthfully."

"What would have happened?"

His jaw muscles bunched, and he turned, fingering some oxygen equipment—equipment such as, if it had been in the back of that fancy Pontiac Consort ambulance, might've saved Agent Perry's life. "From what I've gathered, from confiscated papers and maps…"

He looked at me.

"I'm listening."

"If we hadn't stopped them, or…I know you think we're horrible. I can only assume Washington was in possession of other intelligence, from other field offices, or informants…"

"Go on."

"Dr. King's motorcade was to have been attacked. Along US 80, a bridge very near here. The bridge was a going to be blown with dynamite, behind the last car. Then King and everyone with him would have been killed with automatic weapons fire and rockets."

"The bazooka," I said, nodding.

"There were also plans to jam police communications."

I looked up.

"Coordinated with attacks in other locations, we believe. We haven't sorted through it all yet. It's been very busy, as you know."

"Dr King's been notified?" I asked.

"Yes. We have advised he cancel his trip."

CHAPTER 104

AN FBI MAN FAWNED OVER me like I was Princess Anne and delivered me to the Pine Crest Motel in Alabama not long after seven o'clock Sunday morning. My wedding band and engagement ring were waiting. A little pink bow, even, on the box. I called Fred long distance, and told him what happened. That he'd be hearing about it on the news, if he hadn't already. I told him I'd been hurt, but it was just a scratch, and I'd be fine, not to worry. I promised to drive back first thing Monday, and wondered if he might could be off work when I got there.

We needed to talk.

He said he'd be home.

And nothing else.

I took a nap. When I awoke it was after-church time and I put on a decent dress and limped to my car and drove to Lavonia County. I found Abigail and Henry at home, with their children and Henry's cousin, the tenant farmer. They were eating Sunday dinner, Abigail insisting on fixing me a plate. "Thank you, no," I told her. "Really." I bade her, smiling insistently, to sit back down.

As she lifted her fork, I explained—seated slightly outside the circle, elbows on my knees—that I was on my way home. But they deserved to hear from me—they being my clients, after all—that, naturally, Montie was not guilty of murder. That he had been horribly and fatefully wronged by a white woman he trusted. I shrugged. I apologized, as a white woman, for all white women.

I went on explaining, as a result of that wronging, he and the others had been targeted by an ultraviolent extremist core of the Ku Klux Klan, overseen by John Riley Hobbs, and led by their poor-white-trash county deputy Cecil Loftin. "Their notion," I concluded, "was to commit so vicious a crime, it would light the fuse on a race war. Their hope being to unite enough whites behind them, by hook or by crook, to give them the strength to defeat Martin Luther King, and the Federal government, and the Black Panthers, and all the other violent activists. I doubt they could have succeeded, but the effort would've been a bloody mess. As it happened, they did not even get it off the ground."

I made deliberate eye contact around the table, with the youngsters especially. "The Klan and their hate did not succeed, because of us, white and black. And especially because of men like Bobby Ray Turbeville—who was not a Klansman. I won't say he wasn't a bigot, but he wasn't a Klansman, and in my opinion, he was a fair man, maybe even a good man, who died stopping them."

I stood, raised my chin.

Smoothed my skirt. "I expect formal charges against the men who killed Montie and Dorothy. If that doesn't come to pass, I will see that it does—I promise—or cause a helluva ruckus trying."

Abigail looked up, held it several seconds, then said, "Thank you."

Henry scraped his chair back. Came round and shook my hand.

A firm grasp, and I tried to make mine equally so.

"I'll be going," I said.

"Wait!" Abigail got up.

Disappeared into the kitchen, and returned cradling a wad of Reynolds Wrap the size of a football. "For supper," she said. "Fried chicken and cornbread."

I was half surprised to find the pastor in the chapel at Barbee Creek Primitive Baptist Church. More surprised to find him armed with an old Army rifle. Guarding the church, he said, case of a backlash, retaliation for the weekend's events, or Dr. King's planned, but now-cancelled speech. "Might be some crazy out there, didn't get the word he ain't comin'."

He seemed bitter.

"I don't know what they told you," I said, "or how much of this will show up on the news, but the Klan uprising we stopped—their first target was to be Dr. King, on this trip. They were determined, and armed to the teeth, I assure you. They would have killed him, and then, where would we all be?"

"Armageddon," said the pastor.

Hugging the Garand rifle.

"Hopefully more than one individual stands between us and that," I said. "Anyway, the feeling was Hobbs, who's still at large, might try to carry out the attack anyway. That's why Dr. King isn't coming. I wanted you to know. That it is best he not."

"Probably," he said.

"I'll be going."

I limped out between the pews.

He never thanked me.

Just stood there bracing his gun.

Speaking of guns: mine lay on my bed back at the Pine Crest, recovered from Vance's car. I turned on the TV and ate my chicken and cornbread and drank from a bottle of J&B I'd gotten from the agent manning the office. Perhaps they thought if they got me dead-drunk they could burgle my room, recover the Cal Perry-blooded King itinerary. Probably known as *Operation: Betty*. Never let a good codename go to waste.

I did get drunk, but beforehand I secured the mimeo behind the mirror, under the lid of my train case.

CHAPTER 105

FRED WAS HOME WHEN I got to Murfreesboro about ten-thirty Monday morning. I came through the kitchen and he was standing in the doorway to the den. I wanted my husband to come and take me and hug me in his huge arms. I wore a nice conservative pink shirtdress with a pleated skirt.

He saw my limp from where he was. Asked was I okay.

"Paper said a woman was shot."

Sharp.

Reproachful. I glimpsed the newspaper on the kitchen table. Big headlines:

KKK VS. POLICE GUNBATTLE KILLS SIX
BAMA SHERIFF, G-MAN AMONG DEAD IN MISS.; 10
KLANSMEN HURT; GUNS, EXPLOSIVES SEIZED;
HOOVER LAUDS LAWMEN

"Okay." I looked up, and over. "I got hit in the side of the thigh. Went straight through. Not very deep. End of story." I took a step to show him I could. I even curtsied. "I'm fine. See?" And I kept advancing thinking I might need to be the one doing the arms putting around. "You can even help me change my bandage." Gave him some hubba-hubba brow bouncing, looking up, as I got close.

"Don't make jokes."

Fred turned, off into the den.

I followed. "Wait. What's this about?"

I stood on the carpeted floor as he rotated down into his swivel recliner.

"What in God's name did you do to your hair?"

"My hair…?"

I thrashed my head.

I couldn't even…*God!*…come close to commenting on that, after witnessing seven savage killings—two men blown up!—and various and sundry beatings and brutalizations. "Is this about you being worried? Scared for me? For which, Fred, I humbly and appreciatively apologize. Or is this about…about you thinking, well, a woman who'd go out and get herself shot is, well …"

I let, as I panted, the question hang.

Like maggoty meat.

"Let's say you're warm," he savaged.

I gaped, spasming with emotion. Breathing carefully, I circled over, and sat on our couch. "I'm…very glad to be home Fred. That's the truth."

"Your choice to go."

"I know." I smiled funny. "Because I felt I had to. But, Fred, does that mean I can't be glad to be back?"

"Means it must not've bothered you awfully much."

"Fred, what about…what about like a man who gets drafted and has to go off to war? He doesn't want to go, but believes it's his duty…"

"Don't be silly; that's got nothing to do with this."

"Silly? Fred, what do you think I've been doing?"

"Haven't the foggiest goddamn idea."

"Okay…" Jerkily I nodded, gesturing myself and Fred to cool it. "Just, you haven't seemed all that interested. I'll tell you every—"

"What I'm interested in is a wife who's home. If not home, at least not gallivanting off with other men."

I blinked.

"Okay. I can understand—"

"Can you?"

"I said I could. Look, honey…"

I smiled prettily.

"You respect Martin Luther King, right?"

I waited.

"Right?" Prodding.

He sighed.

"Sure."

Palpable skepticism coming through. "This may not make it into the news," I explained carefully, "but I think I helped to stop a Klan plot to kill Dr. King. That is what I was doing out there."

Fred rolled his eyes.

Flung hands.

"I'm rather proud," I said, "of that!"

"Jesus Christ," he said.

I stood. Clawed fingers round my head. Gritted teeth. Then I paced, pink skirt rustling quietly. I spun. "I know this hasn't been easy. We've got problems. Maybe most of them are my fault. Okay? I admit that. But I want us to work them out." My arms curled in front of me as if to envelope someone who was invisible. The invisible man, whom I wanted very much to hug. "I'm home Fred," I said intensely.

Shook my arms.

He wasn't even looking.

"I talked to a psychiatrist."

"What?" I yelped.

"I talked to a shrink—man my father knew as a kid."

"You talked to your father, then to a psychiatrist—about me?"

"He says it's very simple."

Fred darted his face up. "Says it's classic."

"What is classic?" I said gutturally.

"You not being able to come to terms with your basic feminine instincts."

Bringing up my hand, I pressed the heel of it hard into the center of my forehead, and clawed my nails and closed my eyes, and said:

"Reason I wanted you here when I got home, Fred…"

Then I dropped the hand, and looked him in the eye squarely. "Is I wanted to tell you I really don't want to have a baby. I am so sorry." Crossed hands over my heart. "Maybe later, not now. I know that hurts you. I'd give anything to not hurt you. Some things happened down there I want to tell you about, Fred. So, maybe, you'll understand. Why I feel this way, why I—have to go on the pill."

He didn't speak nor move—fifteen, perhaps twenty seconds lapsing. Then he rose.

Knocked me aside storming past. I rotated, huge longing hazel eyes. But he continued through the kitchen, out the mud room. Screen door squealed and banged. I listened, his truck cranked; he backed out our driveway and drove off.

I went and lay in our bedroom, and cried.

Fred didn't come home that night.

Tuesday, I called a gynecologist in Nashville—actually, he was an abortionist who'd once offered me a job, which I hadn't taken, but would've if I ever needed the money enough. He agreed to call me in a prescription for Ortho-Novum to Green Hills Market and Pharmacy. No one in Murfreesboro need know. I felt better about that—though the Supreme Court had ruled it unconstitutional to deny a married woman contraception. That Tuesday was also Ruthie Mae's regular day.

"Least Montie can rest in peace. Maybe go to heaven. He wudn't perfect, I know. But do you think Miss Sherry he could go to heaven?"

I smiled across the enameled-top table:

"Not the one to ask, but I think it's possible. Surely God can see the good, through a little bad."

She nodded.

Drank from the coffee I'd made.

"Hope those men fry."

"This may seem crazy," I shrugged, "but I don't think, I were you, I'd worry about the Klan."

"How—?"

"They're their own worst enemy, is what I'm saying. The more crazy, violent acts they commit, the more the sane public turns away. The more their leaders get convicted, the more laws get passed, to hobble them, and empower the Negro, the more blacks get elected to public office... What I'm saying is, really, the Klan has done more for civil rights than moderate whites, and most blacks have ever done. See?"

"I guess…"

"The Klan is in decline. Its power is proportionate to the helplessness of blacks; the less helpless you become—through better jobs, education—the more strength gets sapped out of the Klan. Montie was singled out—not personally, not directly, but just the way things happened to fall into place—doing something highly threatening in the Klan's world view. He was trying to better himself, become a property owner. They killed him for that, and when they did, it was one step forward for them—but many more steps back."

I swallowed some coffee.

Leaning back.

"Least, that's what I think."

I felt a…

Disturbance…

A change…

I reached across, patted the back of her hand on the table.

She gave me a sharp look, stiffening, withdrawing the hand.

"Ruthie Mae…"

"Miss Sherry, don't take this wrong. I 'preciate all you did for Montie and Dorothy, and I know you did it for me too. And Lawd knows I need this job…"

My brow twitched.

"But…?"

"You don't have the slightest idea what we're fighting for."

I pulled my neck back. "Beg your pardon?"

"You don't understand no better than my husband does, or that brother-in-law, Henry, a' mine."

"They're both good men."

"Course they are. They work hard and they provide. And they lick the soles of your shoes, Miss Sherry."

"What!"

"What we're asking for, are tired of asking for—and finally are fighting for—is equality."

"I've treated you as an equal!"

I looked horrified.

She humphed.

"*Haven't I?* We hired you as a maid, but—"

"That's not what I'm talking about."

"What?"

"Through this whole affair you done what white liberals always do."

"You asked me to help."

"Help—yes—and please don't take this wrong, I am grateful…"

"But?"

"You treat me like a child, like you're this great white mother out to save the Negro. You think us inferior. You are insensitive. We need equality, not parenting."

She shot up from her seat. "Excuse me, Miss Sherry, I should go finish my work. If you want to fire me, I'll more than understand. All I ask is you pay me for what I've done." And she marched from the kitchen, me screwing my head around, listening as she resumed scrubbing and sloshing in the bathroom.

I faced back.

My breaths short, sharp, quiet…

CHAPTER 106

J. EDGAR HOOVER, THE SEVENTY-two-year-old director of the Federal Bureau of Investigation, had attended every presidential inauguration since Calvin Coolidge's. He had overseen the creation and honing of the world's most formidable law-enforcement organization. Adopting and perfecting every conceivable advance: centralized fingerprinting, ballistics testing, fiber and handwriting analysis, even systematic note-taking, and recordkeeping. Hoover was a devout Presbyterian, who had long ago appointed himself the all-powerful guardian of the nation's morals.

That fall "Burrhead"—a Hoover codename for Dr. Martin Luther King Jr.—was plotting a triumphant return to the National Mall, where King's gift for oratory had glowingly peaked, in the speech at the Lincoln Memorial, the speech that had borne him to glory. The "I Have a Dream" speech.

The Gettysburg Address of the twentieth century.

By late 1967 J. Edgar Hoover's hatred of Martin Luther King had burned for a decade. A high FBI official had once actually mailed King an anonymous letter urging suicide. The black leader's plan for a Poor People's Campaign—to march on Washington, camp on the Mall, engage in nonviolent disruptive acts—was a final straw. The FBI director considered the Poor People's March a threat to the republic, a vandal attack on the nation's capital. Perhaps the start of a Negro revolution. Perhaps

411

the Soviets were backing it.

Hoover warned President Johnson: MLK was "an instrument in the hands of subversive forces seeking to undermine our nation."

Burrhead had to be stopped.